I0562417

THE

Comic History of London,

FROM THE EARLIEST PERIOD.

Illustrated with Numerous Engravings.

LONDON:

BOYS OF ENGLAND OFFICE, 173, FLEET STREET, E.C.

THE
COMIC HISTORY
OF LONDON.

*Extracted from Dreadfully Ancient and Fearfully Authentic
Records.*

By WALTER PARKE.

EDITED BY EDWIN J. BRETT.

I.

INVASION OF BRUTUS—HISTORY OF LONDON FROM THE BEGINNING—AND EARLIER.

SHORT history of the good City of London, narrated in our peculiarly felicitous, facetious, and veracious style is such an essential necessity of life, that it is wonderful our readers have so long contrived to exist without it.

We hasten, therefore, to set matters right by prescribing for them a course of historical knowledge to be taken in weekly doses, hoping it will cure every complaint at least as well as many of the patent medicines daily advertised

The facts are these.

Somewhere about 2100 B.C. (which means, of

course, B-eyond C-omputation), Brutus, a renowned chief of the Trojans, and grandson of Ænas, was wandering about the world on a voyage of discovery.

His fortunes were in a very shady condition, and his creditors wanted him badly; his rival in love was thirsting for his gore, and altogether he didn't know nor care what was going to become of him.

In this unenviable plight he ran ashore at an uninhabited island, longitude something and a half east by west; latitude uncertain.

Having camped for the night, the soldiers turned in, but their general sat up an hour later in order to sacrifice to the gods.

But at length he fell asleep, with his head gently reposing among the ashes of the camp-fire.

Of course he saw a vision.

Who should rise up but the lovely, potent, and benevolent goddess, Diana, who forthwithly addressed him as under—

"Brutus, in your unpleasant sit-u-ation,
　The best of remedies is emigration;
　There lies, far out where Northern oceans swell,
　An isle where giants and wild beastes dwell;
　Go, land there, plant your flag and blow your trumpet:
　The natives, p'rhaps, won't like it—let them lump it!
　Fight, conquer, seize the island as your prize,
　Build, settle, cultivate, and colonise.
　And found a kingdom great as fallen Troy;
　Farewell! henceforth I'll stand your friend, my boy!"

The general woke up in the morning with a splitting headache, and the words of the goddess ringing in his ear.

He told his comrades, and asked their advice.

They tossed up, and the verdict was "Go."

So they set sail at once.

But the island was a long way off, and they put in at all sorts of places, and had no end of fights, dangers, hair-breadth 'scapes, &c., to go through before they got to it.

At last this "beautiful isle of the sea" rose in sight.

And ah! it *was* a bright and lovely spot then.

The wild denizens of the forests, consisting of bears, lions, wolves, boars, mammoths, and alligators, lived there in all the calm and peaceful innocence of primitive nature; and the human aborigines, shaggy savages clothed in skins, and so tall that they used to knock their heads against the tree-tops as they walked along, were sweet creatures to meet on a fine day.

Their king was named Gogmagog; his height nearly thirty feet, weight about seven tons; complexion fiery; colour of hair, a lively orange; eyes green, with a beautiful cast towards the left; disposition uncertain, but generally sanguinary.

He was so strong, that he could pull up a large oak with one little jerk, and then use it as a club, and he generally took four bullocks at each meal; you couldn't have helped liking him.

When Brutus and his three thousand followers saw these nice people waiting on the shore to receive them, their hearts might well have quailed.

But no; the Trojans were heroes down to their very finger-nails.

Undauntedly they landed, and were received so warmly by the giants, that they didn't feel the cold weather at all.

A fight ensued. Such a fight never before, since, or otherwise, occurred in all history.

The Gogmagonian Britons were firmly resolved to smash these pigmies to pulp, and eat them in the form of sausages.

The Trojans, on the other hand, meant to conquer or perish in the attempt; perhaps both.

So they " went for " the giants heavily.

They couldn't reach higher than their shins; but these they so barked and wounded with their swords, that the colossal warriors roared, danced, and at last got tripped up, and sent sprawling on the earth, where a body of Trojans were ready to set upon each and finish him off at once.

These tactics were successful.

Ten hours of hard fighting, and the giants had become, like angels' visits, few and far between.

> " It so fell out they all got killed,
> The rest they ran away."

But the king, Gogmagog, lived yet; and as he could smash ten Trojans with one blow of his club whenever he aimed straight, it seemed probable he would die hard.

At last Corineus, the fraternal friend and chosen chum of Brutus, doubled up his sleeves with the intention of doubling up the giant.

He first skirmished lightly round him, stirring him up by hacking away here and there at his legs and ankles, till the giant, irritated at these proceedings, bent down his head to see his little enemy more-clearly.

He got rather too near that time; for Corineus, suddenly giving a mighty bound in the air, drove his sword up to the hilt in the giant's throat, and separated his jugular.

With a roar like the whole Zoological Gardens at feeding time, Gogmagog fell down, mortally done for, causing quite an earthquake by the ponderous weight of his fall.

Corineus, who was strong for a weak man, took up his corpus, staggered with it to the edge of a high rock, and hurled him over.

This was the first *hurl* ever known in England, and Corineus was the first *duke*, Brutus giving him, for his bravery, the Duchy of Cornwall, otherwise Corineus's or

Cornishland, so called from this hero, and not, as some historians assert, because the ancient natives suffered very much from corns.

But don't make any mistake.

The race of British giants were not yet extinct.

Gogmagog belonged to a great family, and a great family belonged to him ; for he left twelve sons and ten daughters, let alone cousins, nephews, &c., who henceforth retired to the caves and mountains, and from some of these were descended the redoubted Gog and Magog of our present history as you shall see anon.

Well, at all events, the giants were killed, put to flight, and bottled up in general for the time being.

————

II.

FOUNDATION OF LONDON—LINE OF BRUTUS.

AND so Brutus took possession in the name of his noble self, and decreed that the island should from him be henceforth called Brutain, Britain, or Britannia, and its inhabitants Britons.

Then he set out on an exploring expedition.

It was hard work getting along, for the forests were so thick that one could hardly breathe in them, and the wild beasts so numerous and troublesome, that they " interviewed " the visitors with most unpleasant frequency.

However, difficulties were made to be overcome, and Brutus and his men marched on to the site of London, or rather the opposite of it, on the other bank of the river.

He was delighted with the " silvery Thames," which was

silvery then, and not so much like pea-soup as oft-times nowadays.

"Suppose we build a city here?" suggested Brutus, as they halted.

"Yes; it's just the *city*-wation for it," said Corineus, approvingly.

All the army called out—"Hear! hear!" whether at the joke or the proposal is unknown.

So the general began taking measures—six-foot ones—to *mete* out the ground in a manner that would *meet* general approval.

As that very ancient chronicler, Jheo Muggynnes, says, in his antiquated lingo:—

> "Whenn wunce ye citie was begunne,
> Ye builders sett toe wurke lyk funne;
> And roes of howziz uppe didde runne
> Ere yow coud saye Jakke Robbinsunne!"

The city was called New Troy, so as not to confuse it with Old, though there wasn't much fear of that, for Troy had been des-*troy*-ed long before.

The houses, like the "Boy's of England" journal, contained many *storeys*, and were planted in rows like scarlet runners.

The rents were low, so were the ceilings, and, for the matter of that, so were many of the inmates.

Every attention was paid to the inconveniences of life.

The chimneys didn't smoke, because there were none, and, besides, smoking had not yet come into fashion; and I'm sure there was a plentiful supply of water, for sometimes the Thames overflowed, and flooded the ground floors to the depth of **fifty feet.**

As for King Brutus, he built for himself a palace of a composite order of architecture, something between a coal-shed and St. Peter's at Rome.

Brutus carried out the Goddess Diana's commands to the letter.

He came, comprehended, conquered, constructed, cultivated, and colonised; he sent home for his good lady, Ignoge; his men also had their wives and families imported (in sealed packets on by the Parcels Post), **and London grew prosperous, populous, and portentous.**

DIANA GIVES BRUTUS A LIGHT.

It was evidently under the special patronage and favour of Brutus's celestial friend, the Goddess Diana, who once appeared to him again in a vision (after a supper of roast pork and cold lobster salad), and in sweetly benignant style, told him he was a good boy, patted him on the helmet, and even lit his cigar for him by means of a patent candle moulded in ancient Greece.

The wild beasts were gradually exterminated, at least round the capital—all except the immortal British Lion, who is not dead even yet, and don't mean to be.

Long may he wag his tail!

King Brutus reigned long and gloriously, and when he died, divided the kingdom among his three sons, and became the founder of a long line of kings.

Of these the most famous were Locrin, Hudibras, King Lear, Gorbuda, and Belinus. Ebraucus, a monarch of the same dynasty, was quite a family man. He had twenty sons and thirty daughters.

Mustn't his nursery have been extensive, and his baker's bill awful to contemplate?

To give you an idea how long ago it was when all this happened, we may mention that at the same time King David was reigning in Israel, and was pretty well, thank you.

———

III.

THE MERRY OLD DAYS OF GOOD KING LUD.

THIS brings us to the days of King Lud the Great, the monarch and second founder of London.

He lived 0072 A. D. (A-ncient D-ate) more or less.

New Troy had become pretty old by this time.

Indeed, it was in such a shaky, seedy, tumble-down condition, that it was a marvel it could hold out in a gale of wind.

So a deputation of citizens, going to the king, said—

"Good Lud, the city wants rebuilding."

To which the monarch replied—

"Good *Lud!* so it does!"

And gave orders that they should give commands to give instructions to commence the beginning of the preparation for this great work.

It was not much trouble to dispose of the old city.

A dozen strong men had only to stand at the street corners, set up a loud shout, clap their hands, and stamp their feet heavily, and the whole of the edifices came down with a run.

The inmates, of course, had removed their goods first.

Then they carted off the remains, and began with new bricks, which, like new brooms, are always expected to do wonders.

The houses were run up with wonderful rapidity—so were the expenses.

Many important improvements were made, and the rents were raised by hydraulic pressure.

The new town was called Lud-town, which in the fullness of time became modified into Lundun, or London, though it is now sometimes spoken of by roughly-refined people as the Metrollopus.

It was at that time surrounded by high and mighty walls, but of these not a brickbat nor a ha'p'orth of mortar remains, unless we consider the "Hole in the Wall," the *Wal*worth Road, and the cata-*wauls* sometimes heard on the tiles to be relics of them.

Lud was a great king in battle.

His sword always *sawed* its way to the front of victory, and at his fights he played an excellent knife and fork—knife, at least, for forks were then uninvented, except *pitch*forks, which would hardly do to *pitch* into your dinner with.

The engraving on page 10, taken from an antique basso-relievo, dug up under a water-butt of the Bank of England, represents King Lud at one of his *gorgeous* feasts, a *gnawful* spectacle to our more civilised eyes, especially when we turn to the contrast of our own lord mayor, the modern king of London, and see how he conducts himself during his *recherches* spread.

Thus doth civilisation change the habits of men.

King Lud lived till the very day of his death, and was buried at Lud-gate, which he had built previously.

Peace to his cinders.

It dates from his time that the Attorney-general and other

big swells of the law courts are always addressed " my lud," or " your ludship."

KING LUD, A.D. 72. | LORD MAYOR, AD. 1872.

A CITY FEAST—TWO WAYS OF DOING IT.

And now we come to stirring times in our city's history, the times when Julius Cæsar had brought all the world and his wife under his victorious sway, and was pursuing his *victorious way* in Gaul (now called France, or the Land of Mossoo.)

Casting his eagle eye over the British Channel (he was a far-seeing ruler, was J. C.), somewhere about the year 54 B.C., his glance rested on this " right little, tight little island," and he said—

" That place looks healthy for an invasion. Suppose that, now we've come so far, we just run over and conquer it, eh? won't take long, you know. By Jove! I'm determined to ' Rule Britannia, and Britons ever, ever, ever shall be slaves.' "

So he and about ten thousand of the " noblest Romans of them all " embarked one fine night and reached Dover " so early in the morning, before the break of day."

At this time though the Londoners were comparatively

well posted up in civilisation, the majority of ancient Britons were downright barbarians.

They wore their hair *long*—sometimes six months, before they cut it—and their only coats were *coats* of paint, of which they could bear three or four even in the hottest weather ; for, in sooth, they not only killed their enemies in battle, but they *dyed* themselves—in all sorts of fantastical patterns in fast colours.

They dwelt in huts, on a delicious diet of acorns and cold water, and lived to the age of one hundred and twenty or so, provided nothing fatal happened to them before.

We have all heard of their priests, the Druids, knowing old cards, who pretended they could foretell the *future,* provided they received a *present ;* who burnt their prisoners in honour of their gods, which they called the rite of human sacrifices, though I consider them very *in*human sacrifices, rather *wrong* than *rite.*

Well, it was those warlike innocents that formed the main part of the army of Cassivelaunus, brother and successor of King Lud, and now lord of London, against Julius Cæsar.

The great victor had with difficulty landed in Britain, and penetrated as far as the Thames (he was a man of great penetration), and was now hurrying to London.

IV.

VISIT OF JULIUS CÆSAR TO LONDON—WARM RECEPTION.

UNCLE CASS (as his royal nephews called Cassive-launus) luckily heard of Cæsar's approach in *Cæsar-nable* time, and prepared accordingly.

He had a neat dodge that could not possibly fail if it only succeeded.

He fixed a lot of great iron and wooden stakes upright in the bed of Father Thames (the old gentleman couldn't have liked it much), artfully concealed under the water.

Consequently, as soon as Cæsar and his fleet got fairly in view of the city, they fell nicely into the trap.

The first ship that tried to pass, stuck against the upright pins with a jarring sound and stuck fast.

"Holloa," cried Cæsar, mounting the paddle-box, "bless my soul, what's all this?   Go on a-head there."

"Can't, your honour," was the reply.

"Then turn her astern!"

"Can't again—by all the gods she's stuck, impaled, filling, sprung a leak, and we shall drown like rats, if we don't take to the boats."

Such was the fact, and it was soon found that the whole fleet was in the like condition.

Confusion prevailed, rather, and if Julius Cæsar didn't swear, it's a pity.   (N.B.—And so it is if he did.)

Just at that moment, too, Cassivelaunus and his gallant Britons, who had fixed themselves on the banks of the river, opened a volley of arrows, darts, sticks, and stones on the invaders, peppering them in a style that Professor Pepper himself couldn't beat.

Cæsar and his men, however, succeeded in landing, and then there was somewhat of a shindy.

Britons and Romans, horses and chariots, javelins, arrows, spears, swords, oaths, cries, howls, blows and bloodshed, were all mingled together in one hotchpotch of deadly conflict.

The Britons fought like blazes, and the Romans like all vengeance.

Nennius, a young English military swell of the period, and nephew to Cassivelaunus, longed to distinguish himself, and extinguish the hated Cæsar.

So he looked out sharply for the prominent Roman nose of the great *conk*eror, which always loomed large on the field of battle.

When the two got up close to each other, an exciting thing in hand-to-hand fights was confidentially looked for.

Nennius's own account of this great affair, taken down from his own lips by the special reporter of the "Boy's of England" journal, is highly sensational.   Says he—

"Shouting the British war-cry, 'Let them have it!' I plunged into the thickest of the fight, cutting the enemy into thin slices as I went along.   At last I forced my way up to Cæsar. 'Die vehillian!' I cried, seizing his powerful nasal organ, and thereupon I drove my sword through him no less than six times, and broke

AWFUL STRUGGLE—THE ROMAN CÆSAR
AND THE BRITISH "SEIZER."

every bone in his skin.   He was rather discouraged, but not conquered.   He had a wonderful constitution, and wrapping his toga round him, artfully pretended not to feel any of his wounds. Still retaining hold of his Wellingtonian proboscis, I lifted him bodily out of his saddle, and held him aloft, barely alive, but most decidedly kicking. One moment more, and I should have cut him in half, and finished his career, when, suddenly he plunged his sword into my forehead, and left it sticking there. I drew it out, of course, and then, pitching away my own sword, used the now unharmed Cæsar's weapon against himself (rather neat that, I think.) But when he saw this, he pretty soon galloped off, while again I urged on my wild career. I swung the conqueror's sword round my head, and killed on an average ten enemies a minute."

Cæsar's account of the affair was rather different.

He said that he didn't care any more for Nennius than he did for a bluebottle fly, nor felt anything of his wounds, beyond a slight and rather pleasant tickling.

He added that this "Young Man of Great Britain" had a powerful imagination unchastened by a due regard for veracity, which means in plain language, he told awful crammers.

However, Nennius paid the penalty of his rashness.

He never got over Cæsar's sword being driven into his skull.

He took to his bed, and only lingered fifteen years, when he died. "Bury me in my grave," were his last words. And they did so.

Cæsar actually did succeed in conquering London and part of the rest of England, but he never made a complete conquest of this island, as he intended, but in the end had to draw off his army into Gaul, much *galled* at his failure.

———

V.

TREATING OF CARACTA-CUS, AND OTHER CUSSES OF THE PERIOD.

A CENTURY or so then elapsed, during which the Britons were pretty well let alone, suffering the infliction of *a tax*, but no *attacks* from the Romans.

At last the Emperor Claudius sent his armies to see after the tribute, in the payment of which Britannia had got rather behindhand, and didn't seem at all inclined to come forward.

Battles ensued, of course.

One of the greatest of the ancient British heroes was Caractacus, who, for *nine* years, *tena*ciously kept the Romans at bay, but at last, being overpowered, was sent a captive to Rome.

When brought before the emperor, he looked around at the gorgeous palace, and said, boldly—

"It's a hard case that a big swell like you, who wollers in this here bloated magnificence, can't let poor coves like us Britons alone. Am I right?"

"Very much so," responded Claudius, melting into sympathy. "It is a shame, now you put it in that light. What ho, there! Take off his chains, and give him a glass of ginger wine. Caractacus is free!"

Another mighty leader, or leaderess, of the Britons was the renowned Queen Boadicea, who being, as some said, "done out of her rights" by the Romans, appealed to arms.

(You see, there were at that time no law courts, as at present, where everybody can get their wrongs righted in no time, and at the most trifling expense.)

No less than two hundred thousand Britons joined

Boadicea's standard, and, marching in formidable battalions, when they found any Roman settlers, they gave them a *settler* which they didn't like.

London was at that time garrisoned by the foreign foe, whom Boadicea and her forces blockaded up as fast as maggots in a cheese.

The Roman general Suetonius (called *Mutton Suetonius* in derision by his foes, on account of his being so fat), tried to assist his allies; but it was no go.

Boadicea, who was of a fiery disposition, and burning for

A BURNING SHAME—QUEEN BOADICEA SETS FIRE TO LONDON.

vengeance, set London on fire, including the Thames, as some historians say.

However, our capital was soon reduced to a very small figure indeed; nothing but a heap of ashes, and the inhabitants had to choose between being fried or smashed.

For some time Boadicea carried on her victorious career, but at last her whole army of two hundred thousand was defeated by the Romans.

When she heard that all was up, she out with some cyanide of potassium, swallowed a strong dose, and was picked up an hour after on the battle field.

"A cup of cold p'ison it lay by her side,
  With a document a-stating that by p'ison she died."

Despite all this, we benefited vastly by the advent of the Romans, who were a very polished people, so *polished*, indeed, that there was sure to be a *shine* wherever they went.

They taught us civilisation, though the lessons were rather dear.

London began life afresh.

As soon as the capital could be raised, of course the capital that had been *razed* was raised once more, and *capital* indeed it looked, when some great improvements were made.

Chimneys were built, and made to consume their own smoke.

Drains were well looked to, though this sober people, unlike the moderns, never took any "drains" at public-houses; besides, glass wasn't invented, so of course nobody could ever take a glass too much.

The streets were beautifully paved with mud, a custom prevailing to the present time whenever it's wet weather, and the 'cute Britons soon learned how to *drive* a bargain so as to *derive* a good profit out of it.

For a few centuries after these events history records nothing about London or the Londoners, a sure sign that affairs were going on all right; for you'll always find that it's only when people are kicking up rows, getting into scrapes, and tumbling into hot water generally, that we hear much about them.

As soon as they are comfortably off, they leave off letting us know.

In the next chapter we shall go in for the Saxon and

Danish period, and begin describing the deeds of Gog and Magog, who were all *a-gog* at that exciting epoch.

VL

AFTER THE ROMANS.

NO sooner had the Romans gone home to their various mammas, than this "tight little island" began, as an old chronicler graphically remarks, to "drop in for it."

The predaceous Picts and the sanguinary Scots swept down upon us like an avalanche of black beetles.

They regarded the strong wall we had built against them no more than so much lath and plaster, and, having once got through, any hope of driving them back again was downright ridiculous.

Full soon they were all over the North of England, murdering, robbing, and devastating, in the style then so highly fashionable, and driving the British before them at railway speed.

In vain the Britons asked them what they would take to keep quiet.

They wouldn't keep quiet, and took everything they could get.

Then the killing went on *ad lib.*

In one battle alone the Britons lost 15,000 men, till, seeing plainly they would all be exterminated at that rate in about three weeks, they bolted southward, leaving the barbarians in possession of all the land north of the Humber, a very *Humb*(er)*ling* defeat for us.

Added to this a famine broke out, and though the cause

of it was entirely owing to there being a scarcity of anything to eat, the fact itself affords the historian ample food for reflection.

London began to feel nervous, I can tell you.

Everybody from all parts of everywhere were crowded within her walls, and the city, unlike the starved inhabitants, was full to bursting.

It is true her walls were strong, thick and air-tight—none of your stucco in those sturdy days—but whether they could keep out the Picts and Scots, was a quadruped of another colour.

In this *strait* or rather this *crooked* state of affairs, the Britons applied to the Romans for assistance, but the emperor sent back a neat little note with his compliments saying that it was "*non possumus*," or impossible, as far as the Romans were concerned, for they were exactly in the same pickle themselves.

The Goths, Huns, Vandals and other gentleman of that sort, were battering away at their gates, and it was no use their saying they were not at home; therefore, though the Romans couldn't help the Britons, the Britons might help them, if that would do as well.

So the Britons next applied to the Saxons, a race of very warlike people indeed, who at that time occupied the German fatherland and kept the Watch on the Rhine, occasionally pitching heavily into the French, an example followed by their illustrious descendants.

Wittigizzle, the Bismarck of the period, having consulted his pals as to the Britons, replied that the Saxons would be only too happy to help them out of pure benevolence, provided their expenses were paid; and Hengist, his son, undertook the expedition, declaring that he wouldn't leave England—

> " Till every Pict
> And Scot was licked,
> And back to Caledonia kicked !"

The terms were accepted, so thereupon 1,500 men, led by the renowned brothers Horsa and *Hengist*—not a chicken-hearted fellow, though his name may imply it, but a regular " cock of the walk "—landed on our shores, feeling very sure of success.

Both of them caught cold on the voyage (the sea, you see, is always damp), and by the time they landed, Hengist was very hoarse, but still his brother was *Horsa.*

[N.B. This joke was patented at the time, but since then the copyright has run out.]

Well, these doughty warriors not only landed on our shores, but landed on our enemies pretty severely.

So that the members of the Pictish and Scottish Company, Limited, soon caught something worse than a cold.

In fact, they got, as the Yankees would say " consumedly larrupped," and had to " cave in," and retreat to their native hills, following, thereby, Hamlet's advice that it is " better to endure the *hills* we have, than fly to others that we know not of."

The Saxon warriors returned victorious to London, or Augusta, as the Romans, metaphorically considering the city as a lady, had christened her.

It was a proud day for England, though rather wet.

The city was in a blaze of triumph, and all the way from Ludgate Hill to one o'clock in the morning, bells rang, minstrels sang, and all the public pumps ran pale ale.

Vortigern, King of London, Kent, and thereabouts, received the Saxon leaders with open arms, and swore eternal friendship.

" This day," he said, " cements the British and Saxon

nations together as fast as all the patent 'three sticks a penny' that were ever advertised could possibly do it!"

There was a grand banquet, in which everything was got up regardless of expense.

Hengist and Horsa's German brass band played a variety of operatic and other selections, including the Dead March in Saul, and the Live March out of it.

The scene at the king's palace at London utterly knocks over our descriptive powers.

Vortigern, attired in full fig, sat upon a raised daïs, and the glitter of his royal get-up was enough to *daze* anybody, and nothing in these *days* can give any idea of it.

His *guests*, as may be *guessed*, were treated with vast hospitality.

The viands and beverages were well in keeping with the company; for if the dinner was well-dressed, so were the eaters, and if the wine was bright and sparkling, the drinkers were the same; moreover, if the wine was considerably drunk, several of the imbibers were unmistakably ditto.

Some capital speeches were made.

Vortigern remarked that he was unaccustomed to public speaking, and that this was the proudest moment of his life—two brilliant flashes of wit which have been repeated at various festive gatherings ever since.

Hengist replied by toasting Vortigern as a "Jol, jol, jolly good fellow," and so said all of them, and very thick were the tones in which they said it.

VII.

GOG AND MAGOG MAKE THEIR DEBUT—GRAND SUCCESS.

THEN there were all sorts of entertainments; minstrels and bards sang their lays, comic and sentimental, warriors jousted, and " fit," and quarter staffed, and kicked up their male clad heels in the merry dance.

There was noticeable among the attendants of King Vortigern, a gentle youth, tender in years, but already a tough customer personally.

He stood about ten feet two in his sandals, and of proportionate breadth of beam.

His name was Gog, and he was one of the latest—if not the very last—of the race of British giants.

Vortigern had caught him wild in the west of England, during an expedition against some of the refractory chiefs, and trained him up in the way he should go, in the capacity of *light* porter.

" That's rather a fine young fellow over there !" remarked General Hengist, leaning back and criticising Gog scrutinisingly through an imaginary eye-glass.

" You're right," responded the monarch : " but he says he is small and degenerate compared to his ancestors, some of whom stood fifty feet, which was rather too much to *stand*, so the smaller invaders exterminated them."

" Yes, my lord," broke in Gog, in a tremendous voice that was heard above the German band—even including the big drum, " they were conquered, but it was all done by a fluke ; in fair fight, each of my family was equal to one hundred ordinary-sized men, and no mistake about it."

" What's your fighting weight, my little man ?" asked Horsa, condescendingly.

" Only fifty-two stone at present, your honour !" was the reply.

" Strange if true !" observed Vortigern, dubiously.   " But, there, don't tell me ! there isn't such another young giant as Gog in all the world.   I'll bet you my crown on it ?"

" And I'll bet you mine (when I get one) that my giant

will beat yours in fair fight !" replied the Saxon chief, bringing down his hand ponderously on the table.

" Done !"

" No, it's not done, for they haven't begun yet," said the cautious Hengist ; " however, I accept your bet. What a pity that young Magog (that's my fellow's name) is not here to decide the event."

Just at this crisis there was a noise in the street outside.

A blowing of trumpets, neighing of warlike steeds, mingled with the trampling of heavy boots, and the resonant bray of the majestic moke.

" Bless my soul, I forgot !" cried Hengist, suddenly springing up. " It's my niece, Rowena, just landed at the docks. She promised to come and grace this festival with her delectable presence."

" Honoured. I'm sure. Trot her in !" cried King Vortigern.

In a short time the royal lady appeared, and was received with all due honours.

Her beauty amounted to that of Venus, Annie Laurie, Rosalie the Prairie Flower, Polly Perkins, and Jessie the Flower of Dumblane, all knocked into one harmonious whole.

Added to this, she was dressed in robes of regal splendour, so gorgeous as to be bad for the eyes.

What King, who was at all soft about the heart, like Vortigern, could gaze on so lovely a vision without internal damage ? He could not.

She came—he saw—she conquered.

" Roey, my dear," said Hengist, " kneel down, according to custom, and present our most gracious ally, the King of the Britons, with the golden cup of Rhine wine.

" And look here," he added, whispering in her ear as a

private cue, "mind you don't spill any of it, as it spoils the effect."

Graceful as a swan, Rowena knelt down (not that swans ever kneel), and having first taken a sip herself, presented the goblet to the king, with the old Saxon toast, "Waes hael!" to which his majesty, much confused, replied—

"Don't mention it; no trouble at all, I'm sure," and actually drank it all off, giving at the same time a bow so profound that he was obliged to hold on to the table for fear of pitching on his head.

"But about our bet, my liege!" said Hengist. "Here is Magog, come over in my niece's retinue. Now, what do you say?"

Everybody looked at the two young giants.

They certainly were alike, though Magog was, if anything, a trifle the tallest, but Gog made up for it in breadth.

"I think they're a match for each other," remarked Horsa.

"Yes, and a very considerable *match*, too, and one warranted to *strike* well," answered Vortigern, whereat his courtiers, as in duty bound, laughed.

[N. B.—They always laughed at the king's jokes, and he considered it in their wages.]

The two giants introduced themselves to each other, and agreed to oblige the company with a friendly mill.

"So, Magog," said his master, "pull yourself together, for you'll now be able to do as people often tell you, 'hit one your own size.'"

"Shall we have it out with fisteses?" asked Magog, sparring round the room as a preliminary.

"I'm agreeable, young 'un, if our masters say yes,' responded Gog. "How's that for a fist, do you think?" he said, triumphantly clenching his hand, which was then about the size of a seven-pound leg of mutton.

"Suppose, first of all, we see which of them can throw the other," said Vortigern. "What ho! clear the hall there for a wrestling match on a large scale."

VIII.

THE MATCH—THE MILL—THE DISCOVERY—THE SENSATION.

THE hall was cleared accordingly, and Gog and Magog faced each other.

After a mutual survey of each other's strength, they closed.

It was a spectacle of physical force.

Their mighty chests heaved like a volcano on the *eve* of an eruption.

Their muscles stood out like so many Atlantic cables, and they gripped each other as tightly as a couple of boa-constrictors in a death struggle.

A GIANT CONTEST—PUGILISM ON A LARGE SCALE.

Never was seen such wrestling before, never will it be seen again, for the giants that survive in these days, and are shown about in caravans at a penny apiece, are as inferior to

Gog and Magog as a puppy-poodle is to a full-sized New-foundland.

The issue was long and doubtful.

Once Gog nearly went down, and Magog's chance of success accordingly went up; then Gog tried to trip Magog up, but he didn't take the *trip* that time, till, finally, Magog, having grasped Gog's waist so tightly that he declared after-wards he could feel himself meeting inside, knocked him out of time, and the British giant went to the earth.

Shouts of triumph pealed from the Saxon party, and Vortigern confessed that his man was licked.

Gog didn't feel like himself for ten minutes afterwards, till what he called a "mouthful of wine," viz., half a gallon, being administered, he picked up wonderfully, and declared his readiness to continue the contest.

"See if you can get on better at boxing," suggested Hengist, secretly chuckling over the fact that Magog was great at fisticuffs, and sure of victory. "My liege, my bet's almost won."

"Not quite, though," answered Vortigern; "let the mill proceed, and then we'll see about that."

At it again set the two young giants, and it behoves us to describe the mill in language sublimely appropriate to the occasion.

Six rounds altogether were fought : in the first the fistal weapon of Gog visited Magog's proboscis with considerable effect, whereto Magog replied by a rapidly-discharged battery on Gog's lower lip, disturbing the equanimity of his grinders.

In the sixth, and most eventful round, the two gallant fellows, now considerably disguised by bruises, both came up grinning.

Gog's artistically-constructed mauleys planted a liberal assortment of injuries on the majestic features of Magog, who then, letting out with his left, tapped the claret liber-ally; he was answered by a reminder on the nasal organ.

Resenting this, he paid Gog a long bill—two black eyes being among the items—to which Gog gave him a receipt in full, and at last, just after a splendid round of well-planted hits, wound him up by a finisher in the bread-basket.

Time was then called, and it was found that Gog's victory was so complete, that his opponent had the floor all to him-self.

Vortigern was delighted.

"A purse of gold for you, Gog," he cried; "and the appointment of my head porter, for you have nobly vindicated the honour of your country. Hurrah! Britons never will be slaves."

"Softly," interrupted Hengist; "it's only a half victory, or rather a tie, and we are quits. One won, and the other won too."

"That's rather confusing," observed the king, who was rather bad at figures. "I suppose they had better have another set-to to settle it."

"Hullo!" cried Horsa, suddenly; "look at them now."
Everbody did so.

Gog was leaning over the fallen Magog, helping him to rise, and as he did so, gave an exclamation of surprise.

"Whoo! What's this I see?" he cried, opening his eyes to saucer-size. "Have *you* got a cucumber-mark on the back of your neck?"

"To be sure; I've had it ever since I was oorn."

"And I've got just the same, at least it's not the same because it's another one—but look here, isn't it rum? There's some mystery here."

"What family are you of?"

"I've heard I was originally British, or Pictish, or Scottish, or something. I was brought up by the Picts, and sold to a Danish pirate, who appointed me his head powder-monkey," said Magog.

"And I," returned Gog, "lost my twin brother mysteriously ; he was taken away when quite young and tender, by a giant neighbour of ours, who was hungry——"

"And never returned ?" asked Magog, breathlessly.

"Never. It was famine time. The giant in question was our bitterest enemy, and had a very large appetite, so, under the circumstances, the fate of the child was thought to be certain. However, the giant himself was killed next day, and his house entered and robbed by the Picts, who might have *picked* my little brother up."

"And sold him into slavery ?" cried Magog. "Exactly ; it's as clear as pea-soup. *I* was that identical infant."

"Then you are indeed——" cried Gog. "No, can it be ?"

"Oh ! whoo," he added, blubbering with emotion, like a tender-hearted elephant. "This is too much ! But, ha ! Oho ! He, he !—yes, it must be so—we're long-lost brothers, both of us. Let us embrace."

And they did so, the embrace in question being like a railway collision of two powerful engines.

No one with a heart in him could stand by and witness so affecting a scene without the big briny tears bubbling out of his eyes, and rolling down to his very boots in copious showers.

"Of course we can't think of fighting after this," cried Gog. "Our valour has been already proved, and we will make friends, and never, never part, but be hand and glove henceforth, like our royal masters."

"Agreed, agreed," cried the company, unanimously. "Hurrah for Gog and Magog ! Three cheers for the Britons and Saxons !"

"Especially the Saxons," added Hengist aside to Horsa, who winked in reply.

Thus it came to pass that the two brothers, Gog and Magog, became part of the body-guard of Vortigern, who, with great difficulty induced Hengist to part with Gog in return for 1,000 pieces of gold, and the title of Prince of Margate.

IX.

A WEDDING AND A WHACKING.

NOW this Hengist was as deep a card as you'd find anywhere; his head was full of the most unscrupulous dodges, and he always had some speculation in his eye.

He had arranged that his niece Rowena should captivate the heart of Vortigern, which she did, as we have seen, and so rapid was the operation of the spirit of love that he proposed at that very banquet.

She accepted, of course, and forthwith Hengist said:

"Bless you, my children, may you be happy. He's booked," thought he then. "Just

"BLESS YOU, MY CHILDREN!"

let Rocy become queen, and I shall have him under my thumb, and then—ah !"

The marriage took place with immense *eclat*, and Gog and Magog, who attended in the procession, sported wedding favours as big as cart wheels.

Hengist was made prince of all Kent, and Horsa Earl of Sussex, on the same day that Rowena was crowned.

Soon after Hengist, who had all this time been sailing under false colours, put up his real flag.

He openly imported over an immense reinforcement of Saxons, and, when all were landed, told Vortigern to take a month's warning on the spot, and suit himself with a new kingdom somewhere else.

So the Britons and Saxons came to blows, and a long battle was fought at Aylesford, in which Hengist was defeated, and Horsa was killed, after having a *horse-or* two killed under him.

Gog and Magog did great deeds in this and the succeeding engagements, Magog willingly fighting against his treacherous former master.

Vortigern's party soon after came in for an awful defeat, and retreated to London, where they boxed themselves up close as rabbits in a burrow, hence an important part of the metropolis has been called the *Borough* to this day.

Hengist now rode the high horse rough-shod over the liberties of the Britons.

He called himself King of Kent, and by way of showing himself fit for that post, plundered and ravaged right and left, and a great deal more left than right, I should say.

It is said that he pretended to make friends with Vortigern again, invited him to a regal spread, and when he and his lords had got their legs safe under his mahogany, he whistled, and in came a band of assassins to kill him. This may be true, but we won't vouch for it, as our special correspondent was not there.

Vortigern fled, and Hengist seized London, and continued to hold his court there till 498, till he was turned out by the hand of Fate; in other words he demised, after reigning thirty-three years.

Such is the ingratitude of man, that the Britons now turned round upon poor Vortigern, and said that his being outdone in that way by the Saxons proved him to be, politically, a duffer.

They then elected one Ambrosius Emperor of the Britons, and he, joining with the great King Arthur, lord of the west of England, who, as history kindly informs us, was either his son, nephew, brother, uncle, or no relation at all, pitched into the Saxons and Vortigern individually.

Arthur was a wonderful warrior, if five per cent. of what we hear of him is true, which I should say it isn't.

At one battle he is said to have killed 440 men with his own hand—a rather hard day's work, and which shows immense perseverance as well as strength. We should hardly want Armstrong guns or ironclad rams if we had many such fellows nowadays.

As for poor Vortigern, he fled to Wales, lamenting with pathetic *wails* his sad fate, and shut himself up in a castle, which being besieged and burnt by Ambrosius, the old king (unless he escaped) met with the same fate as an overdone loaf; we may, therefore in truth say, peace to his ashes; he was totally uninsured.

Ambrosius now took London, to the great joy of the Britons, and lived there peaceably till war broke out, which wasn't long first; then he went forth and died game in a battle in Hampshire.

After this history records the names of a whole ocean of

kings and chiefs that swayed in Britain. There was Octa, and Ella, and Ida, Ubba and Bubba, and Uffa, and Buffer and Duffer, and Stuffer, and many others too numerous to mention ; and now, ere plunging further into the stirring events of metropolitan history, the hunter after authentic facts must hark back a little, or rather pull up a minute or two, and survey the scene of his operations.

What was London like in those merry old days?

Firstly, though a capital place, it was not *the* capital of England.

York, Winchester, and Canterbury—especially when St. Augustine had turned the natives of this isle into Christians and set them building cathedrals in those towns—were considered great things, while London was but small potatoes ; but come to build a palace, and St. Paul's, and Westminster Abbey, and matters began to look more blooming.

The Venerable Bede (who was said to have been appointed the first beadle of the Burlington, but this is untrue) describes it in 604 as the right sort of place for trade, a fact particularly exemplified by everything being so awfully dear there.

Forty years after the city was ravaged by a great plague, and after that by a fire—which is even a greater plague still, in its way. No less than four times in that unfortunate eighth century was the city burnt to the ground, and though history don't say that it was built up again each time we suppose it was.

The great cause of this was that the houses were mostly built of wood, and consequently *would* burn—whether the inhabitants liked it or not.

Fire engines were not invented, but the people used *water*-engines instead, which did as well, or nearly.

IX.—(*continued.*)

T that time the City was built all on the south side of the river—a very one-sided business that—and was in form a square oval, arranged parallelogrammatically.

The famous Roman Road, called Watling Street (Watling's pork pies will enable you to remember the name), ran from Dover to London, where it began at the town and ended at Ludgate; and talking of that, I think I had better end here, too, for the time only stopping to say, by this period Rome had fallen, and the power of the Cæsars was as dead as the defunctest bloater of the briny ocean.

———

X.

ARRIVAL OF SCANDI-NAVIANS AND OTHER (K)NAVES.

WHEN the Saxons had fairly—or rather, perhaps, unfairly—taken root in Britain, when the whole island was taken by them, they 4thwith divided it into 7 kingdoms, which soon began to 8 each other. In short it was found that these divisions of the land were the cause of a good many other divisions—of opinion—and quarrels, fights, heart-burnings, bilious, and other attacks were continually taking place between the seven kings, whose dominions formed what was called the Saxon Heptarchy.

We should now notice that Britain had changed her name

to England, after the Angles, a tribe of Saxons who had come over here to angle or fish for whatever they could get, and gave their name, and very little else, to the whole country.

In all the quarrels between the native chiefs, the Londoners wisely took the right part—namely, their own; for depend upon it, the best side of a quarrel is always the *outside,* and for the weaker parties especially, it is wisest to keep out of it altogether.

At last these various royal *birds* who had feathered their nests in England, were all brought under what they considered the *hard yoke* of the great *Eg-*bert, King of Wessex, who knocked the seven kingdoms into one, thus proving that seven into one would go—a remarkable arithmetical discovery, and of *sum* importance in history.

He made London the capital of England, and never has *capital* been productive of more *interest.*

This was in the seventh century.

So things were going on bloomingly, when suddenly the proud and hardy Dane did condescendingly *deign* to look with favour on this isle, and each piratical rover in Denmark did, from his *den, mark* how things here were looking.

So, very soon did some *fresh* foes come across the *salt* sea to as-*sault* the English, and put our affairs into a terrible pickle.

We have all heard of "Ada with the golden hair," a highly attractive female, but these golden-haired masculines were not *aiders* at all to us; they were inv-aders, which made all the difference.

They sailed up the Thames as far as London Bridge Railway Station—that is, as far as they would have been if built at the time—and the Danish chief had at all events a long *train* of followers.

King Egbert instantly summoned a *Witenagemot*, or Parliament, to London, to decide what should be done against those *Dane*-gerous enemies.   The decision was "Smash'em!"

But this was easier said than done, and the "hardy Norsemen," despite all opposition, continued to do as they darn please in the metropolis.

No less than thrice during this reign did the Danes pay us visits, leaving substantial marks of their affection in the way of houses plundered, property devastated, and people slain.

The third time, however, these Danish wolves found themselves confronted by an English wolf, namely, King Ethel-*wolf*, who, with his son Ethel-*bald*, so called because he never had any *heir* to his *crown*, faced the Danish troops and cut them into pieces, securing one great *peace* for himself by special treaty.

For the next fifty years (with a holiday sometimes, of course) the Danes kept on at their work of harrassing Britain, till at last that glorious royal brick, King Alfred the Great, assumed the position of schoolmaster to the Danes, and by repeated *thrashings*, taught them a valuable *lesson*—to let their neighbours alone.

He rebuilt our walls, and so embellished the city that it would have been "beautiful for ever," had it not been burnt down a few years afterwards.

But each time it rose from its ashes with *ash*tonishing rapidity, and improved each time, so that its frequent destruction was the making of it.

In 994, the kings of Norway and Denmark, those potent Scandanavians—who, however, as they had such a large fleet, can scarcely be called *Scanty-navy-'uns* at all (Oh!), were seen a-sailing up the Thames, with the intention of *assailing* the Metropolis.

But it was "no go," or rather it *was* a "go," as far as they were concerned, for the Britons made them go back again a wee bit more speedily than they came.

Again, in 1015, in the "merry old days, the merry old days of King Canute," the Danish fleet of 200 vessels—and vessels of wrath they proved to be—attacked this city of ours, but were defeated by the heroic Edmund Steelribs, otherwise Ironsides, the original inventor of iron-clads.

But King Canute prevailed afterwards, and got all England under his royal thumb.

On London he poured the weight of his vengeance to the tune of £10,000 taxes—a heart-rending sum in those times, and not paid with that ecstatic delight which we take in settling with the tax-collector nowadays.

Subsequently, King Canute came to the same end as Queen Anne—he died, and thereupon "the powers that was" assembled in London, and after putting their heads together, placed the crown on that of Harold.

In the same way that Hardicanute and Edward the Confessor were chosen kings in London, which had now started a mint, and had the privilege of both coining its sovereigns and crowning them.

In 1052, Earl Goodwin—who was wrongfully named, for he was neither *good*, nor did he *win* in the contest—turned against his rightful sov., and showed fight.

He sailed up the Thames and threatened London; blood would have flowed, to a very dead certainly, had not Ned and Goody, as Edward and Goodwin affectionately called each other, come to a little arrangement, so that the effusion of gore was mercilessly corked up in time.

Edward the Confessor died in 1065, having proved himself a little too good for this world, and thus different to most of the rulers of the period, who were too much the other way.

He rebuilt Wesminster Abbey, and lived *abbey* ever afterwards.

May he rest in peace !   His old boots are still to be seen in wondrous preservation.

We now come to the *stormy reign* of King Harold the Second, when the political barometer was prophesying squalls and things in general looked uncomfortably black.

Among many others, William, Duke of Normandy, held the opinion that Harold had no more right to the crown of England, than he had to that of the Sandwich Islands, which were not even discovered.

So, overflowing with pure benevolence, the Norman conqueror took ship, and all the men he could get together, and set sail for England to set matters straight.

We all know the result, how he came, saw, and conquered, and altogether proved a second *seizer*.

As the old chronicler hath it, "Ye Saxonnes at ye battaile of Hastyngs, got wun of ye moste treemendus bastings," ending "Grand Tableau—Death of Harold—Victory of the Normans, curtain descends amid blue fire, and raptures of applause."

William marched to London highly victorious, happy and glorious, and he not only *Marched* there, but he September'd, and October'd and December'd there as well, and on the always-to-be-remembered Christmas Day of 1066, he was crowned king in Westminster Abbey.

Proceed we to give an account of the coronation—one of the greatest *spectacles*—gold-rimmed or otherwise—ever witnessed in this country.

XI.

THE CROWNING OF KING BILL.

IT was a very fine day—the weather having been specially ordered beforehand—and everything in nature had put on its dulcetest aspect, and its most beaming smile, when Duke William the Norman rode *forth*, or rather, rode *first*, to Westminster Abbey to be crowned.

There had been a considerable difficulty to get this disinterested and self-denying personage to accept the crown at all.

He had come over here, he said, with his 5,000 or so of armed men, from motives of pure benevolence, and didn't expect to get anything by it—oh, dear, no, of course not! And as to making himself king, he really—upon his word—well, he'd hear what his friends said about it.

Of course they saw which way the wind blew, and advised him accordingly.

"Accept it by all means, my lord," said the Bishop of Winchester, piously turning up the ivory whites of his reverend optical organs. "Don't you know we are commanded in this world to take all we can get? I do religiously."

"Well, you're about right," responded the duke, "and I think, from what I've heard, the crown of England will fit me very well; at all events I'll try it on, and I can but bolt back again if I find the honour really too great."

So the long and short of it was that the ceremony was fixed for the 25th sharp, and all was done to prepare for it.

London was turned into a scene as dazzling as the "Boundless Realms of Blazing Brilliancy" represented in the pantomime.

The best Brussels carpets were laid down in the streets of London. Every house was newly painted, the combined perfume, being of course, delicious—*festoons* and many other *tunes* were perceptible everywhere, and bags and flanners— we beg pardon, flags and banners—waved from every window and chimney pot. The bells rang a triple bob-major, the braying of trumpets and of donkeys resounded through the welkin, and the dulcet hurdygurdy chimed in with its pleasing note.

As to the crowd, it was immense. One special correspondent, standing at a street corner, counted 20,000 persons passing, in five minutes only. There was a general holiday, and everybody felt it a point of duty to be as jolly as possible.

But though the public houses had been ordered to supply liquor gratis, and every drinking fountain ran half and half, nobody was drunk—not yet—but perhaps that wasn't their fault.

Of course all the seats along the line of procession had been let out at fancy prices, and the shop windows had had their goods taken out, and eager spectators put there instead—some of them being ticketted up as " in this style 7s. 6d. ; a great variety within."

And now, clad in his " corronacyione toggerye," as the old chronicler spells it, the duke with his train hove in sight. He was mounted on a magnificent Botany Bay charger—a thoroughbred Roman-nosed, camel-backed, high-stepping pacer he was—with trappings of mauve velvet turned up with silver ; his outer robe (the duke's, not the horse's) was of cloth of gold, lined with ermine, and silver fox skin, and fretted, filagreed, and faltheralled in a highly imposing manner. His moustache had been beautifully curled by machinery and stood out like a corkscrew, and his hair had been highly scented by Rimmel and Co's Patent Perfume Pump.

For William rode bare-headed, as a sort of hint how ready he was to thatch his ducal nob with the Britannic crown.

Attending him on each side were the Constable of England and the Lord Chancellor, carrying the swords of Mercy and Justice.

And behind came a long string of earls, baronets, knights, squires, yeomen, pages, and a hundred other more or less swellish retainers, too numerous to mention.

The cheers that greeted every step of the regal candidate's charger were absolutely deafening.   They shook every house to its foundation, and were visible, it is said, at twenty miles' distance.   You may be sure that the police had enough to do to keep order among the crowd, taking up those who pushed too far forward, and *taking* them *down* a peg or two as well.

Gog and his brother, Magog, clad in the awe-inspiring togs of the " Crusher " of the period, had enough to do to larrup the street-boys, who kept " a-climbing on the lamp-postes," and otherwise keeping the motley throng in something like subjection.

" What !" the bewildered reader naturally exclaims, " were Gog and Magog there ?   Why, they must have been several hundred years old by that time ; hang it all, this won't do, you know ; we can't swallow *that*, whatever we may do to our dinner !"

But oh, incredulous peruser, know ye that all related in this history is true as Gospel—even the Gospel according to St. Benjamin (if you know where *that* sacred book is to be found).

We, your chronicler, resemble the extinct elephant that used to sleep upright because he had no bend in his legs—

we are utterly *incapable of lying*. The explanation of the fact is in this wise.

The ancient Britons were, as we have said, a hardy and long-lived race. Each attained the age of 120—some say 150 years.

Now Gog and Magog, though confessedly degenerated from the stature of their ancestors, whose average height was about thirty feet, were nearly fifteen feet (still a tidy size, mind you), and when fairly measured up, through, and across, their dimensions were exactly equal to those of ten men of ordinary size.

Now, in any case, a person of fifteen feet high is likely to live *longer* than people of common stature, and it stands to reason that a giant ten times as big as an ordinary man will live as long as ten men put together.

This would give them 1,200 years to live, so that at the time we speak of they were just in the prime and vigour of manhood. They had, in sooth, grown somewhat since their celebrated tussle in the halls of Vortigern, and were now unmatched in all England for size, strength, and stamina.

All the kings who had successively reigned in England had appreciated their value, and they were appointed perpetual head-porters and everlasting body-guards to each monarch in turn.

Edward the Confessor was their last master, though they had fought a little under Harold, but the King William graciously pardoned them, and retained them in their posts.

They were in full rig on the Coronation Day, and as they walked down the street like two moving towers, it was a sight to make street-boys slide down the lamp-posts with a run, and induce pickpockets to levant up side-courts with all their speed.

The king-elect and his company marched up the beautiful

central aisle—the organ playing "Beautiful *Isle* of the Sea,'' that is, the *see* of the Bishop of London.

Stigand, the Archbishop of Canterbury, wanted to have the crowning job himself, but having offended the pope, that potentate had, so to speak, put him in the corner like a naughty boy, and commanded him to do nothing till he was ordered.

For you must know that in those days, whenever the Pope issued a *bull*, the whole world was *cowed* into submission.

So Aldred, Archbishop of York, succeeded to the honour, and a great success it was.

The duke and his folks marched solemnly along the *naves* that led to the *altar*—many *knaves* used to go to the *halter* in those hanging days ; and, in spite of the half concealed frowns of many of his Saxon subjects, the duke was as cool as a cucumber, and the crowd *went on*, and the affair *came off* with what the historian calls " a bust of éclat."

Our friends, Gog and Magog, now splendidly clad in state dress, as chief of the king's personal retainers, stood on each side of the throne to give effect to the imposing spectacle, and an imposing *pair of spectacles* they looked, better than any manufactured by the best makers.

The Archbishop first asked the English, or Saxons, whether they would have the Duke of Normandy for their king, which was rather unnecessary, since they couldn't help themselves, and they knew very well that if they said "No," there would be a row in the house, or rather in the cathedral, so they consented.

The Normans of course gave their consent with loud cheers, and cries of " Rather !" " Bill's the man !" " The genuine and only," &c.

To which the duke responded by some of the finest bows that were ever performed, and a look of general bene-

volence all around that was worth taking a guinea ticket to
see.

Still, there were one or two little hitches in the proceedings.

The crown didn't fit so well as it might ; the sacred oil
was a little too rich, especially when it anointed the ears of
his new majesty, and trickled all down his back.

Still the king was rather nervous, and seemed sometimes
as if he didn't exactly know what he was about, or what he
was saying.   When asked how he would take the oath of
fidelity, he replied—

" Warm, with sugar, please."

At which the Archbishop was so shocked, that his *mitre*
fell right over his nose, and he said it *might ha'* blinded him.

However, the king begged 10,222 pardons, and answered
at last that he would take the oath standing at the altar, as
per usual.

" Now," said the archbishop, " will you swear to govern
this kingdom right down to the very sea-beach in conformity
with all the laws hitherto made, and several others of your
own composing ?"

" I does," responded the king.

" Will you promise faithfully to take all the cash, lands,
revenues, and other possessions you can possibly get hold
of ?"

" Rather !" winked his majesty.

"And to bring over all your relations, friends, cronies,
favourites, partisans, and supporters ; and put them into the
best billets, and divide the whole country amongst them ?"

" I will so !" was the royal reply.

" Then," responded his grace, " you'll make the very best
king that ever was manufactured, whether native or
imported."

When the crown was put on, and all the other royal fixtures were duly set up, the king was so bowed down by his emotion and the weight of the honours conferred upon him, that he fell right off his throne, and was *thrown* on to the floor sprawling.

It was a sad thing to see him, and his crown, and his sceptre, and his ermined robes all lying *holus bolus* on the Brussels carpet.

His dignity and his shins were both very much hurt.

However, Gog and Magog soon saw his case, and promptly stooping down, they hoisted him into his throne as easily as if he had been a babe of ten months old.

When he sank into the luxurious velvet

THE THRONE, AND THE KING "THROWN" OFF.

cushions there was a loud cheer, and "God Save the King" was struck up, very much out of tune, for it wasn't actually composed till centuries afterwards.

The king then granted the people of London a new charter—embodying all sorts of privileges—and went home to dinner.

The crowd having cheered till their throats ached, and bonneted several policemen, dispersed with an "ugly rush," and sought the romantic seclusion of the various public houses.

After that they went home, and there were holly and mistletoe, and plum pudding, and all other ingredients for keeping a "jolly Christmas," according to the custom of the " good old time."

The reign of the Norman monarch, which commenced in the highly successful manner we have so graphically described, continued brillaint to the end, and shines out in the page of history like a prime quality composite candle.

Those were lovely times for the city too, for, except three great fires that nearly burnt it to ashes, the plague once or twice, and a few trifling calamaties of this sort, London got on as comfortably as one o'clock.

———

XII.

THE CURFEW—LONDON IMPROVEMENTS.

WE have spoken of the priviliges the king granted the citizens, prominent among which was the license to bruise their own oats, adulterate their own beer, and double up their own perambulators.

Still they considered themselves aggrieved in many respects, especially in the introduction of the curfew, established it was said, in order that there might oc-*cur few* fires in the metropolis.

The law was that at the ringing of a bell at eight o'clock or so, everybody should at once put out their fires, pipes, cigars, or other smokables or burnables, and turn off their gas at the main.

Any youth who ventured forth after the prohibited hours

with even a fragrant cigarette between his adolescent lips, ran a chance of being tightly nabbed, and it was dangerous even to display a *fiery* red head of hair or to allow one's eyes to "flash *fire*," when the bell had rung.

Any gay young *spark* who was *burning* with love had to be very careful not to put too much of the *fire* of genius into his melodious serenades.

No wonder the Londoners looked upon the curfew as a Norman nuisance, and the death knell of English liberty.

THE CURFEW.——"PUT OUT THAT LIGHT AND THEN———"—— *Shakespeare.*

As Shakespeare very justly observes :

> "Hear it not, London, for it is a bell
> That summons thee to Heaven or to——well,
> I won't say where."

The first thing William did when he was fairly fixed on his throne, was to make a survey of all the lands in England, and put it all down in a big book which he intended should last for ever, and so called it the Doomsday Book, and I think if a modern reader were to study till Doomsday he wouldn't understand it ; besides, as it contains nothing about London, I can scarcely see in what way the attempt would benefit the present history.

Many important buildings were begun by the great Norman Bill, who may be thus considered a great Norman *Bill*-der.

It was he who commenced the construction of the Tower, which he generously placed *at-our* disposal, providing good accommodation for prisoners, including rack, thumscrews, and other instruments of torture, free of charge.

It was first called the White Tower—which it was externally, and thus presented a lively contrast to the *black* deeds too often committed inside.

Likewise did King William rear up the now dilapidated St. Paul's, sparing no expense, as the money did not come out of his own pocket ; yet alas, and alack ! in the year 1086, this fine cathedral was burnt down, it was supposed through the *warmth* of religious zeal shown by the clergy.

The ruins were piteous to behold, and many opinions were expressed as to the best way of remedying the disaster, till one acute alderman suggested that the cathedral should be built up again, for which happy thought he was presented with a putty medal on the spot.

A little before this Alwin Childe (not a very young *Childe*, as he was nearly seventeen), founded Bermondsey Priory, the first monastery since the conquest, and after that religious houses sprang up all over London as plentifully as blackberries, but a great deal bigger.

Queen Maud, Henry the First's good lady, built a few of them, besdies the hospital of St. Giles's, Bow Bridge, and other architectural fakements.

But we anticipate. Hop we back, therefore, for a paragraph or two to King William the First.

He reigned twenty-one years, and then gave it up.

He never got very far into the hearts of the English people.

They knew that though a *stout* man, he had *slender* claims to the throne—many of them hated him for being a Norman, (as if he could help that), likewise they objected to paying him so large a screw, forgetting that when once people accept a *Bill*—royal or otherwise, they have to pay for it, *willy-nily*, as the saying is, and it was more *Willy* than nily in this case.

However he's dead now, so it's no use talking.

After his dissolution in 1087, he was succeeded by his *dissolute* son, called William Rufus, called the *Red Heir* to the throne, from the brilliant hue of his flowing locks, which threw that of the carrot far far into the shade.

He did some good for London, enlarged the Tower so as to accommodate more prisoners, built London Bridge, and also Westminster Hall, which was more important than *Hall* the rest of his works put together.

The *Roof* of St Paul's was also repaired by *Roof*-us.

In 1109 the First Harry, surnamed *Beauclerk*, because he dressed so gorgeously, and wrote a beautiful round hand, seized the crown by a fluke, ousting his elder brother Bob in a manner that very naturally caused a *bobbery*.

He said he would have to keep in with the Londoners, whom he treated therefore to a liberal allowance of soft soap, and so won them over to his side.

The city guilds were first established in this reign, which, if not a *golden* age, was certainly the age of *gilding*.

Oh! for such times again; why, enough corn to feed a hundred people at four meals, was sold for twelve pence, or one shilling. (It would be a rare *sell* to try and get it for such a price now, eh! reader?) And fourpence, by the same rule, would buy a live sheep, or forage to last a horse twenty days.

Monasteries, churches, and hospitals, increased in London at a surprising rate, about this time, and Bartholomew Fair was founded, together with many other *thorough-fares*, which was a *fair* sign of prosperity.

In the reign of Stephen, London had a bad turn of luck.

The king taxed his subjects within an inch of their lives. Some people found the place too *hot* to hold them, especially when the city was burnt down, which happened several times at this period.

But people began to get used to it, like eels do to skinning.

At last the mild and refreshing reign of Henry the Second began.

London prospered again. She grew rich, and started a stone bridge, which was supported by the *peers* of the realm, and every *arch* separately blessed by the *Arch*-bishop of Canterbury.

Clean sheets were also put on the bed of the river, 1157 A.D.

Cheapness still prevailed.

What do you think of a sheep for sixpence, a tidy horse for three shillings, and a fat ox for four shillings? A quartern loaf was sold for a half-penny.

What the price of lucifer matches could have been passes my comprehension; you would have wanted very strong spectacles to see the coin, I'm thinking.

XIII.

FIRST   LORD   MAYOR'S   DAY.—FULL   PARTICULARS.—SPECIAL
REPORT.

ALL this brings us to the reign of the first Richard, the most thorough royal British (Cœur de) Lion in all history.

As a warrior, his equal was not to be had for love or money. He was never at peace but when he was fighting; never felt at home but when he was abroad, and almost all the time he occupied the English throne, he was several hundred miles away from it.

Consequently he did not spend much time in England, much more in London, and when he did come, it was generally to borrow money for his crusading speculations.

While he was away, his ministers played the very dickens, especially one Chancellor Longchamp, who made himself an emphatic nuisance.

He had the cheek to set to enlarging the Tower so much that it took in all the surrounding ground, which was a regular *take in* altogether—and threatened, if proceeded with in that style, to swallow up the whole city.

There was a row, and Longchamp got the sack, which was ex-*sack*-ly what he deserved.

The Londoners were so grateful that they started a subscription to get King Richard out of pawn—he was pining away in an Austrian prison, literally a " pretty dickey " in a cage, for we know by the Blondel affair how he used to sing in captivity.

When he came back to his loving London subjects they

gave him a grand reception, " on a scale of magnificence hitherto unattempted," as the advertisements said.

Great improvements had been made in London ; even the wooden houses were now built of stone ; the streets too, had been so wonderfully improved that the mud was never more than a foot deep, and in very hard frosts you could walk along without wetting your boots.

But now we come to a most important event, the invention of Lord Mayor's Day.

Previous to this the title of the chief magistrate had been simply that of bailiff, and it is said that he wore a *bay leaf* wreath by way of eminence, which we *bay-lieve* to be true.

But now, in 1194, the Lion-hearted king, knowing that he owed the citizens a debt of gratitude and 2,000 crowns, agreed to allow them to appoint the first Lord Mayor of London.

They fixed upon Henry FitzAlwyn, son of Simon Alwyn, who was a descendant in a direct line from the celebrated Simple Simon, who immortalised himself by meeting the pieman, and other gallant deeds.   Henry was styled Fitz, because, in riches and generosity, he beat into *fits* all the other aldermen put together.

By trade he was a grocer, tailor, floor-cloth manufacturer, or something of that kind.

But, be it as it may, he was as popular as money itself, and a rare treat was promised the citizens on the 9th of November, 1194, when they intended to do him honour, besides giving a grand public reception to their liberated monarch, thus killing two very big birds with one stone.

For the benefit of those of our readers who were not alive seven hundred years ago, we will give a full description of the ceremonial, and the high jinks performed in London on that eventful day—extracted from an old chronicle, so worn and torn that we can't make out a single word of it.

However, here it is—

" City decked out as usual; banners, scarfs, flowers, ribbons, etcetera, etcetera, as before; streets cleared, traffic stopped, crowd kept in order as much as possible.

" First came a band of trumpets, each with a man behind it, who, with considerable cheek, was blowing his own. On each side of this cymbals, drums, pipes, flutes, concertinas, gongs, and triangles, all playing out of tune or time, and outdoing Babel itself.

" Next, a detachment of mounted spearmen, *speering* round at the crowd, and other mounted warriors, carrying flags of gorgeous tints; then the men in brass, hired from the Drury Garden Theatre, for the day, at a bob each, and everything found.

" Next, the Lord Mayor's footmen in their full uniforms of a bright *liver*-colour—and thence called *liveries*, and with their calves newly stuffed with the very best straw.

" Then all the City companies, smoking short pipes and carrying long flag poles.

" Then a lot more officials, staggering under the weight of banners and other encumbrances, and looking about as uncomfortable as they knew how.

" Last, but not least—far from it—came the Lord Mayor himself.

" He rode a fine mouse-coloured ambling palfrey, the *state* coach being then in a future *state*—for it hadn't been introduced yet.

" Over his lordship's head was borne a canopy of crimson silk, fringed with gold, to keep off the rain (if any).

" The supporters of this were no others than our old

friends Gog and Magog, very old friends they were by this time, but they carried their centuries wonderfully.

"The renowned giants were still in the personal service of the king, who, however, generally lent them to the Lord Mayor, or other City magnates, on big occasions.

"They were specially on their mettle to-day, as report went that the king had brought home from the East a couple of terifically-ferocious Moorish giants, who boasted that they could 'double up' any number of English ones in half no time.

"Grand indeed looked Gog and Magog in their full uniform, and with their glittering weapons; and grander still, if possible, looked his lordship the Mayor in his majesterial 'get up,' all crimson velvet, at I don't know how much a yard, and furred splendidly; round his worshipful neck was a rich collar of S. S. (signifying Splendiferous Swell), with an immense diamond hanging wiggle-waggle from the front of it; a massive double chain of warranted twenty-five carat gold was wound twice round his chest.

"Beside him came the man with the mace, the bearer of the City sword, the *crier* (who was *laughing*), the sheriffs, bailiffs, aldermen, and above all in splendour, the awe-inspiring City beadle.

"Punctually at five-and-twenty minutes after the proper time, his Majesty King Richard started forth from his palace at the Tower, on a grand Royal progress through the City; all was serene—weather, people, flags, and even the temper of the much-tried policemen.

"Gallant and gay was the monarch's mien as he tooled along on his celebrated Syrian Barb, Kahfoozelum, an animal of such tremendous mettle that he almost knocked out his own front teeth with his fore legs, he took such high steps.

The king wore his Sunday crown, and his brother, Prince

John, who immediately followed him, clad in 'gorgeous bright,' might have been observed to cast his eye on that crown very long and longingly."

Our best plan, in order to bring this grand spectacle before the eyes of the modern public, is to quote from contemporary authorities the programme of the procession—

Police to clear the way.

Two Family Heralds.

Detachment of Royal Horse Guards Green.

Yeoman of the Palace in Togs of State.

His Majesty's Private Band, playing *inaudibly.*

The King Himself.

The Queen Herself.

Swells and Swellesses in attendance.

Field-Marshal H. R. H. Prince John, K.C.B.,
K.D.G., K.L.M., K.Q.X., &c.

Princes, Dukes, Barons, Knights,
And Pages of History.

The Archbishops, Bishops, Chancellors,
Chamberlains, and other exalted Parties, all
Mounted, except those on Foot.

Blondel, the King's Minstrel, performing **a**
Rondolletto on a three-stringed Flute.

Funnidawg, the King's Fool, or Court Jester,
cracking Jokes, to Choruses of Laughter.

Royal Horse Guards Brown.

The King's Elephants (two), led by a couple of Gigantic
Moorish Attendants, warranted (in their own estimation) to
take the shine out of Gog and Magog.

Band of the very Cold Stream Guards (shivering).

Master of the (Towel) Horse.

Mistress of the Royal Wash-tub.

Band of the Hot Stream Guards (perspiring).

The British Lion.
Two Pages to hold up the tail of ditto.
Copper Stick in Waiting.
Groom of the Dust-bin to H. R. H. Prince John
Keeper of the King's Conscience (in a box).
One-humped Camel in Waiting.
(Of course preceded by a Band playing—
"The *Camels* are Coming!")
The Foresters, led by Robin Hood and Little John
in person.
Two-humped Camel in Attendance.
Bean-Stick in Waiting.
The Astronomer Royal (with telescope complete).
Cats of the King's Palace.
Kittens in Waiting.
More Soldiers, Servants, Bands, Policemen.
Tag-rag and Bob-tail in Waiting.

The great point to be noticed in this splendid procession, is that the king went first, or nearly so, and not last, in accordance with the senseless modern custom.

The cheers were deafening, and the shouts of the millions set the flags waving like a nor'-easter.

Flowers were spread in the king's path so plentifully that the royal steeds could hardly get along for them, and the number of loyal mottos hung up everywhere was absolutely bewildering, especially as to the spelling of them.

The lord mayor met the king at Aldgate, or thereabouts, and forthwith knelt before him, a rather difficult feat on horseback, handing him the city fire-irons as a token of loyalty.

The king thanked him, saying he was much obliged all the same, but didn't want the bother of carrying those cumbrous specimens of ironmongery about with him.

He then knighted the lord mayor on both shoulders, with the pair of tongs, and told him to be off.

Sir Henry did so with pride on his brow, and prepared to lead his lawful sovereign through the capital.

While the king of England and the king of London thus met and greeted, Gog and Magog, the city giants, and Mumbo and Jumbo, the two big blackamoors in the king's train, were brought face to face.

Mumbo and Jumbo were ten feet high, at least, and in strength looked fully equal to their British rivals.

" How are you ?" asked the latter, wishing to do the civil to the distinguished foreigners.

They replied in their native language—

" Ram chumderee bunderee bago."

Accompanying this with a fierce look, and a significant pointing to the handles of their big scimitars.

" Oh, that's it, is it ?" cried Gog.   " I'll tell you what, my festive Christy Minstrels, if you're on for a fight, we're your men ; and if our royal master agrees, we'll differ at once, and have it out with the mawleys."

As he accompanied these words by clenching his hand, which, big at any time, was of course *twice* as big when *doubled*, the two darkies " *comprennied* immediate."

The king and lord mayor being asked, replied that nothing would please them more than to witness a contest between the four giants, to ascertain whether those two English *wights* could conquer the two Moorish *blacks*.

" Have it out by all means !" cried King Richard, heartily. " Black to win."

———

XIV.

THE FIGHT—THE BANQUET—THE RIDDLE—THE GONG.

"I BACK white, your majesty, for 2,000 dollars!" exclaimed the lord mayor.

"Done!" responded Cœur de Lion, who thus saw his way out of the heavy debt he owed the City.

Almost everybody else was too loyal not to take the king's side, but the lord mayor was confident of victory on the part of the City giants.

And now began one of the strangest combats ever witnessed in any London street.

Mumbo and Jumbo, who apparently didn't understand fist fighting, drew their scimitars, and, not content with this, seized a further advantage by vaulting on to the backs of the elephants, and expressing by the words "Falderee, cholderee lol," that they meant to have it out mounted.

"Very good," replied Gog and Magog.

So one drew his formidable mace, and the other his stout staff, with a chain and spiked ball at the end, and without more ado attacked the blackies at a disadvantage. In sooth, the latter ought to have beat; everything was in their favour.

They were not only in such an elevated position that they could easily get a "good swipe" at their adversaries, but they had great skill with those murderous crooked swords of theirs, and, in addition to this, they had taught their elephants to assist them by bringing down their trunks and tails heavily on the heads or other parts of the enemies' anatomy.

"Ah! would you?" cried Gog to Jumbo's elephant. "I'll

soon stop that game !" and, seizing the trunk in his mighty hand, he held the animal tight while, with the other, he belaboured the Moor with his ball club.

Magog in the same manner felt himself being nicely knocked about in the small of the back by the tail of Mumbo's elephant, while the master of that quadruped was trying to slice his head off with his sabre.

Turning round fiercely, Magog cried, " I'll soon bring your tail to the last chapter," and so, exerting all his strength he tied the offending member into ever so many tight knots which the elephant could *not* untwist, tug as he would, and this kept him busy, and allowed Magog more opportunity to peg away at the swarthy rider.

SLAUGHTEROUS AND ELEPHANTINE COMBAT BETWEEN THE GIANTS
(From a picture recently hung at Guildhall by Calcraft.)

Mumbo and Jumbo, finding themselves repulsed, swore a terrific African oath, and grasping their scimitars, resolved to send Gog and Magog to the *scimetar*-y (!) by killing them at once.

Long and ferocious was the contest that ensued, till at last Magog, taking advantage of the elephant's quandary with regard to his tail (which was made worse by Magog twisting his trunk into a knot too), and the consequently helpless state of the animal, leaped on his back and attacked Mumbo on his own level.

The darky soon found himself disarmed, and Magog, flinging away his club, wrestled with him in a close struggle.

After a time the Saracen felt himself giving way, and, despite his efforts, he was at Magog's mercy, who at last gave him such a mighty kick, that he flew right off the elephant's back and fell to the ground ten yards off, as heavily as half a ton of coals.

Then Magog, untwisting the elephant's tail and trunk, gave the animal a few encouraging pats, and ambled victoriously away, amid the cheers of the spectators.

Meanwhile Gog, with difficulty avoiding the slashing cuts of Jumbo, nevertheless gave the snout of his elephant such a long and strong pull that that animal objected by means of a loud roar.

Jumbo got several staggering blows from Gog's spiked ball, but still kept his perch, till at last, worked up to fury, he stooped over his elephant's head, and gave such a wide whirring sweep of his mighty scimitar, as would have inevitably slithered off our friend's head in a jiffey, if it had not missed, but it did miss, and the consequence was that the Moorish giant overbalanced himself, and fell headlong to the ground.

It was lucky for him his turban was thickly stuffed, or his brains (if any) would have been knocked clean out.

"Hurrah?" cried Gog, jumping on the riderless elephant's back, "all's fair in war. We've changed places, and it's my turn to give you a little cavalry charge.   Come on !"

But the Moor declined any *more* of it ; he grew *moor*-ose and sulky, and giant as he was, began to feel as small as Tom *Moore* himself.

Gog and Magog, therefore, came out of the contest with flying colours ; the people cheered lustily and made heroes of the two giants, who had thus upheld the honour of England.

The king looked rather serious at finding he had lost his bet, and doubled his debt to the City.

But he soon regained his customary good humour, and declared himself so pleased with the City giants that he would appoint them honorary keepers to the royal menagerie.

The procession now moved on, the two beaten *blacks*, who were beaten *black* and blue, falling to the rear, and slinking behind their elephants in a a very crestfallen manner.

The king went by water to Westminster, in a splendid barge that seemed like a big floating lump of gingerbread. It must have looked *sweet*, mustn't it ?

He returned by land, and was entertained at the town hall by one of those grand feasts, which when once eaten, are never forgotten.

The turtle went down beautifully, the roast beef of old England smoked on the board, and fat haunches of venison killed in Sherwood by Robin Hood himself, graced the festal table-cloth.

To give a catalogue of the wines, and the prices of them would be downright impossible.

The king, becoming wondrous affable and condescending under the influence of the festive scene, rose at exactly the proper moment, and, addressing his host, the lord mayor, said—

"My lord, can you tell me what is the difference between

yourself, in the capacity of magistrate, and this golden goblet ?"

The lord mayor cudgelled his brains, but couldn't guess the riddle for the life of him ; no more could anyone else, not even Funnydawg, the royal jester, who was good at such puzzles.

"Well," said the king, "I'll tell you. You are a *beak* and this is a *beaker*."

Then he raised the vessel to his lips, and winking over the rim, drank the lord mayor's health.

Of course every loyal subject laughed at this joke till he rolled under the table ; and the lord mayor, when he had sufficiently recovered, gave "The health of our most gracious and facetious monarch, Richard the First."

FIRST LORD MAYOR'S DAY——KING
RICHARD'S RIDDLE.

Drunk with all honours. *Readers are entreated not to give it up.*

"And now," continued his majesty, "I'll give you a song. Blondel, tune up your weapons of harmony, and prepare to come in at the right cue."

Then, in a deep, manly, royal, *basso profundo*, which, in the lower parts, seemed to go down to his very boots, the king trolled the following lay, concerning the celebrated occurrence of his captivity and release :—

Air.—"Partant pour la Syrie."

"It was King Dick the (ahem!) young and brave,
    Came home from Palestine;
But first they caught and shut him up
    In prison near the Rhine.
Till one fine day he heard a flute,
    That played a well-known air;
He climbed the grating and looked out,
    And who do you think was there?"

Blondel (striking in)—

Air.—"The gentleman that, &c."

"The party that you heard,
    Who warbled like a bird,
A-sitting on the stump of a tree;
    With pleasure and surprise,
    You soon did recognise,
A gentleman that looked like me.
    Sure—as—*you're* alive
    Lucky 'twas I *did* arrive,
    England did *thus* contrive,
To set Cœur-de-Lion free-ee.
    Oh! the party that you heard,
    Who warbled like a bird,
Was the gentleman that looked like me.
                    (*Chorus twice over.*)

King Richard (joining chorus)—
    "Oh! the party that you heard, &c."
                    (*Chorus twice over.*)

And, will you believe it, this chorus was taken up by every voice in that large assembly, and even taken up by the policemen outside, though we don't know whether they took it to the station house.

However, the reception of the king by the City, on the first Lord Mayor's Day, went off altogether (and so did several fireworks, by the bye) in such a brilliant style, that it deserves to be recorded for evermore, or "to the grand everlasting," as the French say.

So now let us draw a veil over this picture of festivity in

the good old times, and get on with the progress of events in our very much unparalleled history.

XV.

THE HISTORY MAKES A FRESH START.

AFTER Richard, the next monarch on the cards was John, an artful card himself, and by no means the Jack of Trumps he was at first supposed to be.

In fact, it was soon apparent that he wasn't so good but what he might have been a great deal better without hurting himself *much*.

Instead of being an upright king, he was a *downright* despot, oppressed the people *desp'ot*-ly.

Still he was rather benevolent to the people of London, especially when he wanted them to lend him money.

Jews came in for it heavily. If they objected to hand over the coin, there was a Jews (*deuce*) of a noise. They were clapped into prison, and tortured till the blood came, so that John used to *bleed* the people in two ways.

All this, as you know, roused the British lion, and made that noble quadruped so wag his tail and open his mouth, and give such loud growls, that the king was frightened into signing Magna Charta.

It was a bitter pill, and he never got over it to the last day of his life.

London was to the *fore* in *for*-cing the king to this just measure, and one of the clauses in the charter provided that the City should enjoy all its ancient privileges, meals, &c., as aforetime of old.

You see we had come to know Master John by this time,

and it wouldn't do to trust him much further than we could see him.

Why, when we had a row with the Pope, who insisted upon being paid from John no less than 400,000 marks of gold (besides 100,000 marks of respect), the king made the City pay a good deal more than its share.

XVI.

THE TRUE AND EXCITING NARRATIVE OF MAUD THE FAIR.

IT behoves us to recount, now that we are in the reign of King John, "a norrible tale" of real life, which occurred at that period within the boundaries of the good city of London.

Reader, do you know Baynard Castle?

Did you ever, on some fine, seasonable November night, when the thermom. registered 21 degrees below zero, and the fog was as thick as cold pea soup; or when the snow was rapidly covering the earth with a coating of flake white —did you ever, I say, stand on the summit of that lordly pile, and gaze adown the broad expanse of the Thames in the sanguine hope of being able to see something?

If you *have* done so, I trust you will excuse me saying that you must be a born idiot, and well qualified for admission to Hanwell.

Nevertheless, the castle is a fine place.

A nice, dark, gloomy, feudal, hard-hearted looking fortress, situate on one of the banks of the Thames—the only sort of *banks*, by the way, known in those ages.

In one respect, too, this renowned edifice resembles a coffee cup in a sloppy saucer—it stands in its own *grounds*.

XVI.—(*continued.*)

It WAS born—I mean built—by one of that doughty nation who, in the eleventh century, devoured and " chawed up " England so completely, and in the *teeth* of difficulties, that they were rightly called *Gnaw*mans.

In short, the original founder, Ralph Baynard, came over with the Conqueror, and when he got here, " came over " the Conqueror to let him have this and a few other desirable family residences in the City.

His grandson, Henry Baynard, having a quarrel with

"BOYS OF ENGLAND OFFICE," AS IT APPEARED IN THE 13TH CENTURY.

(*See page* 84.)

another Henry—viz., the first English king of that name—this monarch "confisticated" Baynard's property, and turned it over to Bob Fitz-Dick, or in long, Robert Fitz-Richard, grandson of an Irish peer, Gilbert *de Clare*, who is *de-clared* to have been the king's cup-bearer-in-waiting.

He called himself Lord of Baynard and Baron of Dunmow, and had a son accordingly.

This son had another, who was Robert Fitz-Walter, the chief of the *barons* who hatched that anything but *barren* conspiracy against King John.

That nobleman's daughter, as you will come to see, was the indirect cause of Magna Charta.

Her name was Maud the Fair, *alias* Matilda Fitz-Walter, *alias* (to *very* intimate friends) " 'Tilda dear."

She was the pride of her native parish of Dunmow, in Essex.

Nor was there, in all *S X*, one of her *S E X* who was, in the slightest degree, able to hold a candle to her—not even a farthing rushlight.

Her beauty was more than you could draw with the assistance of the very best pencils ever manufactured.

It was lucky that she didn't often go to London, for when she did, every merchant or clerk who happened to meet her was unfit for business all the rest of the day.

It was no uncommon thing to meet hundreds of these unfortunates wandering about the streets, imploring passengers to tell them which way the Lady Maud and her attendants had gone, as they wanted to follow her to the ends of the earth.

They either forgot their way home entirely, or when they did get there made such fearful mistakes in their accounts as often to bring on bankruptcy.

It was this peerless damsel with whom King John (who

was by that time quite old enough to know better) was badly smitten.

We all know, by this time, what sort of a monarch King John was.

He was such that the things he didn't do were a good deal better than those he did.

In fact, he was a king whose virtues blushed entirely unseen, and you might have known him for ever so many years without finding them out.

He quarrelled with all his wives (who numbered three in regular succession), and doubtless would have quarrelled with more if he had had them.

In one of these tiffs with Isabella of Angouleme, he went off in a huff, swearing that he would cut the matrimonial noose, and send the queen back to France, carriage paid.

Her successor, if any, should, he resolved, be none other than Maud, the Fair, and he thereupon went to the baron's castle to see about it.

Both Fitz-Walter, and his daughter discouraged the king's *suit*—though, of course, it was made by the very best court tailor—whereat John was riled, though he pretended otherwise.

The baron Fitz-Walter always rapped out an oath whenever he heard King John's knock at the front door.

But what could he do?

You can't turn a king out of the house as you would a cadger, or refuse him admittance on the plea of "we don't want anything in your way this morning."

So King John continued to call, lured by the attractions of the young lady, and the old wine the baron had in his cellar.

But both served him out—the young lady was severely frigid in her demeanour, and the old wine made him walk slantindicularly over night and gave him a headache the next morning.

One evening Maud was alone on the castle terrace, feeding one of the peacocks which her papa had brought from the East on his last crusade, when King John approached.

It was plain to see that his majesty had been drinking rather over than under the average, even if a goblet half full in his hand hadn't been there to tell tales.

"Come into the garden, Maud," sang the king, trying to imitate Sims Reeves in that melody.

And she came accordingly, and they meandered adown the winding path of that blooming paradise, where the cabbage-rose was now in full blossom, and the early spring cauli-flower reared its fragrant top.

"Maud," said King John, presently; "wherefore this coldness of demeanour—this Arctic manner of treating me? I love thee to distraction."

"To which, my liege?" asked Maud, pausing, ere smashing a destructive earwig.

"De—dis—trac——"

This time the word stuck in the throat of the king like a couple of pills, so that he swallowed the remainder of the wine, and it quite finished him. He grew awfully senti-mental, and went down on his knees with as much grace and elegance as an elderly gentleman of over 12-stun-4 could be well expected to.

"Fly with me, sweet maid," he said, "far away to the beauteous bowers of Battersea, or the peaceful shades of Lambeth Marsh. Thou shalt be my queen, and wear robes with eight yards of Genoa velvet in the skirt, and we will sit on a golden throne and quaff imperial Tokay out of a goblet crusted all over with diamonds. Is that it?"

"No, it isn't," she replied. "Since your highness is so fond of flying, you had better take a fly by yourself. Good evening."

And off she went—or would have went—towards her pa's ancestral halls, but the king sprang to his feet, and cried—

"No, you don't."

Whereupon, without more ado, he seized her by her locks of gold, which were done up in a sort of tower, or Duke of York's column, on the top of her head, and thus came remarkably handy. Then, dragging her towards the gate, he gave a loud whistle, promptly answered by one of his minions who was always ready waiting round the corner.

"Away with her," cried the king, "to the—you know."

And the expressive wink of the man whom he spoke to, showed that he did know only too well.

And before Maud could even scream, a coloured pocket-handkerchief, at $2\frac{3}{4}$d. per yard, was gagged over her beauteous lips, and she was carried away by this herculean ruffian, placed in a pony-cart, and still further concealed by being wrapped up in a railway rug, which—the cart, I mean—was then driven off at full speed.

Of course Maud fainted—it's a way heroines have got on such occasions, and a very good thing too; saves a deal of bother, and enables them to be carried off easily.

As to King John, he thought it would be rather awkward to face the baron just then, so chalking up on the pales—

"Sudden indisposition—urgent business in London.—J. Rex,"—he mounted his horse at the side gate, and followed in the wake of the cart.

———

XVII.

CONTINUATION OF DITTO, DITTO.

WHEN Maud came to herself, a very uncomfortable come-to it proved to be.

She was in a large, gloomy chamber, hung round with tapestry, and well populated with rats.

"Where am I?" cried the bewildered girl.

"Why, in the Tower to be sure, miss," cried a doddering old jailor, who was the only person present, and even *he* was not wanted.

"The Tower! Oh!—murder!—fire!" shrieked Maud, frantically, trying to pull the *grate* bars of the *great* window, which were un*grate*ful enough to resist all her attempts.

"'Tis no use, Maud, my bird, thou art caged," said the king, entering at this moment. "Why try to fly out? I brought you here because I thought a little change of scene would do you good."

"Oh! I implore your majesty, send me back to my papa," was the only reply.

"First let me ask a question," said King John. "Do you love me then as now?"

"Every bit," was the response; "my feelings towards your majesty have never changed."

"Come, that sounds encouraging, at all events," thought the king.

Dusting the floor, he knelt down again.

"Lady M. Fitz-W., it's no use appealing to your father, all rests with you. Say but the word, and I will divorce the queen, and thou shalt become my number 4."

"I thought your majesty mostly looked out for number 1," replied the daring young lady.

"Oh, a joke; and to my face?" he replied, in rising wrath. "But, seriously, what are your objections to this brilliant offer?"

"In the first place, with the utmost respect, allow me to observe that your majesty is considerably too old, and a great deal too ugly, and besides (here she got the steam up for a clincher), I love another!"

These words made the king bounce up like a cricket ball.

"Death and daggers!" he shouted. "What other. Where does he live?"

As he thundered forth these words, the king, in his fury, rushed at one of the figures worked upon the tapestry, and stabbed it to the heart.

"Lady Maud Fitz-Walter, look here. I'll teach you to make a fool of me. You have defied your rightful sovereign. No more mercy."

And he gave the bell-handle such a furious pull that it brought up the head jailor like an emetic.

We know very well that when tyrants on the stage want to punish anyone, they always say—

"Away with him to the deepest dungeon of the castle."

John reversed this process, and said—

"Away with her to the topmost turret of the Tower."

And a fearful place it was, the coldest, bleakest, chilliest den imaginable, where the wind habitually blew in such a cutting manner that scissors were quite unnecessary, and so high and steep that it would have made even an eagle giddy to look down from it.

Here poor Maud pined for many and many a long day.

Of course the Baron Fitz-Walter was struck all of an aristocratic heap, on hearing that his daughter had disappeared;

he guessed the real state of affairs, and gathering all his friends together, got up an unlimited liability company of the king's foes, whose game was vengeance.

All agreed that John wanted putting down.

As for the gallant young knight, Sir Walter Fitz-Robert, Maud's seventh cousin and first lover (who, you perceive, had been christened after his uncle, *backwards*), he was particularly angered against his rightful (?) sovereign, and felt that the smothering of King John would be a little holiday to him.

His majesty treated all the baron's remonstrances and letters with profound contempt, and, hearing of the coalition he had formed, accused him of high treason, sent men to secure him, and others to besiege his chief residence, Baynard Castle.

We don't intend to describe that scene, as sieges have been described before, and they generally end in a victory, or a defeat, or something of that kind.

Suffice it that the castle was utterly demolished, and until it was built up again, looked very much like a ruin.

As for Lord Fitz-Walter, finding that it was impossible to rescue his daughter, and looking upon himself as a *great gun* he *went off* as soon as he found himself *charged* with treason.

It was well for him he did, or otherwise his *head* would have paid the penalty of his *feat*, and had the king *caught* him, he would have showed him very little *court* favour.

For his majesty, angered at Maud's rejection of his suit, was now in a state of tremendous fury against everybody in general, and the Fitz-Walter family in particular, as the ballad of the period expressed it—

> " For he was so awfully wild, you know:
> In fact he was regular riled, you know ;
> His temper was perfectly spiled, you know,
>   Oh, it made him so HAWFULLY wild !"

He had taken up his abode at his palace in the Tower of London, where every morning he got up with the resolution of having Maud's head off without delay ; but by the time he had her death-warrant written out, he thought better of it, and concluded he'd stop a bit.

One day after dinner, just as the royal tooth-pick was being served up on a clean plate, a man of murderous aspect sought admission to the august presence, on business of great importance. Leave was given, and he entered.

Never in the annals of Newgate was a more horrific being seen.

He looked a mixture of tiger, wolf, and rattle-snake, with a dash of the alligator.

His complexion was so dark that on moonless nights it must have been quite invisible ; and his teeth grinned a horrible grin, as he opened his mouth from ear to ear, or rather, perhaps, from *here* to *there*.

His moustache reared up like a sort of doubled-headed snake on each side of his bronze-coloured cheek, and his eyes shot forth lightnings that seemed to crozzle up everything within range.

He was clothed from head to foot in black armour, and wore two swords, three daggers, a heavy mace, and a pike that looked capable of splitting a man into pieces like *pi(k)e-crust.*

This promising individual, on being asked by the king what the——he wanted, replied—

" Please, your effulgence, I've heard that you require a new jailor in the White Tower, and I make bold to say that I've been recommended by the royal headsman, the London hangman, and the Tower torturer, and beyond that, I'm not at all particular what I do, and I'm a mortal enemy to the Fitz-Walters !"

"Just the fellow to look after Maud, the Fair," mused the king. "If the very looks of him don't frighten her into obedience, then my name isn't what it is. Sirrah," he said aloud, "I think you're likely to suit. Name the wages you require, and let me take off twenty-five per cent., and you can enter into your duties at once."

XVIII.

SAME STORY CONTINUED—A WONDROUS ESCAPE.

AFTER that, the king conferred privately with his new satellite, and put him up to his work.

He began mounting guard over the captive lady's prison that very afternoon, at twenty-two minutes to four o'clock.

If Maud the Fair hadn't been a girl of a great deal more pluck than you or I—supposing us to belong to that delightful sex—she would have passed the remainder of her captivity in shuddering at the horrific countenance of her jailor.

She would have shrieked whenever he came near, in which case you would have been quite right in calling her a beauteous *screecher* (creature?), not but what he frightened her quite enough as it was.

Whenever he approached she shrank up against the wall as close as if she formed part of the paper pattern—only they didn't have any in those days.

Poor Maud! she was particularly to be pitied, mewed up in the terrible top turret of the White Tower.

What made it worse was that the king had now ordered

her to be kept entirely without food—a refinement of cruelty which came very cheap.

But yet, whenever he came to pursue his suit, she rejected him with the same scorn as before, only a little more of it.

Reader, have you ever gone without food for three weeks?

Did you ever feel that vacancy within which has led you to reflect how true is the saying about the *emptiness* of all worldly things?

Did you ever hear the still, small voice crying out that it didn't care much about silver forks, so long as there were provisions of some sort served up?

Did you ever begin to wonder what eating was like, and long for an opportunity to try it merely by way of experiment?

Yet time is a wonderful soother.

Only go without long enough, and in process of time you will become so thoroughly used to it as really not to need anything any more.

The persecuted Maud was rapidly approaching this condition.

As the weary hours went by, her strength went by also, till she was that feeble that to brush away a fly that ever and anon danced a waltz, all by its little self, up and down the sleeve of her velvet *jupon*, would have been for her too great an exertion even to think of.

What, then, was her joy one morning to see the terrible jailor entering with something on a tray?

"His majesty has suddenly grown merciful," he explained. "He says that your *short* commons have continued too *long*, and so intends to melt you with kindness into gratitude and love. Accept this new-laid egg as a first instalment—a foreshadowing of meals to come."

And dear reader it *was* an egg.

There was never seen one *egg*xactly like it, and if I were to give you its dimensions, you would declare I was *egg*xaggerating.

An ostrich needn't have been ashamed of it.

"There," said the jailor, setting down this ornithological curiosity; "that's the first this season. Our fowls don't often lay, but when they do, they pay attention to it, and do the thing in style."

"It looks nice," exclaimed Maud, venturing a little nearer.

"Will your ladyship require my assistance to crack it?" asked the jailor, with sudden politeness.

"No, I can manage it, thanks," was the response.

And Maud took up a silver spoon, with the royal arms and legs stamped upon it, preparatory to giving the top a tap.

Ere the first semi-spoonful had reached the roseate portals of her fragrant mouth (this is poetic), the jailor rushed forward and slapped the spoon out of her hand.

It fell ringing to the floor, while the portion of egg it contained flew up to the ceiling and stuck to the white-wash.

"Ah, what's that for?" cried the lady, in a disappointed and indignant voice.

Now did she perceive that her jailor's manner had undergone a wonderful change.

Not only had he carefully locked the door, but his voice, generally as harsh as a saw-mill, now sank to a whisper as low and sweet as the cooing of a silkworm, while his eyes might have melted wrought iron into love and sympathy.

"Lady Maud, this is a dodge—the king's just outside there—the egg is poisoned—he has *egged* me on to do it! Look!"

He emptied the egg on the floor, and immediately a

blackbeetle, who had only been biding his time, came out and began to eat some of it.

Finding the egg good, the blackbeetle whistled for his pals, who all came out and joined in the feast.

But one by one they all rolled over on their backs, dead as doornails.

"We must escape at once," cried that strange man, pulling a rope ladder from his waist-coat pocket and tying it to the table-legs.

"How?— why?—which? — wherefore ? —where to ?" cried Maud, her mind con-fused by the horrors of her position.

"Hark! me-thinks I hear the royal foot-steps on the stairs !" he cried. "Quick !"

AN ELOPEMENT: HOW TO GET OUT OF PRISON.

With superhuman strength he shook one of the iron bars of the grating till it was quite loose, and broke it away altogether.

This left an aperture big enough for exit, and he lowered the rope ladder.

"Now, then," cried the jailor, seizing those convenient golden tresses, but more gently than King John did it; "away! away!"

And away they went, reaching the bottom so quickly that it was rather before they started.

They fell safely into the moat up to their necks, but clambered up the farthest bank with still greater speed.

"Free, free, so far!" cried her companion.

"But who?—which?—where?—why?—what means this, most gallant being?" she sobbed; "who are you?"

He for one instant removed his hideous mask.

Yes, 'twas he; the brave young Sir Walter Fitz-Robert, her seventh cousin, and one who ever would remain hers truly till death!

"I disguised myself and got the place with the sole intention of setting you free," he explained, "and now I've done it.   Oh, joy!"

They got in time safe to France, and lived more or less happy ever afterwards.

I am well aware that some historians give quite another version of this interesting affair.

They say that Maud was really poisoned, that the egg ended her *egg*-xistence, and the only remains of the maid were her own remains—dead; and that she now lies at Dunmow, Essex, but might it not be the historians that lies, and not Maud?

XIX.

SHOWING HOW TO KILL A KING.

KING JOHN himself didn't continue in office very long after those sensational events we have recorded.

Everybody knows of the other great events of this reign, how the barons laid their iron-capped heads together, and by a united course of action, drove the king into such a very narrow corner that he was obliged to put his name to that great bill which was ever after being presented to him for payment.

Magna Charta was duly signed at *Rummy*-mead, and the tyrant never new a happy moment from that hour, or a happy hour from that moment.

How he died is among the things not generally known.

Some say he fell ill on his journey to the Wash, in Lincolnshire, where he was taking his linen to the royal laundress.

The river rose in a flood, and carried away the lot—bag and baggage, basket and clothes, pegs, and all.

Others again say that, putting up at Swineshead (nick-named Pigshead) Abbey, he was received with wonderful hospitality.

In the abbey grounds they grew peaches and nectarines, of which the king was very fond (query, who isn't?)

Again it is said that a monk, who was a-*monk*-st John's most secret enemies, privately put the poison of a *toad* in a glass of wine, and went up to the king in a *toady*ing manner, saying—

"My most gracious sire, taste this. It came over with

the Conqueror, and has laid in our cellars ever since, because
it is such splendid stuff that nobody here will presume to
drink it.   It's only fit for some high, mighty, potent,
benevolent, angelic monarch——"

"That's me!" exclaimed the king.

SWEEPERS OF THE OLDEN TIME—(NOT MAY-DAY SWEEPS).
(*See page* 96)

"Exactly; therefore, your majesty, take this cup of
sparkling wine.   As the song says—

> "This is the wine
> That's made from the vine
> That grows on the bank of the German Rhine;
> And I opine
> It's in your line!
> Oh, nothing on earth is so divine,
> As the wine,
> The wine,
> The gen-u-*wine!*"

"All right, Father Slifoxious," returned the king, "but
if it's so wonderfully good, why don't you take a drink
yourself first?"

The monk changed colour a bit.

But he was so determined on his dark scheme that he didn't mind killing himself to get rid of John, which is something like cutting off your head to be revenged on your feet.

So he half emptied the cup.

The king, thinking all was right, refilled it to the brim.

A WET DAY IN THE FOURTEENTH CENTURY.
(*See page* 89.)

He drank it off to the dregs, and then wished he hadn't.

For he felt inside and all over a sort of——

Oh, he was *that* bad you can't think.

"Stretchery ! stretchery !" he cried, seeing the monk *stretched* on the floor in *strong* convulsion, though very *weak* himself. "I'm poisoned ! fetch a pummack-stump—I mean a stum——"

"Too late," said the abbot, exultingly; "you are done for. Die tyrant."

And for the first time in his life, King John obeyed one of his subjects.

He died.

"Another way" (as the cookery-books express it) in which King John is said to have been disposed of, was by the abbot presenting him with a dish of pears, some of which, though ap*pear*antly as good as the others, were in reality strongly charged with prussic acid, or something equally murderous.

The king, naturally choosing the biggest, began at the thin end, and gradually worked his way through four, at which he stopped, and never ate any more pears, or anything else, all the rest of his life, which lasted just half-an-hour.

Whether this account is any truer than the first, it is difficult to say.

But all historians are so far agreed that John did die, and that nobody was particularly sorry for it.

"But what has this to do with the History of London?" you ask.

Not much.

So proceed we forward.

———

XX.

HOW LONDON GOT ON AFTER THAT.

HENRY III. took after his father, that is, he took the throne after his father had done with it, and kept it a tidy time—fifty-six years.

You see he was only 9—a 10der age—when he unexpectedly came into the royal property.

He was not a brilliant character, and, therefore did not illuminate the page of history so as to make it very light reading.

An immense number of convents and monasteries were built in the capital in his reign, and all sorts of friars, black friars, white friars, grey, brown, blue, and purple friars, and even *friers* of bacon and sausages, were seen.

The City had grown very rich and strong by this time, and the king and his barons, who were often " parlous harduppe," became jealous of the merchants' wealth, and only wished they could find some excuse to pitch into them, *sack* the city, and *bag* their money-bags.

They were always borrowing. The king had to pawn his crown once, and couldn't get it out till Saturday night.

After Harry Three came Ned One, a rearing, tearing, fighting monarch of the Cœur-de-Lion species, who conquered all Wales, and would have dittoed " bonny Scotuland" but for Bruce and Wallace, and the " Scots wha ha' wi' the aforesaid gentleman bled," as the song says.

Nevertheless, Edward did some good for London. He came down stiff upon those " mean cusses" who in those very far gone times actually used to adulterate the goods.

Says the song (Air—" Choose to be a Baby ")—

> " King Edward used to take them
> And drill them through the ears,
> And nail them to the door-posts,
> Despite their cries and fears.
> In pillories he'd fix them,
> And all the mob allow,
> To pelt them with dead cats and stones—
> Why don't they do it now?"

In 1235 one Le Bruin, the original village blacksmith, set up his forge in the Strand, and agreed to pay to the crown, by way of rent, six horseshoes, with nails complete ; hence the expression " down on the nail ;" and as long as he paid it, the government let him work his forge as much as ever he liked without indicting him for *forgery*.

When he shoed the royal horses, each quadruped used to give a little *stamp* by way of receipt.

I believe that Le Bruin and his shop are both gone away now; but the custom of paying six nails annually is still kept up.

Say we somewhat now of the ancient aspect, sports, &c., of our unrivalled metropolis.

The following facts are mostly gleaned from a very rare and costly volume, intituled " Lunding as it Used to Was."

London was so different then to what it is now, that it will be worth while to take a special train of thought far back into the past to have a look at it.

Nothing like so big, of course, as the present metropolis. No music-halls, union banks, gas companies, nor telegraph offices. Ne'er a railway station to be seen for miles, not even with powerful telescopes, which, besides, were not invented.

Belgravia was all forest, and it was dangerous to walk in St. John's Wood after dark, on account of the bands of robbers and other wild animals of ferocious demeanour.

Houndsditch and Shoreditch were all real ditches then; and the Fleet river, which was very *fleet* in its course, or wide enough for a *fleet* to sail along, meandered its way along like a stream of rather thick pea-soup.

Above all, there was no " BOYS OF ENGLAND " in those days—at least, there were boys, but no journal devoted to them. Fancy that !

What a sad benighted state to live in !

Consequently, by the rules of logic, there was no publishing office at No. 173, which was then a range of blooming hedgerows, bounded on one side by the Fleet, while on the other were grassy meads, wherein ecstatic mokes kicked up their heels, and munched the festive thistle.

We ought to say something about London street names, and how they came for to be so.

Thus Moorgate Street was so named because when all the city gates had been built they built one *more gate* to make up the number.

Bell Savage Yard was so called from a large bell that once hung up there, and made people savage who rang it and couldn't get in.

The "Bull and Mouth" was so named from an Irishman, who always had a *bull* in his mouth.

Charing Cross was the place where *cross char-*women were sent to.

Of the other streets in London, we may briefly mention that Cheapside was so called because the inhabitants always charged twenty per cent. more than other people.

KING JOHN FALLS IN LOVE AND ON HIS KNEES. (*See page* 68.)

This little weakness—so people say—they haven't *quite* got over even yet.

Birchin Lane was the locality where most of the school-masters lived.

Hatton Garden was so named from a gardener who used to keep his *hat* on before the king.

Long Acre alludes to a very extensive double tooth that was pulled out by a dentist of the period, and which is *said* to have caused quite an obstruction in the street.

Millbank is said to have come to its name from two Bankers who had a mill there, all along of some disputed property.

Newgate was so called because it was so old.

Pall Mall was where the *mal*-contents and their *pals* used to assemble to hatch conspiracies, &c.

Many other places were named from many other circumstances, all more or less remarkable, and worthy of being recorded by those who have time to go in for it.

The ancient sports and pastimes of London in the good old times really *are* interesting, and whoever says they are not I should like to—but to proceed to particulars.

In the first place, theatrical exhibitions, rather of the Punch and Judy order, perambulated the streets, to the delight of the pick-pockets of the period.

Then there was a good deal of hunting in the forests round London.

N.B.—We should have to hunt *for* the forests instead of *in* them nowadays.

But at that time stags, wild boars, and ferocious bulls were to be seen in abounding numbers *abounding* about the suburbs.

Then, among other zoological sports, there were the combating of the courageous cock, the baiting of the beauteous badger, and the rousing of the rapacious rat.

Cock-fighting was a special delectation, and " living like

fighting cocks " came to be a proverb for a particularly jolly existence.

Balls took place in the green fields—I mean footballs, not dancing balls, though there was naturally a good deal of *kicking up.*

Besides this there was leaping, in which both sexes took part, for even the young ladies would often *jump* at a good offer, especially in *leap* year.

They also sounded the loud timbrel, and tripped it on the light fantastic.

Wrestling was an exercise wherein the esquires and merry apprentices of old much excelled, and therefore woe be to those that didn't.

Javelins, stones, and other missiles were also thrown by way of exercise, and prudent folks got out of the gangway on these occasions, especially when the performers were rather uncertain in their aiming.

Archery was, of course, the grand sport, for were not those the days of Robin Hood and all his company (limited)?

Precisely; and, of course, Bow and Harrow were the favourite places for the recreation with the *beaux* of the period.

Besides this, there was plenty of horse-riding in the course—*in course* there was.

The swells had their tilts and tourneys, which always came off well, and so did many of the riders when they were unhorsed.

In the Easter holidays, aquatic sham fights and water tournaments took place on the river—that is, the tilters *rowed* in a boat on the water for the same purpose that they *rode* on a horse on shore.

The object, and a funny-looking object, too, was to strike a target fixed to an upright pole in the middle of the stream, and whoever tried and failed found it very striking indeed, for he was sure to be knocked *out* of breath and *into* the water.

However, they always had a hook and line ready to fish him out again, and then he was hung up to dry.

However fine the weather might be, such a disaster made it a *wet* day for him, at all events.

Skating was, by special act of parliament, only allowed to take place in cold weather.

On hot July days it wasn't permitted, on any account.

Velocipides and Rob Roy canoes are to be particularly mentioned as *not* being in use at this period.

XXI.

THE reign of Edward III. was so long that the historian is obliged to take a six-foot rule to measure it, which, as Edward (being a tall man) might be considered a six-foot *ruler*, come in very appropriate.

He was a man who, take him for all in all—or otherwise—we shall not look upon his like again in a hurry.

When I say that he swayed his sceptre over the whole of England at once, and that he supported the entire weight of the government (somewhere about a ton and a half) on his shoulders, the reader will gain some faint idea how big and strong he was.

Such a monarch was likely to do much for London, and he did it accordingly.

He not only granted two charters, each written on the very best parchment and beautifully done up with red tape, but gave the lord mayor special permission to spend as much as he liked out of his own private income, to support the dignity of the city.

He likewise graciously condescended to accept 20,000 gold marks from the citizens to carry on his French wars.

In 1346, the people of Holborn took it into their heads to grumble concerning the condition of that thoroughfare, which was in such a terrible state, that in trying to get along it, carts and carriages went up and down—and especially down—like vessels at sea in a storm.

Somebody went and told the king, who immediately *tolled* the thoroughfare, by laying a *toll* of a halfpenny or so on everybody and everything that went by.

This plan succeeded; the road was mended, and in process of time, people could actually walk along it without sinking deeper into the mud than up to their shins.

To keep up this enviable state of things, each true citizen was enjoined to sweep round his own doorstep, paddle his own canoe (if he had one), and not to throw orange peel on the pavement.

This last pernicious habit (which I am sorry to see is only too prevalent in the present day) was then carried on so extensively that the poor policemen were always slipping down when on their beat, and that's how they came to be called *peelers*.

They were obliged to *appeal* to the people's feelings, to be more careful about their peelings—which is rhyme and reason.

In 1354, the lord mayor was first allowed to have gold and silver maces carried before him, instead of copper ones, as heretofore.

Of course everybody was delighted at this great privilege, except the mace-bearer himself, who began to grumble at the extra weight.

Out of gratitude for all these high favours from his majesty, the Londoners raised a volunteer corps of twenty-five knights, armed *cap-a-pie*, and five hundred archers, and after a little practice at sham fighting on Easter Monday they set sail for France, and considerably astonished the "mossoos" at the battle of Poictiers.

The Black Prince, when he had done fighting for a little while—everybody wants a slight spell of rest now and then—came home, and entered London with all his followers in grand procession.

He brought with him, as prisoner, the king of France, whom he had chivalrously grabbed after a tough struggle on the field.

Still he treated his prisoner wonderfully well, and would even have treated him to liquor at every "public" they went by, but his majesty answered "*Merci*, monseigneur, but I haff not the *necessite* to dreenk heem," to which the prince answered in the same lingo—

"*Tray bong mossoo votre majeste* has the right."

And so they passed on through the streets, which were crowded, and crammed, and choked with people to that extent that it was ridiculous to think of breathing, and many people left off trying.

The street decorations were "things of beauty and joys forever," or, at least, till they were taken down.

Nevertheless the cheering, and drums, trumpets, and other harmonious sounds all going together, were rather bad for the headache.

Let us hope that no one in that dense throng was suffering from that malady.

To show his own humility, the Black Prince mounted his royal prisoner on a big dray horse, while he himself rode on the smallest Shetland pony that could be had.

The king being rather a little man, and the prince weighing twelve stone ten without his armour (which he had on), the contrast was wonderfully effective.

Indeed, it was rather too much so for the much-enduring quadruped that carried the prince, which was observed to look every now and then at the king's horse enviously and beseechingly, as much as to say—

"Don't I wish we could change riders."

In the year 1360, there was a great invasion panic in London.

The news was that the French, to the tune of some twenty thousand men, had landed on the coast of Sussex and played "old gooseberry," or rather French champagne, to a considerable rate.

They entirely conquered England; that is, they would have done if they could, but the Britons, who had come to a resolution never—never—never to be slaves to a foreign conqueror, wouldn't hear of it. At least they did hear of it, and acted accordingly.

Foremost of all the gallant City of London came to the rescue.

She started a fleet of one hundred and sixty sail, and fourteen thousand men, who, besides administering an English beating to the French invaders, paid them out in their own coinage, by landing at Boulogne, and considerably astonished the very large cocked hats which the natives were then in the habit of wearing.

XXII.

SIGNS OF THE TIMES.

SO great an event as the following deserves to be recorded.

In 1363 the people of London had their loyalty strung

up to sensation pitch; no less than four kings came to London at once to visit the lord mayor, who, as king of the City, might be considered to make a fifth. Leaving him out, however, and counting only four, it naturally follows that the people were four times as loyal as usual, and that instead of giving "three times three" cheers as their majesties drove along, they gave "four times four," with a little one in for the lord mayor.

Edward the Black Prince, who had carefully washed his face for the occasion, and now shone out a dazzling white, was of the party, and a vast number of other parties followed, some so high in rank that it made one's neck ache to look up at them.

These heavier swells were heavier still when they came back again after dinner.

Some historians say that as King Edward III. grew older his temper became soured like beer does in a thunderstorm, and certainly those times were so stormy that one cannot much wonder at it.

An undoubted fact is, that when he became to be sixty, he spoke a great deal sharper to the people than he used to do when a gentle infant of six weeks old.

You will find this often the case; in fact it is only natural, so we need not blame Edward III. in particular.

The city was in a very flourishing state indeed at this period.

Money was plentiful, meat cheap, and there is not the slightest doubt that if the underground railway had been in existence, it would have paid well.

In those days there were a great many signs and sign-boards in London, especially the signs of the times, and signs of prosperity.

Not only the *inns* but the *outs* also had their signs.

Besides this the butcher, the baker, the candlestick maker, &c., each had their special signboard.

The butcher had painted up the representation of a pound of mutton suet, or a silver-side of beef on a blue ground; the baker's sign was generally a penny roll, rampant with the motto—"All hot!" and the candlestick maker sported a chamber one, with snuffers and extinguisher complete.

The tinker generally hung up a gilt kettle over his door, and the tailor's symbol was a beautifully fitting pair of—scissors, or something very much of the same shape.

The apothecary showed a box of golden pills, and the bootmaker, the effigy of one of the ram's-horn-toed patent leathers of the period, with the legend—"How doth youre poore feete?"

As to such people as the receivers of stolen goods, they were so modest that they did not hang up any sign at all, which was in itself a suspicious sign at all events.

At that lively period, as I have before intimated, a menagerie was kept in the Tower, consisting of lions, tigers, leopards, bears, porcupines, elephants, crocodiles, and other "entertaining little cusses" of that species.

I think I before told you that our good friends, Gog and Magog, had the looking after of these distinguished zoological foreigners.

It was a post splendidly fitted for them, and of course the extra trouble involved was "considered in the screw," which was paid with *screw*-pulous regularity.

Talking of signboards and menageries, we must note how large a number of heraldic animals were visible about the streets at this time.

That favourite Roman bird, the eagle, seems to have been *eagle-ly* caught up as a London sign. Plenty of variety as to colour; there were black eagles, white eagles, red, blue, and golden eagles, besides those whose complexions had turned a fine deep brown through want of being cleaned.

Then there was the swan with two necks, and the crane with three heads, and altogether a very curious lot of birds must have been hatched in those times.

Lions, too, of various breeds, now quite extinct, such as the red lion, white lion, and golden lion, very often with an unicorn opposite, seemed to have prevailed considerably.

These remarkable creatures were generally perched up over the doors, or on the tops of the roofs, where they stood bravely defying all weathers, and did not cost much to keep.

The wild boar was another sign so frequently repeated that it must have become a *bore* indeed, and enough to make anybody *wild*.

It is a wonder they *bore* it so long. And of course you are aware that the boars with the large tusks came originally from *Tusc*-any.

Besides such effigies, there were specimens of human sculpture in the good old times, such as at this time we sometimes read about but very seldom see.

In St. Dunstan's Church, Fleet Street, standing in niches not one hundred miles from the clock tower, there used to be a couple of wooden giants, armed with clubs, which were nothing like so polished as the modern *clubs* at the West End.

With these little implements — each weighed about twenty pounds—they used to strike the half-hours and quarters—rather hard upon the latter, wasn't it? I wonder they didn't strike the giants back. But, perhaps, strikes were not so common in those times as the present, although some striking events, or, at least, so it strikes the historian, took place then.

These two wooden giants had the impudence to suppose

they could beat Gog and Magog, and to feel *stuck up* because they were perched some thirty feet from the ground.

"Sich is human wanity?" as the ancient philosopher observed.

In 1377, Edward III., having emigrated from this mortal sphere, was succeeded by his grandson, young Richard II., son of the Black Prince.

He didn't take much after his father—perhaps his father had not left any.

At all events he was about as fit to be a king of this nation as the man in the moon, and I, for one, would undertake to rule England better with my eyes shut.

But, fit or unfit, king he was for the time, and the people had to make the best of a bad bargain.

The first great event in Richard's time, and one much concerning the good City of London, was the celebrated insurrection of Wat Tyler (1381), which "present company" could say a great deal about but don't feel inclined.

The reader is referred to the soul-stirring narrative of "Wat Tyler ; or, Who's your Hatter?" recorded by the same chronicler as now writeth, which narrative is always to be found in the BOYS OF ENGLAND, Nos. 184 to 197 inclusive.

Therein the whole achievements of the great Wat, all he did, and all he did not, are faithfully and tragi-comically described.

All we need say at present on the matter is that, looking upon that great rebellion by the light of historical criticism, it cannot be denied that one party or the other, if not both, must have been in the wrong, and that if Wat had succeeded in killing Richard II., at the time in question, that monarch would not have reigned so long as he did.

We defy anybody to prove otherwise.

Richard did some shadow of good for the City of London.

He saw or smelt that by this time the streets had got

into a shocking state again, and wanted cleaning very badly.

They were filled with all sorts of ordure, and the king consequently *ordured* it to be removed.

To hear was to obey ; so the city went through a regular ablutionary process, and came out as clean as a new pin, and bright as an old needle.

To crown the edifice of prosperity, the lord mayor was allowed to rank as an earl, and made to pay twenty-five per cent. extra taxes for it, an immense honour and privilege.

Several guilds, or trade societies, were started at this time, and, among others, the Skinners' Company, so called, it is said, from their dexterity in skinning flints.

The skin itself was largely used to make ladies' bonnets, being a beautifully thin and light material for summer wear.

Somewhere about this period of history, too, or within one hundred years of it, more or less, the present system of trial by jury was inaugurated.

It was laid down by law that the jurors should be chosen from among those persons who had plenty to do at home, and didn't want to leave their businesses, and who were likely to know nothing whatever about the cases tried.

This system has kept on to the present day, and we sincerely hope it will keep on until it stops—the sooner the better.

And now we come to one of the finest of the city stories, that about our old friend, or, rather, our *young* friend, Dick Whittington.

I am going to give you such an account of him and his whole history as you never heard before, and which is worth committing entire to memory, and repeating every morning before breakfast. Dick was—but no, we will wait for our next page, and commence with a chapter to his memory.

XXIII.

THE TRUE AND REMARKABLE BIOGRAPHY OF DICK WHITTINGTON.

DICK WHITTINGTON was born in the year uncertain, in one of the towns of England—some say 1353, at Taunton, in "Zummerzetzhire;" and I should be the last to say they were not telling the truth.

He had two parents, but beyond this his pedigree is rather hazy; and whether his ancestors "came over with the Conqueror"—or any other man—is now unknown.

Probably the Whittington family had "seen better days"—but if so,

GALLANT ONSLAUGHT—WHITTINGTON'S CAT ROUTS THE ENEMY.
(See page 116.)

they didn't go on seeing them long—and thus it occurred, somehow or other, that the poor lad had to set out to seek his own fortune.

After this he found that a playmate of his had been to London, and professed to be able to tell what the "Metrollopus" was like.

He informed him that the streets were paved with gold—laid down in good thick slabs—while the middle of the road was generally of silver, hall marked.

"And don't people ever steal these golden paving stones?" asked little Dick, who took all this in without the slightest idea in the world that he was being taken in himself.

"Not they," responded the other; "in the first place don't you see that they are so heavy that no mortal being could lift them? and though there are some depraved indiwiddles who sometimes try to chip bits off, the majority of folks in London are too honest ever to do anything of the kind, and you might trust 'em with your cash-box any day in the week."

"Well, they can't get much out of *me*, at all events," observed young Richard, contemplating his own entire stock-in-trade—2½d. and a blunt knife.

So without bidding farewell to all at home—for he knew they wouldn't like to part with him—he put his rattle-traps together overnight, and started off one fine morning, just when the excursion trains—had there been any—would have been blowing off their parting whistle.

Richard whistled himself a bit, too, for his heart was light; and the idea of seeing the world, at the outset, is always nice.

Yet, as he got farther and farther away from his home, he felt a sort of melancholy feeling, "still so gently o'er him stealing," as he thought he might ne'er again behold either his parents or the mud hut they lived in.

But a rest of half-an-hour at a milestone, and an *al fresco* snack, consisting of a hard-boiled egg out of his wallet, and a drink out of the neighbouring brook, enabled him to pluck up his spirits and face the future manfully.

Presently he overtook a carrier's cart, which was also on its way to London, and looked as if it might be expected to get there about in time for the Day of Judgment.

The carrier allowed our young adventurer to walk behind his vehicle all the way—which was very kind of him indeed, though Dick thought it would have been even kinder to give him "a h'ist up" for a few miles.

It was one hundred and fifty altogether to London, and though the roads were "not so dusty," and the weather amiable most of the way, Dick was best part of a week doing the journey, and often and often he "woulded he were a burrud," so that he might get on a little quicker.

Alas! alas! how disappointment ever dogs the footsteps of mortals!

Dick Whittington soon found that all his friend Bob Longbow had told him was a long way outside the truth.

The streets of London were not paved with gold, but with mud, or at the best, very hard-hearted paving-stones, and the people seemed much more inclined to give him an aggressive fist than a helping hand.

It is true that the carrier at parting gave him fourpence.

Now, fourpence is a sum which will *not* last forever, be you as economical as you may, and it's no wonder that Whittington found himself one night wandering hopelessly along the streets with nothing in his pocket, nothing in his provision store, only something in his eye—viz., a few tears.

He sat down on a doorstep.

Had he been seen, there is no doubt that some passing peeler of the period would have told him to "move on !"

But the stone porch was deep, the night dark, and little Dick had smuggled himself up so closely in the corner, that it would have required a night-telescope to find him out.

Here, therefore, he slept, as well as he could till dawn, when he was awakened by a remonstrative voice that said—

"Well, I'm sure, this is imperance ; to be a-roosting on our steps. Now off you go, for I'm going to clean 'em."

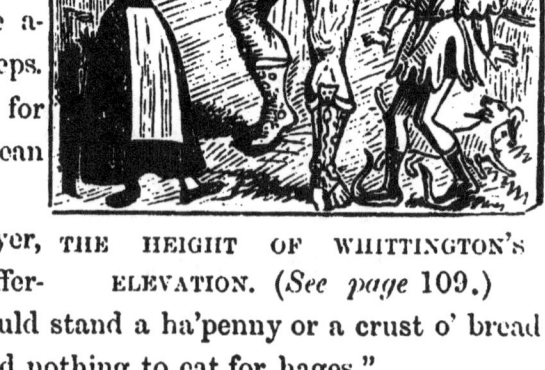

THE HEIGHT OF WHITTINGTON'S ELEVATION. (*See page* 109.)

"I'll do it for yer, mum," said Dick, differentially ; "if you could stand a ha'penny or a crust o' bread to a chap 'as ain't had nothing to eat for hages."

The housemaid reflected.

After all, step-cleaning was not what she was partial to

herself, and, besides, there were some stale bits of bread in the pantry that would bear getting rid of.

So she agreed to Dick's terms, and forthwith he set to using the hearthstone with all the strength left in him—which wasn't an alarming quantity.

But he didn't leave off till the steps were as bright and shining as a sheet of cream-laid note paper, and so smooth and polished that they were dangerous to walk upon.

The servant declared herself satisfied, and thereupon introduced our hero to Mistress Cicely, the cook, who introduced him to the expected breakfast.

It consisted of several young crusts of bread—at least, if not *young*, they were not more than a week old—and some of the day-before-yesterday's milk, which had been standing till it was beautifully rich and high-flavoured.

Most people would have fought shy of such a meal as this, but Richard was *in extremis* (which, in this case, is the Latin for starvation), and hunger makes us acquainted with strange eatables.

After ten minutes or so of soaking, the venerable bread slid down his throat like a letter into a pillar box.

Scarce had he finished, when the cook suddenly exclaimed :

"Ho ! good gracious !   If here ain't Miss Alice !"

Miss Alice it was, in all her glory.

She was more than beautiful, but not more than fifteen ; she had just come home from a highly fashionable boarding-school, where she had gone through the whole *curriculum* of studies, and become so excruciatingly genteel that you would have taken her for " the daughter of a hundred earl's " instead of one merchant.

Her dress was something startling ; she sported a gold-mounted eye glass, walked with a Grecian bend, and talked with an " awithtoquatic lithp."

"Haw! Whom have we hee-aw?" asked this young lady, elevating her eyebrows slightly.

"Only a young ragamuffin, miss, as I've had in, out of pure benevolence," said Cicely, the cook ; "and I'm going to turn him out presently."

"Don't you think, cook, it would be an impwoovement if his face were washed?" suggested Miss Alice. "I think he wouldn't be altogether hideouth then."

Poor Richard, meanwhile, covered with confusion down to his very heels, rose and made the very best bow he had about him, and remarked that if he could in any way perform any service for the young lady, he would only be too happy.

She said that that sounded very pretty, and he would improve in time.

It strikes me that Miss Alice, at breakfast that morning, must have mentioned to her papa and mamma—otherwise Mr. Hugh and Dame Maud Fitzwarren—that there was a slightly nice boy in the kitchen, for both these personages came down afterwards, and took a survey of Whittington.

When they had asked him all the appropriate questions, such as where he had come from, and where he expected to go to, they said he could stay a week on trial, as scullion and errand boy.

It wasn't a magnificent post, but it was a slight improvement on starvation, and Richard accepted it thankfully.

He was to sleep in a "garret near the sky," eat whatever was given him whenever there was time, and yield implicit obedience to Mistress Cicely, the cook, who, as to size and strength, could have doubled him up like a trussed turkey, if he turned "obstroperous."

Both servants contrived to make him very useful.

Instead of getting up at six o'clock, as formerly, the

housemaid never turned out before eight, and if Dick had not got all the fires lit, and the kettle boiling by that time, he might expect a litttle hot water of another kind.

After that, he commenced the boot cleaning of the establishment, beginning with the merchant's big ram's-horn-toed Wellingtons, and gradually working his way down to the dainty blue kid *bottines* of Mistress Alice.

The knives and daggers were next operated upon, and as those implements, at that time, were used not only for cutting dinners, but throats (when necessary), they often required a good deal of cleaning.

By the time these pleasing duties were performed, dinner began looming in the distance, and for two mortal hours, at least, Dick had to turn the spit, till it's-pit-eous to think how tired he was.

After dinner, of course, the pots and pans, and such like gear, must be cleansed and put away ; and between whiles, all sorts of errands had to be run, and odd-and-end jobs to be performed.

There is no use denying the fact that Dick Whittington led a dog of a life at this period ; he was at the beck and call of everybody, and especially of the cook, who was a regular tartar, and used to blow him up sometimes as if she had swallowed a charge of gunpowder.

And to add to the day's wretchedness, instead of being able to rest of a night, poor Dick found that his bed-room was the last place in the world to sleep comfortably in.

For, let alone that the wind and the rain could come in whenever they felt inclined, it was so infested with a rabble of mice, that it made him quite *mice-rabble**

After having been kept without sleep for a fortnight, he determined to put a stop to it.

* Query. " miserable ?"

"I must get a cat," he said, *mew*-singly; "though as I've got not a farthing of money, it puzzles *me-how* * I'm to get one."

Now it chanced that on that day a gentleman came to the merchant's to dinner, a young City swell, who was supposed to be casting sheep's eyes at Miss Alice.

He had arrived in such a hurry that his boots were uncleaned, and he asked Dick to polish them off "for a consideration."

Whittington made them shine like a couple of walking mirrors, and the gentleman gave him a penny.

That don't seem much to us, but remember that a penny then was equal to at least sixpence of our deprecated currency.

As luck would have it, Dick presently met in the streets an old woman, with a remarkably fine young tabby.

On finding Dick eager to buy, she laid on the price rather thick, but ultimately came down to a penny, and as it was all he had, I don't see how he could very well have given more.

Dick returned to the merchant's, hugging his prize under his coat.

The chief difficulty was how to smuggle in puss "unbeknownst" to the cook, who hated cats as much as if she had been a mouse herself.

However, Dick contrived to reach his attic in safety, and deposited the quadruped in a band-box, whence he let her out when he came up for the night.

Then began a regular mouse chase.

It was very exciting, but hardly conducive to repose, and Dick, as he lay in bed, by the light of his farthing candle-end, watched it without attempting to go to sleep.

---

* Query, "me-ow?"

Puss proved a capital mouser, and the animal made "lovely havoc o' the warmints," as the cook might have expressed it, had she known.

The mice, with a sprinkling of rats, were so numerous, that puss had quite enough to do, and was always well provided with provisions, especially as Dick now and then contrived to smuggle up modicums of milk, as well as some titbits pocketted in the kitchen.

There was a trap-door, too, in the attic, leading out on to the roof, which was highly eligible for a promenade; and altogether, no cat could have been more happily situated.

But all that Dick could do could not prevent the animal occasionally *maciouwling*, and though his attic was so high up that this was not likely to disturb the *rest* of the house, the cook, whose dormitory was nearest, once heard the sound.

When Dick was questioned, he explained that this *mew*-sic proceeded from his practising on a violin that somebody had lent him entirely for his own a-*mews*-ment.

Of course, the cook believed this; but she told him he had better not do it again, or there would be "a row in the house" even more unpleasant.

But at last the cat-astrophe came.

Miss puss was tired of her state of confinement, mice were getting scarce, and the door was accidentally left open, so she slowly strolled downstairs, and entered the kitchen, with the intention of asking for some milk.

Passing on to the front of the premises, she very excusably helped herself out of the "three-ha'porth" which the milkman had left down by the area railing.

Ah! you should have heard the *railing* of the cook when she came in!

Observing that the animal had a blue ribbon, with

"R. W." on it, tied round the neck, Mistress Cicely guessed all.

It was Whittington's cat, and she determined to pay out both.

Whittington being out, she began with the cat.

No doubt you have read the prescription of the doctor who, on being asked what was the best cure for indigestion, recommended this gentle exercise —

"Shut all the doors and windows, then take a birch-broom, and chase a cat up and down-stairs till you *steam*."

Mistress Cicely carried this out to the letter ; never was a poor pusy so *pussy*-cuted as was Whittington's unfortunate animal on that occasion.

The cook kept on till she—being stout—was pretty well exhausted ; while the cat, being thin, had nimbly retreated to the top railing of the stairs.

When Cicely came up to him for the last time, it was literally "coming up to the *scratch*," for puss turned round on her, and *clawed* her face with a ferocity which *Claude Duval* himself couldn't have surpassed.

The shrieks of Mistress Cicely were enough to rouse the neighbourhood, and at this unlucky crisis in came Whittington.

He flew upstairs to the rescue of his pet, and only by skilful dodging escaped the weighty consequences of Mistress Cicely's fist.

"Get out of the house, you owdacious young willain, and your nasty, wicious animal into the barging. Come, troop, both of ye, or murder will be done."

To add force to her admonition, she threw at him three blacking-brushes, one copper-stick, four knives, and a pair of his own hob-nailed boots.

It was a mercy that Dick was able to dodge these missiles,

and, seeing more coming, he thought it would be expedient to evacuate the premises with all dispatch.

So he rushed up to his attic, hastily gathered together his worldly effects in a red cotton handkerchief, tied at the end of a crab stick, and snatching up the cat under his arm, bolted through the back way, leaving Mistress Cicely still cutting out slips of diachylon plaster, and calling down Heaven's vengeance on that much-enduring quadruped.

XXIV.

WHITTINGTON "OUT IN THE COLD."

YOUNG DICK crossed through the crowded streets of London, and soon came to Smithfield, Bunhill Fields, Lincoln's Inn Fields, and other verdant spots, which were literally fields then, though now paving-stones grow there instead of grass, and houses instead of trees.

In time he got to Highgate Hill, sometimes pronounced " 'iget 'ill ;" and feeling rather tired, sat down under one of the elms that grew numerously there in those days.

London presented a fine prospect from this point, much better than Dick's prospect in life now.

Where was he to go, what was he to do?

He didn't know any more than Adam's grandfather, and even the cat couldn't tell him.

As he and the cat sat *mew*-sing together, they heard the bells of Highgate church ringing merrily.

Dick listened, and couldn't help fancying he heard them say—

"Turn again, Whittington, thrice Lord Mayor of London."

Which so flabbergasted him that he listened spellbound, and utterly left off breathing in the intensity of his interest.

"Hullo, young fellow, what's your complaint?" cried a loud and hearty voice, while a gigantic shadow loomed overhead.

Looking up—and a long way up, too—Dick recognised Magog, the celebrated City giant, and chief of the metropolitan police.

Dick wasn't frightened. He knew that, big as the giant was, his heart was in the right place, and he wouldn't hurt a fly unnecessarily, much more a Whittington.

"I ain't doing any harm, Mister Magog," protested Richard, "and not much good either. I'm cast on the world without a penny in my pocket, and don't know which way to turn."

"Then why don't you——" began the giant, reflectively, plucking some of the top leaves of the elm tree; "why don't you——"

"Hark!" interrupted Dick, "there's the bells a-ringing. They're at it again, I declare. It's strange—it beats the Bells at the Lyceum Theaytre. Don't you hear what they say?

"Turn again, Whittington, thrice Lord Mayor of London!"

"Ha! ha!" laughed Magog, "you don't look much like a Lord Mayor now, but who knows what may happen? Perhaps some of these fine days, me and brother Gog may have the pleasure of walking beside your carriage to Guildhall. And are you going to turn back?"

"Well, the bells keep on telling me to——Hark, again! that's the third time. Then I think I will, not that I know where I'm going to if I do, and I'm about as tired as a post-man on Valentine's Day."

"I'll h'ist you up on my head," suggested the giant, "and we'll make tracks for London, where I'm on duty. Up you go."

And forthwith, Dick was set a-straddle on the ponderous head of the giant, where he felt as comfortable as a good rider in a saddle, and looked as little as a canary perched on the top of an elephant.

In one hand he held aloft Miss Pussy, and in the other his stick and bundle, making a capital balance.

Inspector Magog, A 1, then began to set in motion his leviathan legs, and they strode down the hill at a brisk seven mile an hour.

In this triumphal state, Whittington re-entered London.

The folks were so much struck by the novelty of the sight, that they gazed on in astonishment. Many shouted "Hooray!" and waved their hats, and some, seeing the shadow of Magog and his burden pass over the first floor blind, rushed to the window to see what was up.

The affair of Whittington and the bells on Highgate Hill has been often described.

But one remarkable fact concerning it is not generally known, namely, that the celebrated verse chimed by the bells, though they meant the same, sounded differently each time.

Thus, at first, it was plain enough—

> "Turn again, Whittington,
> Thrice Lord Mayor of London!"

The second time the bells they rang backwards, and made it sound like this—

> ,notgnittihW ,niaga nruT "
> "! nodnoL fo royaM droL ecirhT

And the third time, having run up and down the scale,

they got into a sort of mad ecstasy, and mixed it up in this jumblified style—

"Tu a n, Whittin gton, cel dma flon
    rn gai thri or yoro don!"

That is the true fact about the bells, though you may not *bell*ieve it.

For three days Whittington and his cat put up at the residence of the giants, next door to the head police-station, where they became so popular, that nobody wanted to part with them.

It so happened that Mistress Cicely, the cook, had been in very ill luck lately.

She got a holiday the day after Dick's departure, and on some occasion or other she got into a row, and ran foul of the police.

Waxing wrath, she upped with her fist and knocked down Constable Lambkin, XX 19, and was forthwith had up for creating a disturbance, and assaulting a public officer in the exercise of his duty.

Dick was in court when she was brought up, and now would have been his time for vengeance.

But he was of a forgiving nature, and, instead of taunting her, he used his influence with the police to have her fined instead of imprisoned.

A night in the station house had much brought down the pride of Mistress Cicely.

She went into violent hysterics, implored Mr. Fitzwarren (who came to look after her) not to turn her out of her situation, and overwhelmed Whittington, including his cat, with blessings.

As if to punish her, ever since Dick and puss had left, the mice had made awful invasions into the kitchen, eating up all the candles, butter, cheese, and other domestic commodities, to the great chagrin of the cook, who didn't like any living creature to purloin those articles except herself.

The cat would be of some service now, and the end of it all was that they agreed to take back Whittington and his feline companion, on the agreement that the former was to be better treated than formerly, and the latter was to have the run of the kitchen and scullery with all perquisites thereunto appertaining.

Now, it so happened that Mr. Fitzwarren's ship, the "Unicorn" (A 1, copper-bottomed, and carrying an experienced surgeon), was off to unknown lands on a trading cruise.

She was laden with every sort of English merchandise, from carpets to nutmeg-graters, and from British brandy to cold-drawn castor oil.

The merchant had a custom of letting everybody in his service put their little venture in the craft.

If it was only a sixpenny thimble, it might bring back some profit.

Everybody put something.

The apprentices ventured their last "tips" of five bob or so, or the latest thing in scarf-pins.

The workmen invested the price of those pints of beer which they didn't have.

Mrs. Fitzwarren risked exactly the sum she felt disposed to, and Mistress Alice some jewellery that she happened to be tired of.

The cook sent two pounds of the best dripping and an electro-plated brooch, the housemaid an old cap and six valentines, and the groom three pairs of cast-off horseshoes and a used-up betting-book.

It was calculated that all these articles would rather astonish the savages, and fetch fancy prices.

XXV.

CRUISE OF THE "UNICORN."

BUT when Whittington's turn came, what could he contribute?

Nothing but his cat, and though it gave his heartstrings a pull to part with her, he saw nothing for it but that pussy must be sacrificed to the capricious goddess of fortune.

THE LORD MAYOR. THE CARDINAL

"HOW DARE YOU BE LORD MAYOR?" SAID THE CARDINAL.
(*See page* 130.)

So, with tears in her eyes, which made the beloved animal look rather wet, he resigned her to Captain Cockletop, the master of the ship, and went entirely off his feed for the next three days out of grief.

The "Unicorn" set sail from Quilp's Wharf on the eleventeenth ult., and was gone over two years.

Meanwhile our hero stuck close to his work, rising, in process of time, to be head sculleryman, and afterwards to be a fourth class apprentice in the shop itself.

He advanced in the favour of his master and mistress, and even succeeded, to some extent, in soothing the savage breast of Cicely, the cook.

As to Miss Alice, he was only too delighted when she gave him any little commission to execute, and as he always contrived to get his face washed, and his hair manipulated, before appearing to her, her opinion of his personal appearance went up many per cent.

There were not wanting persons who averred that the

"HOLD ME WHILE I FAINT!" CRIED WHITTINGTON.

(*See page* 120.)

first dawn of love was lighting up in the hearts of both of them, and indeed, the blush that arose on the cheek of each whenever they met, gave some colour to that supposition.

Even Mr. Moorgate Leadenhall, the young swell merchant, who thought he had only to speak to be accepted with joy, began at times to feel a bit jealous of that rising youth, R. W.

Shift we now the scene to the sunny shores of Afric, that

beauteous land, where niggers, alligators, and yellow fevers are always to be found when wanted.

Hitherto the English didn't know much about it, and there was no Livingstone in those days, but our traders, to turn an honest *penny*, would *pene*trate anywhere, and so it came to pass that the " Unicorn," one fine morning, found herself anchored in the bay of Mogador, while the captain and officers found themselves in the bloated presence of Moorish royalty.

His Majesty Selim Sinbad Ali Baba Mahomet Camaralzaman Saydassayd (with ever so much more of it), King, Emperor, and Sultan of all the Barbaries, and next-door neighbour to the sun and moon, sat in audience on his divan, or royal perch, as fine as a poll-parrot in pairing-time.

Lords and swells, slaves and guards were located around.

A little way off, and on a humbler, but still gorgeous seat, attended by ladies and she-male negresses, was the beauteous Sultana Fatima Leila Zuleika Yungazelle Balroubadour, a lady of *vast* attractions, merging on to fourteen stone and a half, and correspondingly *extensive* in attire.

They all sat on rich carpets, embroidered with gold and silver, cross-legged (we don't mean that the gold and silver were crossed-legged, but the people), and what with the colours and the sunshine, and altogether, the scene had a magnificent Arabian Night sort of effect, very taking to the eye.

Captain Cockletop unfolded his wares, his Derby cotton reels, Paisley shawls, Sheffield blades, and Brummagem brooches, Banbury cakes, Yarmouth bloaters, and Wenham Lake ices.

The king and company didn't seem to go into hysterical raptures of delight over any of the goods, or inclined to bid high even for the best ; but the captain had such an insinuating way with him, that the more people didn't want any-thing, the more he would make them buy it, and at last he pretty well cleared out his stock, at a good percentage.

The king then proposed that they should clinch the bargain with a regal spread.

Solid gold-topped tables were therefore brought in—pillauf, rice, jugged turkey-cocks, roast alligator, and other delicacies of that clime, including the most luscious fruits and ginger beer, that was positively seraphic, were all duly prepared; when, lo, and behold! from every corner of the room a regiment of mice and rats, of gigantic size, came swarming, overran the table, and walked bodily off with everything in the least degree eatable; they thought no more of running up the king's sleeve and snatching the very best tit-bits out of his hand or mouth than they did of winking.

In two minutes they had devoured the whole dinner, which the cook had been all the morning preparing.

All was confusion, of course; the ladies screamed and jumped anywhere and everywhere out of the way; the king swore, and the English officers drew their swords, for, brave as they were, this invasion of so many enemies at once rather startled them.

"Dear me," cried the captain, "we don't have mice and rats with so much check in our country. Do they always come to dinner uninvited like this, or does your majesty encourage them?"

"They don't want much encouraging," answered his majesty. "We only wish we could get rid of them.

> "'Twas ever thus from childhood's hour;
> I never had a banquet brought
> To glad me with its flavour nice,
> But when it tasted as it ought,
> 'Twas eaten up by rats and mice."

"Well, I think I know of a perfect cure," remarked the

captain, looking at the king as he did so; "there's an animal on board our ship that would kill as many rats and mice in an hour as a Chinaman could eat in a month?"

"Ah! Where is this animal? What's it's name? Where is it? Let me see it, quick!" cried the sultan, jumping up eagerly; "what is it like?"

"Like! why, like a cat, to be sure?" answered Captain Cockletop.

"And what's a cat like when it's at home, Seegneor Eengleez?" asked the Oriental potentate. "Remember, I've never seen one. Is it any larger than an elephant?"

"Not very much," said the captain, cautiously, "but it makes up for the size in sense and daring, but your effulgence shall see it at once."

He sent off the third mate to the ship, and very soon Pussy appeared.

To one who had never seen a cat, the sight was heavenly.

So *graceful* an animal was like a *grace* before meat, and from the way the ladies of the court fondled and *stroked* her, the captain knew that he had done a fine *stroke* in bringing her here.

"Now you shall see what you *shall* see," said Captain Cockletop.

By this time a fresh banquet was placed on the table, and no sooner was it there than the rats, as before, came in swarms, and overran everthing.

But Pussy was on to them like lightning; spreading out all her claws, she let out right and left, and soon scattered the enemy and made 'em fall, to such good purpose that thirteen out of every dozen gave their last kick.

Then, jumping down from the table, Pussy *puss*-ued them all round the room, and lucky were they that got back safe to their holes.

"By the toothpick of the prophet!" exclaimed the sultan, "this creature's a perfect wonder! What will you take for her—ten times her weight in gold?"

"Ten times!" cried the captain, turning pale with sheer amazement; "did your majesty say ten times?"

"Yes! but if you don't think it enough, we'll fix it fifteen times, and your pick out of my finest crown jewels."

The captain thought that he was dreaming when he received this overwhelming offer, but, disguising his surprise, he said, in an off-hand tone—

"Well, your most gracious highness, I won't say your offer isn't liberal, but this animal is so rare and highly valued in England (Oh! what a—— ! ! !), that I am not sure its owner, the Lord Richard de Whittington, would part with her at any price. However, I'll take the responsibility, and say 'done!'"

"Done it is!" responded the sultan, heartily, and at once gave orders to his treasurer to bring in his golden scales, his largest treasure chest, and his crown jewels.

The ladies went into ecstacies over the cat; they declared its fur was softer than the down of a sucking dove, that its eyes outshone the emerald, that its purr was *purr*-fection, and that it's very mew was like the voice of the angels.

The captain artfully took care that Pussy should be well fed before weighing, so that her price should come all the heavier.

It was a sight to see the gold, silver, jewels, and valuables of all kinds brought in.

The entire amount paid was equal to about £300,000, which was thought a vast sum in those days, and, indeed, is reckoned a good deal now.

Some greedy historians don't seem to consider even this enough, and try to make out that the Sultan of all the

Barbaries sent home the good ship " Unicorn " loaded to her very bulwarks with diamonds, rubies, and pearls.

I should be inclined to think that this is cutting it too thick, since a vessel loaded in this way would never have reached England. She could only have steered in one course—viz. to the bottom.

However, there is no doubt that Whittington's cat fetched more than any other Tom or Tittikins that ever wagged its tabby or tortoise-shell tail before or since. Now change we the scene once more.

It is England ; it is Fitzwarren's house ; it is Whittington's room. The mice are gone, but misery had not quite departed, for Dick has still to bear a good deal of ill-humour from the cook, a great deal of hard work ; and besides, he had never got over Pussy's departure, nor had her parting "molrow " ever ceased to echo in his ears.

It's true there was a new cat downstairs, but where or when could he ever hope to find a cat like the one he had lost ? Not in this world !

" I wonder how much they sold her for !" mused he ; " in a place where cats are rare she might fetch, say two half-crowns, or even (only it won't do to expect too much) seven and sixpence."

Then he heard his name pronounced below in loud and exciting accents.

" They're a-calling of me," he said, " they're a-calling of me. I expect it's that Mrs. Cicely wanting to blow me up for not polishing off that pair of master's boots quicker. Ah, well ! mine's a hard lot—hard as nails, and no mistake," and he gave a deep, deep sigh.

When he descended, he was surprised to see Captain Cockletop and his men, and everybody else assembled in the parlour, and evidently bursting with some good news.

"Mr. Whittington," began his master.

"Mister? why, he never can mean me!" exclaimed the humble Dick, all in a quiver of astonishment.

"I have to congratulate you that your—I mean my ship has come home," said Mr. Fitzwarren, "and our—I mean your success has been astounding. Your cat is sold!"

"Who bought her, and how much for, sir?" asked our hero.

"The King of Barbary, who gave—guess!"

"Eight bob?"

"No."

"Ten?"

"No."

"Fifteen?"

"No."

"Great goodness, you don't mean to say as he forked out a real golden sovereign?" said Whittington, breathlessly.

"He did, though, and another on the top of that, and another afterwards, and so on. In fact—not to keep you in suspense—what ho, there! bring in the price received for the cat."

And in they brought it, trays and baskets, and bags, and bowls full of gold, and silver, and diamonds, and rubies, and pearls, and emptied it on to the floor in heaps.

"Oh, mercy! I'm dreaming!" cried Whittington. "It can't be true! I wouldn't believe it on your oath! And yet—yet it is solid gold and jewels, and, I declare the very shining of it nearly blinds me! What might be the full amount?"

"I should estimate it at about three hundred thousand five hundred and seventy nine pounds," said Captain Cockletop.

"Hold me while I faint!" cried Whittington, and he went off in the arms of Miss Alice.

She had caught him just in the nick of time, for she saw what a good *catch* he would be now.

When Richard came to himself, he was almost smothered with congratulations.

Everybody suddenly discovered that they loved him better than their own father. Even Mistress Cicely, the cook, declared that she had doated on him all along, only didn't like to show it.

Miss Alice, about whose affection there never could have been the slightest doubt, covered his marble brow (it *was* marble now, you know) with rapturous kisses, saying that disguise was now useless.

"Bless you, my children!" cried the delighted merchant, even before anyone had asked him for it. "Be happy! This day seven years, Richard, you will be of age, and then the marriage shall take place. Meanwhile, you must go to college, &c., and be educated into a Universal Crichton. Then I'll take you into partnership, and we'll speculate largely in blacking."

"We will! we will!" cried Whittington, flinging himself into the arms of the merchant.

He gave a champagne supper that night, inviting everyone he knew, and many that he didn't.

Whittington's altered appearance and manner on that occasion made it almost difficult to identify him even on oath.

Toasts were drunk, speeches made, and happiness pervaded the entire house.

Only one heart was there tinged with any gall and wormwood.

It belonged to Mr. Moorgate Leadenhall, the young swell

merchant, who had hitherto looked upon Alice as booked for him, and was jealous of Whittington altogether.

But even he ultimately gave in to the general festivity, and congratulated everybody.

All Whittington's fellow servants, including the cook, were presented with a handsome bonus, which they received with three cheers.

Of course, from that time Whittington bade adieu to blacking-brushes, knife-boards, and dripping-pans.

He was promoted from the scullery to the dining-room at one step, though there were three flights to get to it.

Henceforth, his life was one long express journey on the road to prosperity.

He went to college, and became so learned that he was able to tackle the stoutest professors on any subject from Political Economy to Billiards.

Then he went into trade as the merchant's partner, and became the lion of the Stock Exchange.

The new firm prospered well, and Whittington and Fitz-warren's blacking became so popular, that Crosse and Blackwell's marmalade stood no chance against it.

When Richard came home, he went to court Alice again, after which he went to court to see the king, and was equally successful in both cases.

King Edward III. showed him great favour, and borrowed money of him frequently.

He said that there wasn't a man in his dominions whom he liked borrowing of better than Whittington ; he had such a pleasing way of handing over the amount, and asked such a small interest.

On one occasion, Whittington was dining with his majesty when these little matters had mounted up to £60,000.

Bless you ! this was a mere trifle to Whittington now !

"Never had king such a subject," exclaimed the grateful monarch, as he pocketed the last instalment.

"Never had subject such a king!" retorted Whittington, as he burnt the receipts at the oil-lamp.

"Upon my word that is a neat saying of yours," cried the king, gratefuller than ever, "and your repudiating the debt has won my heart."

Seizing a toasting-fork that lay providentially on the table, the king then smote our hero over the left shoulder, saying—

"Rise up, Sir Richard Whittington, and next year I'll get them to elect you Lord Mayor!"

So he *did* rise up Sir Richard Whittington in style that showed him to be a *rising* young man indeed.

In truth, he had grown so tall that Mistress Alice declared she would never *look down* upon him any more on account of his low birth.

The marriage took place at the time appointed with greater magnificence than anything of the kind since the Deluge.

Of course, Whittington's parents joined in the universal prosperity.

He had them both up from Zummerzetzhire, and had them created Lord and Lady Whittington by special patent.

They let their country cottage, and took a mansion instead.

Everybody knows that Whittington was Lord Mayor three times ; that Gog and Magog carried him through the streets on their heads, one foot resting on the head of each, tumbler fashion, so that he could be seen by all.

The cheers of the populace were very gratifying, but rather too loud for people with weak nerves ; and the Lord

Mayor's Show on each occasion was a thing of beauty and a joy forever.

To give a list of all Whittington's good deeds, of the hospitals, colleges, prisons, and other establishments he founded, and of the honours that were paid to him to the end of his life, would be really overwhelming; something like reading through the Post Office London Directory.

Suffice it that he did all this, and more.

Reader, I've done.

There are some miserable wretches who declare that the whole story of Dick Whittington and his cat is one gigantic crammer; that he never was a poor boy, but that his father was a big swell of a baronet, who could well afford to pay a good premium for his apprenticeship, and leave him a large fortune.

As for the cat, they say she was only an imaginary animal like the nightmare and the golopossomus; or that he had a vessel named "The Cat," that traded in *cat*-tle to the shores of *Cat*-alonia, and this gave rise to the story.

All that is nonsense; you must believe every word of the succinct narrative above recorded; for even if it hasn't been true up to this time, it must be so now *I* say it!

XXVI.

A GREAT DEAL OF CROWNING.

RETURNING from the peaceful brooklet of Sir Richard Whittington's biography to the main current of London history, let us relate (in strict confidence) what else occurred at this period.

Towards the close of the fourteenth century, a variety of circumstances, a great deal too numerous to mention here, had brought the people of England to the unsatisfactory conclusion that Richard II. wasn't a good king.

They were a long time—somewhere about eleven years—finding this out, and even then they couldn't make him see it himself.

However, when another eleven years had passed, taking advantage of his being out of town for a holiday, they invited over one Harry Bolingbroke, who, after a good deal of political palavering, gently kicked his cousin Dick out of the throne at the point of those long-toed boots then fashionable.

The surprising thing is that Richard was ever allowed to be king at all, when there were others ever so much better, especially Old John of Gaunt, as thorough a brick as ever appeared on the extensive brickfield of English history. (N.B.—We are now speaking figuratively—very much so indeed.)

He would have been next king after Richard, but he had to wait so long for the throne that he could not wait any longer, so he died.

Thereupon his son Harry took up the business of pretender to the English throne, and made a decided hit of it.

And it was quite time for a *change of heir* to the English crown.

What with his follies and his favourites, England was glad to see the last of the Plantagenets.

His extravagance was something awful.

Why, it is said he used to keep two thousand cooks—quite enough to spoil the broth, and no mistake—yet, although Richard II. didn't improve himself so much as he might, he made some great improvements in London.

In particular, he built Westminster Hall, and kept Christmas and several cash-boxes in it.

Literature flourished greatly at that period.

It was the age of Chaucer, the "Father of English Poetry," who had a large family of descendants, whereof W. Shakespeare was the biggest and most promising boy.

The "Canterbury Tales," all about the pilgrims that started from the famous "Tabard Inn," at Southwark, are notable for their delicious spelling—

> "Whylomme uppone a seasonne onn a daie,
> Att Sowthw'k at the 'Tabbard' as I laye."

And so on for a thousand pages.   I advise you to read them on some spare afternoon.

The new king Harry IV.'s coronation was on such a scale of magnificence that the present historiographer is devoutly thankful at not being personally called upon to pay for it.

It is not thought worth while to describe the ceremony in full ; the description of William the Conqueror's crowning, allowing for differences, will apply very well.

Nevertheless, it was a grand sight, and cost a *grand sight* of money.

————

X X V I I.

TREATS OF LORD MAYORS, KINGS, DUKE HUMPHREYS, ETC.

RICHARD II., the poor unfortunate ex-king (alas ! that little letter X is *ex*-actly what makes all the difference), took off his crown, and, handing it to his cousin, said—

"Bolingbroke, I declare you have nearly (Boling) *broke* my heart."

To which the new king replied that "he didn't go to do it, but political considerations" (here he turned round the crown to find the right way to put it on) "left him no choice.   Duty," he added, giving the crown a smart tap when on, "is what England expects every man, king, or t'other, to do."

Noble sentiments, were they not?

The hearers thought so, and cried—

"Long live Henry IV.!"

To which he replied—

"Thanks, good people, I will, as long as I can."

Nevertheless, he knew that his hold of supreme power wasn't a very tight one; so he had the crown rivetted on, and wore it night and day.

It was a rather hard sort of nightcap.

Its weight and the jewels made it awfully uncomfortable.

Hence the saying recorded by Shakespeare—"Uneasy lies the head that wears a crown."

He never got thoroughly used to it, and even when, for the sake of ease, he at last got into the habit of taking off his crown, and laying it under his pillow, his sleep was disturbed by the constant fear of burglars.

Nor was he far out, as we all know, for his wild son, young Harry, coming in one evening, found the crown propping up the royal bolster, and the king asleep.

He couldn't resist the temptation of "trying it on"—the crown we mean.

So he managed with great care to slide it out of its resting-place, putting the boot-jack there in its stead.

He then cried—

"Here goes for Henry V.!"

And put on the crown before the big looking-glass.

"Splendid, by Jove!" cried the prince, in boundless admiration.

When suddenly up rose the king, who, catching his young hopeful in the act of placing the diadem on his curly wig, snatched it away in regal wrath, and gave him a good *wigg*ing for it.

Henry IV. began his reign with the best intentions towards the metropolis.

He set up markets, granted new charters, and had the old ones burnt as waste paper, and gave the Lord Mayor the keys of Newgate, Ludgate, and Billingsgate to do as he liked with.

But, better than everything else, Guildhall was built in this reign, 1411, by Sir T. Knowles, Lord Mayor.

Henry No. 5 succeeded No. 4 in 1413.

In his youth he had been about as wild as a New South Wales kangaroo, and cut as extraordinary capers.

He was the bosom chum of Poins, Bardolph, ancient Pistol, Sir J. Falstaff, knight, and other "jolly dogs" of the day (see Shakespeare), and was generally called the "madcap prince," but, on becoming king, he changed his madcap for a sensible crown, and became so sharp that he cut all his old friends.

What he liked above all things was fighting the French, and what the people were particularly fond of was helping him.

Think of the battles he fought! Lives there an Englishman who can ever forget the glorious victory of Agincourt? If so, what a bad memory he must have.

When the king came back from that starring exhibition of conquest, you should see the reception the Londoners gave him!

The people turned out in such numbers that you would

have thought the whole population of the world had a holiday.

The decorations of the streets surpassed themselves.

The people considered their king a regular hero of heroes, able to do much greater deeds than Julius Cæsar, especially now that Cæsar was dead.

They proposed to carry his (Harry's, not Cæsar's) helmet through the streets, with all the dents and holes in it, so as to show the populace that he really had been fighting, and there was no deception.

But the king declined this honour, being contented with the other honours which the lord mayor and aldermen, and citizens in general lavished upon him.

After this triumphal entry, some of the flags that had been carelessly hoisted fell down and got trampled upon.

The pedestrians found them such soft walking that they thought it would be a good thing to have flags laid down all over the pathway.

Such was the accident that first suggested London pavements.

It also began to strike some brilliant persons that if the streets were lighted it would not be quite so dark at night, and might prevent some of the garrotting and robberies that were then committed as regularly as clockwork.

Six lanterns, illuminated with halfpenny rushlights inside, were accordingly hung up all along the route, and the inhabitants came out in their thousands to admire this grand illumination.

It was evident that the Dark Ages were coming to an end at last. But, alas, just as everybody was congratulating themselves on the *bright* aspect of affairs, another calamity happened, as will be seen by the following :—

XXVII.—(*Continued.*)

IT is a rather remarkable fact in history, that whenever we get hold of a good king, something happened to prevent him reigning so long as we should have liked—it was only the bad ones that were hard to get rid of.

So it happened with Henry V.

He was just winning all the people's affection for himself, when he was cut off like a blighted lily —far, far away on a French battle-field, with no great grandmother near to smooth his expiring pillow.

The people of England, and especially those of London, wept and mourned, but after all they had nothing to reproach

DINING WITH DUKE HUMPHREY.   (*See page* 132.)

themselves with, as it wasn't their fault.   If kings *will* go into battle, you know——

What made the worst worse still, was that Henry VI., the new king, was a minor, not a *coal* miner— for he wouldn't have been strong enough for the work—but an infant, a piccaninny, a babby, a "tiddy ittle sing," a small rosebud of humanity ; in point of fact he was only eight months old and little enough at that.

Of course he was far too young to be anything but an inside passenger in the stage coach, while the reins of government were held by older and tougher hands.

Extreme youth is a bad complaint for an absolute king to suffer under.

But Henry gradually got over it, and by the time he was twenty-one, might be considered quite cured.

The first London row in the sixth Harry's reign arose from the "obstroperousness" of Cardinal Beaufort, an ambitious prelate, who wanted to play not only "first fiddle," but most of the other instruments in the orchestra as well.

So he pretended that as Lord Mayor's Day had passed off rather flat of late, he would try and make it more lively.

Accordingly, choosing the memorable 9th of November, 1400 and something, he set out with a very large number of his boon companions, for the purpose of meeting the procession as it went along and having a fight.

"How dare anybody be lord mayor," he exclaimed, with *ire*, that rose *higher* and *higher* every moment, "without consulting me ?   Pretty state of things, indeed."

"Your lordship is right, as usual," responded the mayor, who had good reasons for wanting to keep in with the cardinal ; "but since I've been elected, I don't intend to be turned out a minute before I can help it."

He then protested how much he respected his eminence,

especially at a distance, and at last managed to talk over the proud cardinal and prevented a general shindy.

The lord mayor, preceded by his own corporation, then led the cardinal back to Westminster in great state, and further soothed his anger by presenting him with 1000 marks of gold and 10,000 marks of respect, besides two splendid ewers of solid silver, with the appropriate remark, " these were *mine* once, but now they're *ewers.*"

In 1426, the lord mayor was Sir John Rainwell, a capital name for the king of the City, who carried it out by *reigning* very *well* indeed. He found out that the Lombard merchants were in the habit of adultering port and sherry with tobacco-juice, Spanish liquorice, boiled mahogany chips, clarified blacking, and other foreign substances, which may be very nice in themselves when kept separate from wine, but they don't go well together when mixed.

The lord mayor exclaimed, indignantly—

" *Butt* me no *butts* of such stuff as this," and ordered no less than 750 butts to be thrown into the kennel.

It was done, and as the beverage was acknowledged by all to be totally unfit for human consumption, the only persons who lapped it up were the dogs, who, of course, thought that whatever was put in the *kennels* would be their especial property.

The consequence was that they all got drunk, and couldn't bark without hiccupping, and kept running round and round, and none of them could find their way home, or, even if they did, found that they had lost their latchkeys.

They *were* " jolly dogs," with a vengeance.

This lord mayor was kind enough to give away a number of houses and lands, to pay off a heavy tax that was demanded most from those who could afford it least.

We always think of him, and wish he was alive now, when

we hear the tax-gatherer's inspiring knock at the front door.

Baynard Castle, the scene of the pathetic history we have already recounted, was destroyed by fire in 1428, and built up again by the Duke of Gloucester, the king's uncle, and generally known by the title of the good Duke Humphrey.

He tried the plan of beginning to build the castle at the bottom, and working his way gradually up to the top ; this was considered by the architects of the time a very neat idea, and it has been carried out with success ever since.

The good Duke Humphrey will now occupy our attention.

He was a man whom I should like to know very much, but I'm afraid it is late in the day to think of cultivating his acquaintance.

He was much renowned for his great hospitality.

He was always inviting people to dinner, though, strangely enough, he sometimes forgot to provide the necessary provender.

Of course, politeness forbade the guests to tell him of his mistake, so they pretended to like it, and loudly remarked to each other how splendidly the large joints were cooked.

You will thus perceive that dining with Duke Humphrey was not so very different from going without altogether.

The dinner service was, however, of the very best quality, and with the trifling exception of the dinner itself, there was nothing left to be desired.

The good Duke Humphrey at first played the part of "heavy father" to the youthful monarch, Henry VI., but Cardinal Beaufort got the young king so completely under his thumb, that he was able to twirl him round in any direction he pleased.

So the government was divided into two parties—nothing like so agreeable as evening parties, dinner parties, &c.

The only thing that they agreed about was that it would be advisable to provide the king with a con*sort* of the right *sort*, who might be able to make him do as she liked, if they couldn't.

Such a one was the celebrated Margaret of Anjou, who was chosen not without great opposition.

When she came over, she joined the Beaufort party, and they all turned fiercely against the poor unfortunate Duke Humphrey.

His duchess was accused of witchcraft, of *which craft* she was entirely innocent; and she, being condemned, was sentenced to walk through the streets barefoot and bare-headed, attired in a robe of penance, and holding a wax taper to throw a light on the subject.

She got to St. Paul's without further accident, except being pelted with stones, dead cats, and rotten eggs.

Of course the poor lady caught a violent cold, and was laid up with rheumatism ever afterwards.

This was a great blow to the duke, who, seeing it was all through the king and his advisers, would, you might think, have felt ready to smash them all; but instead of this he forgave his enemies, and held his tongue, only rapping out an oath, or wiping away a tear when he was alone, and no witnesses handy.

A parliament then met to see if there wasn't some neat way of hurrying the duke out of the world without killing him by violence, blood being often apt to make a mess on the floor, which is some trouble to wipe up.

The plotters agreed what they would do; so, one day, when the duke was going to his club, he was suddenly arrested and thrown into prison.

After having been confined seventeen days without any trial, though I should think he had been through *trials* enough already, he was found to have popped off the hooks of existence.

If it wasn't a case of poison, my name's not Aristogonius Polyasterisk.

The fate of the good Duke Humphrey is a warning to all men not to try and do anything for the public good, as they are sure to get in for it.

Let each look out only for himself, and permit others to do the same, and he will always be rewarded, promoted, and praised to the skies.

This is a rule with very few exceptions.

X X V I I I.

ABOUT SERFS, JEWS, CHRISTIANS, AND OTHER INDIVIDUALS.

ALL of the foregoing didn't prevent several good laws being made in this reign, with regard to London.

One was, that all serfs who had resided a year and a day in the city should be considered to have *serfed* their time, and be set free—and easy ; another was that nobody who had less than thirty shillings a-year income should be considered as belonging to the bloated aristocracy, and that beggars should not on any account be allowed to ride in their carriages, as it didn't look well.

At this period there were a great many people in London who belonged to the He-brew and She-brew persuasion ; in other words, Jews and Jewesses. Most of them lived in Old Jewry, not a *Grand Jewry* by any means.

I must say that they were badly treated.

Of course all my readers have read " Ivanhoe," or, at

least *I've-a-no*-tion that they have, and they will remember how shamefully they served out poor old Isaac of York because he didn't like roast pork, and was supposed to have some surreptitious hoard of lucre stowed away in a snug corner.

Well, that's a general specimen of how the children of Israel were persecuted by the English Pharaohs of the dark ages.

No end of rods were in pickle for these unfortunates, if they didn't hand over the *John Doradoes* just whenever the great barons wanted them.

The way of serving the descendants of Israel is really too bad.

Why, King John had a Jew locked up, and one of his teeth drawn out every day till he told him where his *Rhynoceros*, or treasure trunk was kept.

A number of these Iraelites having ventured out to look at King Cœur de Lion's coronation, were set upon and mobbed by the infuriated populace.

Not only did the latter kill about one hundred, but burnt their houses, seized their property, and altogether demolished them by way of showing themselves devout Christians.

It seems to me that it would have been a great deal better if they hadn't been quite so religious.

Certainly there were enough churches at the time to convert all the Jews in England.

For the Norman period was the grand time for church-building, and cathedrals, chapels, churches, nunneries, monkeries, priories, friaries, colleges, retreats, seminaries, &c., &c., &c., springing up all over England as if they'd been sown thickly, and watered every morning.

Five hundred monastic edifices were reared in this country from 1066 to 1210 only, and if they had kept on at that rate till now we should have all been too religious to live.

All sorts of pious brotherhoods, sisterhoods, unclehoods, and monkhoods, not to mention Tom Hoods, Robin Hoods, and little Red Ridinghoods, were visible in London.

Grey friars, white friars, brown friars, red friars, and black and blue friars, and friars of everything else, even including *friers* of sausages, soon swarmed in the streets of London.

There were even *crutched friars*, so called not because they went on crutches, but because they wore a cross on their backs, and some of them looked cross in the face as well.

Readers, pull yourselves together, open your ears to their widest, and prepare to fix on your historian an attention so intense and concentrated that an earthquake wouldn't disturb you.

We are about to enter into the sensational history of Jack Cade, who, according to documents recently brought to light after immense researches, was originally christened John.

He was born in ould Ireland, begorra he was ! though, as his parents happened to be travelling in England at the time, he never considered himself anything but an Englishman.

His father, it is said, was a bricklayer ; and besides laying bricks, he was a *brick* himself, and belonged to the *mortar*mer (Mortimer ?) family.

He was also descended from the Lacies, who, because they always *stayed* in Ireland, were called *stay-Lacies*.

Of Jack Cade's early years we don't know much, and if we do, intend to keep it to ourselves.

But this we will stick to, that from his very cradle he exhibited an aspiring soul, and was determined to rise high in the world, even if he had to go "Up in a baloon" to do it.

He commenced his career by poaching, and would soon have ended it on the gallows.

But he managed to escape to France, whence he came to Albion's isle, otherwise " Britannia the pride of the ocean !"

Now, it so happened that things in England were just in the right state to get up a jolly good rebellion.

Peace had been made with the French, but people-in-general's blood was so thoroughly up that they determined to have it out on somebody, so fixed on the king.

Henry and his ministers fell so far *short* of what the nation wanted, that the said nation determined to stand them no *longer*.

Added to this, Richard, Duke of York, had a beautifully artistic design on the crown, and so he stirred up the British lion with the long pole of ambition.

The Londoners, who, you will perceive, were always to the fore when anything like civil war was coming, took the lead as usual.

Jack Cade, having come to London on the extreme quiet, had a private interview with the Duke of York, up a side court leading out of the Strand, at which the duke—under the incog. of John Jones, Esq.—told him that if he would rebel like blazes, and turn London as much upside down as possible, he would stick to him like the very best cement.

As this friendly declaration was accompanied by various drinks and a hundred pounds in cash, to be repeated in a month's time if all went well, Cade jumped at the offer like a bird.

The very next day he fixed up his standard at Blackheath, where, by making a splendid speech, he soon gathered a thousand people round him.

Another thousand soon came to look at the first thousand, another to look at that, and so on till altogether twenty thousand were collected.

Cade began by saying that his name was Mortimer, that he

was the rightful heir, not only to an earldom, but to the throne of England, his pa being the Earl of March, and his ma, of course, the Countess of *April*.

He said he had been changed at birth, and his supposed parent, Mr. Cade the bricklayer, had only taken care of him, and not much care either.

"But I know it's no use setting up as 'claimant,'" continued Cade, putting on a Wagga-waggish air of jocularity; "because it would take about seven years and fifty thousand pounds to prosecute my claim, even if I didn't get prosecuted myself afterwards; and it would be too much to come down on the public to pay my law expenses—I couldn't do it, for I know I *Orton* to.

"No, my present game is patriotism—down with everything in general, and up with everything else in particular.

"London people and country people must be united; the present ministry must be turned out—neck and crop, root and branch, bag and baggage—and if the king won't give them the *sack*, we must commit *sacrilege* ourselves, and say—

"'Now then, out o' that throne!'"

All approved.

The shouts were deafening, and had a fine effect at the distance of ten miles.

Cade then raised his flag, which was of a brilliant red, enough to send any bright-spirited bull—even an Irish bull—raving mad.

It had the cap of liberty stuck on the top, with the name "liberty" on it—of course in *cap*ital letters—and underneath Cade's own motto—

"When Adam worked, and Eve as well,
    Pray, who was then an idle swell?"

the meaning of which was, everybody had a right to strike,

and all those who were rich and did nothing, would have to look out.

In short, Jack Cade was determined to play the same part as the ever-to-be-renowned Wat Tyler, of whose history he had heard with rapture, crying—

"Hear! hear! Splendid! My feelings to a spoonful! By Jove! this will bear doing again!"

And that's how he came to do it.

Well, not to make a short story long, the procession set off towards London, and Cade's rebellion soon became the sensation of the day.

The city was in commotion, the West End was roused, the suburbs nearly went distracted.

The name of Cade was on every lip, and echo repeated it till the poor thing got regularly tired out.

When King Henry heard of it he happened to have his shoes off, or he would certainly have shaken in them; but, as it was, his stockings did pretty well for that purpose.

He was certainly much taken aback, and knew no more what to do than an elephant that's lost his trunk.

So he blew the royal whistle, and his *train* of courtiers, instead of *going off*, *stopped* a little longer, perceiving that there was danger on the line.

None of the statesmen present could give the king any good advice at the crisis.

So Henry's only resource was his royal spouse, Margaret of Anjou, a lady who was equal to several men in most things; indeed she was too many for some of them.

She belonged to the very strongest minded order.

She stuck up for the rights of woman to that extent, that the rights of man were nowhere.

Thus the king could sometimes feel compassion for his oppressed subjects; he knew what it was himself.

The exterior appearance of this remarkable female was overpowering, awe inspiring to a man of weak nerves.

It seemed as if to say much to her when she was put out would be like entering the lion's den and trying to make off with the eatables.

Her very manner as she swept into the room, dragging a rich train—three and a half yards of purple velvet, stiff with gold—after her, her very manner, I say, said as plainly as manner could say—

"If you dare to aggerryvate me, look out."

"My dearest life," faltered the fond monarch, presenting to her Cade's petition, just sent in; "we're in a fix. The rebels ask more than we can possibly grant, and I don't want to kill the poor misguided fellows."

"The traitorous villains, you mean!" answered the queen. "Let me see their petition. Great Jupiter alive! Grant all this? I should think not indeed! Why, it couldn't be done at any price. Well, I know what would happen if I were King of England."

"What, my dear?" asked the royal patient, anxiously.

"Their heads would come off at once; something in this way," replied Margaret the majestic, snipping off the tops of two geraniums with a pair of golden scissors.

"Quite right, my beloved," approved the king. "But mercy is the royal prerogative, and I prefer catching the rebels first, at all events, before I kill them. It's only fair. We must try negotiations. Suppose we send some reverend gentleman to talk them over, and tell them how naughty it is to rebel against their rightful ruler, My Lord Bishop of Chi-chichester, you'll go, of course?'

"Not if I know it, your majesty," was the response of his grace. "If you want to kill me right off, do it, but don't —oh, don't ask me to expose myself to death in that way!"

And he dropped a tear into his mitre, which he had taken off for the purpose.

"Well, perhaps, after all, a man-of-war sent amongst them would be best," said the king. "I don't mean a *ship*, of course, unless your lord*ship*"—turning to him of Warwick—"would venture on this unpleasant but necessary duty."

"I will," replied the earl. "Why should I fear? Odsdaggers are dumplings! who's Cade, I should like to know? All the Cades that ever walked, and all the mobs that ever talked, wouldn't frighten me! I'll undertake to settle the rascals; and if I don't bring home Cade's head under my arm, done up into a neat brown paper parcel, you may—there, you may choke me with castor oil!"

"Bravo! encore!" cried his majesty, clapping his royal gloves together approvingly. "Would that there were many like thee, my lord, in my court. I should get on like three houses on fire. Go, and take my blessing; it won't weigh very much. Tell these dissatisfied and unreasonable rapscallions that their petition won't wash with me; tell them that if they lay down their lives, I'll spare their arms. No; I mean—but, there, tell them what thou wilt. Thou requirest followers. You, my Lord Say, and you also, my Lord Scales, must accompany him."

(N.B.—Lord Say was a nobleman apt at speech, able to *say* the right thing at the right moment, and therefore always employed in difficult negotiations.)

Lord Scales was often called *fish* scales, because he lived in Fish Street, where his of-*fish*-ial duties were very ef-*fish*-iently executed.

Both these two noble lords wished they were somebody else just then; but they couldn't disobey the king's commands.

So in a short time they and their retinues were ready to go, though perhaps not willing.

"Be merciful to the poor rebels," were the last words of the compassionate king.

"And take as many as possible into custody," added the dispassionate queen.

With these parting injunctions, the king and queen departed for Kenilworth, which, being a hundred miles from London, his majesty thought would be a safe and pleasant retreat for the time being.

So he set off away from London to *Warwick*, while *Warwick* himself went into London.

Meanwhile Cade kept up his *march* to London, with a war-like pomp and circumstance which couldn't have been surpassed by the Earl of *March* himself.

Wherever he came, the citizens received him with open arms and open mouths, and that blissful feeling which people in the good old times always experienced when they saw a chance of getting their heads broken.

London Bridge was the first point of attack, and a struggle took place there "whose like we ne'er shall look upon again."

There were no steamers then.

But the rebels went at it "like steam," and the royal party, consisting of only one *beat* of loyal policemen, soon had to *beat* a retreat, on account of being *beat* themselves.

Having gained London Bridge, the rebels again urged on their wild career, and soon reached the Monument—or rather, would have reached it if it had been standing, and Cade would certainly have knocked it down.

People flew from houses, shops were shut up with all speed, rich merchants buttoned up their pockets and bolted, and in short, London seemed to have gone distracted on Cade's arrival.

Cannon Street was soon reached by the victorious mob.

It was lucky for them that there were no *cannon* in it at the time.

The next points in the programme were the Tower, Smithfield, and a few other churches, all of which would be reached in due time.

But now let us say a little about the principal fellows Cade had with him.

First, there was Tom the smith.

[N.B.—No relation to the Mr. Smith *you* are acquainted with.]

Next stood Dick the butcher, a very valuable member of the band, inasmuch as he was good at *killing*, ready to take part in any *joint* conspiracy, and made no *bones* about any desperate course that happened to *meat* his views.

Kit the carpenter *saw* a *plane* course in the matter, and knew how to hit the right *nail* on the head.

Best the tanner warranted that he would well *tan* his enemies, and give their *hides* the *best leather*ing they ever had.

Bill the baker was prepared to *do*(*ugh*) some *dough*ty deeds in the contest.

He saw that Cade would *need* the *flower* of London's valour to assist him, and that, however *depressed* the swells might feel in the West End of London, there would be a splendid *rising* in the (*y*)*east;* while Jimmy the weaver, armed with his *beam*, presented anything but a *beam*ing face to his enemy.

As to George and Joe, and Mike and Pat (for siveral rale Oirish lads followed in the *wake* of Cade, so they did, intirely), and all the rest, they were of one mind, and agreed to have nothing but their own way right on to the end.

With such a band of trusty followers, it was no wonder that Cade felt as sure of carrying all before him as a leg of mutton is of being eaten.

He paraded through the London streets as confidently as a cock in a farmyard, only that those interesting birds

"NOW, MY FRIENDS, DO YOU ACKNOWLEDGE ME AS KING?"

(*See page* 148.)

don't in general ride on horseback, nor wear chain armour and hat and feathers.

When he reached London Stone, the great rebel chieftain voted for a rest, with a running accompaniment of beer.

He also unfurled his standard to the inspiring breeze.

His own words on the occasion were—

"For London stone
Shall be my throne,
And none shall rule but I alone."

Then he rose and made a speech thus—

"My name's Lord John de la Cade de Mortimer, the rightful Earl of March, and still more rightful King of England!"

"What a crammer!" murmured a certain individual in the crowd.

Only he took care that nobody should hear him.

"If anyone disputes it, show him in. I'm ready," continued the insurgent leader, clutching his stout cudgel energetically.

GRAND EQUESTRIAN FEAT—CADE JUMPS OUT OF DANGER. (*See page* 157.)

Nobody, of course, made any objection.

But one enthusiastic voice ejaculated—

"Brayvo, Cade!"

"Don't Cade me!" exclaimed the illustrious John; "or you'll come in for it. Don't I tell you I'm one of the Mortimers?"

"By Jove! anyone would think you were all the Mortimers

put together, from the *big* way you talk," mused the observant party before mentioned.

"Londoners," pursued Cade, "I've come to save you from oppression. You've been ground down like coffee—trodden under foot like blackbeetles. Don't put up with it any longer. Strike—strike, like blazes! This is the age of strikes. Everybody and everything is striking nowadays. Why, the very clocks are striking; hark at 'em! Even lucifer matches strike sometimes, though it is only on the box. And so why shouldn't you?"

"Hear, hear!" they cried, for these sentiments suited them very well indeed.

At length after a pause, Cade continued—

"Men of Kent, you who have been the prime movers in this insurrection—very *prime* movers indeed—I am proud of you." (A voice—"The same to you, and many of 'em.") "I intend to reward you at once. Now, I'll just tell you what it is I mean to do."

It was just at this very interesting point that trumpets and tramps of hoofs made themselves perceptible, and up came the Earls of Suffolk and Warwick, Lord Say, Lord Scales, and many other big men of the king's faction.

The Earl of Warwick, who looked as *stern* as the *back* part of a ship, rode first, and approached the redoubted rebel far more fearlessly than you, reader, would walk up to a hungry tiger.

Reining up his gallant charger, the earl threw the petition at the head of Cade.

"Thief, rebel, villain, miscreant, traitor, and——"

"I say, my lord, draw it mild," remonstrated Cade, "or you'll rowge the British lion" ("or rather the Irish bull," murmured the party in the crowd) "within this here breastplate. Besides, if you must return the petition, you might

have handed it to me on a clean plate.   Never mind, I forgive you.   Go on."

"The king rejects your outrageous demands," continued
the royal emissary, "and says that if you don't lay down
your arms, your head and shoulders must dissolve partnership."

"No, they won't," answered Jack.   "They get on too
well together for that.   Now, do you mean to tell me that
the king puts on the deaf ear to our petition, that he don't
intend to kick out the present parliament, and grant reforms
all round?"

"He'll see you made into sausages first," responded the
resolute statesman.

"Then witness all, great and small, I mean to kick him
out and be king myself," cried Cade, bringing his fist down
a clencher on the stone, to show that he meant it.

"I'll be crowned at Westminster to-morrow, and compel
all London to swear allegiance."

The cheek of Cade actually made the *cheek* of Warwick
turn pale, although he did belong to the *red rose*-y
party.

"Men (women included, if any) of London," said Lord
Say, turning to the mob, "will you own as leader a man
whose father was a bricklayer?"

"Was he?   Then here's one of his bricks for you," cried
Cade, hurling a good-sized one at the nobleman, who managed
to dodge it neatly.

"Will you rebel against your lawful king?" continued
Lord Say.   "Goodness gracious! why it's rank felony, not
to mention battles, murder, and sudden death.   Don't do it.
Go home, put your heads in a bag, and reflect calmly."

"Ya-ah!   Go home yourself!" responded the insulted
crowd, while Cade, rising, cried—

"At 'em, boys! Pitch into the nobs! Drive 'em off! Stick up for London and liberty!"

His words acted like a charm.

A skirmish ensued, and the Earl of Warwick, despite the fact that he had been in more battles than he could remember all at once, soon found himself utterly unable to cope with the rebels; not but that he would have held out to the last, or longer, but when he saw all his friends and followers desert him in a sudden panic—when he saw that the rebels were about ten to one, and well provided with such artillery as dead cats, rotten apples, and flint stones, he thought a retreat movement would be good policy.

So he dignifiedly rode off, the rebels following him with a wild hulloo!

" Ha, ha !" laughed Cade, enjoying the spectacle, especially as an egg he had dexterously thrown went smash against Lord Scale's helmet. " See how they run ! Three blind mice was nothing to 'em. Hi, my boys, after 'em, after 'em ! and half a sovereign for the first person brought back !"

While the more adventurous spirits joined in the hue and cry, Jack Cade turned to the steadier ones, saying, as he quaffed out of a half gallon mug to the health of all present—

" And now, my friends and followers, let's continue my speech. Do you acknowledge me as king ?"

" We does, we does !" exclaimed the excited crowd, few of whom had learned grammar.

" That's right. I mean to go in for reforms on a large scale. Grant petitions on all sides. From this very hour everything shall be cheap, and adulteration be punished with a ducking. Seven ha'penny loaves shall be sold for a penny."

" Then how the dooce can they be ha'penny ones ?"

mentally asked the mysterious individual in the crowd, who, to let the reader into a profound secret, was by trade a corn chandler.

"Every three-hooped drinking cup," pursued the new monarch, "shall have ten hoops in future."

"Three hoops on a ten-hooped cup; another Irish bull," commented the corn chandler, inaudibly.

"And whoever drinks small beer shall be deemed guilty of sacrilege in the first degree."

"Hooray!" was the hearty response.

"Nobody shall ever pay any more rents or rates, or taxes, or bills, or—by jingo! there shall be no money at all. I'll keep everybody, and find them in clothes, food, lodging, and washing, now and for evermore."

"Amen!" echoed the delighted and pious crowd.

It was precisely at this moment and no other that Dick the butcher, and a number of other rebels, came up with great commotion, hauling along a small and exceedingly frightened man, who wished himself a hundred miles off.

"Please, captain—I mean, your majesty," bawled out Dick, "we've caught a——"

"A Tartar, I suppose?" suggested Cade.

"Not a bit of it. A lawyer, leastways, a lawyer's clerk, from Clerkenwell. Let's make an example of him."

"Aye, aye; vengeance on the lawyers!" cried everybody, with one voice only.

Trembling all over like a jelly, and his hair as straight as a bundle of pipelights with sheer terror, the clerk of Clerkenwell was brought before the redoubtable Cade.

"Now, you pettifogging, six-and-eightpenny yard of red tape, what do you mean by it? How dare you be a lawyer?"

"Please, sir, I was put to it," protested the poor fellow.

" It ain't my fault.   You must blame my father, who's dead these ten years."

" It's well for him he is," observed Cade, " for he would get in for it nicely if he were alive.   But ah, oho ! what's this?   A quill and ink-horn ?   Why, you know how to write then, you villain !"

" Ye-es, my lord ; but please, sir, I can't help it, it was taught me."

" I don't care," cried the rebel leader, " I can't write myself, and I don't see why *you* should.   I've made it a law that whoever does *write* does *wrong*, and must be strung up instanter."

" Oh, please don't !" cried the unfortunate scribe ; " think of my poor grandmother, my bereaved uncle, my——"

" Why, here's a book !" exclaimed the herculean smith, who had been searching the clerk.   " I shouldn't wonder if he could read as well."

" Read !   Worse and worse !" roared Cade.   " What, thou fiend in human form, dost thou know reading as well as writing ?"

" A few," replied the clerk, timidly ; " but I can't help it, you know, they *would* make me learn it."

" Ha !" cried Cade, frowning like thunder, " we've had readin' and 'ritin', we shall get to the 'rithmetic next. Answer this, miscreant, do you know that too ?   Can you do sums ?"

" To *sum* extent," responded the persecuted scholar, who now knew what the poet meant by saying—

" A little learning is a dangerous thing."

" But please, don't kill me for it, it was my master's fault for teaching me.   I'll never add up another two figures as long as I live."

" Which won't be long," answered Cade.   " You've

confessed your guilt, and stand convicted of the very worst crimes.

"I've heard so much of the London School Board, that I'm school-*bored* to death at the very thought of that a-*bhorred* institution, and I've sworn to make an example of the first prisoner I took that had even anything to do with education. You're the man, so away with you. String him up, my men, to yonder lamp-post, and tie his ink-pot round his neck."

This terrible order would have been at once executed—and it certainly would have been an *ink*-credibly *black* deed, and quite in-*neck*-scusable—but for the timely arrival of a prisoner of more importance, namely, Lord Say, who had been run down after a hard chase, in the tail of the retreat.

Cade was delighted with this opportunity of serving out the aristocracy, bloated or otherwise.

"Now, Lord Say, what have you to say for yourself?" asked Cade, trying to look as much like the Lord Chief Justice as possible.

"I decline answering," replied the nobleman. "Think I'm going to be cross-questioned by a fellow who don't even wear spectacles and a wig? Where's your authority?"

"Here," answered the new king of London, grasping the thick cudgel, which suited him better than a sword or even a sceptre. "I should like to see you dispute it.

"You're one of the ministers we, the people, are particular down upon. *We* remember all about your doings in the House of Lords. Who sold us to the French? Who raised the taxes? Who stole the donkey?"

"Who, indeed?" said the bloated aristocrat, mockingly.

"Who opposed the nine-hours movement?" Cade went on. "Who was it declared that universal suffrage wouldn't do, and costomongers ought to sell taters without a licence? Who was it?—*Say!*"

"It wasn't *Say*," cried the nobleman, roused to opposition. "I didn't do any of it—and if I did——"

"Away with him," cried Cade. "and chop off his head ten times; once isn't enough. Dick the butcher, you're the fellow to do the job neatly; and while you're about it, call at Sir James Cromer's house, with my compliments, and tell him I want his head as well, and don't come away without it, mind."

"We won't, we won't," shouted they.

And away went the smith and his myrmidons on this pleasing errand.

"And this is slow work after all, sitting here and delivering judgment," said Cade. "I'm for action. Let's knock down a few houses. But I'm tired of walking; besides it ain't dignified. What ho! there, a hoss, a hoss! my kingdom for a hoss!"

"Won't a donkey do?" asked a considerate coster, who had one handy.

"A donkey, indeed!" cried Cade, firing up. "What, do you think I'm going to ride on *your* back? What next? No, I must have a horse, not a towel horse, but a right down, blue-blooded, red-breasted charger, up to any weight, and able to leap like a kangaroo."

"Bring forth the horse," cried Jimmy, the weaver.

And of course the horse was brought.

In truth he was a noble steed; something about half way between a racer and a Barclay and Perkins.

Cade mounted.

He had learned to ride while managing the stables attached to the horse marines out by the Nore—a capital school of *naval* horseman*ship*.

When fairly seated, he certainly looked a most eligible party, and reminded everybody a good deal of Wat Tyler, though none of them had seen him.

Away then the rebels went again, fighting their way through the streets at a tremendous rate, upsetting everything and everybody, smashing windows, and tying tin kettles to the tails of unoffending dogs.

This sort of thing went on longer than I care to describe or you to hear.

The great people of the City itself, such as the lord mayor and aldermen, didn't exactly side with the rebels.

But they dared not go against them, so they shut themselves up out of the way, and the lord mayor in particular, who, it is said, went off to bed with a bowl of his favourite turtle soup under his pillow.

The West-Endians—that is, the more extensive nobs—were in Westminster, where they summoned a *Westministerial* meeting to decide what was to be done at this crisis.

Few noble lords, having in view the fate of Say and Cromer, cared about exposing themselves to the beheading powers of the insurgents.

But at last the brave Duke of Buckingham volunteered to face the danger, and talk to them "like a dutch uncle."

So, with three hundred men, so heavily armed at all points that their horses could hardly stagger under them, Buckingham entered the City, and reaching Smithfield Market, found Cade in all his glory.

A trumpet being sounded to produce silence (rather a queer way of doing it, by the bye), the duke faced about to the crowd, and began—

"My good people——"

"Go it, old *Buck!*" shouted the crowd.

[N.B.—This was their short for *Buckingham*.]

"I've just had a telegram from our most gracious sovereign. He says he'll love you all for ever after, if you will only stop this riot. He promises a free pardon to everybody who gives up this audacious rebel's company and comes over to the right side."

"Don't listen to him, pals," cried Cade. "Mine's the only right side. Stick to your own Mortimer (myself, I mean), the lineal descendant of Alfred the Great—ahem!"

"Friends," pursued the duke, "if you listen to all the lies this rapscallion tells you, you'll have enough to do. Your only rightful lord and suzerain is Henry VI., king of England, France, Ireland, Anjou, Aquitaine, Jersey, Guernsey, Whitechapel, and——"

"Stop his mouth with a fire-plug, somebody!" cried Cade, getting riled. "Cut it short, Buckingham, or I'll cut *you* short!"

"Will you follow a base-born miscreant, who can't prove who were his ancestors, or even whether he had any or not? Whereas our good king, Henry VI., can trace his pedigree right on back to William the Conqueror, and so on back as far as King Solomon, who was the wisest monarch that ever lived."

"Then I'm blowed if Henry takes much after him!" exclaimed Cade. "Look here, Buckingham; I don't care for you, nor all the rest of the king's lardy-dardy, kid glove courtiers put together.

"If you don't instantly do me homage as your liege lord, and if you dare say another word to alienate these my trusty subjects, especially that lot there, who are men of Kent——"

"Then all I can say is that it's hard-upon Kent to have to own such ragamuffins!" cried the noble duke.

"Don't interrupt me, sir! I say, if you say another word,

I'll off with your head, and then it will be 'so much for Buckingham,' and no mistake."

Do you think the duke heeded this threat?

Not the slightest.

He gathered together all his wind for a mighty blast, and shouted out *fortissimo* —

"Seize the rebel! A thousand pounds reward for the head of Jack Cade!"

The effect was like a peal of lightning.

Many a sturdy rebel, who, the minute before, would have annihilated anybody who said a word against Cade, now turned over to the other side.

The coin was too tempting to be withstood.

A simultaneous movement was made from all sides to seize Cade, who stood (on horseback) defiantly in the middle.

"Ah, would you!" he cried, putting on an air of injured innocence. "Do you call this sticking to your colours? Bah! be off! Such followers are not worth having! I'd kick you all round if I had time! But rally round me, all you real, right-down Englishmen, and fight, if necessary, till there's nothing left but your eyelashes!"

And they did so.

Dick the butcher, Tom the smith, and a few more—principally Kentish men—gathered round Jack, and a fight—that is to say a struggle—otherwise a contest—to wit, a combat—or, to speak more plainly, a skrimmage—ensued.

Cade fought as never a man had fought that hadn't any chance;
Oh! his ranks—his ranks were breaking, and they never could advance.

In short, after a sharp tussle, Cade found himself flying down Cheapside at the top of his speed, followed by his few remaining followers, with the enemy following them.

He had all but reached the Mansion House, when, at the

extremity of the thoroughfare, he suddenly beheld two objects that seemed like a couple of towers—only towers don't walk, nor wear armour, nor slash about right and left with swords—so Cade came to the conclusion that they must be no other than the renowned City Giants, Gog and Magog.

Yes, they, on their own responsibility, had undertaken to catch the arch rebel.

He was going along so quickly that he hadn't time to pull up or put the break on, before he rode slap up to them, when, by a sudden move, they caught him in full career.

" Ha !" cried Gog, clutching his horse's throat.

" Ho !" exclaimed Magog, seizing the rebel's right arm.

The appearance of the two giants at that moment was something awful to contemplate.

Cade gave himself up for lost.

He could defy most things, but two such enemies were *two* much, and fairly took his breath away.

" Hurrah, we've got him, my lord !" shouted Gog, in a voice that was plainly heard by the Duke of Buckingham, who was then at the other end of Moorgate Street.

" Hurrah and hooray !   Cade's caught."

A deafening shout of triumph from all quarters showed that this news gave universal satisfaction.

To make the fact more apparent to the public, the two giants lifted up Cade and his horse—much as Magog had done with Whittington and his cat—high above their heads.

The weight was a mere nothing to them.

But they were not prepared for what followed.

X X X.

SAME KING AND SAME "SUBJECT" CONTINUED.

JUST as Gog and Magog were inwardly chuckling at the thought of the reward—£500 apiece would be a nice little haul—and just as the Duke of Buckingham and other royalists were thinking how triumphantly they would seize their prisoner, Cade gave his horse a spur, and the agile quadruped, dealing Magog's head a parting kick that made him roar, gave a mighty bound into the air, and leaping over an adjoining house, disappeared—rider and all, of course.

You doubt the fact, but why should you?

Remember it was not like jumping over a house from the ground.

Cade, when held aloft by the giants, was over twenty feet high ; the house was not much higher, and the steed, besides being naturally spring-heeled, was a *roof-jumper*.

He had been practised by a late master (for, of course, he had been "the property of a gentleman gone abroad ") to clear a row of chimney pots at a bound, or keep his footing over the most slippery tiles.

It was rather a sell for Gog and Magog, and they felt it acutely, in fact it cut them to the heart.

Cade, alighting safely in a bye street, tore along like a second, or rather, perhaps, a first Dick Turpin, and seemed just as likely to get off, and perhaps escape as far as York itself.

There was a hue and cry, of course ; but, besides the difficulty of catching the flying rebel, many of the Londoners had still a "sneaking kindness" for a now fugitive and ruined man, who, say what you like, was at all events brave enough.

When they saw Cade take the river, and swim across as easily as a Muscovy duck, the royalist party thought they would give him up for the time, knowing that at all events his game was played out, and besides several of his comrades had been secured.

Gog and Magog were the only inconsolable persons; they "went on a good un," as the latter expressed it, and I'm afraid rapped out not a few oaths proportionate to their size.

The shades of evening closed not o'er us on a more important day than that had been in London History, and the darkness favoured the fugitive, who was soon, doubtless, in the wildest parts of Kent, though they couldn't be *wilder* than his disappointed enemies.

The Duke of Buckingham posted down to Warwickshire to tell the joyous news of the end of **the** rebellion to the king.

That examplary monarch had been all that day, and the one before, bewailing his fate and the anxieties he had to endure, in a style that made him a royal nuisance to everybody.

His Majesty, as the duke entered, was heard to complain in the following beautiful and pathetic lines—

> " Oh, what a tremendous humbug 'tis to say,
>   A king is happy as the livelong day !
>   Try it yourselves, my friends, for goodness sake,
>   And see how soon you'll find out your mistake !
>   I eel so wretched now that I could die,
>   If 'twasn't for my wife and fam-i-*lie.*

How true that sentence that my grandpa said—
'Uneasy lies the crown that wears a head.'
Stop, that's not right—I've turned it upside down—
'Uneasy lies the head that wears a crown.'"

And, bursting into tears, his afflicted majesty sought to lay his drooping head in the queen's lap ; but that resolute female, who didn't sympathise with such weak despondency, sternly told him to "hold up."

"Yes, hold up, your majesty," echoed the Duke of Buckingham, breaking in at this crisis, and breaking out into blank verse at the same time.

"Cease your loud wail, and dry your tearful eyes,
For Cade—the rebel Cade—is brought to bay ;
Corner'd run down, smashed up, completely done.
He's bolted, mizzled, fled, dispersed, levanted !
We've seized his followers—got them safe in quod ;
And if he ain't caught soon, it will be odd.
A hunted and deserted fugi-*tive*,
I don't think he will long remain alive."

"Why, the goodness can't you speak plain English, my lord ?" said the queen, "instead of going off into that Shakesperian tagrag and bobtail stuff ? Do you really mean to say that this riot is over, and its leaders arrested ?"

"I do, your majesty," the noble duke replied.

"Oh, joy !" cried the king, starting up. "Away, grief ; take the pocket-handkerchief somebody—I don't want it any longer. My tune's quite changed now. How easy lies the head that wears a crown ! Ha, ha ! I believe you, my boy," he added, winking at the duke. "Let's have a dance."

"But how came you to let the principal culprit escape ?" asked Margaret of Anjou.

"We didn't let him, madam ; he went of his own accord —hopped away like a bird on a twig just as we thought we'd fixed him. I'll tell your majesties all about it."

X X X I.

CADE'S FINAL PERFORMANCES AND EXIT.

WHILE this passed at Kenilworth, hie we away to the wilds of Kent, and follow the desperate fortunes of the escaped (?) rebel.

After a ride of six hours, his steed could stand it no longer, so fell down and refused to move another inch.

All Cade could do wouldn't induce him to budge ; and as it was the middle of the night, and the middle of the road as well, with mud a foot deep at least, Cade was obliged to get out and walk, and leave the animal to his fate, while he himself sought rest under a hedge.

For three days he led much the same sort of life as a hunted fox, only he was, if anything, rather worse off, for he had no safe hole to creep into, and couldn't catch wild rabbits to eat.

Every place he came near was too hot to hold him, though the weather was not particularly oppressive. The name of Cade was in every mouth, and every mouth watered for the £1,000 reward.

In this unpleasant style of travelling, he at length got as far as Rochester, and after the very narrowest escape from the " crushers " of the district, who seemed determined to *crush* all his hopes, he concealed himself in the thick woods of Kent, finding nothing to eat for several days but unripe blackberries.

At last he chanced upon a spot that made his heart dance a polka with sudden delight.

XXXI.—(continued.)

E had come upon a splendid garden.

In it grew the finest cabbages ever seen, all set in rows; and, besides these cabbage *rows*, there were other *cabbage roses* as well in great variety.

Turnips were also there in beautiful profusion, reminding any one forcibly of the garden of Eden.

Such, in fact, it was, all but one letter; for, though not the garden of *E*den, it was the garden of *I*den, for that was the name of the market gardener who lived there.

He was a well-to-do fellow, and, by a strange chance, ormerly knew Cade over in France.

But J. C. De La Mortimer, *alias* Jack Cade, knew nothing of all this.

HISTORICAL TABLEAU—JACK CADE'S LAST KICK.   (*See page* 164.)

No. 6.

He only knew that he was as hungry as a hunter and a whole pack of hounds put together.

Consequently, in creeping through the hedge into this garden, utterly disre*gardin'* the notice "Trespassers will be pulverised," he thought he had dropped upon a good thing.

Without stopping to deliberate, he took things exactly as they came, beginning first with a couple of big apples from the central tree, next working his way through half a dozen lettuces, which brought him to a cabbage-bed, flanked by red and white currant bushes; till, gaining strength as he went along, he pulled himself together for a vigorous assault on a large pumpkin-frame, for the purpose of taking it by storm.

"One might as well be hung for a horse as a pony," he remarked, cramming the last cabbage-leaf into his mouth. "I'll clear out the garden before I've done, and then make off, for fear the owner might appear and say something unpleasant."

Alas!

Even while he spoke, what sound was that which made him drop a cold pumpkin like a hot potato—which set him trembling like an aspen, and pierced him to the very (vegetable) marrow of his bones?

It was the voice of Iden!

Cade knew it at once, and, as soon as the gardener appeared, was completely satisfied of his *iden*tity.

Diving down, Cade hid himself behind the cucumber-frame, while Iden, looking on the scene of desolation around him, grew very wroth indeed.

"Caterpillars again!" he exclaimed. "Drat the varmints! They'll eat me out of house and home soon! Hang it, you know, this is too bad! Oh, won't I give it' em!"

And seizing the biggest sword ever seen in this world, he searched round the garden in every hole and corner, prodding here and stamping there, and killing caterpillars by the dozen at every step.

"Hullo!" he suddenly cried. "What's that—a boot?—it can't be—but, by the hokey, it is. Some ragamuffin trespasser got in here for prigging purposes!"

And giving a pull at the boot aforesaid, he pulled the owner out into the gravelled walk, and Jack Cade *stood* (or, rather, *lay*, for he couldn't *stand*) revealed to his enraged vision.

"Ah! oh! ugh! What, can it be possible?—Jack Cade?" Iden exclaimed. "So *you* were the caterpiller, eh? By jingo, I'll——"

"Oh, please—please, Iden—good Iden!" implored Cade.

"Yes, I'll give you a *good hidin'* if you talk to me! Surrender, rebel—you're fairly cotched."

"Never!" cried Cade, gathering his remaining strength for a last struggle. "Alick Iden, I didn't think it of you. Pitch into a man that ain't had anything to eat for a *week*, and is naturally in a *weak* state? Where's your mercy and fair play?"

"I can't help it," answered Iden. "Duty's duty, and a thousand pounds is ten hundred, so come on."

"And I'll give you two," cried Jack Cade, grasping his sword, which was now all he had in the world.

The last fight of Cade's was an exciting spectacle, only there was nobody to see it except the caterpillars aforesaid, and a few observant sparrows on the trees.

Cade did pretty well considering.

He gave Iden a number of raps which filled the latter with anything but *rapture*, and to which he responded by a series of *whacks*, which made Jack Cade *wax* desperate, and feel as if he was undergoing the process of *waxina-tion*.

This could not last.

The odds were against the exhausted Cade, who ultimately found himself full length on the ground, badly bruised, with Iden's heavy boot on his stomach.

"Surrender?" again cried Iden.

"I won't; I'll die game," was the reply. "Iden, I ain't afraid of you, even now. Take my blessing backwards. May all your hopes be blighted, your cabbages be devoured by slugs, and your ribstone pippins perish of the dry rot! There!"

With which frightful malediction Cade lay down stiff.

It's no use disguising the fact; he died soon after this, and while his decapitated head was taken away by the triumphant Iden, and given to the king (who said it was a most *headify-ing* spectacle), the body of Cade was buried where it fell, under the biggest apple tree.

From that day forth the shape of the tree changed and changed, till it assumed the exact shape of a gallows, and every apple that grew on it was of the precise aspect of Cade's head.

This is a wonderful botanical fact, well worthy the consideration of all practical gardeners.

So ended Jack Cade.

Reader, don't go and do likewise, on any account.

XXXII.

A FLOWERY PERIOD—THE WARS OF THE ROSES.

WE are now entering upon the period of the great contest known in English history as the War of the Roses, the point of which was, as everybody knows, what coloured flower the king of England should stick in his royal crown.

All the roses that then existed, from the celebrated "Coal Black Rose," to the "Last Rose of Summer," took part in this gigantic struggle, which was the means of bringing forward many he*roes*, not to mention she*roes* as well, who *arose* from the ranks of people, and joined the *flower* of the army.

Henry VI. was not, as you have seen, a particularly warlike king.

He objected, on principle, to having an arrow pierce his brain, or a sword run through his body; and when the first note of war resounded through the land, he wished for the time that he had been Emperor of China, or monarch of the remote and peaceful region of Timbuctoo.

Queen Margaret was far more of a military mind, and indeed throughout the whole campaign she was the commanding officer, the king being at most only second in command.

XXXIII.

THE SMASH-UP OF THE LANCASTER PARTY.

MARGARET rode just behind the king to the field of battle, to keep him up to his work, and see that he didn't shirk the toils and dangers of the situation under the plea of nerves, corns, or anything of that sort.

But his career as a " Bowld Sojer Boy " soon came to a *finis*.

In the very first encounter he was defeated and wounded, and found himself entirely at the mercy of the Duke of York, which he considered a very (Y)*ork*ward predicament.

However, he stood it like a lamb ; too much so, Margaret thought, who, on her part, resolved not to stand it at all, but to resist, like a real British lion.

Various contests then followed 'twixt the two great parties, in all of which one or the other, or both, or neither became victorious, till the Duke of York, having been killed by about twelve sanguinary wounds (minutely described in the report), the gentle Margaret began to entertain hopes that all would yet be well.

But all her endeavours were knocked into nothing by the renowned Earl of Warwick, the very *last* of the barons (see Lord Lytton's famous tale), though one of the first men in England.

He favoured the young Edward of York, a prince who now set up as the *Claimant* to the kingly title and estate, and who, by a remarkable coincidence, though thin enough then, became very stout afterwards.

Lucky for him he had gained his cause first.

Creating a favourable impression by his affability and stylish "get up," he entered London in triumph, the citizens being mostly ready to bet ten to one on York, and leave Lancaster out in the cold.

At St. John's Fields there was a monster meeting, at which the Earl of Warwick, introducing the royal claimant, said that "his right to the throne was as clear as the best filtered Thames water."

The prince made a speech to the same effect, and the assembled throng gave three cheers for Edward IV., in a tone that made such of the spectators as belonged to the Lancastrian party feel very far "down in the mouth."

Another great fight taking place after this somewhere in the north, Edward took the title of king, and the checkmated Henry was ignominiously conducted to the Tower on a wretched moke, his royal legs being tied together under the animal's stomach.

Several years passed, in which the kingdom was about in the same state as Mount Vesuvius during the pauses of an eruption, that is, always threatening to break out afresh, till at last the expected calamity came in the form of an explosion of rage on the part of the great Earl of Warwick.

For King Edward, instead of marrying, as proposed, the Princess Bona of Savoy, who was, of course, one of the *Bona*parte family, or even espousing Warwick's niece, a young lady o'er whose alabaster brow some seventeen and a half summers had sweetly passed, actually took it into his head to marry the widowed Lady Grey, thereby giving *grey*ve offence to Warwick.

Thereupon that puissant earl did what the ferry-boats do, he *went over to the other side*, and so worked the oracle that very soon Edward had to make a little excursion to Holland, strictly *incog.*

Once more poor Henry VI. was dragged out of prison, and fixed on his ricketty throne.

This state of things lasted till a change came (which, somehow or other, is generally the case), when Edward once more got the upper hand, and Warwick, having got a full stop put to his existence on Barnet field, the White Rose again bloomed victoriously.

When Queen Margaret heard of all this, she burst into tears (her first experiment in that line), which cast quite a damper over the spirits of her followers.

Her after fate, and that of poor Harry, who was so *harried* about for so many years—as well as a good many other things, can be ascertained by reading any book that treats of that subject.

(N.B.—The best way to make sure of finding it is to look for the right page.)

London was not much put out by the great national struggle, but kept on much in the same way, notwithstand-the frequent changes of government.

In other words, " business was carried on as usual during the alterations."

November 9, 1454, was celebrated for being the first time the lord mayor launched his barge, and was rowed in it to Westminster, himself taking a turn at the oar, and proving himself to be the noblest *rowman* (Roman?) of them all.

Previous to this, he generally rode a horse *there*, and in returning rode a *horse back*, and that was one reason why he was called a *mayor*.

The fashions in those times were something alarming, and beat ours into convulsions.

The ladies wore peaked head-dresses, so high that they seemed designed to poke out the stars, and trains so long that not more than three could go in one street.

The gentlemen's boots were so lengthy and pointed at the toes, that they loomed in sight several minutes before the wearers were visible.

At last they became so outrageously long that the clergy resolved that they should not be worn *any longer*.

They preached against them, and at last stationed men at the street corners to cut off these elongated toes with shears, after which they *sheered* off, bearing away that portion of the boot as *booty*.

XXXIV.

TREATS OF KING EDWARD AND OTHER SUBJECTS.

EDWARD IV. didn't do very much for London beyond knighting the lord mayor and sheriffs, in 1473, and even that, it was said, he only did when he was far gone in the liquor of the period.

The lord mayor, Ralph Josceline, was one of the right sort.

He not only built up some of the walls of London at his own expense, but would not let the other great citizens have any peace till they had done likewise.

Another lord mayor, Sir William Hampton (no relation to Hampton Court), seeing that the stocks in which vagabonds' legs were confined were getting out of repair, ordered a fresh supply of *stocks* (and perhaps *wallflowers* as well) to be planted near the Mansion House and elsewhere.

In 1474, the first book was printed in England by a press brought over from some foreign land, it being found that there was a *pressing* necessity for it.

William Caxton, the introducer of printing in England, was by trade a mercer, though you mustn't conclude from this that he was *mercer*nary, but quite the reversenary.

He deserves all our gratitude, as long as we have any, for it is more than probable that if the printing-press had never turned up, you would not be luxuriating on the pages of this incomparable journal, or revelling in this delectable history at the present moment.

After studying the subject hard for seventy-five years, I have come to the conclusion that Edward IV. was not a particularly good man.

He had a way of stringing people up in bunches, like grapes, whether they committed any crimes or not, which impresses us with the conviction, that in him, at least,

"The quality of mercy was not strained;"

or rather, seemed to have been quite strained out of him long before.

Every time you walked the streets, you saw that each gate was decorated with traitors' heads or criminals' bodies.

And the king, as he rode gaily by with his retinue, to go to dine with the lordly chancellor, or some other extensive party, used to look up and say that these species of ornaments made the place quite lively; only it was a very *deadly* sort of *lively* according to our ideas.

I might say a good deal about the famous Jane Shore, only I'm *sure* that you have heard all about her before.

I might also give a list of the unfortunate beings who were executed at Tyburn, but as this would occupy about fifty columns, I think we had better leave it over to some fine day when time is no object; suffice it that Edward IV., after "carrying on" quite his own way for about twenty-two years, was "carried off" himself at last.

I don't know which way he went.

Edward V. was a nice little fellow, when his hair was brushed and his clean pinafore tied on.

He was at school when his pa died, but when he heard that he was now king, his master thought he had better go home for his holidays.

He didn't enjoy them much.

Uncle Dick, for now it is that the double-dealing duke, hence called *double Gloucester*, though he wasn't at all the *cheese*, now steps on the stage of history—Uncle Dick became Dick-tator of England.

He pretended to be so fond of the young king and his little brother York, that he would stick to them till death, which he did, for he had them murdered soon after.

The historical tragedy in the tower is not, I think, a highly amusing narrative, nor calculated to put you in good spirits, so we had better leave it till some time when we're too cheerful and want a little depressing.

Nor need much be said here about Richard III.

Shakespeare has gone into the subject pretty extensively, and I don't think I could improve upon him much.

If Richard hadn't done quite so many murders he might have been a wiser and a better man.

He gained the throne entirely by a fluke, fair play being out of his line, for his deeds, like himself, were of a dark complexion.

The only occasion on which a lord mayor of London was guilty of disgraceful conduct occurred at this period.

Being bribed heavily by Richard, this chief magistrate, whose rascally name was Sir Edward Shaw, got his brother, a parson, to preach at St. Paul's on the text "Is the Duke of Gloucester an angel?" making out that he was, though the private opinion of the congregation was that he rather belonged to the *other* species.

However, some bribed ones got up a cry of "Long live Richard III. !"

Talk of the—angel, you know, and he is sure to appear, and, sure enough, at this moment in walked the duke just as the clerk said, "Amen."

Looking round with the same expression as a hungry lion, the duke then said, "Let us prey," and as nothing could *prey*-vent him, this *rogue* had the *prey-rogue*-ative of being king of England.

London didn't improve much during the reign of King *Dick*, whose *line* of action was calculated to set it on the *Dick-line* (decline).

The principal public works carried on metropolitaneously in those sanguinary times were executions.

The Tower became the busiest place in London, and the trade of Hangman, Headsman, or Torturer, flourished more than any other.

Sometimes a citizen, who didn't want the trouble of going out to be hanged, was kindly allowed to have an execution in his own house.

Money was tight, downright drunk sometimes.

The treasury was *banco-rupto*, and even the rich citizens were now poor.

Roads were neglected, children strayed away from school, and people in general forgot to have their hair cut.

The houses had got into such a dilapidated state that every main road looked like the original road to ruin, for it was hardly worth while having your house repaired when, for all you knew, you might be hanging out at Newgate next day.

But this wretched state of things disappeared like butter before a hungry cat, when Harry of Richmond, having proved at last that Richard III. had some brains, by knocking them out, took up the business of royalty in England.

His reception in London was on a grand scale.

The new king was very affable.

Nothing pleased him so much as going to dine with the lord mayor, or any other man, but when it came to returning the compliment, his majesty's face began to look of the longest.

For, in point of fact, Henry VII.'s great weakness was an over-fondness for coin, otherwise lucre, otherwise cash, otherwise the root of all evil.

He was a man who liked to get his shilling's worth for tenpence, with a discount for ready money. The citizens soon found that the new printing press was nothing to the way in which the king put the screw on when he had any claim against them.

Harry Tudor, now that he had become king, was suddenly discovered to possess a great number of merits (both wholesale and retail) which nobody had ever suspected him of before.

The nation received him with open arms.

The first time he proceeded to Westminster to meet and entertain the lord mayor and companies, he went in great state, and some say he came home in a nice *state* as well, but this I don't believe, for Henry VII. was very sparing in the use of wine, especially when he had to pay for it himself.

Still the banquet went off well; the lord mayor and aldermen declared that they had enough of everything, which alone shows there must have been abundance. The company did not go home till morning, when they all went, according to immemorial custom, to see the sun rise from the top of Primrose Hill.

Pretenders to the throne were not backward in coming forward in this reign.

The first was Lambert Simnel, who said he was the son of the Duke of Clarence, a great gun who came to his (*butt-*) end by drowning in a wine-*butt* in the Tower.

Some people believed in him (for some people will believe anything), but a battle in the county of *Notts* proved that the impostor was *not-so* successful as he expected to be. His army was killed, and himself taken prisoner. The king, instead of removing his skull from his shoulders, mercifully gave him a situation in the royal scullery.

Perkin *Warbeck*, who got up a civil *war* at the *beck* of the Duchess of Burgundy, was another sort of party altogether.

It never was known for certain whether he was an impostor or not, for English law wasn't clever at finding out that sort of thing. But whether he was the true king of England, or an *untrue* humbug, I solemnly declare that I don't care *that!*

The Londoners generally disbelieved in him; and, spite of the king's screwiness towards them, they uncorked their *purses* in a most *purse*vering style to furnish him with coin to send an army against the rebel.

The Duchess of Burgundy and the king had a quarrel on the same subject.

The consequence was, trade was stopped between here and there, and this led to a skrimmage between the English and German traders in London, during which they dealt in very *hard* ware indeed—viz., blows.

Another riot soon after (nearly) took place in London, all through Perkin, and so hot was the dispute that, if it hadn't stopped just short of a fight, 200,000 people *might have been* killed.

Perkin at last, being driven up into a narrow *corner*

somewhere near *Corn*wall, was offered £100 reward to give himself up.

The king said he'd give him the sum.

He meant over the *left*.

But Perkin thought it was all *right*, so agreed.

He was brought to town, and made to read in public a confession, declaring that all he had said was lies—though his saying so might have been, for all we know, the greatest lie of all.

Henry would doubtless have saved his life, for he was of a very *saving* disposition.

But that very fact made him consider how expensive it would be to keep him as a prisoner, so he had him hanged at Tyburn.

When cut down, Perkin Warbeck was placed on a splendid *bier*, and it has ever since been a matter of dispute among historians whether the *beer* of Barclay is as good as *Perkin's*.

Among other City improvements under Henry VII., the River Fleet was rendered navigable up to Holborn Bridge, toy boats being able to sail on as far as Temple Bar.

In Finsbury, large artillery-grounds were laid out, in which practised bowmen were allowed to shoot anything, from the moon to a cocoa-nut.

Talking of *arch*ery, an *arch* was also built over Houndsditch, so that the game of throwing dead dogs into that salubrious stream—which didn't smell *quite* like *eau de Cologne*—was put a stop to for ever more.

Sir John Shaw, lord mayor in 1503, improved Guildhall immensely, building one chamber so lofty that Gog and Magog could walk in it with their hats on.

This proved Sir John to be a man of *high* notions.

King Henry VII. had a great many dealings with the City concerning the all-important subject of £ *s. d.*, and he generally managed to get the best of the bargain, for he was awfully *sharp* where *blunt* was concerned.

His stinginess increased with age, till at last he became so *near* that the citizens wished him *farther*.

Even his piety was carried on at the public expense.

He built Henry the Seventh's Chapel, Westminster Abbey, entirely out of his own pocket, only the money had first been put there out of other people's.

HIS MAJESTY IS SHOCKED AT THE LANGUAGE OF THE COSTER.

(See page 177.)

He also built up Baynard Castle afresh, for he knew that, on the political chessboard, the *castle* is often very useful to the *king*.

It was in this reign that bricks began to be largely used in building.

Also *flints* (especially skin*flints*, after his majesty's own heart) began to be extensively employed.

The London chimneys were also greatly improved, having

been hitherto so wretchedly built that the inhabitants con-
sumed a good deal of their own smoke, whether they liked
it or not.

Education was much neglected at this time, the London
School Board taking thirty years to deliberate over building
each school, which seems rather too long.

The king, himself a profound scholar, was much concerned
at the great want of learning that prevailed.

He had noticed that grammar was in a dreadfully neglected
state, and nobody would pronounce their words properly.

THE KING, THE COURTIERS, AND THE CULPRITS.
(*See page* 184.)

Happening, as he walked in the streets, to hear a coster
bawling out—" Ya-ah ! here's yer sparrer-*grass*, brocker*low*,
and cowkim*ber*," instead of asparagus, brocoli, and cucumber,
his majesty's nerves were so shocked, that he ordered four
grammar-schools to be built immediately.

This is all that need be said about Henry VII., the first

of the Tudors—for historians generally count them as one *Tudor*, two *Tudor*, three *Tudor*, &c.

He was a man, take him for all in all, we shall never look upon his like again—unless his ghost walks occasionally.

———

XXXV.

LONDON UNDER KING HARRY THE BLUFF

OUR historical London researches have now brought us up to the reign of Bluff King Hal, who it is generally (*II*)*al*-lowed, was the most powerful monarch in England since his predecessor, King (*II*)*al*-fred the Great. Henry VIII. was as different from his father as chalk and cheese, though which was chalk and which was " the cheese," it is difficult to say.

Henry VII. was a very thin and *lanky* individual (a peculiarity he inherited from the family of *Lanky*-ster). Henry VIII., in his fattest days, resembled a good-sized waterbutt, imbued with Divine right.

They were unlike in all respects.

One was much older and one much younger than the other—one liked getting all the money he could, the other liked spending all he got ; and to crown all, one had but a *single* wife, and the other six, who were *married.*

Never was there such a time for public feasts, royal processions, grand tournaments, and other high jinks of that sort, as the reign of this king.

But at first corn was getting scarce in England, and bread

consequently went up at such a rate that it was expected to reach the moon in due time, leaving us poor metropolitan mortals to starve. Thereupon the good lord mayor, Roger Achily (pronounce this with a sneeze), saw what wanted doing and did it.

He got all the corn and grain of every kind, by every means, from everywhere, and stored it in Leadenhall, the city granary.

Thence he sold it to the people " at the lowest price consistent with good quality," as the grocers say in their advertisements.

By the introduction of this *corn* the Londoners, who hitherto had *bar(e)ly* sufficient to support life, soon had plenty to *(wh)eat*, and were no longer inclined to be *rye*-otous.

All honour to the citizen who thus prom-*oats* the public welfare.

Nor was this all the good lord mayor did.

He ate his dinners sometimes, and besides this, he built pavements and causeways and bridges in all the most traffical portions of the city, all at his own expense.

Men like this deserve to be encouraged.

In 1514, some of the lords of the manor round the metropolis, declared that no *man-or* woman or child should by any manner of means enter their preserves, and so they fenced them in, thereby giving great of-*fence* to the citizens.

For in those days such places as Islington, Hoxton, and Shoreditch were rural hamlets (nothing to do with *Hamlet's* ghost, you know), where gentle apprentices and city clerks used to take their sweethearts on Sundays and holidays, and no doubt treat them to *sweet-tarts* and other delicacies of the season.

It was hard to be debarred from these *al fresco* places of

recreation, and the people resolving not to stand it, agreed to strike.

The cry was "Down with the palings!" and a desperate mob, headed by a fellow in the disguise of a jester or Tom-fool of the period (many people said the dress suited him to a T), made a grand rush, armed with bludgeons, cudgels, and shovels, and other agricultural implements, soon demolished the gates, and, rushing in, got up a pic-nic on the lawn in the Roshervillian style, declaring the grounds "just the place to spend a happy day."

Another great riot took place in London only three years after, but which, perhaps, was long enough to enable the city to get over the first.

I allude to what was called the "Evil May Day," 1517.

The time of which we are speaking was remarkable for the great number of "furrineerin' coves," as the populace called them, who came "Over the sea" to this "Isle of beauty," otherwise England, much the same as the Communists do now.

Many of the citizens objected to this kind of thing, and as these *strangers* soon monopolised all their trade, it would have been *stranger* still if they *had* liked it ; so, *egged* on by the more desperate *birds* of the metropolis, the citizens *hatched* a pretty *nest* of mischief.

On *May Day* they *made a* desperate attack on the foreigners, that is to say, they would have done so, had not those alien parties made themselves scarce.

They had heard the day before, that the "weecked Eengleesh," had determined to massacre them all, and so they concluded they had better be absent on that occasion.

Cardinal Wolsey, who was at that time on the top of the *tree* in England, and wielded *tree*-men-dous power, gave orders that nobody should leave his home all that day, but—as, by the time the police were thoroughly awake, the row was already " on,"—it was rather too late.

It began by a number of lads playing at bucklers near Bucklersbury, and an alderman, who interfered with their sport, was at once " cheeked " by the youth who was chief offender.

The alderman said that the youngster required taking *down*, so ordered a policeman to take him *up*.

But ere 'twas done, the cry of " 'Prentices! clubs!" was raised, and the alderman soon found he had to run in a style that took away his breath, and made him feel as if he were swallowing lucifers.

The mob, having once collected, wouldn't separate without having done something that would make them go down to posterity, so the cry of " Down with the foreigners! murder 'em all!" resounded through the welkin.

A pretty set-out then followed.   The rabble rushed down St. Martin's-le-Grand.

There was no General Post Office there then, though one of the *Generals Posted* some officers there when he saw a riot coming on.

The lord mayor and sheriffs put on double-plated armour, and tried to argue with the mob; the lieutenant of the Tower lined the road with his very best cannon, but all to no purpose.

Every true citizen thirsted (it was hot weather) for the blood of the obnoxious foreigners, who, however, having heard previously how much they were wanted, deserted " Laister Squarr," (as they pronounced the name of their favourite " hang-out,") and made tracks for other and safer localities.

The mob therefore had to content themselves with smashing windows, wrenching off bell-handles, rooting up lamp-posts, emptying the contents of shops into the road, and hanging all the cats they could catch, without a fair trial, or any counsel for the defence.

This, however, was quite enough to do, and a very pleasing holiday pastime for a fine May day.

The king who was at *Sheen*, near Richmond, when informed of what was going on, said—

" This must be *sheen* to."

So he deputed two *earls* to set out *early* to London, where, with their *forces*, they arrived about *five* o'clock.

By that time, however, the riot was over, and the streets were as quiet as a mouse when the cat's in his immediate proximity.

The fact is, the rioters' exertions had made them rather hungry, and they had adjourned for breakfast.

Thus ended the London row on " Evil May Day," which, harmless as it passed off, *might have been* the death of a good many people if they'd got killed.

But you mustn't suppose that the parties concerned had heard the last of it.

Two hundred and eighty persons had been arrested on a charge of disturbing the public peace, and breaking several heads, the private property of certain persons specified.

Thirteen, which is always supposed to be an unlucky number, were condemned to die.

But the king, in whose youthful heart mercy then dwelt (of course, without paying any rent), only had the leader strung up.

The other twelve were at once brought before him, with their *ropes* still round their *necks*, and their (*h*)*opes neck*st to nowhere.

" Well, what do you think of yourselves?" asked King

Henry. "Don't you feel that you deserve to be drowned twice over and then blown up in a powder mill?"

"Please, your majesty, we didn't mean to do no harm," protested the spokesman, a worthy grocer from "Vitecheppel," as it was called in days of old.

"There, be off?" thundered the bluff monarch; "and congratulate yourselves your heads are still on your shoulders; they may not be there long. I haven't made up my mind yet. Meet me next Thursday at Westminster Hall, and you may, or may not hear something to your advantage."

The citizens departed, guarded by policemen, and passed, as you may be sure, a most agreeable week of suspense.

"To be (hanged) or not to be, that was the question" for them.

Only the king had power to solve it.

When the fatal Thursday came, a more solemncolly spectacle was never seen.

The entire metropolis seemed going into *mourning*, and a very gloomy *morning* too.

All London was bent upon showing how sorry it was to have offended its liege sovereign, the king.

The lord mayor, sheriffs, and aldermen, were all in their inkiest black, even down to their boots, which had been covered with blacking, but not polished, and up to their faces, which were deeply begrimed, *a la* Christy minstrels, with soot.

As for the prisoners, they followed in a very undress uniform—just as if they had stripped to have the cat-o'-nine-tails applied externally—and bound hand and foot like professors of the Davenport trick.

The noose was still round their necks, and only wanted one leetle pull and up would go the criminal.

The king, who was sitting on a splendid throne, and putting on an expression which made everybody present feel how uncertain is human life, was surrounded by soldiers, courtiers, and Cardinal Wolsey.

The procession fell on its knees before him (the king, I mean), and kissed the hem of his robe as if it liked it, and cried out for mercy with all its lungs.

"What shall I do?" asked the king, turning to Wolsey.

"Kill 'em, to be sure," answered the proud prelate, in whose stern eye not a spark of pity was anywhere to be seen.

"Somehow I don't like to do it," mused the king, who hadn't got used to signing death warrants yet.

"But recollect they've offended ME," argued the great churchman; "and if that doesn't deserve death, I should most certainly like to know what does."

But here the lord mayor, sheriffs, aldermen, and other chief Londoners, got up a chorus of entreaty to be spared, keeping such beautiful tune and time, that the king felt that it was like hearing a concert for nothing.

"Well," he said, at length, "depart. You are spared; but mind you don't do it again, for if you do, I shan't."

(What he meant was that if they did as they had done, he wouldn't do again what he was doing then, viz., spare them.)

Loud were the shouts that then burst out from great and small throughout the hall, and made it ring. "God save the king! we shan't be hung!" Each rope was flung up to the roof, a striking proof how glad they were this sad affair had ended so. Then off they go, with dance and skip, and "Hip, hip, hip! hurrah, hurray! we've gained the day."

(Note.—These poetical fits will come on at times, and any

reader who knows of a cure for the complaint, is respectfully asked to send the recipe to our office.)

If the length of our history would permit, we might enter into full particulars as to the life, character, and career of the great Cardinal Wolsey.

Showing how he rose from nothing, went up high as he could go, and came down with a run ; but we forbear, and only notice that this great man was very kind to London.

His palace of Whitehall was fitted up in a style of magnificence that must have made the hearts of upholsterers and carvers and gilders leap with joy when they sent in their little accounts, and leap higher and higher still when they came to be paid.

Whenever King Henry wanted money, which was tolerably often, he used to *prime* his *prime* minister to squeeze it out of the rich people in the city.

In 1521, the cardinal came to raise the wind in this fashion.

He called the chief citizens together, and said that if the clergy would come *forth* with a *fourth* of their property, and the *lay* people would *lay* a sixth of theirs before him, he and the king would be satisfied.

But the ungrateful Londoners didn't see the affair in that light at all, and began to back out so very decidedly that at last the king thought it prudent to draw in.

So he sent a letter to the lord mayor, saying that he wouldn't deprive the citizens and others of their money on any account, but he trusted to their benevolence to give him a little, say 20 per cent. or so.

But even then these unreasonable monsters grumbled, and told the lord cardinal that they felt very sorry that the king wanted money so badly, but feared his majesty would have to be graciously pleased to go on wanting it.

As for benevolence, they didn't keep it at their shops, and it looked so much like taxation that they couldn't tell the difference.

"Bravo, London!" cried all the rest of England, and a general opposition to such extortions sprang up, and though the king and cardinal were ready to kick everybody else with rage, they feared a revolution, and so pretended to be quite pleased.

You should have seen London in the days of "Bluff King Hal."

It was a place and no mistake.

It wasn't large, indeed so small that the modern metropolis would look "very like a whale" beside it; but it made up for size in joviality, especially on May Days, which were not all *evil* May Days—very much the reverse.

Ah, there was some rare old sport carried on then!

XXXVI.

"LARKS" OF LONDON IN THE OLDEN TIME.

HENRY, accompanied by whichever queen happened to have her head on at the time, used to set forth a-Maying to Shooter's Hill, which, at that time was, so to speak, one hundred miles out of town.

The City archers went through their performances, and though they drew a good bow, and dressed themselves up as Robin Hood and Co., they couldn't hold a candle to those renowned outlaws, who appeared to have taken out a patent for shooting farther than anyone else.

Then there were wrestling matches.

Did you ever see one? If not, take an ordinary match (Bryant and May's, for preference, because they will only ignite on the box), stick it up on end, and see if it will wrestle; then, of course, it will be a wrestling match.

This pastime is very exciting.

Then they used to play at bowls, there being in each district a large bowling green, though not quite so *green* as many of the players who used to lose their money on it.

Quarterstaff was another favourite sport.

Two could play at that game.

Each staff was about thirty feet long, and as thick round as the bowsprit of a small schooner.

You grasped it in the middle and swung it round your head like the sails of a windmill, and when your opponent came up, you let him have it.

He did the same, and whichever had his head knocked off, or two of his ribs broken, was thought by critical judges to have got rather the worst of it.

This gentle exercise required a somewhat thick skull, as a "topper" from a quarterstaff was apt to let daylight into those particularly unlucky heads that it might happen to drop upon.

Apprentices in those days were kept strictly up to the mark; they were scarcely permitted even to sneeze without their master's written permission.

They were condemned to wear a plain dress, and were not allowed swords; at all events, if they dared to *wear* them indoors, they didn't dare to *air* them in the streets.

Still they were not unhappy.

Each of them carried a thick stick or club, with which

he could give a friendly crack to any pal he happened to like best.

On May day they had full liberty to do just as they pleased, within bounds, of course; for if they had tried to shoot the king, set fire to the City, and stone the House of Lords to death, they would have been considered guilty of carrying their little game too far, and somebody would have talked to them a bit.

The lord mayor used to ride out to see the wrestling, etc.

He went in state, and took all his relations, down to the cat, all dressed in their Sunday clothes.

His lordship was conducted to a front reserved seat at Smithfield, and patronised the sports benevolently for three hours.

When he went home to dinner everybody was invited.

He usually made a speech to the citizens, who cried "Hear! hear!" so frequently that nobody really *could* hear anything of it.

Gog and Magog were all there on these merry May meetings, and, of course, even Gog was *May*-Gog during that happy month.

Such was London then, and why ain't it so now?

Alas! the world, like a shop till, is *full of change.*

Time is always altering everything, turning the world round, and in and out, and upside down, and topsy turvy.

Ah, me! what a pity it is!

Excuse, reader, these tears.

The historian is obliged to be sad sometimes when he looks backward into futurity, or forward into the past; when he compares things as they used for to were with things as they continues for to be.

Where are all the good old sports of London gone to?

Why can't we have such little games as our ancestors went in for?

Why, if you, for instance, were to set up practising archery at Cheapside, or Charing Cross, or play ninepins in the middle of Oxford Street, where would you expect to go to?

And echo answers—

" Afore the beak !"

There is no archery shooting in London now, except when the Metropolitan Railway trains *shoot* through the *arches* of the Underground ; no *bowls*, except the flowing *bowl* that is sometimes filled at the public house ; no wrestling, though the strongest men have a *fall* sometimes when the pavement is extra slippery ; and no tournaments and tilts, though a cab sometimes *tilts* over through furious driving.

The only consolation we have is that our heads are, generally speaking, our own, while in the good old days the king would have had them off in the twinkling of an eye if he happened to feel ill-tempered.

Change we the subject to a more cheerful one—the celebrated episode of the King and the Cobbler.

XXXVII.

THE EPISODE OF THE KING AND THE COBBLER.

BE it known to all men, past, present, and to come, that Henry Tudor, number eight, *alias* Bluff King Hal, *alias* Burly King Harry, *alias* &c., was very fond of going about in disguise.

Nothing pleased him so much as to lock up his crown, robes, and other royal rattletraps in lavender, don the attire of anything, from a duke to a dustman, and set forth to have a private squint at affairs in general.

Night was the time for this sort of thing—"a starry night for a ramble," as Lord Alhambra Fitz-Canterbury, the court poet of the age, describes it in his matchless rhymes.

Once his majesty was out on the *qui vive* in this way.

All was serene.

Not an inch of fog disturbed the equanimity of the atmosphere ; not a cat was heard ; not a garotter was seen ; and the royal latch-key was lying snugly in the royal pocket.

At a safe distance—say ten yards—behind him came the captain of the guard, who, though disguised as a mild merchant scarcely able to kill a fly, had, in reality, enough weapons under his cloak to settle the hash of all the robbers in London, besides a coat of mail that would stand bullets.

He kept his eye on the king, who had not only disguised himself capitally, but had pinched in his otherwise extensive waist, and walked in a rolling, semi-nautical fashion that made him look something between a lawyer's clerk, and a bo'sun's mate.

If he ran foul of any danger, he had only to whistle, and up would come the captain with his weapons to see about it.

Many and various were the scenes the king saw that night.

Not only did he walk up and down the streets and through

all the back ways of the most aristocratic snuggeries, but he steered due east, prowled round the Tower, sought the salubrious region of Wapping, and woke with his heavy footsteps the sleeping fish in Billingsgate Market.

Whenever he found one of the old watchmen asleep at his post, he gave him a flip on the ear, and shouted, in royal accents—

"Hullo, wake up, there! Fire! murder! treason!" etc.

Till the fellow, so suddenly roused, would jump nearly out of his skin, and promise he wouldn't do it again.

In this way several hours elapsed, till it was nearly all over with the night, while in lieu thereof the first *streaks* of dawn spread over the sky, making it look like fine *streaky* bacon.

At this time his majesty found himself *streak*ing along the Southwark Road.

The melodious sounds of a hammer struck the royal ear, and casting his inquiring eyes around, the disguised potentate perceived a stall, fixed in the cellar of a large grocer's.

Over the place was this inscription—

KRISTERFER JOBSON.

Gents boots sold and eeled on the shortist notiss.

Repairs neetly xeqted.

And there sat Jobson himself, working away like one o'clock, though it was nearly half-past three, and a hazy morning.

"How happy that fellow looks," murmured King Henry. "I really wish my boots wanted mending, so that I might have an excuse to make his acquaintance."

And as luck would have it, just at that very moment the high heel of the royal Wellington got fixed in a plug-hole, and there it stuck as fast as a cork in a sealed bottle.

In vain the king strained and pulled—
> He gave a tug,
> And then a lug,
> But couldn't escape from that there plug.

At length, with a tremendous wrench, he got free his boot, including his leg, but the heel, broken off, remained where it was.

"Now, the boots got no *heel*," said his majesty; "so I'll take it to the cobbler, and *he'll* mend it."

For this he bent down over the *stall*, which was quite overshadowed by his *tall* figure.

"Hullo!" said the cobbler.

"Same to you, I'm sure," responded the king. "You work early."

"Yes, I have been working *early* of *late*," replied Jobson. "Pressure of work on—ten pairs to sole and heel before next Christmas."

"I hope you're not too busy to attend to me," said the apparently humble customer, as he described his accident. "I've lost one *heel*, and as I don't want to have to hobble, I wish you would apply the *heal*ing remedy."

Well, not to spin it out, the cobbler did the job while the king waited, and was paid threepence. Nor was that all.

He got talking to his customer, who so won his heart that he declared he was "the nicest bloke as he ever see."

The cobbler asked invitingly, "What do you say to a Welsh rabbit?"

"Well, I think it's the cheese," was the reply.

"Ha, ha! the *toasted* cheese, you mean," laughed the jovial cobbler.

So they proceeded into Mr. Jobson's domicile, to discuss the viand aforesaid, and wash it down with the best table beer.

Thither, gentle reader, let us follow them, for Harry has some game in view worthy of our notice.

XXXVII (*Continued*).

ENRY and the Cobbler talked and sang, but it was in a whisper, for the cobbler explained that his wife Joan wasn't up yet, and if woke too soon, she had a way of making the house an unpleasant one to live in.

Then the k——, I mean the cobbler's customer, proposed they should adjourn to the "Blue-faced Lion," an early pub., where carriers, ere starting on their journeys, were enabled to *carry* out their intention of

"HERE'S OUR OWN HEALTHS," SAID THE KING.   "JUST SO," SAID THE COBBLER."—(*See page* 194.)

carrying away some liquor with them. The cobbler's customer stood treat.

"Let's drink our own health's first," he said.

"Just so," said the cobbler.

And they did.

"Now the health of the king," proposed the cobbler; "and may he keep always in the same way. I only hope as how he's like you, sir, cos you're the real sort. By-the-bye, I didn't ask your name."

"Harry Fitz-Harry Ap-Tudor," replied the other, readily. "I belong to a very ancient Welsh family."

"Welsh, eh? Then that accounts for your being so fond of that there Welsh rabbit. Ha, ha!" laughed the jovial cobbler, who next proceeded to troll forth this appropriate stave—

> "Let lordlings so fine
> Brag over their wine;
> A cobbler, though maybe he's ruder,
> Can laugh, drink, and sing,
> Long life to the king,
> And likewise to Harry Ap-Tudor."

"Here's to you again, sir, for you really *air* one of the nicest indiwiddles as I ever knowed."

"Ditto to you," responded the disguised one, drinking. "Come and see me some day at the palace" (this slipped out unawares, when his stout majesty was not a *thin-king*).

"Who? what?" cried the cobbler, opening his eyes. "The king's palace!"

"Yes; at Whitehall; there's where I hang out. I'm groom of the back kitchen window to Sir Jeremy Joggins, who is deputy assistant secretary to the Lord Blundergoggles, who is third silver-stick in waiting to his most gracious of majesties."

"Who's a-goin' to remember all that, do you think?" asked

the cobbler. "Howsumdever, I'll come and see you, as sure as a gun, for you're one of the primest blokes as ever stepped."

"All right; be sure you come. Make it Wednesday week, 12.30 P.M., sharp; for, look here," he added, in a confidential whisper, "perhaps I'll be able to show you the king."

"Splendid!" shouted the cobbler. "I'd give anything to see him, as I've never sawed him yet."

The fascinating party went away, and the cobbler returned to his wife Joan, who *was* up by this time.

He told her all about his customer, and the invitation to the palace.

"And look here, old ooman," concluded the cobbler, "I means to keep in with that chap, for he's the delightfullest party as ever wore shoe-leather."

The cobbler was so impatient for that grand visit to the palace, that every day seemed sixty-four hours long.

At last the important date arrived, and his cobblership prepared for a holiday.

He got himself up regardless of expense.

First he stepped over the way round the corner, and indulged in a prime twopenny dip at the Lambeth Baths.

Then he called upon the barber next door, who operated upon his head and face till he looked almost as handsome as the waxen head in the window.

Returning to his beloved Joan, he got that exemplary woman to officiate as his *valet de chambre pro tem.*—in other words to help him on with his best togs.

The cleanest shirt ever known in the annals of history was put on, and nextly, his best hat, coat, hose and various *etcetras*, till the cobbler was at last so much improved in appearance, that his own uncle, who died when he was three months old, wouldn't have known him.

Walking proudly down the street in this gallant trim, the honest cobbler thought himself somebody and a half, I can tell you.

The cobbler's heart began to beat double quick as he rang the gate bell of the main entrance of Whitehall.

It was opened by a terrible-looking porter, all plush and pomposity, who asked him in a grand tone what he might presume to want.

" Is Mr. Ap-Tooder at home?" asked Jobson.

" Mr. who?" responded the gorgeous being in plush. "Don't know the party. Hand hif he his, what might be your business with him?"

" Merely a friendly call," was the answer. " He treated me to a pot or so the other day, and invited me here. If you doubt my honour, here's my card."

And he brought out his trade card, which wasn't quite as clean as fresh cream-laid paper, and handed it to this extensive flunky.

" No, thank you," said that personage, elegantly declining it.

" I don't know the name of Haptoodor in the pallis; but I'll binquire."

He did so, and returning, told the cobbler to step this way.

He did step this way and no other, and then the porter, having handed him over to half a dozen yeomen of the guard, they led him on through marble halls and magnificent passages, floored with the very best patent oilcloth, and hung with tapestry, and in some cases lined with soldiers.

Gog and Magog now came forward to escort the cobbler, and Jobson felt ready to sink into the earth with fright at these two tremendous fellows, each of whom looked, in his eyes, as tall as a lighthouse at least.

At last they came to a magnificent hall, such as few if any could describe.

Gog whispered to Jobson in a true giant's voice—

"This is the presence chamber of the king."

"Oh, Moses! you don't say so?" exclaimed the cobbler. "It's an awfully grand place; quite knocks me over, and I feel I have no business here.

"But I want Harry Ap-Tudor, and I don't expect to find him among all these noble lords, swells, and big pots of aristocratic breed. He's a plain man, is Harry, and between you and me, the pleasantest chap I ever diskivered in my life."

"I'll fetch him to you directly," said Magog, and he forthwith went and raised the awful curtain that stood before the throne.

The cobbler felt his knees beginning to give way.

"It's all over with me now," he murmured.

"They're going to bring his most gracious majesty here, and if he asks me how I dare walk into his house like this, what shall I say? Why, that I am guilty of high treason at least, and he'll have my head off as sure as it's on now I see how it is, that Ap-Tudor was a-hoaxing of me; he don't live at the palace at all. I must bolt right off."

He did so, and before anyone could prevent him, got to the ante-chamber, and through that into the passage beyond, and tried to steer for the main door. There was a hue and cry, and several of the officers of the palace tried to stop him, which only made him run the faster.

He got so confused and bewildered, that he took the wrong turning, and ran bolt up against the royal cook, who was just bringing in the king's morning snack.

This functionary, meeting the sturdy cobbler full butt, went over like a nine-pin, spilling the luscious boiled chicken and trimmings, including the delicious gravy, on to the floor.

"Treason, murder, assault and battery!" yelled the cook, and the cobbler, more frightened than ever, ran on, but was soon caught by the intrepid Magog, who held him in a grip like that of a boa-constrictor.

It was no use struggling, and the cobbler was taken before the king, who had now come out into full daylight, surrounded by his courtiers and attendants.

Now as Henry VIII. was six feet two, and sixteen stone, with gorgeous robes on, and a frown (when he liked) that was as good as a death warrant, it is no wonder the cobbler began to feel as if he was near the end of his mortal career.

"Presumptuous varlet!" cried the king, in deep, bass tones. "How dare you trespass in my palace, and kick up this disturbance? I'm a good mind to have your head off before dinner."

"Oh! don't, most gracious suvering," implored the cobbler, going down on his knees. "If you do, how will my business and my wife carry on?

"I swear I didn't go to commit no crimes; it's all through that Harry Ap-Tudor that I have got into this scrape."

He glanced up at the king's highness.

But what with the change of dress, and the change of voice, and the king's frown (which was quite of the Richard III. order), he didn't recognise him as the Ap-Tudor of the week before.

"Away with him!" cried the king. "Away with him, to the deepest cellar beneath the palace; there to await the deadly sentence."

"My snakes and gracious!" exclaimed the cobbler, and fell to the floor in a fit.

* * * * * *

His majesty went back to his private room, and laughed consumedly.

*　　*　　*　　*　　*　　*

When Jobson recovered his wits he found himself in a cellar filled up to the ceiling with big wine casks, giving forth a mingled flavour of the most delicious and intoxicating wine.

He noticed that one cask had the tap in, and there was a flagon in the window-sill, so he filled it, and was just about to drink, to recover his spirits, when several human beings entered his cell.

The first he recognised at once, and, dark as it was, as no other than his friend Harry Fitz-Harry Ap-Tudor, dressed in his usual plain suit, though strange to say, his companions were noble lords of the court with their hats off.

"Oh, Harry Ap-Tooder," cried the cobbler, "haven't you led me into a fine lot of hot water? I'm done for, and all through your invitation. Do you think you can do anything to get me off."

"I don't know as I can, but I'll try," said the other. "The king may revoke your sentence; it all depends on the humour he is in. At all events, if you are hanged, you'll have the consolation of knowing you've seen the king, and that's something."

"Precious little though, when it comes to that," murmured the cobbler.

"Well, you may as well make yourself as comfortable as you can," was the reply. "Sit down, and troll us forth one of your jolly catches."

The cobbler, under the influence of the splendid wine,

was soon again in singing order; but his song naturally turned on his own misfortunes.

> "It's a ticklish thing
>   To offend a great king,
> In the palace I've been an intruder;
>   And now it's gone goose,
>   And my neck's in the noose,
> And it's all through that Harry Ap-Tudor."

His companion took up the refrain with the following startling verse—

> "Cheer up, honest blade,
>   And don't be afraid:
> No longer I'll be a deluder.
>   You soon shall go free,
>   And believe me to be
> Your friend and your king, Harry Tudor."

Just then a gleam of daylight, getting through the grate, fell on the royal frontispiece with a sort of halo that showed there was no mistake about it.

"What!" cried the cobbler, gasping. "Is it really and truly his high mightiness? Great goodness! and I've been a-treating of England's monarch just the same as any other man!"

"Never mind! you didn't mean it," said the king. "I'll forgive you. Use no ceremony with me; I have quite enough of that at home. What ho, there, my lord butler, tap a fresh cask, and we'll have a few gentle tastes of wine."

The butler brought forth the treasures of the cellar with the utmost *celer*ity, and they all tasted the wine till their spirits rose to about ninety-two in the shade.

Songs, and glees, and catches were poured forth, the cobbler doing quite his share, and the king joining in when required.

Before Jobson went home the king gave him ten gold

pieces ; told him he'd let him mend all the boots in his household, and even, perhaps, after a bit make him a courtier.

———

XXXVIII.

THE COBBLER AND THE THREE MONARCHS DISPOSED OF.

HE also told him to bring Mrs. Jobson when he next called.

His head half turned by these favours, Jobson went home to tell his wife Joan and his neighbours the marvellous adventures he had met with.

"There's no mistake about it," said the cobbler, as he walked proudly along ; " the king is the biggest trump ever known in this here universe."

The cobbler's fortune was made from that hour, for depend upon it, reader, when a king not only asks you to dinner, but tells you to bring the "missis" as well, you may calculate that you're in the right shoes.

· And so it was with our honest friend, Christopher Jobson.

His wife Joan was at first so struck all of a heap at the bare idea of having entertained his most gracious majesty under her humble ceiling, and more still at the idea of returning the visit, that she actually forgot to take the potatoes off the fire till they blew up of their own account.

She passed the morning in going round to her neighbours, telling them the marvellous news under the promise of strict secrecy, well knowing that to be the surest means of getting the affair spread about.

She began already to feel three inches taller, and all her friends agreed that the Jobsons were in luck's way.

Honest Christopher prepared for a much-increasing business, and already looked forward to the time when he could take a shop in the main thoroughfare.

Just at this nick of time up came an individual, who said he was a tanner and leather-seller, and offered to supply some capital pieces of leather on credit.

Christopher jumped at the offer, and he got talking with the tanner, who wouldn't take so much as a *tanner* on account, and found him almost as entertaining as Harry Ap-Tudor himself.

Well, after the bargain, the cobbler asked him to have dinner, saying they'd the finest bloaters, and the very best potatoe pie yet known was a-baking in the oven.

"The worst of it is my own missus expects me," objected the tanner.

"Then come, missus and all," burst out the cobbler, generously. "Our house ain't over furnished, but if there ain't three-legged stools enough for all, I'll guarantee you a first rate egg-box to sit down upon."

Well, not to cut a short story long, Mr. and Mrs. Tanner dined that day with Mr. and Mrs. Cobbler, and the former two were so charmed by the latter two that the party were soon as merry as grigs (if the reader knows what those animals are).

At last, after the fifth time the leather bottle had circulated, the tanner suddenly rose to his feet, and pulled off his false, long beard.

"Ha, ha! sold again," he ejaculated.

The cobbler looked up, his heart standing still.

"The king himself, by goles!" he exclaimed.

"Oh, 'evvins!" echoed Mrs. Cobbler; and with that she gave a loud scream, and fell off her perch.

"Never mind, mum; it was only a wager," said the king, helping to pick her up. "I said I'd take you in a second time, and so I did. Don't make a fuss about it; the queen and I are off now. Here's a purse of gold; come and see us at the palace to-morrow."

And sure enough they went, and had turtle soup, and boiled grouse, and all the delicacies of the season, served on gold plates.

The ways and manners of the cobbler and his wife made some of the grand lords smile; but what were the odds, as long as the company in general were happy?

The cobbler's business, under favour of the king, so increased that he was able to set up a large shoe-shop, and at last became alderman, and lord mayor, and courtier, under the style and title of Sir Christopher Jobson, knight.

To the end of his life he stuck to it that—

"Our most gracious King Hal, *alias* Harry Fitz-Harry Ap-Tudor, is the fust-ratest fellow as ever wore boots!"

Wending again along the main road of our history, we must note that London was well off for lord mayors during Henry VIII.'s reign.

Not only was there always one to be found when wanted, but he was some good when he *was* found.

Under these excellent rulers London improved vastly, and paving-stones were laid down right and left.

The monasteries were also dissolved by order of the king, and the poor priests who were turned out of house and home, were, of course, dissolved also—in tears.

If I were to give a list of all the clerical houses disestablished in London alone, you'd think I was never going to leave off.

To make up for this, several hospitals, etc., were set afloat by one lord mayor, the famous Sir Thomas Gresham, who was quite a second edition of Whittington for liberality.

Many other things, more or less, happened in London at this time, but not worth stopping for.

Well, Bluff King Hal having gone the way of all kings, bluff or otherwise, the crown changed hands—or rather, heads.

Edward VI. was one of the youngest monarchs that ever came to the throne of England, but it wasn't his fault.

What he wanted in age he made up in other things, for he knew more than many people who have lived in the world fifty times as long.

He passed several very salubrious laws concerning his beloved capital London, and would have done an immense deal of good had there been time.

Especially he founded the Blue-coat School, and if he had never done anything else but invent the deliciously beautiful style of dress worn by the boys there, he would still have to be considered as a benefactor to his species.

To give you an idea how things were carried on in the good old times, workmen who dared to strike were fined £10 each, or twenty days; striking a second time, double, besides being pilloried; and if they went at it a third time, one of their ears was cut off.

It is very few persons who could stand such a punishment *ear*-oically.

Butchers also were severely punished for raising the price of meat in the *meat*-ropolis.

According to one topographer of this date, London was

arranged on a plan strange enough to puzzle St. Anthony himself.

Westminster was a separate town of itself, standing between Temple Bar and St. Paul's, which led out on St. James's Park, overlooking the Tower of London on one side and St Pancras Church on the other, while Charing Cross stood in the middle.

In the City improvements (made by special commission in the year 1533½), all of the foregoing were paved back and front, water laid down, and the sewers carried up to the main-building carrying off all the refuse into the water-butts.

(N. B. By historian. We will by no means vouch for the accuracy of the above account, though it is taken from one of the very best authorities. It seems to us to have got rather mixed, and if the chonicler wasn't drunk when he wrote it, at all events we are ready to wager he wasn't a teetotaler).

The reign of Queen Mary I., familiarly called Blo——but no, we mustn't swear—wasn't conducive of much good to London or any other place, rather the contrarywise.

The principal events going on were hangings, beheadings, and burnings, and if you can find any fun in them, do it, for we can't.

If this queen had reigned as long as her sister Elizabeth, it is propable that there wouldn't have remained in England any population to speak of.

London would have been deserted, grass would have grown in the street, and water-cresses sprung up on the Thames banks.

Every house or so would have been shut up, and a notice placed in the window " Premises to be sold on account of sudden death of owner," or " To be let for immediate possession, previous tenant having been executed last week," or "This house to be let or sold. Proprietor gone away to escape the queen's vengeance."

However, as there don't strike us to be much amusement to be got out of this sort of thing, and as nothing of great importance happened in the City in Mary's reign, we will proceed to that of her very successful successor.

XXXIX.

"YE GREAT ELIZA'S GOLDYN AGE."

THERE is no doubt that "Bonny Queen Bess," who now came to the throne (because the throne would not come to her), was the very *Bess*-t queen that had ever yet appeared on this stage of history.

Some historians describe her immediate popularity by saying that her *reign* was *hailed* with joy, but that weather joke is so old now that I think we had better let it rest in peace.

Still, there is no doubt that the advent of Elizabeth *Eliz*-ited much satisfaction on all sides, except among the Roman Catholics, whose adherence to the pope made the prospect of a Protestant reign somewhat un-*pope*-ular.

The queen, on being crowned, swore to keep up the new religion, and at once set the clerical gentlemen to work to compile the church service, which was a very great service, indeed, to the nation.

The Londoners greeted Her Majesty with tremendous joy.

and put their best legs forward to stand on a good footing with her.

Compared with the dark reign of the terrible Mary, the advent of Queen Elizabeth came like delicious jam after a nauseous dose of physic.

In 1561, St. Paul's steeple was struck by a flash of lightning, which had been on the watch up in the clouds for some time, looking out for a good opportunity to spring down.

The consequence was that the fine old spire no longer stood a-*spiring* towards the skies, but came down with a run, bringing its fine peal of bells with it.

It was "look-out *bel(l)*ow," then, and enough to make any one *bell*-ow that they might drop upon.

London had by this time swelled out so much in point of size, that it looked quite a swell place; for all that, in comparison with our present metropolis, it was no bigger than a shrimp is by the side of a lobster.

The city ended at Charing Cross; all beyond was fields till you got to Westminster, which was a town of itself, and all the suburbs, where now we can't see enough grass to feed a cockroach, was then "truly rural," or "toolral looral," as some gentlemen (after dinner) pronounce it.

Why, there were then only forty public houses in all London, and now we have nearly forty miles of them.

Holborn was a separate village, and the Strand was a pebbly beach—something like Gravesend without the bathing-machines—with a few gentlemen's houses and gardens winding down to the placid billows.

Yet, for all this, the queen, as soon as she saw so much building going on, grew alarmed for fear London would become too large! So that Elizabeth, instead of being, as some make out, fond of getting as much money as she could, was actually *opposed to an extension of her capital.*

One reason was that, in those days, the bigger the town, the bigger the chance of fevers and fires springing up, and, indeed, people looked out for one or the other of them as naturally as we look out for fine weather in the summer— only they were not so often disappointed.

LONDON FASHIONS IN THE ELIZABETSYAN AGE.
(See page 220.)

The houses were so built that they would burn beautifully on the slightest provocation, the walls being mostly lath and plaster, about as strong as so much chips and paste, and the roofs of thatch, which, when it once caught, used to blaze away like straw, at an ex-*straw*-dinary quick rate.

Bricks were little used, and cricket not being known, even brick-*bats* were never employed.

Inside, the best houses were about as comfortable as the steerage cabin of a coal-barge; the walls were unpapered, so that, as an aged chronicler observes, "You coulde see the insex a-crorlin about as plain as the noze on yor phace, and as lyvely as kittings."

The floors were covered with rushes, a sight enough to *floor* any modern lady, and make her *rush* away in horror.

THE FIRST PUFF OF TOBACCO.   (*See page* 214.)

Even in the swellest mansions, bones, etc., used to be thrown among the "straw" or "rushes" on the floor, which were not swept up till they were in the most dis——in short, a perfect nuisance.

Elizabeth herself had no better carpet in her very best room than a sprinkling of newly-made hay. "What do you think of that, *hay*, reader?"

Many monasteries and churches, having either fallen down, or been pulled down by Henry VIII., who had such a *down* upon the monks thereof, there was a magnificent lot of materials for building lying about, as cheap as dirt, and very much like it.

The builders ran up houses very fast about this period, and rents ran up too, and even many of the existing tenants suddenly found their rents raised over twenty feet.

(Some of them "raised the house" themselves at having to pay it.)

Many of the City improvements were owing to the great —good Sir Thomas Gresham, who was, in fact, both a manufacturer and a benefactor of London.

All at his own expense he knocked down eighty old houses and built one bran new Royal Exchange, which was certainly an (*Ex*-)change for the better.

The 7th of June, 1566, was a great day in London, for then it was that Sir Thomas laid the foundation stone of this great building.

He was assisted in the ceremony by the lord mayor and twelve aldermen, which shows what a tremendous size the stone must have been.

It's true that our friends Gog and Magog could have done the work as easily as you or I could throw a brick through a plate-glass window; but though they were present, their services were not made available.

The queen came down in great state to see the affair, and dined with Sir Thomas and a large and brilliant company, who distinguished themselves highly by their performance at table.

As soon as the Exchange was built, Sir Thomas handed it over to the Lord Mayor and sheriffs, and wouldn't take a single farthing for it, though he acknowledged that "exchange was no robbery."

Besides this, he built a college and called it after his

name, which name, I hope, will be remembered as long as London knows what it's about.

Sir Thomas was not the only charitable Thomas at this period.

Sir Thomas Rowe, Lord Mayor, 1568, the composer of "*Rowe*, brothers, *Rowe*," and founder of Paternoster *Rowe*, did heaps of similar good.

He first established a permanent watch in the city, and this city *watch* was one warranted to go.

He built pulpits, hospitals, and almshouses in various places, and lent money to poor tradesmen at nothing per cent., which showed that he really did *take an interest* in them, and besides this he so improved the city waterworks that even on frozen-out winter mornings the plug was up early.

In 1569, a public lottery took place at St. Paul's for an unlimited number of silver forks, spoons, and other plate.

This affair went on for several months, and was a decided success, some people realising large purses and having their pockets picked immediately afterwards.

Of course these occasions drew together all the riff-raff of the metropolis, and it was found necessary to have sixteen beadles to keep order.

Some of these desperadoes cared no more for the beadles than if they had been *black* beadles, and the consequence was shindies, broken heads, and friendly visits to the nearest magistrates.

XL.

THE FIRST PIPE.

IT was somewhere about this time that tobacco was introduced into England by Sir Walter Raleigh, who brought it over from "Old Virginny Shore," which was however, new at that time, having only just been colonised.

You must know that at this time the swell place of resort was a tavern called "The Mermaid," where all the wits of the epoch used to meet to discuss a friendly glass or a friendly song, but never a friendly pipe, not till Raleigh showed them the way.

This was not long after he came home from his last voyage, bringing many curiosities to arouse the curiosity of his friends.

One fine evening Captain Raleigh came in as per usual.

All the members of the club, it so happened, were assembled that evening, the absent ones only excepted.

First, for we must put him first, was a gentleman with a forehead like the dome of St. Paul's, an eye that looked through and through everything and right out on the other side ; and a smile, oh, that smile ! To use his own words —

"We shall not look upon its like again !"

Yes, reader, 'twas he, the immortal W. Shakespeare, Esq., then well known as manager of the Globe Theatre, and just bringing out with decided success his new sensation play of "Macbeth, or the Moor of Denmark," in which, as you know, Julius Cæsar is the principal character.

Then there was his fellow bard, "rare Ben Jonson," once a bricklayer, then a soldier, next a player, and now a poet, and ready to turn his hand to anything else that might turn up; Ned Alleyne, the wonderful actor, who, when he was hard up, used to perform the part of a man borrowing money so naturally that it was like life itself.

Several more could be named as belonging to this club, which was not exactly either a Bachelors' Button or Young Married Men's, but mixed.

In walked Raleigh with his usual military-nautical, aristocratical air.

"What ho, waitaw—sirrah, I mean—fetch me a stoup of Burgundy, and be quick, *stoup*id."

To which the attendant responded—

"Anon, anon, your worship," which was the way they had in those times of expressing—

"Yessir; cumming d'rectly, sir."

"Give ye good e'en, gentlemen," said Sir Walter. "How are you to-morrow evening ?"

"To be, or not to be; that is the question," returned a mysterious voice.

"What, Willy Shakespeare, my boy ! Why, you look as if you don't know me."

"Horatio, or I do forget myself?" said Shakespeare, who was thinking of Hamlet.

"Not a bit of it; my name's Raleigh, or, at least, used to be, though there have been so many changes in England lately, that one don't know who one is hardly. Now, friends, I promised that I'd show you how to blow a cloud, in the Red Indian fashion. Here's the entire apparatus complete in my carpet-bag; so watch me intently and don't get frightened."

Thereupon Sir Walter pulled out a bamboo tube about a

yard and a half long, with a big silver-mounted bowl at the end, and a large square box filled with the very best Virginia tobacco.

"I'feggins, and by my halidome!" exclaimed Ben Jonson, "this is a parlous rum start."

"Whatever *is* his game?" ejaculated Ned Alleyne.

"Aye, there's the rub," added Shakespeare.

Meanwhile, Sir Walter Raleigh filled the bowl (it held two ounces), applied the mouthpiece to his lips, and picking out a red-hot coal from the fire with his dagger, lit up.

The others began to feel nervous.

They had never seen anything of this kind before, and thought Sir Walter had got a tile loose during his travels, and was going in for suicide by fire.

So intently did they watch the process that they didn't dare to breathe, whereas Sir Walter Raleigh seemed to be breathing (through his pipe) as heavily as two porpoises.

When they saw the first white puff rise up and *puff*-ume the apartment, they one and all gave an amazed exclamation of—

"Oh my!"

And, as the cloud grew and grew, they began to feel tight on the chest, and set to coughing to that extent that you might have supposed them all to be natives of *Corfe* Castle.

Ben Jonson gasped; Ned Alleyne called for cough lozenges.

Wm. Shakespeare himself, leaning exhausted against the wall, exclaimed—

"Oh, my prophetic soul, my uncle! This is a sight worse than Hamlet's ghost."

And he felt, though he had been through many volumes in his time, these *volumes* of smoke were one too many for him.

At this moment in come the waiter with the stoup of wine.

On his first opening the door, he thought the chimney had got stopped up, but when he saw Sir Walter with fiery flames bursting out of his pipe, and his mouth, and his eyes, and his nose, and his ears, he thought that he had caught fire through spontaneous combustion or something, and that the whole house would soon be burnt to the ground.

So holloaing out in a dreadful fright, he flung the entire contents of the three-pint flagon over the knight, with the intention of putting him out.

In this he succeeded, for Sir Walter was very much "put out" indeed.

So much so that he sprang from his seat, and exclaimed—

"Thou unscrumpscious varlet, take that !"

He administered to the waiter more kicks than he had earned halfpence all the week.

Out rushed the waiter as if the "old un" was after him, and tore down the street, calling out—

"Fire ! fire !" varied by "Murder ! robbery ! and treason !"

This in time collected a crowd, and the startling news that Sir Walter Raleigh had broken out into a fiery eruption like Mount Vesuvius soon reached the queen's ears.

Her majesty, much concerned for the safety of Sir W., who was one of her favourite courtiers, instantly despatched the Lord Chancellor to make inquiries.

That nobleman arrived at "The Mermaid" just as Sir Walter's friends were all in turn having a pull at his pipe, to find out what the sensation was like.

The queen's anxiety was expelled when she saw Captain Raleigh walk in with the pipe in his mouth, and he assured her that whatever she might think he wasn't dead yet.

As Raleigh smoked before the queen, of course the queen smoked after Raleigh, for he persuaded her to take a whiff, so that she would know-*if* (!) it was a pleasant sensation or not.

Placing the amber mouthpiece of the pipe to her regal lips, the Defender of the Faith drew in a fair mouthful of smoke, which, after making her gasp a bit, was seen the next moment to be rushing out of her majestic ears.

At this sight many of the loyal courtiers called out lustily—

" Ear ! ear !" as in duty bound.

But in spite of this the queen wasn't particularly happy.

In short she began to feel a sort of a——I should describe it, in fact, as a sensation like———but you know the sort of thing, I dare say.

XLI.

NEW INVENTIONS, VICTORIES, POULTERERS' BILLS, &C.

THOUGHT the room was spinning round and round, the whole world seemed made of tobacco smoke, and a feeling such as anyone might experience after swallowing a hot brick oppressed Her Majesty's throat.

Flinging down the pipe at last, the virgin queen exclaimed—

"By my father's bootjack, but this won't do. I wouldn't continue this an hour, not to be Pope of Rome and Emperor of China to boot. Take it away. Sir Walter, I find I was not created for smoking, and for the future I'll *get it done for me.*"

Thus was the science of smoking introduced into this truly great country, and grew so widely in public favour that in a few years many children were born with pipes in their mouths.

N.B.—The latter remarkable circumstance, which is described in the life of Raleigh, is *raly* a fact.

Coaches were now first seen in the streets.

At this time they were used too in summer, autumn, and winter, but were without *springs.*

One Boone, a Dutchman, was the first that brought over

these vehicles, and the queen, who thought his invention a very great *boon* indeed, appointed him her first coachman.

Previously she used to ride on horseback behind the lord chancellor, hanging on to the skirt of his robe.

She now appeared in public in a finely-ornamented coach, in shape like a Chinese pagoda on wheels, and not weighing more than three modern omnibuses.

In 1580 a panic was caused in London by a severe shock of earthquake, which destroyed several splendid churches, convulsed society, scattered ruin and desolation o'er many a peaceful home, and turned some milk sour.

The queen, who was going to St. Paul's in her state coach at the time, felt the shock severely.

Her teeth (she had recently taken to a false set) were fearfully shaken, and with a wild shriek, such as only a queen can give, she was thrown forward into the arms of the young and handsome Earl of Essex, who sat providentially opposite.   1588 was the year if you like.

Then it was that the Invincible Armada had proved itself very vincible indeed, for instead of the Spanish catching the English napping as they hoped, they caught a tartar instead.

Admiral Drake was just the bird to gobble them up, and no sooner had he taken to the water than the Spanish fleet knew how *fleet*ing were their hopes of victory.

Drake, in fact, made ducks and drakes of this grand flotilla, and took Don Whiskerandos De Fandango, the Spanish admiral, an abject prisoner.

A national thanksgiving for this victory took place on the 24th of November, and all sorts of jollifications were carried on.

At the banquet at Sir Francis Drake's mansion in the Strand, her majesty was graciously pleased to pledge the admiral in a pint bumper of Burgundy.

Ladies at that time could stand any amount of alcoholic beverages, which would send their weaker descendants into *delirium tremens* in no time.

This was especially the case with the virgin queen, who not only disposed of some very strong fluid, but rapped out some very strong expressions, sometimes *a la* Harry VIII.

If you want to know how cheap things were then, just cast your eyes over a poulterer's bill of the period.

	s.	D.
1 Goose - - - - - - -	1	0
Ditto Rabbit - - - - - -	0	3
4 Dozen Eggs - - - - - -	0	10
2 Pounds of Butter (best fresh) - - -	0	5½
2 Chickens - - - - - -	0	2¾
Total	2	9¼

The bill of fare for the queen's breakfast is still more interesting.

	s.	D.
Bread, 3 quarterns - - - - -	0	8
Ale and beer, 6 gallons - - - -	0	10¾
Boiled mutton, 14 pounds - - - -	0	9
Chickens for gruel - - - - -	0	6
Veal, 3 pounds - - - - -	0	2½
Butter, 2 pounds - - - - -	0	7
Wine, 6 pints - - - - - -	1	3
Total	4	10¼

It makes any one quite hungry to read this sort of thing.

Dress in this period flourished to an extent that is awful to contemplate.

Gorgeour of apparel grew to be a great deal more than extravagant.

It was downright dangerous.

To walk the streets was like running the gauntlet of a haberdasher's shop.

The ladies wore "farthingales," which would have made the biggest modern crinoline look small.

Their ruffs and frills stood up some six inches above the tops of their heads.

They sported as much jewellery as they could move under.

Necklaces like the Atlantic cable, and ear-rings about the size of fine William pears.

Every colour in the rainbow, and some out of it, was to be seen.

Silks, and satins, and velvets, and three-piled cloths, and tufted taffetas, and embossed camlets, were considered quite common material.

And then the fringings, stitchings, lacings, borderings, and every species of filagree work, broke out all over the dresses like an eruption.

It was the same with the *beaux*, whose brilliant colours made them rain*beaux* indeed.

The head was crowned with feathers that reached above the doorway, and plumed over like a fountain.

Slashings, and puffs, and cuffs, and ruffs, in every sort of costly stuffs, and blues, and reds, and pinks, and buffs, were worn alike by rogues and muffs.

Edward Vere, a *verey* great swell, introduced embroidered gloves into England, and he introduced them to the queen as well, who was so delighted to make their acquaintance that she had her portrait painted in them.

One extreme exquisite among the courtiers wore a flower

in his hair, probably to denote himself the flower of the flock.

Hats were of all shapes, from the flat pork-pie to the steeple-crowned beaver; and some were much the shape of an inverted tea-cup, with the saucer worn as a brim.

As to ruffs, they grew so wide, and as to swords, they grew so long, that the queen stationed men at the street corners to cut down every ruff, and smash every sword, that was over a certain standard.

As there were a good many great *roughs* and *sordid* scoundrels in London at that time, some of them dropped in for it.

Laws were made to prevent apprentices and others dressing beyond their means, or sporting sham jewellery, etc., with the idea of " coming it flash."

By order of the lord mayor, all aspiring young fellows found too extravagantly dressed were to be punished by a good. *dressing*, making them *smart* in a manner they didn't like.

Oh, all ye modern youth who are inclined to flashiness, beware, for *that law has never been repealed*.

XLII.

HISTORY OF ESSEX STREET, AND OF ESSEX HIMSELF.

TALKING of this reminds me that it was exactly then that the Strand, hitherto only a lane, was *turned* into a street, with a number of littler streets *turning* into that.

The most bloated aristocrats didn't mind living there then, as our authority explains—

" 'Cos vy, there vosn't no Vest End."

We have mentioned the Earl of Essex.

His address was Essex House, Essex Buildings, Essex Street, Strand, in the *S. X.* district—very easy for the postman to remember.

He was a great man at court, for the queen, though sixty-six at the time, imagined she was only in the first bright dawn of maiden loveliness, and the earl, by calling her the royal rosebud of Virginia, and other fine names, had quite won her youthful heart.

He was very popular with the cits of London, who would have done anything in the world for him, from lending money to blacking boots.

But there is a limit to all things, and when he wanted them to get up a rebellion, *a la* Wat Tyler, likely, if it failed, to become a hanging matter, they didn't see it.

The facts were as follows.

The earl had a slight row with Lord Burleigh, the chancellor, at the queen's palace, at Westminster (first floor front).

They drew their swords, and though the lord chamberlain interfered, though the captain of the guard remonstrated, and though the first mistress of the robes retreated into a corner out of the way, yet, as the song says—

> "And yet them two cantankerous chaps
> Still fit, and fit, and fit,"

till at last the royal grace of England appeared on the hostile spot.

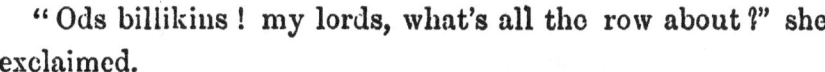

"Ods billikins! my lords, what's all the row about?" she exclaimed.

"Please, mum, it was him," cried Burleigh.

"Oh, you story! it was you," retorted Essex.

"No, it wasn't!"

"Silence!" exclaimed the queen.

And Essex, soon finding that her majesty was inclined to take Lord Burleigh's part if any, got indignant, and by turning his *back* upon her, gave af*front* to his rightful sovereign.

"Well I'm——" began her majesty, and would probably have said something very much in Henry VIII's style, only she pulled up just on the edge.

However, the British lion was roused, and clenching her august hand, she gave Essex the heaviest box on the ear he had ever felt.

"Now go home!" thundered the queen; "and if ever you dare to show your audacious frontispiece here again——"

He saw what she meant, and went at once.

For three days he shut himself up in his house, and didn't take off so much as his collar.

Then he determined to do something.

Gathering all his friends round him, he issued forth and ran through London streets, exclaiming—

"Treason, fire, blood, murder, and treachery! Down with the Burleigh party! Britons, strike home!" etc., etc.

But it wouldn't do.

The Londoners, instead of rushing out and joining his standard, kept indoors, pretending to be fast asleep—a sure sign that they were *wide awake.*

Essex was at last obliged to beat a retreat to his house in

the Strand, where he locked himself up, and prepared to stand a siege from the queen's soldiers.

Ten hours were they at it, without any time allowed for meals, and the commotion all over London was something gigantic.

At last, the royal troops having broken the bolts of the *front* door, many of Essex's friends made a *bolt* out at the *back*.

Then he saw his enemies rush in, and though he declared he didn't care a *rush* for it, his heart sank like an overloaded ship.

So he gave himself *up*, and was carried *down* the river to the Tower.

A mournful case of the *ups* and *downs* of life.

Very soon he found himself, under sentence of death, in the condemned cell, where it was very little consolation for him to know that he was *cell*ebrated.

He never held up his head after this, but the executioner held it up for him after it was off.

Elizabeth never forgave herself or anybody else for their parts in this affair.

She was seventy by this time, and it was too much for her.

And as it will be too much for the reader if we go on much longer, we will e'en turn to London as it was in the reign of James I., Rex.

So, proceed we onward.

XLIII.

JAMES I. now came to the English throne, and as he had to travel from Edinburgh to take possession, we may say he came a very long way to it.

But scarcely had James got used to the comforts of England, after the discomforts of Scotland, when the great Guy Fawkes discovery was made.

CROMWELL REFUSING THE CROWN.—(*A long way after a celebrated Painting.*)—See page 233.

And never did any discovery—not even those of Dr. Livingstone and Mr. Stanley—create a more immense sensation.

Of course I ought to give you a full description of the Gunpowder Plot, but people don't always do as they ought in this world.

Read for yourselves.

There are plenty of accounts, but none more full, true, and particular, than that written by a very near relation of the present chronicler, and published in the "BOYS OF ENGLAND," Nos. 260 to 269.

Therein the whole history of Guy Fawkes, his family, his friends, his private life, his public house, his plots and plans, his feats and failures, and final fate, all this, I say, you may read as easily as A B C and as plain as a pikestaff, in those ten numbers of that never-to-be-sufficiently-studied periodical.

Proceed we therefore with our main narrative.

In 1607, his majesty, having paid all the money he owed to the City, naturally began borrowing again.

It was only £63,000 this time, which of course so rich a corporation could easily lend any day before breakfast, and think nothing of it.

The king was so pleased at the loan, that not *alone* did he grant them a beautiful fresh charter—on a nice *new roll* of parchment, quite appetising to look at—but he gave them a big slice of land seized from the Irish rebels.

It was at first intended to plant it over here, and anchor it on to London, but this not being quite so feasible as you might suppose, colonists went over there from here instead.

These were the *London Irish*, who are now formed into a volunteer corps.

London now began growing at such a tremendous rate, that it must have suffered from the growing-pains terribly.

Smithfield (so called from the immortal Smith, whose descendants are still alive), was built upon; Wapping became a whopping big place, and the celebrated Old Stairs (built, of course, by Lord Stair), now first *stared* travellers in the face; while Holborn stretched out so far that people wondered where it was going to stop and when.

In 1612, a Mr. Sutton, who was so rich that he dined off gold every day (what a splendid digestion he must have had !), gave £20,000 to build the Charter House.

Sir Baptist Hicks also displayed *hick*straordinary munificence by building at his own expense, a sessions house, called Hick's Hall, for which he was deservedly *Hick's-hal*ted (exalted) to the rank of Viscount Camden and Earl Kentish.

But of all the patriotic citizens of the period, Sir Hugh Myddleton was the patriotickest.

Seeing that what London wanted most was water, he organised himself into the first Metropolitan Waterworks Company ever formed.

Casting about for a good place, he began to bore the earth, and *bore* all the expenses too.

The first source he opened was at Amwell, in Hertford.

" That *am well*," exclaimed Sir Hugh, as he first saw it.

By means of this *spring*, he turned the *winter* of our dis-content into a *summer* of enjoyment.

The other branch of the New River came from Ware, and as it was said at the time—

> " How *full* Sir *Hugh's* most *Hugh's-full* river flows,
> It comes from *Ware*, and this is *where* it goes."

Previous to this, one William Lamb, had built a *conduit*

or reservior, not in *Sheep*-side as you might think, or even *Lambeth*, but in *Lamb's Conduit* Street.

Trade now flourished more than ever, and foreign traders swarmed to London like flies to a treacle jar.

Turkey merchants became cocks of the walk.

Levant traders levanted with English goods, leaving in exchange good prices.

France sent over stewed frogs.

Africa exported wool (from the negroes' heads).

Geneva sent watches, jewellery, and the very best Old Tom.

England had likewise a *sole* right to some most valuable fisheries, particularly the Greenland fishery, which prospered suf-*fish*-iently to *net* a large profit.

The cutlery business prospered, under the patronage of Lord Sheffield, Sir John Blades, and Viscount Steele.

In fact, with our good old English knives, we *cut out* all foreign manufacturers, while most of our own *carved* their way to fortune.

Yes ; London was now unmistakably serene.

The police were to be found when wanted ; coals were deliciously cheap, and Shakespeare was still alive, though he had let his theatre and retired into clover down in his native Warwick.

James I left off reigning in 1625 ; but considering that (as the Irishman would say) he wasn't *living* in London when he *died*, his demise does not closely concern our history.

He was not a bad king if you compare him with many worse.

The year 1626, when Charles I., poor man, had begun to be king, was memorable for the establishment, by royal authority, of fifty hack carriages, in London, which was a great *hack*-commodation.

Coffee-houses were also established, the first being the "Rainbow," where the *beaux* of this *reign* soon learnt to assemble, situated at Temple Gate, Fleet Street, not a hundred miles from that venerable and romantic pile, the office of this journal.

Another was kept by a barber at Cornhill, but as he got mixing his two businesses together—stirring up the coffee with his combs, and pouring milk and sugar by mistake on gentleman's heads instead of pomatum—he had in due time to shut up shop. ·

A great deal of building went on in the capital, and much improvement was made not a minute before it was required.

The Earl of Bedford, in 1634, began to build Covent Garden, and the *fruits* of his efforts are still visible.

The great architect at this time was Inigo Jones; don't call it *Indigo*, please, for he wasn't of that colour at all.

His name originated from his being the first to use the phrase "go in and win," and he was called *In-I-go* accordingly.

He repaired St Paul's, Whitehall Palace, and built Lincoln's Inn, and *inn*-numerable other edifices.

And all the time he was erecting these he was of course building up his own fortune as well.

But all this was during the bright days of Charles I., which were soon over, and very dark ones came instead.

In 1640 troubles broke out like all vengeance.

These arose from the king ordering so many *ships* that the citizens declared it a hard*ship* to have to pay for them.

In fact, they themselves became *vessels* of wrath, and were soon transformed into *men of war*.

John Hampden was the first to say that he'd be * * * * * * if he'd pay the tax—which he didn't.

Others took his part, and by degrees there arose a strike

so general that a great many generals got implicated in it, and this national strike grew and grew until the king's head was struck off.

Of course this was a terrible affair, but at the same time it makes a very good sensation drama, and now every night they are s-*Irving* our poor Charles I. at the Lyceum. (N. B.—If you think this is a *lie, see 'um* yourself.)

The great civil war put a full stopper on the bottle of London's prosperity.

Things were now at sixes and sevens, and even worse than that.

Goings-on of a truly awful kind took place in the streets ; riots and window smashings, fights between Cavaliers and Roundheads, some of whom were blockheads as well.

London had strong walls built all round.

Cheapside Cross, that proud edifice, was not only taken down a peg or two, but demolished altogether by a band of furious fanatics, in 1643, and King Charles's statue was kicked over, horse and all, and sold for what it would fetch.

The king, driven to desperation—which is a nasty place to drive to—for want of money, among other things seized about £20,000 lodged at the Mint by certain citizens, who indignantly demanded what he *mint* by it.

This added fresh blazes to the flame of popular wrath, and though the king tried to make up his quarrel with his subjects, and even, we believe, went to dinner with the lord mayor, still he was not happy.

How it all ended you already know ; his dark fate culminated at Whitehall.

Of course, in the general wreck of things, fashion was nowhere ; people wore whatever they could get, and weren't particular how it fitted.

Nevertheless, the ladies' dress was particularly becoming,

and *becoming* more so every year, while the costume of the Cavaliers beat everything seen before or since.

Even our modern chimney-pot hats and funnel trousers were nothing to it.

There was as much difference between it and the Elizabethian mode of toggery as there is between British brandy and good spirits.

Since Queen Bess's time there had been a great fall in collars, which were now worn hanging down and beautifully laced; the hats were now regular brimmers, trunk hose had grown into knickerbockers, and though roses still bloomed on the insteps of the fashionable, boots were often worn with tops spreading out like cauliflowers.

XLIV.

THE CROMWELLITES, AND OTHER LIGHTS OF THE AGE.

NOSES were turned up occassionally, and moustaches too, others had a downward tendency.

In short, these fine old swaggering Cavaliers were got up capitally.

The Parliamentary party, or Puritans—people with particularly prim and puritanical prejudices (a fine crop of *P's* to grow all together) dressed very differently, in all the dingy clothes they could find, and with about as much ornament on them as there is on a kitchen shovel.

But the great distinction was in their way of wearing the hair.

The royal party rejoiced in love-locks, and other locks so luxuriant that it was said a key was required to do them with.

As the old rhyme says—

"Ye Cavaliers their lockes doe weare,
Much longer than they oughter,
Ye Puritannes doe croppe their haire,
Considerably shorter."

And indeed with the Cromwellites, it was the custom to keep their hair short and their faces long.

In 1646 Sir John Gayer was lord mayor.

Like Mr. Stanley, he had just come home from Africa, where he had been to see the lions.

And he saw rather too much of them, for being alone in the wilderness, he saw a fine lion coming towards him, and falling on his knees (the traveller, not the lion), made a vow that if he got safe home he would do something grateful.

The lion, fortunately, had just dined, so he passed on with a friendly wag of the tail, and disappeared into the pathless desert.

Sir John Gayer, who was now much gayer than he had been recently, soon met with a kindly vessel, whereby he reached his native land.

Of course in London he himself became the lion of the day.

He immediately gave £200 to the City, the interest to be devoted to giving the poor bread all the year round, and a sermon once a year.

It is said that the bread is never too short in weight, nor the sermon too long.

Cromwell, when in his hey-day of power, often went to visit the City Corporation.

There used to be grand doings then, and they generally wound up the dinner by singing the 119th Psalm.

One memorable day in 1653, the Parliament assembled at Westminster Hall and offered Cromwell the Crown of England.

He thanked them, saying that it looked very nice, but he was afraid it wouldn't agree with him, as he had known people who found that wearing a crown was the death of them.

However, he ruled Britannia quite as much as any king, and more, until 1658, when he departed, aged fifty-four years nine months.

Various opinions prevail about Oliver.

Some declare he was all the hypocrites and villians on earth, and others that he was the greatest statesman that ever had a wart on his nose.

For my part I steer between, and think him very much of both, if not a little of either.

There is much that he did, which, whether we look on it this way or otherwise, was undoubtedly so rather than not; but, take him for all in all, he did a great deal of good, and London had cause for regret when he died, through an inability to prolong his existence.

XLV.

CHARLES II. AND CO. (LIMITED). ESTABLISHED 1660.

AFTER trying in vain to be ruled well by Cromwell's son, who was more like a rushlight than a *sun* compared to Oliver, people came to the conclusion that they couldn't do better than go in for another King Charles.

No. 2 of that name was therefore invited over from Holland, where he had been hiding himself, keeping his eyes sharply fixed on the vacant throne.

A grand day indeed was that day in May, 1660, King Charles's thirtieth birthday, though it was at the same time *the twenty-ninth.*

As it turned out a fine day, people turned out too in swarms to see the procession, and even those who didn't usually pay their rent, now *rent* the air with their cheers.

King Charles bowed so frequently that he began to feel his head almost as loose as that of his dear departed papa.

One of the new monarch's first London laws was to lay a tax of five pounds on the hackney coaches, which made them so heavy the horses could hardly draw them along.

An act was also passed to enlarge the courts and alleys in London, which were so narrow that until the Act was passed, vehicles could not pass each other.

Charles II., who kept a large *court* himself, could not bear the idea of such small courts remaining in the metropolis.

Another of his majesty's early acts was to give back to the City their estates in Ireland, which had been taken away from them and now came to them again, yet remained in Ireland all the time, which sounds Irish altogether.

Of course he granted the City a new charter, and for some years things in London settled down slowly, like a Seidlitz powder when it has done fizzing.

In 1665 the great plague passed over London, and we shall return the compliment by passing over the great plague.

Were we to describe it, our character for comicality would be irretrievably lost, and the reader would have to provide us with a new one.

The best authority is the "History of the Plague" by

Defoe, who describes all the horrors with *Foe*-tographic minuteness.

The great fire is a good subject to warm up the imagination, especially in cold weather, but there was too much of it, and it wasn't thought at all comic at the time.

Nevertheless, it did a good deal of good in the end.

It burnt away the remainder of the plague, destroyed all the fever-dens, whether insured or not, and London could rise again from her ashes as clean as a new pin, and a great deal more picturesque.

In four years, such was the rapid rate of building, any one wouldn't have recognised the place, especially if they had never seen it before.

Everyone knows that the great fire began at Pudding Lane, and ended at Pie Corner, and goodness knows how much pastry it was greedy enough to consume besides ; so that it is rightly named the *devouring* element.

Old St. Paul's, as we know, was like a cowardly soldier ; it *failed to stand fire*, but got completely burnt down—though, as the conflagration began at the base, perhaps we ought rather to say burnt *up*.

However, now that a clearance was made, was the time for beginning afresh ; so the great architect, Sir Christopher Wren, took London in hand, and completely *wren*-ovated it.

He made the designs for many other public buildings in London, which proved him to be a *designing* man.

Sometimes he concocted some very dark *plans*, that was when he drew them in Indian ink ; but strange to say, instead of being punished when found out, he was rewarded.

He built several churches, especially Temple Bar, which, though a fine structure, is considered by some authorities to be built in a temple-barbarous style of architecture.

It is the last of the London gates now standing, and it don't look as if it would do that long.

When it falls, it is to be hoped that some of our readers will be there ; the sight is sure to be grand.

Go early, and secure a good place underneath.

King Charles superintended a tolerable amount of building in his time.

He founded Chelsea Hospital, in order that veteran soldiers who had lost both legs should have some visible means of support.

Also he established Greenwich Hospital for old sailors in a like condition, on the site of the former palace of Greenwich.

And a very pretty *sight* it is, too, from the river.

This king only built one wing of the hospital ; perhaps he was afraid that if he built two wings it would fly away.

St. James's Palace was now taken in hand, and became a very royal residence, the king and queen always residing there when they were not elsewhere.

Rank and fashion had begun to migrate westward, and St. James's Park became (to speak with elegance) the swellest hang-out in London.

Its present aspect will give no idea of what it was then.

All sorts of grand buildings stood around it, whereof there isn't so much as a ha'p'orth of mortar left.

There was Barkshire House, so called on account of the number of dogs kept there ; Tart Hall, so named by the Baker family, who built it in the form of a jam tart— a *sweet* idea, though we cannot call it (t)*artistic*, and many others.

Leicester Square was then called Leicester Fields, and had not attained its present magnificent condition.

Hay was really sold at the Haymarket; in those days a real windmill stood in Windmill Street.

Bunhill Row was so called from the number of buns sold there, and the number of people that were ill after eating them.

Bermondsey Abbey was still existing, not as a ruined abbey, but suitable for an *Abbey*tation.

When people went to Stepney, they found it was many a *step-nea*-rer the open country than nowadays, and Bow was within a bow-shot of the most truly rural districts.

It is strange to read how Gray's Inn Lane was a nice green lane to walk in of a Sunday, and see the fashions.

People used also to go holiday-making in Red Lion Fields, and though the name is still upon the locality, there are no fields now, and not a vestige of a red lion to be seen anywhere.

Charles II. often visited the City, and some awful gorgeous dinners were given by the lord mayors on these occasions.

Pageants and shows, and spectacles were exhibited, and Jacob Hall, the Blondin of the period, particularly distinguished himself by his tumbling on the slack wire, but never tumbling *off*.

In 1674, the lord mayor had become so jovial at the banquet, through continually toasting the royal family, that he slapped the king on the back in a familiar style, saying—

"Charlie, my boy, here's to you again, and several of 'em!" so that his majesty, who had his dignity to keep up, thought it high time to be off.

He therefore slipped out unawares while the lord mayor was occupied in declaring (for the thirteenth time) that this was the happiest moment of his life.

But finding out his royal guest's flight, his lordship bolted after him, and fairly dragged him back for the purpose of having another bottle.

The monarch, fortunately, was rather used to this sort of thing, and it took a great deal to knock him over, so he complied, and his health was drunk six times six, and two cheers more.

History doesn't tell how the king or the lord mayor felt the next morning.

———

XLVI.

CONTINUATION OF THE CHARLESIAN AND JAMESIAN PERIOD.

ONE great sensation of this time was the notorious Colonel Blood's attempt to walk off with the crown, sceptre, and other royal movables, from the Tower of London in broad daylight—about the coolest thing ever known, except perhaps Wenham Lake ice.

When brought before the king, Blood declared that he didn't at all mind hanging—liked it rather than not, but that should he be executed, his comrades had sworn to take jet-black and double distilled vengeance on everybody.

The king either believed the colonel, or was quite charmed with his frankness, for he not only ordered him to be liberated, but gave him £500 a-year for life.

Thus, to the surprise of all, the perpetrator of this desperate deed got a pension, instead of a *sus*-pension.

(For further particulars see the "Life of Colonel Blood," by Mrs. *Gore*.)

King Charles kept a **very gay court**, and fashion went on regardless of expense.

The " merry monarch " (as they called King Charles) was very popular.   Like the " Merry Zingara," he had " a smile, a smile for all "—though he was not quite so ready in rewarding his friends as he might have been.

He used to walk in St. James's Park every morning and feed the ducks.

You could tell him by his face for one thing, and also by his being followed by a number of the celebrated King Charles's spaniel puppies, as well as several young swells of the court, who were also puppies, though of another breed.

Methinks I see him now.

But enough of this.

We have another King James to look after now, and several historical events to study, of such importance that the reader must not think of having any dinner till he has mastered them thoroughly.

In 1685 James II. set up as king, with the full determination to do as he liked, which turned out to be very different to what other people liked.

He was down upon London particularly hard.

He took away all the City liberties and privileges, hanged one alderman, imprisoned a few more, and wanted the lord mayor to rule only during His Majesty's pleasure.

Nay, it was even said that he dictated what his lordship was to have for dinner, and how much blacking he should use for his boots.

This was coming it rather too strong, and the corporation of the City told the king so ; and one lord mayor, to defy him, kept in office three years *running*—by which time he must have been rather tired, and inclined to sit down.

James's nose was aquiline, but his religion was Roman—so much so that he used to go in state to mass, which offended the *mass* of the people greatly.

He invited over a large number of Catholic priests, who soon swarmed in the streets to that extent that Londoners began to wonder whether London had not suddenly got drifted on to the Continent.

He then sent six English bishops to be tried for compound disloyal heritical high treason, which must have been a very bad complaint.

However, they were let off when brought to trial, and the people of London were so delighted that they raised a shout, which some say was heard by the king at Hounslow—but that is *going rather too far.*

KING CHARLES IS TAKEN DOWN A LITTLE.
(See page 230.)

Well, King James went on in one way or another till at last he went off, for people could not stand him any longer.

You can see him in the Horse Armoury at the Tower any time you like to pay your sixpence.

He is on horseback, and dressed as queerly as if he had got into the wrong clothes by mistake and never found his way out.

What with his helmet and his wig, and his necktie as big as a Christy Minstrel's, and his laced coat and breast-

ENTRANCE OF KING WILLIAM III. INTO LONDON.—(*From a drawing taken on the Spot.*)—See page 242.

plate over it, and his holster pistols, and big boots coming pretty well up to his neck, he looks like a mixture of Oliver Cromwell and Dick Turpin.

We may now consider, without being at all unreasonable, that we've got into modern London.

Alsatia was "away-withed," and the scoundrels therein sent about their business; Greenwich Hospital was nearly completed; and Billingsgate Market arose in all its majesty and glory.

All this was in the palmy days of William and Mary, who

after James II.'s ignominious bolt, came over here with the object of setting things *square* all *round*.

William was a Dutchman.

He had been so as long as he could remember, and his ancestors before him.

But he turned out a very good *king*, and so did his *wife*, for they reigned together, as well as one after the other.

William made a most triumphant entry into London.

He could hardly get along for the enthusiastic crowd.

In honour of him as Prince of Orange, everybody wore orange scarves and dresses, orange blossoms were strewn before him, and everybody pelted everybody else with oranges, which flew about in all directions.

It was a sublime sight, and William felt it as such every time he took off his hat.

You will see by our illustration (which was strictly drawn from the life), that his nose was of the Romanest, but he wasn't a *Romanist* himself, like James, but Protestant to the backbone.

He was soon seated so firmly on the throne, that his father-in-law's efforts to dislodge him were no go whatever.

Queen Mary was also very popular.

Whenever the king went back to have a look at his beloved Holland, she carried on the business of government as comfortable as if she had been a widow.

Thus, in 1692, when his majesty took a trip to see how his Dutch tulips and hyacinths were getting on, his consort got a loan from the City (£200,000) far more easily than he could have done it.

One Alderman Dashwood said he was *dashed* if he *would*n't dub up £60,000 out of his own purse, which he did.

About this time there was an invasion panic in London,

for it was thought the French intended paying us an armed visit.

No monarch was more dreaded at that time than *Louis Quatorze.*

(You pronounce this *cart-horse*, all the others being mere ponies compared with him).

In England they prepared for the worst by raising volunteers in large quantities—Englishmen of right-down valour, ready to march anywhere, even across the Channel, if necessary.

The lord mayor alone raised 10,000 horse, and many other thousand foot, which would undoubtedly have received the "mossoos" in a *horse*-tile and by no means *horse*-pitable manner, and made them foot it.

But, fortunately for them, they thought better of the project, and didn't come.

Our old friends Punch and Judy began to be popular in the streets of London about this time.

Some say that they came over with William the Third, others that they were long before.

Anyhow they proved a decided success.

Each show was followed by vast crowds.

The theatres and Italian operas were quite deserted.

People forgot their meals, their business, their very names, and, worse than all, went to see Punch instead of going to church.

I wonder where they expected to go to after that !

In 1691 the first fire-engine was set up in London, and the citizens set fire to several houses to see how it would work.

There is nothing like testing scientific inventions by practical experiment.

One lord mayor of this period actually did not have any procession at all on the ninth of November.

The name of this miscreant was Sir Humphrey Edwin.

On the 8th of September, 1692, London was startled by a terrible shock of earthquake, which was so violent that it drove the merchants from Change, the people from their houses, spoilt the public appetite, and turned all the citizens, of whatever religion, into *Quakers*.

You must not suppose that King William's new throne was quite a bed of roses.

XLVII.

PLOTS AGAIN, AND ANOTHER LORD MAYOR'S SHOW.

SOME people objected to King William so much that they tried to assassinate him several times, but, having insured his life in a new company just started, he got off safely.

Once there was a plot to stop him on his way home to Kensington, and kidnap him, and ship him off in the night to the undiscoverable islands somewhere in the South Pacific Ocean, but it failed, and the conspirators' heads adorned Temple Bar soon afterwards. Such was the custom of the age.

Our foreign foes were pretty active, too, and once a French privateer, disguised as a coal barge, sailed up the Thames, and nearly captured the vessel that was going down to the Nore with all the money to pay the navy.

It was the narrowest escape on record, and all by chance, for the movements of the privateer had not previously reached the *private-ear* of any of the authorities who would have shed many a *private tear* had they lost their coins.

The Lord Mayor's show indeed surpassed itself.

It was worth seeing for its own sake, and remembering afterwards down to the latest date.

Sir Thomas Abney, a fishmonger, was lord mayor, and, having once gone as far as Gravesend, he considered himself quite a sailor, and determined to have everything as nautical as possible.

First in the procession came old Father Neptune in a splendid chariot made of the largest shell procurable (it measured thirty feet round) for which his lordship had to *shell* out liberally.

It was drawn by magnificent sea horses.

The ocean monarch was personated by our very old friend Gog.

Grand indeed he looked, with a crown of shells and coral on his head, peppered all over with big pearls.

His armour was made of fishes' scales, and glistened like a whole family of rainbows ; and in his hand he bore the trident—that poetical toasting-fork which Britannia holds up on a penny piece, only this one had a magnificent bloater stuck on it.

Magog, as Triton, was similarly got up, and only about one per cent. less splendiferous than his brother.

Time, of course, had somewhat thinned the flowing locks and bent the stalwart forms of the two famous giants, for it is impossible to be 1200 years old without feeling you are getting on in years, and, in point of fact, rather elderly.

But there was life in the old dogs yet, and though they had both retired on pensions (good big ones, you may be sure, according to their size), on special occasions like this they used to come out, and come out very strong, too.

After these came half-a-dozen mermaids, *walking*, of course, as they always do on dry land, and combing their hair to soft music, followed by the *Great Seal* of England and the *Prince of Whales*, with three walruses and a Polar bear in waiting.

Then came a ship in full rig, on a cart, drawn by an aquatic donkey, and escorted by a band of the Royal Sea-Horse Marines, followed by all the sailors, fishermen, watermen, and water sprites that could be collected together.

The lord mayor was dressed in sea green, and his coach was driven by a tar, in a cocked hat of *tar*paulin.

For music they had " Rule Britannia," " I'm Afloat," and " The Sea is England's Glory," and other salt-water minstrelsy, and the streets and balconies were all along hung with sea weed.

In short, a nauticaller procession never stepped, and it made the spectators feel as if they were a thousand miles out on the briny ocean.

William III. survived Queen Mary II. eight years, viz., to 1702, when he finished up his resemblance to William the Conqueror, by dying in the same manner; viz., through a fall from his horse.

It is no use disguising the fact that William was one of the best sovereigns of England, though he wasn't the most agreeable individual in the world, being somewhat yellow and bilious, and of sour aspect, like most of the Orange princes.

Though a little man, he had a great soul, and was a *great sol*dier.

His abilities were large, and his nose ditto—peculiarities shared to some extent by other eminent warriors; viz., Wellington, Napolean, and Julius Cæsar.

But, extensive as was his nasal organ, William never poked

it into other people's business, which, when we compare him with many other kings, does him great credit.

For further information about William, read the " History of the House of Orange," by the late Mark *Lemon* and Sir Robert *Peel*.

———

XLVIII.

THE LONDON HIGHWAY IN THE OLDEN TIME.

WE ought now to say something about the state of London during the last half of the seventeenth century ; how it was off for robbers, etc.

Well, as far as robbers went (and they went rather too far sometimes), there were plenty of them.

Highwaymen were a good deal more plentiful than blackberries.

Why, people used to be robbed in broad daylight, when travellers and vehicles were passing ; the latter didn't dare to interfere, but while the robbers were stealing away the valuables, took the opportunity of *stealing away* themselves

If you got into a hackney coach, ten to one but what the driver was a highwayman, or a highwayman's pal in disguise, and when he had driven you into some sequestered spot, would turn you out and signal to his comrades, who, rushing out, would perform the "money-or-your-life" trick, leaving you with light pockets in the *dark* lane.

It was nothing for twenty "gentlemen of the road" to be in Newgate at once, under sentence of death, but singing and drinking as jovially as possible, and swearing over their cups that they would faithfully *hang together*.

The real original Jack Ketch lived in James II.'s time, and had to give up the place because the work was too hard.

Certainly the most respectable of all highwaymen was Claude Duval, who used to *do val*-iant deeds on the London roads till he was at last *clawed* by the authorities.

Claude favoured the northern quarters of London most.

In Islington he did much as he liked, as if it had been *his*-(lington), actually.

Holloway was a *way* he often went, and Highgate was a *gate* that was always open to him.

There used to be a lane out in that direction called after him, Duval's Lane.

Some pronounce it *Devil's* Lane, but Claude wasn't so bad as that.

He was not so much a devil as a *dare*-devil.

This redoubtable highwayman didn't care whom or what he stopped.

Once he even *stopped* an old gentleman's tooth, because it had some gold in it.

Duval and his gang, which was large, used often to rob his majesty's mails, and his *fe*-males as well, whenever they got the chance.

He was the gallant who once made a lady get out of her carriage, and dance a *coranto* with him (some say it was a *fandango*, and others a *suravando*, but we needn't be *too* particular), and she did it so gracefully, that he let her off the four hundred pounds in her portmanteau.

See how useful it sometimes turns out to have learned dancing.

After a brilliant career, Claude made his final exit at

Tyburn, age twenty-seven, and by a twirl of the *neck*, went into the *next world* (*necks twirled*).

Then there was Jemmy Whitney, called the Handsome Highwayman, remarkable for his fashionable and tasteful way of dressing, which, considering that his clothes were all stolen, and he had to take them as they came, did him great credit.

The same cannot be said of his conduct, for when he was taken, he offered to give up his accomplices.

HOW THEY DID IT IN THE LAST CENTURY.

One who does this deserves more hanging than usual, and accordingly Whitney got it rather slightly at Newgate, in April, 1692.

Among his followers were a baker, and a grocer, a livery stable keeper, a man-milliner, which last was (guess) none other than Captain Blood, the son of the redoubtable colonel.

This showed that the young fellow had a good deal of the *old Blood* about him at least.

Whitney himself was taken at his favourite crib in

Bishopsgate Street, and when driven to *bay*, he wouldn't o *bey* the command to surrender, but kept the "minions of the law" off for four mortal hours with a *bay*-onet.

When they once managed to *wrest* his weapon from his hand the *rest* (and the *arrest*) was easy.

But about the smartest highwayman on record is one whose name doesn't transpire; but he was brought up at the sessions, and convicted of sacrilege, burglary, two murders, three violent assaults, and four acts of incendiarism —all committed in twelve hours.

He was evidently an active and industrious lad, ready to turn his hand to anything, and make himself generally useful.

As a reward of merit, they elevated him, and presented him with the most noble order of the Rope.

In point of fact these desperate robberies in London reached such an awful pitch that people used to boast if they came home from a journey with their throats uncut and their pockets still intact.

Even gentlemen used to adopt this lawless career, and a baronet once took to the highway, which is, after all, a *low-way* of getting a living; and, however people may make heroes of "Knights of the Road," it wasn't so nice on a fine morning to find oneself taking part in a grand farewell performance in public at the Theatre Royal, Newgate.

Turn we now awhile to the fashions of the age, which were something amazing.

King William introduced square Dutch-built coats, and waistcoats reaching to the knee, or *kneerly* so.

Boots were square-toed, and hats had a "cock" on one side, and, for all we know, a *hen* on the other.

But the wigs were the great features of dress at this time, and all other *features* were completely overwhelmed by them.

They were so large that the present Lord Chancellor's wig is a mere tuft in comparison.

Your importance was estimated by the size of your wig, hence the term " big-wig " applied to portentous persons.

It would have been considered the height of coolness for an attorney to sport a wig as big as a judge, or a judge to come out as strong in perruques as the Solicitor-General.

What size the king's wig could have been surpasses comprehension, and won't bear thinking of.

Then the wigs were so extensively powdered and perfumed that gentlemen had it all over their shoulders and shirt-fronts, and thus everyone, soldier or not, " smelt powder " in those days.

Altogether the fashionables of this period looked as stiff as if they dined off starch, and swallowed a kitchen poker regularly each morning.

This was the age of the beaux, or ineffable dandies, who set the fashion, such as Beau Fielding, Beau Wilson, and Beau Nash, who was the original *beau ideal.*

They used to be fond of duelling, and were dead shots, being able to hit their man whether they fired at him or not.

But their favourite weapon was the rapier—that nice, slender, delicate-looking sword that went slick through you and out on the other side before you knew where you were.

The ladies wore their dresses *long*, but not *longer* than they continued to be fashionable.

All sorts of paraphernalia and ornamentation were attached to the dresses, and the hair was frizzed up like the froth of a champagne bottle, and adorned with indescribable lavishness.

Jewellery of all kinds was worn in profusion, but only by those who could afford it, or get credit.

It is remarkable how plainly those ladies dressed whose means did not run to ornament.

The fashions came straight from France, and many of them were so ugly that it is a pity they did not stay there.

XLIX.

THE RUSSIANS INVADE LONDON—AWFUL GOINGS ON.

IT was in William III.'s reign, viz., in 1698, that there arrived in England no less a personage than Peter the Great, Czar of Russia, who was *czar*tainly a remarkable man, and who had previously worked as a sailor in Holland.

In order to learn shipbuilding, he put up in furnished apartments near Deptford dockyard, in the house of the famous John Evelyn.

He wasn't an eligible lodger at all.

He generally went to bed with his boots on, often sawed off the legs of the chairs and tables to practise himself in carpentry, and trundled his heavy friend, Prince Mentschikoff, in a wheelbarrow over the choicest flower beds in the garden.

He and his servants only stayed at Evelyn's three weeks, and when they had gone, it cost John £150 for repairs.

No wonder he was glad there were not *two* emperors of Russia.

Peter used to get up at six every morning, and be off to work in the dockyard; and when he had done in the evening, it was his habit to turn into a "pub." parlour, smoke his meerschaum, and treat his mates to liquor and comic songs.

He didn't stand much on his dignity, which he disguised under the name of Paul Pickaxicoff.

He was fond of mechanics, by which I mean both machinery and the fellows who worked it, to whom he often stood treat like a father.

He was also fond of Greenwich Hospital, which he frequently pulled up the river to have a look at, "shying" big stones through the windows to ascertain how thick the glass was, and frequently de-claring that he wished he were laid up, in order that he might live in so fine a place.

He wasn't quite so pleased with West-minster Hall; and when he heard a great

"HOLLOA !" EXCLAIMED PETER THE GREAT, "WHO IS YER A SHOVIN' OF !"
(*See page 255.*)

sensation case on there, he was quite appalled by the swarms of long-winded counsels in their wigs and gowns.

He asked how many lawyers there were in England, and was told five millions and a half.

"Well, I'm flustered!" exclaimed Peter. "I've only two in all my dominions, and one of them I mean to hang when I get back."

Of course everybody thought what a delightfully law(*yer*)less place Russia must be to live in.

Peter was of a fiery temper, and when we consider that his favourite drink was brandy with pepper in it, drunk steaming hot out of a saucepan, and sometimes flavoured with gunpowder, there isn't much to wonder at in that.

In point of fact, His Imperial Majesty was rather a hard drinker, and a hard eater also, and ditto his companions, who brought their Russian appetites with them.

Once on putting up at a hotel, the party ordered breakfast, which consisted of half a sheep, a quarter of lamb, ten pullets, twelve chickens, salad, seven dozen eggs, and a pound and a half of the best tallow candles.

This was washed down with three quarts of brandy, and six quarts of mulled wine.

Pretty well for a party of twenty-five !

But after all that was only a snack, and they were quite ready for dinner when it came.

It consisted of five ribs of beef, one sheep, of half a hundredweight, three quarters of lamb, a shoulder of veal, loin of ditto, three pullets, eight rabbits, two and a half dozen of sack, and one dozen of claret.

" By Jove !" exclaims the reader, "they must have been like that celebrated American colonel, who was hollow all the way down to the feet, and used to pile in his food upwards till it reached his throat."

Yes, a man would hold a good quantity packed on that system, which is perhaps the fashion in Russia.

I should be inclined to doubt the whole affair, did we not possess, as unquestionable evidence, the landlord's bill for the aforesaid feasts.

It is in the Bodleian Library, and measures six feet in length.

On the same authority we learn that Peter's usual morning allowance of fluid sustenance was a pint of brandy and a bottle of sherry for breakfast, which merely freshened him up, as it were, till lunch time, and when he had drunk eight bottles of port or sherry, he began to feel comfortable.

It is related that once going along the docks in his shipwright's dress, his Muscovite majesty was run up against by a big porter, carrying a tremendous load, which, stalwart as the monarch was, made him stagger and almost fall.

"Holloa!" exclaimed Peter, who had by this time learned correct English, "who is yer a shovin' of? Do you know that you're running up against the Czar?"

"And *Czar*ved yer right, for getting in the way," retorted the man. "Why, we're all Czars here, come to that, and equal to Roossian ones any day."

Peter said no more, but he looked after that porter as if he wished he had him in his clutches at Moscow, where he could give him a round dozen with the knout for such an (*kn*)outrageous piece of insolence.

This incident made the Russian monarch resemble an intoxicated beer drinker; he was *quite knocked over by some London porter.*

One of his favourites was a monkey, which used to perch upon his shoulder during dinner, and help himself from the emperor's plate, or anybody else's for that matter, and when a tit-bit was thus slily appropriated by the animal, while the owner was looking another way, the Russian Emperor laughed loudly.

Occasionally Jacko got a knock for his purloining, and ran howling to his master, who soothed him with all sorts of endearing and crack-jaw Russian names.

We have mentioned that the Czar was fond of machinery, and he was skilful at it too.

He could take a watch to pieces, or even *smash* it to

pieces, with any man alive, but when he came to put it together again, the result was not always happy.

But he meant well.

Having obtained a good knowledge of shipbuilding, Peter departed from the London docks one fine day in the autumn of '98, and took a good many English things and people with him.

His parting words to King William were—

"Take this, old hawk-nose, with my blessing; the anchor's weighed; farewell, remember me!" and he placed in his hand a ruby valued at £1,000, wrapped up in dirty brown paper.

His Britannic Majesty wiped away a tear, and put it (not the tear, but the ruby), into his waistcoat pocket, but ere he could turn to thank the donor, Peter had gone from his gaze, or rather, could just be distinguished in the distance, waving a red pocket-handkerchief full of holes from his boat.

When he got back to Russia, he performed wonders in civilising the nation, but never seemed to succeed in civilising himself.

Of all the illustrious strangers that have visited England, Peter was the most illustrious and the strangest.

L.

CONCERNING THE TIMES BEFORE QUEEN ANNE WAS DEAD.

AND now for the reign of the good Queen Anne, who in 1702, being a personage of some weight, worthily filled the British throne.

L.—(*Continued.*)

ONE of her first public acts was to dine with the lord mayor, on which occasion all was rejoicing; the City train bands were laid out, wearing red uniforms, lined with orange, while they themselves *lined* the road all the way from Temple Bar to Ludgate.

It was forsooth a stirring sight.

Politically and atmospherically these must have been stormy times, and in 1703, broke out the

QUEEN ANNE IS WELCOMED TO THE CITY.

most severe storm ever known in London. It began at ten at night, and kept it up till seven the next morning, just as if it knew exactly the time to come so as to prevent the citizens from going to sleep.

And sleep they didn't.

I don't beleve there were forty winks in the whole metropolis put together on that dreadful night.

Never was such weather before, since, or at any other time.

The sky was black and the wind *blew.*

Over two thousand stacks of chimneys were blown down, paving stones were torn up and hurled into the air, zinc roofings were curled up like brown paper.

The roof of Whitehall was carried away bodily, and with it several foolhardy cats, who, having ventured upon the tiles as usual, found themselves being borne away on the wings of the breeze, whither they knew not.

They were soon whirled out of sight, and never came down again.

The spires of several churches fell to the ground, weathercocks, chimney-pots, and unattached bricks flew about in all directions, windows were torn out of their frames, and the glass blown to atoms by the mere action of the wind, and strong party walls fell down as if they had been built of cards.

Ships, barges and boats on the river were capsized or blown on to the land, and their owners compelled to take refuge in any public-house that sold good liquor.

In short such a breeze was never known before, and it must have been a terrible *blow* to many people, for no less than two millions' worth of property was destroyed in London alone.

———

LI.

MORE EVENTS, AND SUCH LIKE.

I WILL leave you to guess how many ships were wrecked, and how many brave tars wished themselves safely back at Wapping Old Stairs.

It was no use to provide ginger lozenges or camomile tea as a remedy for *the wind*.

It was far too violent for that, nor would any amount of peppermint *drops* make the wind *drop*.

The storm didn't even spare the sacred home of royalty.

The queen herself, as an Irish chronicler said, didn't go to sleep all night, and *even then she woke up several times*, while some of the sentinels outside St. James's Palace suddenly had *tiles* on their heads (blown off the roof), instead of their usual helmets.

About this time, among other events, several insurance offices were established; the original Vauxhall tea-gardens first started, and the City watch re-organised; 583 watchmen were set on, each provided with a lantern, so as to throw some light on the dark deeds of the London robbers, and each carried a halbert, to which the lantern was affixed by a *halbert* chain.

These watchmen resembled the modern policemen in always being on the spot, or at least on *some other* spot, exactly when wanted.

It is needless to say that the damage done to the City by the great storm was not soon repaired, and that the price of bricks went up like a balloon, but notwithstanding, the builders were as busy as bees.

London underwent considerable extension in this reign, in fact seemed to stretch itself out in all directions, like india-rubber.

Bedford Row, Hatton Garden, and various other picturesque spots, were entirely re-organised.

Saffron Hill, in our days the favourite *rendezvous* of organ-grinders, was at that time a rather nice place, thickly planted with saffron trees, upon whose luxuriant branches the mellifluous lady-bird poured forth her enchanting strain.

Alas! how great the change. Nowadays, in going through Saffron Hill, the traveller finds it necessary to hold his nose, open his eyes, and button up his pockets.

Yet here a bishop's palace once stood, and the same may be said of Ely Place, where, of old, his grace of Ely lived in a perfect *Ely*-sium.

At last, however, he found such an extraordinary number of eels on the premises—bred in the neighbouring ditches—that they became quite a nuisance, and the bishop declared that he couldn't stay in such an *Eely place* any longer.

Among other improvements in London, Golden Square was built, some say of pure gold, but we are inclined to think it was only plated, and it has certainly been quite rubbed off by time, for there isn't much sign of the precious metal lying about there now.

St. James's Palace and Park still kept high in the royal favour, and Constitution Hill became the queen's favourite place wherein to take a constitutional.

Among other events—

> "A heavy duty now was laid on coals,
> And from the proceeds churches built in shoals"

all over London.

Lamps on posts were now first used, instead of the old style of swinging lanterns to a chain slung across the streets; and these nice new lamp globes afforded the street boys excellent opportunities for a shy, of which they were not *shy* to avail themselves.

Parish engines were also first instituted, and the firemen of London became almost as great favourites as the watermen.

The reign of Queen Anne is usually spoken of as the Augustan Era, after Augustus, the Roman emperor, who lived nearly two thousand years before, and consequently hadn't much to do with it.

It was certainly an age of great men, for then lived the renowned Duke of Marlborough, who won so many victories over the French that he couldn't count them up; also Lord Go*dolphin*, a big *fish* in the political world.

Then it was that there flourished Richard *Savage*, who was so awfully *wild*, you know, in fact, an ancestor of the present Baron *Wilde* (?); then did Sir Richard *Steele* do wonders with his *quill*; then did *Pope* the poet rise into *pope*-ularity; then did Mat Prior prove himself a *pryer* into state affairs, and a good diplo-*mat;* then did *Locke* find a key to the Human Understanding, and *Newton* prove that he *knew a ton* at least of the heaviest learning.

Last, but not least, was the celebrated Dean *Swift*, who was so *swift* at writing, that it was said he got through all "Gulliver's Travels" without taking his pen off the paper, *except at intervals;* and to this we must add Add-ison, the acute "Spectator," who first introduced us to that "fine old English gentleman," Sir Roger de Coverley.

Nor was the great architectural genius, Sir Christopher Wren, dead yet, by any means.

He only finished St. Paul's in 1710, after having been

hard at it for twenty-five years, and even then it wasn't finished.

The dome, for all it looks so overwhelming, is only lath and plaster, and if a lot of stout men went up it together, or if two earthquakes came at once, or anything of that sort, there is no knowing what might or might not be the consequence.

———

LII.

SAME SUBJECT, ONLY MORE SO.

THAT reminds me of another historical event.

We have all heard of the Gunpowder Plot, and also of the Meal Tub Plot, and now there was another conspiracy called the Screw Plot.

The object was privately to unfasten the iron bolts or screws from the top of St. Paul's Cathedral, so that when the queen came to church the dome should fall in, and her majesty be *domed* to death.

This screw plot naturally *rivetted* the public attention for some time, for things were so unsettled, what with the Pretender, and the Whigs and Tories, and what not, that most people agreed there was a *screw loose* somewhere, if not in St. Paul's.

However, the plot turned out a mere hoax, and Queen Anne wasn't dead yet.

Poor old Newgate really did fall down in this reign, at least, partly, for the stone lion and unicorn—animals weighing about half a ton each—fell off their perches, with such force that it would have rather shaken the system of anybody who might have been walking underneath.

As it was, the huge mass tore up the pavement, and buried itself in the ground, quite out of sight.

In 1709, a certain Dr. Sacheverel made himself an emphatic nuisance by preaching against the government, in sermons so long that many of the congregation fainted through sheer exhaustion, and had to be carried out.

He was tried for high treason, but the law was not so cheap, rapid, and satisfactory as it is in our days, and consequently his trial dragged on till it promised to be as long as his sermons.

At last the public declared themselves sick of it, and threatened if it lasted much longer, they would break into the Bank, the Houses of Parliament and St. James's Palace, lynch the Lord Chancellor, and play the very Charles Dickens with everything.

The commotion, like the Duke of Marlborough, *became general*, and even the bakers resolved to follow the example of their own yeast, and *rise*.

The volunteers were called out, together with the regulars, foot and horse, and people began to look out for lively times in the city.

However, it was all settled by the rebellious doctor being found guilty and sentenced to be suspended, not from a rope, but from his clerical office.

Shortly after a sensation was created by the arrival in London of four Red Indian kings, feathers, war paint, tattoo, tomahawks, wampum belts, and all the rest of it.

They were introduced to the queen, and shown all the sights of the town, though they were in themselves a *sight* more interesting than all the other lions in London.

The tawny chiefs answered to the interesting names of Chuck-ah-lar-oo, Hoh-kippo-kewang-ke-fum, Burrio-boo-le-gar, and Skinno-ma-linka-lee.

Their lives must have been a perpetual joy.

Eight hundred hackney coaches were licensed in 1712, and they were so strictly looked after that the poor oppressed drivers were never allowed to charge just as much as they liked, which is the proud privilege of our cabmen now-a-days.

Two hundred sedan chairs were likewise set going.

You are aware that a sedan was a kind of box without wheels, with poles attached.

One of the bearers took hold of the southern pole, and another of the north, and carried you along as smoothly as skating.

Ladies used to go out to parties in this style, especially if they couldn't afford a carriage.

These chairs originally came from Sedan, and were just the thing for people of *Sedan*-tary habits.

In those days, and a good many days before, it was the custom for our monarchs to Touch for the Evil, a complaint which it was supposed would disappear like magic if the sovereign laid hands on the patient.

Charles II. is said to have touched 2,400 people in four years after his Restoration, though, whether this resulted always in *their* restoration (to health) we don't know.

They used to wait for him in shoals at St. Paul's Cathedral, so that he might touch them as he came out.

It must have been a *touching* spectacle, eh?

William III. was not above humouring this little whim, though, as a man of sense, he must have known it to be all nonsense.

Queen Anne was the last to " touch " for the evil, and this

sort of mesmerism is now only used by quack doctors, and such like.

It is with extreme regret that we now have to record the death of Queen Anne, which took place in the autumn of the year 1714.

For some time her majesty's constitution had been so damaged that she could no longer be considered a constitutional sovereign.

Her fate, even at this distance, deserves a tear.

She was the last of the Stuarts, though her brother, styled the Pretender, might have succeeded her had he *succeeded* in seeing her in time.

Queen Anne left no family, though, as she had seventeen children (who died), it wasn't her fault.

Her character was good, and if she wasn't altogether as clever as Elizabeth, she knew where the clever men were to be got hold of.

She would have been a better ruler if she hadn't let the Duke and Duchess of Marlborough *rule her* so much.

Anne is said to have been rather too addicted to anti-teetotal beverages, but I don't believe it, or even if so, what has that to do with the history of London?

There are many statues of Queen Anne about the metropolis, especially that one which stands in St. Paul's churchyard, to delight the eyes of the weary traveller.

The royal nose is rather dilapidated, and her majesty looks altogether like those respectable laundresses, who are always advertising that they " want washing."*

The application of a mop and pail of water would make Queen Anne shine out again in all her pristine beauty and magnificence.

---

* "WASHING WANTED, by a respectable laundress."—*See Daily Papers.*

She holds in her hand what is intended for the orb of regal sway, but which at present, looks rather like a pumpkin that has been dipped in the mud.

She is dressed in royal robes, as is usual in her portraits, but with regard to the costume of every-day life it was very much the same as in the time of King William.

Ladies still followed up French fashions as close as their little lapdogs followed them.

Tie-wigs for gentlemen were introduced.

Stockings were worn rolled up over the knee; the wrists of the beaux, like their tempers, were sometimes very much *ruffled*, and sleeves were worn so short that if the tailor happened to send home a coat without any, it was not noticed; beyond this, the fashions underwent little change.

Talking of *little change*, it was for a long time supposed that Queen Anne's farthings were so rare as to be worth quite a fortune; that if you chanced upon one you were almost as lucky as Sinbad when he found the Valley of Diamonds.

Once a man travelled all the way from the north of England, and another from the south, each taking one of these precious farthings to sell in London at a splendid price.

Another man left his son a Queen Anne's farthing instead of a £500 legacy.

All these unfortunate parties found themselves sold, for in reality these farthing are nothing like so rare as was thought, and if you get a few shillings for one, you may count yourselves among the lucky ones.

So, coin collectors, beware; "all that glitters is not gold," and the same sage remark applies to copper.

———

LIII.

BEGINNING OF THE GRAND GEORGIAN ERA—MAGNIFICENT DOINGS.

AN act of settlement having settled the Pretender altogether—at least it was hoped so—George Louis, Elector of Hanover, being electable to the English throne, and (*d*)*electable* to many of the English people, came over here to reign over us.

All the arguments in the world couldn't prove him to be an English monarch, since he had been born abroad, and was as thoroughly German as a real meerschaum pipe or a cheap concertina.

King George entered London on September 20, 1714, was met by the lord mayor, Sir Peter King, and the two kings went on in grand procession to St. James's Palace.

At the first meeting the City authorities presented their new monarch with the following loyal and sublime address:—

" Most dreadfully high and mighty sovereign lord king.— We, the lord mayor, aldermen, and common councillors of the good City of London, and the most humble and insignificant of your majesty's subjects, crave that your majesty will pardon us if we fail to express adequately the ecstatic bliss, heavenly felicity, and thrilling delight which your most gracious arrival causes us.   The very first sight of your majesty's angelic physiognomy made our souls leap sky-high with joy, and every step your majesty makes leads your majesty further and deeper into the heart of a loyal, brave and enlightened metropolis!"

To which his most gracious, but decidedly German majesty replied—

"Meinherrin and milords Eengleesh, I gannot egsbress the gradest blezzure I veel to zee thus this grade and disdinguished gumpany. *Ich bin sehr glucklich*—I mean, I am ver' 'appy and ver' proud thus to gome to be king off England.   Blezz you, mine children.   I vill be unto you like your own varther."

Despite this exchange of compliments, and this most tender reply, King George's reception wasn't quite so satisfactory with everybody.

Some of those depraved individuals whose motto was "England for the English and no Germans!" mobbed the new king when he went to "dissolf Barliments," as he called it, and made deprecating allusions to German sauerkraut and German sausages, and had the still greater audacity to mimic his majesty's broken English.

The sight of such a swarm of grafs, herzogs, meinherrs, madames and frauleins, as came over with the king's court, was rather displeasing to many of the citizens, and when they began to hiss them, his majesty, unable to stand it any longer, popped his head out of the carriage window, and said—

"Mein goot peoples, vat for you go hi-sh-sh-sh! zo? You should know dat we gome over here vor your own goods."

He meant that he and his followers had come to this country from a benevolent desire to benefit the English nation, but the individual who led the mob pretended to understand it very differently.

"Ha! ha! Our own *goods!*—yes, and chattels, too, let alone our money ; for you and your meinheers will get plenty of all of them, and feather your nests pretty warmly, I warrant !"

But why should we repeat the treasonable utterances of the disloyal few ?

A large majority, particularly those who had been promised nice little situations under the new government, were as staunch as the needle to the pole, and shouted—

"Hurrah for King George !" till their throats were as dry as the interior of a baker's oven.

In 1715 two things broke out, an extensive fire and a Jacobite rebellion, the latter being considered by far the worse of the two.

No sooner had King George begun trying to master the English language than he felt himself called upon to master the Scotch.

For the Pretender, *alias* James III., had landed and stirred up insubordination in the bonny north, and was expecting soon to pay London a visit.

Here was a state of things !

The metropolis was in commotion.

Troops were called out, the City watch doubled, and nervous old ladies had extra fastenings put to their houses.

On the other hand, the members of the secret Jacobite clubs in London rejoiced, of course.

They had been active in getting up the affair, and over their cups of *green tea*, had been long hatching this new *gunpowder* plot, not against King James, as Guy Fawkes's was, but in his favour.

They used to drink the health of the king "Over the

water," viz., in France, and those who liked stronger liquor used to do it over the *brandy* and water.

It was dangerous in those times to confess that your favourite name for a king began with a J. instead of a G.

However, the Pretender never came to London after all.

The Duke of Cumberland, setting out to meet him, succeeded in giving him a very extensive check, which wasn't quite as profitable to him as a *cheque* on the London and County Bank.

In fact, he lost more than he gained over it.

James III. had to give in, and his kingship was for the time utterly wrecked.

He had to go back to France rather quicker than he came, with a flea in his ear, and a price on his head.

There is no doubt that if he had been caught, the old Pretender would have become *the hung* (the young) Pretender as well.

Yet for about fifty years, the Jacobites were a sort of *bites* almost as much feared by the government as the bites of mad dogs, and when the police broke into their little clubs, there was a rare piece of work.

The clubs were mostly held in coffee-houses which were the " pubs " of the period, and were at this time in full flourish.

Every class had its own especial.

Noblemen's *heirs* went to the *Whigs'* coffee-house ; tailors to *Button's ;* lawyers to *Will's* in Great Russell Street ; butchers to *Old Slaughter's ;* rustics went to *Giles' ; green* people went to *Forrest's ;* spotless virtuous beings were to be found at *White's ;* old maids of the tabby-cat order used to go and scandalise each other at *Tom's ;* and by the rules of contrary, young people went to the *Old Man's* coffee-house ; while people over sixty mostly put up at *Child's.*

It was in honour of the Duke of Cumberland's victory over the Pretender that Tom Dogget put up his coat and badge to be rowed for every first of August.

Tom was an actor and an Irishman, with the "rale Cork brogue into him."

"He danced like a fairy and sang like a bird."

He first came out at Bartholomew Fair, and got on to the regular stage in the latter *stage* of his career.

———

LIV.

EVENTS, AND THINGS OF THAT SORT.

TOM DOGGET could act anything, from Old Mother Hubbard to Lord Foppington, and his acting was funny enough to draw laughter from a wooden image.

Of course it drew money as well, and so Tom retired on a considerable pittance.

The waterman's prize was to be an orange coat and a silver badge with a white horse, the arms of Hanover, on it.

Whichever waterman won the badge some facetious persons used to nickname the *badger*, but this was only one of their atrocious jokes.

The custom goes on still, and a particularly fine sight it is from the bridge, only mind you don't get your pocket picked when you are looking on.

Sometimes the tide is against them, and then we should not be (*h*)*erring* to call it a *hard row*, and admire how he-*row*-ically they get through it.

All honour to Dogget, his coat, and his badge !

Up to this time the lord mayor used to go on horseback in his processions, but now, thinking himself too great a man for one horse, he started a coach and four.

Further on, the number got to be six, and modern lord mayors, not contented even with this, have increased the number to half a dozen.

It used to be the fashion, when the sovereign went to dine with the lord mayor, to meet the lady mayoress on the steps, and bestow a kiss upon her ladyship's roseate check.

BIRD'S EYE VIEW OF A LONDON JACOBITE CLUB.

(*See page* 270.)

Queen Anne first broke through the custom, and King George didn't know whether to carry it on or not.

Her ladyship of the year 1715 was not quite as beautiful for ever as Madame Rachael's customers, nor as young as she had been twenty years before.

However, there she stood right in the king's way, with her countenance fixed exactly at the right angle on the

Guildhall steps, and the king was undecided what steps to take.

It is even said that she had decorated her head with a mistletoe bough, by way of a still more forcible reminder of the good old custom.

He therefore resigned himself to his fate, and shutting his eyes, performed the ceremony with as much grace as a stout German of fifty-four could manage it.

His heart gave quite a bound of relief when it was over.

WOMAN'S RIGHTS IN 1738.—PERILOUS POSITION OF THE LORD CHANCELLOR.—(*See page* 279.)

The queen followed next, and the lady mayoress naturally expected the high honour to be repeated, but her majesty disapproved of such customs, and murmuring—"None of *your* cheek for me," passed on.

Her ladyship thereupon considered herself insulted, and began "letting on" in a style that proved how true it was that she had come originally from the neighbourhood of Billingsgate.

"Here, boy," she said to her page, "hold my *bucket* (bouquet?). I shall be off. If I ain't as good as a parcel of imperant German madams, it's a pretty state of things, and no mistake."

So saying, she flounced into the house, and even declined to adorn the banquet with her distinguished presence.

In 1715, as we have said, there was a considerable fire in London, that did as much damage as it could, and was very much "put out" because it couldn't do ever so much more.

By way of compensation for so much warmth, there was a great frost on the Thames next year, and so, in turn, by way of keeping themselves warm, the Whigs and Tories got up mutual riots in the streets, broke into a meeting-place called the Mug-house, and wouldn't be dispersed till the military put in an appearance.

The Riot Act was read in a loud voice.

———

LV.

ABOUT BUBBLE COMPANIES, PANTOMIMES, AND OTHER BOTANICAL SUBJECTS.

IN 1720, London was convulsed, not with laughter or earthquakes, but by the celebrated South Sea Bubble.

This was a company started to lend money to the Spaniards at 600 per cent., *if they could be induced to pay it.*

The prospectus was so beautifully got up that it took amazingly.

Everybody began investing their " little all " with the idea of making a *big* haul out of it.

They expected to make their fortunes rapidly, ordered expensive goods on credit, and began to cut all their poorer friends.

South Sea Stock went up to 1100 per cent.—a height no *stock* or even *wallflower* in our garden ever reached.

London was all excitement.

Nothing was talked of but the grand things that would be done when the ship came home from the West Indies, laden down to the water's edge and bursting out of her very portholes with the riches of Mexico and Peru.

But alas ! in a very short time these golden visions were broken like eggshells, the value of stock came down with a run, and the whole affair turned out a swindle, as neat as brandy before it is watered.

On arriving at the office of the company, a crowd of speculators found the place shut up, and " Ha, ha ! Sold again, and *we've* got the money," written on the door.

They broke in, but found that the directors had vanished, and all the cash-boxes with them.

Hundreds were ruined, people of all ages, sorts, and sexes, were engulfed in a common smash ; many a child of six weeks old found, on looking over his account-book, that he was thousands to the bad, and vast numbers of persons formerly rolling in wealth had now to roll in poverty.

The government took up the affair—and the police took up the directors.

Two millions were recovered, but that was hardly three-quarters of nothing in the pound.

Several other grand specs. started on the same principle—

or rather want of principle—turned out just as successful, and bankruptcy became as common a complaint as influenza.

Moral—Never lend money at a higher rate than you can get.

The British Drama now began to look up.

What was then called " the theatre in Drury Lane, Covent Garden," was established in 1719, and long since then this one establishment has been knocked into two.

The "ltttle theatre in the Haymarket" also opened its doors under Sam Foote, somewhere about 1721.

Foote was one day out hunting, when he happened to break his leg, and remained a lame Foote all his life.

However, the accident was not altogether a false step, for the Duke of York, a kind prince, who was present, promised that, by way of salve for the broken leg, he would leave Foote a *legacy*.

However, as a present *standing* in the world and a *footing* in society were of much more consequence to Foote just then, he was presented instead with the full patent and monopoly of the Haymarket Theatre.

It was opened accordingly, and filled so immensely that the house burst—but it was only into fits of laughter.

At this period of our history pantomime was instituted.

The first harlequinade was produced on Boxing Day, 1717, by John Rich ; such a funny Harlequin that had you seen him, you would have declared that he really *was* Rich.

Columbine came over some time before, Pantaloon followed, and with him came our old friend Clown, who, though only fourth fiddle at first, gradually worked his way up to the front rank in pantomime, where he still wields his red-hot poker and string of sausages, to the delight of the juveniles.

About this time the notorious Jack Sheppard (of whom more anon) was the terror of London.

George 1., who ruled on to the year 1727, wasn't so bad a king.

He did all the good he could, especially for himself and his German cronies, and the welfare of the English nation was only next in importance, as he thought, to that of his beloved fatherland.

He confessed himself a *plain* man, which he certainly was.

Some called him downright ugly.

We refrain, however, from going as far as that.

In temper he was *grave*, for his father was *Ernest*, and he took after him.

Another thing which he took after his father was snuff in considerable quantities, and another thing which he couldn't take at all was a joke.

He was of moderate size, all but his wig, which was enormous.

He stuck to his friends much closer than ever the Stuarts did, even when he couldn't get anything out of them.

We have seen that he spoke broken English when he first came over here, and never was able to mend it properly afterwards.

His queen, Sophia of Zell, to whom he was not very *zell*ous in his affection, didn't grace our metropolis very often.

LVI.

THE LADIES AND THE LORDS, WITH OTHER DIVERTING PARTICULARS.

RARE doings went on one day in 1738 at the House of Lords, when the first Woman's Rights agitation ever mentioned in history broke out.

It appears that, considering that the spectators' galleries were limited, and the ladies, with the big hoops then fashionable, took up a great deal of room, it was made a rule that they must not be allowed to come in.

Accordingly, when next a lot of them came to listen to the debates as usual, the chancellor said he was very sorry, but there was no admittance except on business.

The words had barely issued from his lips ere a howl of execration (of course in a ladylike strain) arose, and a threatening attitude was assumed by all.

No words that ever were invented would give any idea of the inward trepidation felt by Sir William Saunders, lord chancellor, in his critical position.

His soul trembled beneath his official robe, his teeth

knocked together, and his heart sank almost into the pocket of his long waistcoat with the intensity of his fear.

But he proceeded, in his sternest, judicial voice—

"Yes, ladies, it is my painful duty to inform you that the question of right of entry having been lately canvassed at the High Court of Sequestration, it has been decided, after a lengthened discussion, that the act 25th Henry VIII., Chapter 503, applying to this case, is rescinded by a special clause in the statute of Habeas Corpus, which is equivalent to a decree *nisi*. So you see it is impossible I can let you in."

"What do you mean by that, sir ?" exclaimed the Duchess of Queensberry, who led the fair squadron. "We have always been accustomed to come in here when we please, and come in we will, spite of all the trumpery lawyers in the universe. Make way there, or——"

Her grace raised her fan to knock over the chancellor, who being a little man, looked up at her with some terror, and dodged the weapon as well as he could. But still he heroically repeated—

"I won't."

"You won't !" said the duchess. "Very well then ; you'll have to stand a siege, for we mean to keep here night and day, till the door's opened."

"And we mean to keep the door shut till you go away. So raise the siege, or we'll starve you out."

Well, will you believe it, those resolute ladies, two dozen of them, the least of whom was a baronetess, remained outside that door without any refreshments, for over five hours !

Nothing would induce them to give in.

They kept up the siege gloriously.

They proved themselves excellent *foot* soldiers by the way in which they kicked at the door.

They knocked at it, rapped at it, rattled the lock, and expressed their indignation one after another through the keyhole.

The lords couldn't hear themselves speak, and were so agitated that they repealed the law of "a man may not murder his grandmother" by mistake, and made it obligatory to do so.

The row outside was deafening.

At last it suddenly lulled and died away into a dead and buried silence.

"We've conquered at last," exclaimed the lord chancellor, in triumph. "They have gone away. I thought they couldn't keep it up all this time. And now we may venture to open the door, for, to tell the truth, it's past my dinner time, and I'm getting hungry."

And were the ladies gone after all? Ne'er a bit of it.

The noble duchess had thought of a capital dodge.

She told her companions to be as mute as mice for half an hour, and the lords, hearing no sound, would suppose they had gone, naturally concluding that for twenty-five women all to be silent for half an hour at a stretch would be sheerly impossible. The plan succeeded.

The door was opened at last, and instantly all the fair besiegers rushed in a body into the house, and perched themselves in the very front rows of the spectators' seats.

O resolution of woman!

There they sat till eleven o'clock at night, listening to every word of the debates, and often commenting on them in no complimentary terms.

From that day forth there has always been a place reserved in the house for lady spectators; and it is most appropriately called a *gallery*.

LVII.

THE SAME EXCITING SUBJECT CONTINUED WITH OTHERS.

IN 1740 there was a great frost on the Thames, during which streets of shops were built on the ice.

Jolly young watermen began to be jolly cold, and took to driving coaches along the ice instead of their trim-built wherries.

The frost gave everbody a nip, and all who could afford it got a nip of brandy as a remedy.

THE FASHIONS—PALL MALL IN 1750—(*See page* 282)

Nobody was seen without skates, and when once fastened they were frozen to the feet, and couldn't be got off again all the rest of the winter.

The most remarkable part of the affair was that it was not until a thaw came that the ice melted.

Scientific men couldn't make it out.

Great improvements were made in London now.

New parishes were formed, new beadles appointed.

Fleet Ditch was filled up, and a general lighting took place ; even the cats were allowed *lights.*

The houses on London Bridge, which had got so old and shaky that it was dangerous to sneeze in them, were taken down and sold for firewood.

Westminster Bridge and the Society of Arts were inaugurated, and the present Mansion House built at a cost of £42,628 18s. 8d.—especially 8d.

Captain Coram, an old *salt,* whom we ought always to keep *fresh* in our memories, built the Foundling Hospital ; and Ironmongers' Hall, Fishmongers' Hall, and Scavengers' Hall, and Rogues' Hall began to rear their imposing heads.

In 1753 the British Museum was raised by subscription, and White's club house was *razed* by fire.

In the latter catastrophe, such inveterate gamblers were the club men, that, fire or no fire, they still fired away at their game ; and it was only when the table had caught alight, and the banknotes were beginning to frizzle up in the devouring element that they thought it time to go.

Costume under the early Georges had reached a *g(e)orge*ous pitch of magnificence.

Powder and patch, wigs and high-heeled boots, were rampant and triumphant.

In fact, the dandies and fine madams of the time got themselves up very much like those figures we often see in stone china.

Putting the ladies first, as in duty bound, their dresses were so stiff with brocade and other rich ornamental work, that they could not only stand upright when off, but even walk about by themselves.

Their tub-hoops were a size larger than most water-butts,

and so covered with horticultural and verdant decorations, that the wearers looked like Jacks-in-the-green.

Dresses were worn so lengthy, that the poor scavengers complained that "they'd got no work to do," for now ladies did their own sweeping.

The hair was worn powdered, and built up in the form of a pumpkin or a beehive, only of course much bigger, and so plastered with jewellery, that the fair fashionables looked as if they had first covered their heads with cement, and then dipped them into a bag of diamonds.

Talking of bags, these majestic dames wore sacques, which were introduced here from *Saxe*-Coburg, and then, what with puffs and puckers, flounces and furbelows, frizzles and ruffles, cuffs and muffs, long hanging sleeves, and long stays, the life of a fashionable lady was rendered as miserable as she could possibly desire.

Mob-caps were in favour, so were fly-caps, so called because they were ready to fly off at any moment.

Hoods of scarlet or other hues *used* to be much worn, especially on horseback, so that there were plenty of Little Red Riding Hoods, and big ones too.

The tight lacing was something awful.

Some ladies actually looked to be gliding about in two separate halves, their waists being entirely invisible.

Boots had heels so high, that it was said some ladies had to go up a ladder to put them on, and down a flight of steps to get them off again.

Black court plaister patches were still stuck on to the face, and on the tip of the nose especially must have looked delightful.

As to the beaux, they were dazzlingly got up; and if fine feathers didn't make fine birds in those days, it wasn't their fault.

The wigs were of all shapes, and some of no shape at all.

One sort had one lock hanging to it almost as long and heavy as " Locke on the Human Understanding."

Another sort of wigs were like Turkish sheeps tails, and must have made the wearers look very sheepish.

Bag-wigs were worn so large that you might as well " go home and put your head in a bag " at once.

Then there were the Ranelagh wig, the Ramilies wig, the nightcap wig, the riding wig, cauliflower wig, tie wig, scratch wig, bob wig, and frizzle wig, not to mention the *ear*-wig, which was the most lively-looking of them all.

As for the coats, they were square cut and Dutch waisted, turned up with silk, embroidered and laced, and sprigged, and embossed within an inch of their lives.

Flowers were set all over them, which came up beautifully on a dark background.

All this made the coats as stiff as buckram, and made the price pretty stiff, too, you may be sure.

At the marriage of the Prince of Wales some of the richer noblemen wore velvet or gold brocaded tissue, running to the tune of about £500 a suit.

George II. came out grandly on the same occasion, wearing gold brocade turned up with silk, and a high nose turned up with contempt.

One good point about King George was that he would only wear real British-made clothes.

" None of your Vrench vashions here," said he. " Noding is so goot as de British manuvacter."

You see that, though this monarch used to boast " I speege Engleesh berry bell," he wasn't quite up to the accent.

LVIII.

CONCERNING COSTUMES, CUSTOMS, CONJURORS, AND CONSPIRATORS.

L ARGE cocked hats still went on *ahead*, or rather on a great many heads, and in particular those with the Cumberland cock (so called from the Duke of Cumberland, a great fighting cock about this time).

Some hats were cocked on one side, some on the other, and some were cocked all round, giving the wearer of them a very cocky appearance.

Boots were still buckled, and very stout men who couldn't see their feet, ran a chance of getting their buckles stolen, if valuable.

Sedan chairs still continued to be the order of the day with fashionable folks, who took to keeping their own chairs, beautifully adorned and emblazoned with the family arms.

They certainly came cheaper than carriages, and took you along as smoothly as a garden roller over a gravel walk; the only thing to be feared was that the bearers might be drunk, or inclined to be up to their larks; and to be turned over in your sedan, or left in the middle of the road, or set down under a rain spout on a pouring day, was what Pat would call " moighty unconvanient."

You remember the Irishman who thought he would try a sedan, and they gave him one with the bottom out, so that he declared that only for the look of the thing, it wasn't much better than walking.

Ladies had to have the tops thrown back when they went out to fashionable meetings, the head-dresses being so lofty.

The longest journey in one of these machines was that of one of the princesses, who, being told by her father to go to Bath, went in a sedan.

It took her a week.

The manners of the Georgian age were stiff, and the customs not always agreeable.

Gambling went on at an awful rate.

Everybody gambled, from a duke to a dustman, and even ladies of quality kept gaming-houses.

The king thought nothing of card-playing in public, some times staking his only crown on the event.

Princesses of the blood royal, aged three and a half years, often lost their dolls at five-handed whist, and cats might be seen risking their little all at cats'-cradle.

All kinds of stakes, beef steaks especially, were played for, and some people made it a rule never to rise from the table till they were forcibly kicked out for cheating.

Among the noted belles of the Georgian era there were several of high pretensions, but none surpassed the Viscountess of Coventry, save and except her sister, the Duchess of Hamilton.

So striking was her beauty that one glance of her eye went straight to its mark like an electric shock.

Wherever she lived, palpitation, ossification, and other diseases of the heart became epidemic.

Wherever she went she was mobbed by crowds, who thronged at windows and doors, climbed up lamp-posts, and put themselves in peril of their lives to catch even the slightest glance of her beauteous physiognomy.

If it hadn't been for the guard of military that surrounded her, she would soon have been either kissed to death or suffocated with bouquets.

Whenever she went to a theatre the attraction was so great that the house was sure to be crammed with spectators, eager to bask in the sunshine of her angelic gaze, and it wasn't necessary to have any performance on the stage at all.

Seven hundred people sat up all night at an inn in Worcestershire, so as as to have the supreme felicity of seeing the duchess get into her post-chaise in the morning.

The shoemaker who manufactured her shoes made three times their value beforehand by showing them at a shilling a pair to eager spectators; no bad dodge in a commercial sense, let me tell you.

It was a rare treat to see the folks assembled in gala dress in Vauxhall or Ranelagh.

These gardens were the places where the flowers of fashions came out and flourished most luxuriantly.

Ranelagh was opened in 1742, and a few years afterwards, peace being concluded with France, the proprietors concluded that they would celebrate the event by a grand jubilee.

Tents, flags, streamers, fireworks, waterworks, boats, barges, and gondolas were set going like fun.

Maypoles were danced round, air-balloons sent up, cannons boomed, bonfires blazed.

All was pipes and patriotism—beer and benevolence.

Every kind of masquerade, harlequinade, lemonade, and other aids to festivity, were brought into action.

The king, queen, princes, and lords honoured the affair with their presence, and the king was so well disguised that some people thought he was a pickpocket, and others said to him—

" Here, you rascally waiter, how long am I to wait for that hot water ?"

Vauxhall was so named from some circumstance over which we have no control.

It was for a long time known as Spring Gardens, till the name was altered one summer.

In 1732 a Mr. Tyers took the gardens, and to his un-*tyer*-ing energy the prosperity of the place was en-*tyer*-ly owing.

When Frederick Prince of Wales came with four hundred attendants in masks for an evening spree, the fortune of the gardens was made.

Everybody thronged there to see the Prince of Wales, and, even if they couldn't get near enough to see himself, they could have a good look at his carriage and go home happy with the intention of coming again.

An organ was set up in the middle of the gardens with an organ-grinder attached, and both wound up to concert pitch.

Artificial ruins of cut cork were fixed up, and a cascade of real glass made as near an approach to wild nature as could be done for the money.

The celebrated Vauxhall slices of ham were now first instituted by an experienced cutter, who boasted that he could cut them so thin as to cover the whole garden (eleven acres) from one ham.

People with good eyes could easily read print through these slices, and took a dozen sandwiches to get the slightest taste of ham into the mouth !

LVIII.—(*Continued.*)

RANELAGH GARDENS were still worse for hungry people, because they didn't pretend to give you anything to eat at all, only tea and coffee, and the fashionables, after drinking a few cups of coffee in the open air, usually left the grounds.

Marylebone Gardens (the name has been much improved in our time, and is now pronounced "marrer-bun") was another favoured metropolitan resort.

AWKWARD MEETING BETWEEN THE YOUNG PRETENDER AND GEORGE II.—(*See page* 292.)

No. 10.

The bright stars of fashion went there in such numbers that no lamps were required.

It was here that old King George II., who was fast losing whatever common sense he had, went down on his knees on the gravel walk to declare his love to Miss Chudleigh, a maid of honour so angelic that people said she looked only fit to be sent off to Heaven by the earliest conveyance.

His majesty's wig fell off in the earnestness of his declaration, and while he was picking it up, the lady had resumed her mask and was gone.

Some of the conjurors, vaulters, and acrobats that exhibited in these gardens were really wonderful.

One of them could stand on one leg, or even no legs at all, could dislocate himself piece by piece, and then put himself together again, tie himself into three knots at a time, kick the back of his own head with his heels, roll himself out flat like the dough for a pie-crust, or stretch himself out into a line twelve feet long.

Anyone could scarcely believe all this did we not possess evidence which no solicitor-general could knock over.

The humbler folks meanwhile had their London fairs, as it was only fair they should.

Smithfield and Southwark Fairs, and especially Bartholomew Fair, were the most popular and populous.

"Old Bartlemy" was a rare place for fun.

Started in Henry I.'s reign, it was not put a stop to until seventeen years ago—a tolerably long run.

Here appeared Faux, a noted conjuror and posture maker, who, after tumbling about a good deal, fell upon his feet at last, for he retired with £10,000, and from that time forth had more to do with banks than with *mounte*banks.

When money was tight, or business slack, he used to perform on the *tight* rope and *slack* rope alternately.

He could draw anything, from a cheque to a waggon, and, more than all, could draw the public.

Here, too, appeared Topham, the strong man of Islington.

He was a wonderful fellow; he undertook to pull first against one, and then against two horses, and was so successful, that not only did he pull them over to his side, but pulled them clean in half.

He could break a thick iron wire by just bending his forefinger, lift up a pound weight with his eyelashes, and break an ostrich's egg endwise.

He could bend a kitchen poker by striking it against his arm, and then pull it straight again in a moment.

It is no wonder that by the time the poor fellow was ninety-two, he began to feel the advance of premature age.

He died a few years after, cut off in his prime, a victim to his own strength.

All this time the Jacobites had been keeping quiet, as it looked, but in reality they were always plotting, drinking the health of "Charlie over the water, Charlie over the sea," till at last he really did come over the water.

But prevention is better than cure, and so the Government thought it wise to stop Charlie.

In short, no sooner did they hear that a number of *tartan*-clad warriors had crossed the *Tweed*, and *played* (plaid) the very deuce in those regions, than they sent troops to give them a *check*. Everyone knows the result by this time.

The firm of James III. and Son had to go politically bankrupt, with nothing in the pound, and many of their poor deluded followers were present (by compulsion), at the various executions that took place in London.

In 1750, the young Pretender paid a secret visit to London, calling himself Mr. Smith.

He kept as quiet as he could during his visit.

Once he took a turn in the Mall and met King George, who was taking his morning stroll.

Would he escape recognition ?

The king passed him with merely a slight wink of recognition, which went to his heart.

LIX.

THE ESCAPE—THE HOAX—THE EARTHQUAKE.

GEORGE II. in fact thought he'd let off the Pretender with his head this time, and say nothing about it ; for as the government had already executed about a hundred of the prince's supporters, and killed some two thousand more, King George felt that he could afford to be merciful.

The Pretender, declining the offer of a few conspirators to get up a revolution, went peacefully back to France, congratulating himself that his head was still on his shoulders.

A tolerably good practical joke was played off in 1749, showing that people could be gulled even in these times.

Some noblemen for a game put an advertisement in the papers, stating that a certain distinguished conjuror, who could play tunes on a walking stick, and give farmyard imitations on a fire-shovel, would wind up his miraculous performance by squeezing himself into a quart bottle.

It took immensely.

The theatre was crammed ; but when the money was all paid and the audience all assembled, it appeared as if the conjuror wasn't going to appear at all.

The gallery got impatient, and began cat-calling, and chucking orange-peel about ; the pit and boxes grumbled like tigers at the delay, and at last they all threatened that if much more waiting was to be done, they would begin tearing up the benches.

At last somebody came forward on the stage, and announced that the signor would shortly appear, and if the audience liked to pay *double* prices, they should see him get into a *pint* instead of a quart bottle.

However, as he still didn't show up, the audience shrewdly judged it to be a sell altogether.

So they hissed, groaned, tore up the benches, pulled down the scenes, broke the furniture, and altogether seemed slightly inclined to have it out in damages.

If it hadn't been for the providential arrival of the military, just too late to be any good, there is no doubt that something unpleasant might have occurred.

As it was, there was no mischief done, the theatre was *merely* demolished.

It must have cost a good deal to repair.

Moral—practical jokes don't often pay.

In 1750 a fearful earthquake came over here on a visit.

It caused a great sensation, and made some noise in the world.

Bells began ringing, dogs howling, fish leapt clean out of the water, and the funds went up like a rocket.

A good deal of crockery was broken, and several false teeth shaken out of their owners' heads.

Lord Sherryport, coming home late from a convivial party, declared that he felt the earthquake distinctly; the very ground *rose up* and struck him in the face, and he couldn't find his own latch-key.

Sir Robert Walpole, who was a notoriously late riser, was seen wildly rushing about the streets at five o'clock in the morning, and his friends knew that nothing short of an earthquake could have turned him out of bed at *that* hour.

Nothing but the earthquake was talked of.

Earthquake coats, earthquake hats, boots, and bonnets, were advertised for sale, and of course they were of *loud* and *violent* colours.

One quack doctor (who probably came from *Holloway*) made a grand stroke with his patent earthquake pills, warranted to keep off the shock.

George II. left off his long reign after thirty-three years of it.

He was benevolent, but of an awful temper.

Perhaps the enormous quantities of strong snuff he took got into his system.

When his ministers offended him, he would kick and cuff them right and left, and he was also in the habit, when enraged, of kicking his hat about the room.

To hear him swear in high Dutch was a treat.

He turned his son and heir out of doors, solely because he wanted one of the children christened Heliogabalus, and the prince wouldn't stand it.

After all said and done, however, King George II. is dead now, and we needn't worry him more.

Peace to his periwig!

LX.

PERILS OF THE KING'S HIGHWAY.

STREETS, previous to the middle of the last century, were not exactly like walking down a smooth gravel walk in the garden of Eden.

In the first place, they were so narrow that a man of any breadth was certain to knock his elbow against one side or the other, if not both.

If he happened to be going out to dinner, or for any other reason, dressed in his best clothes, he was pretty sure to run up against a coalheaver or a sweep, the footpath being too narrow to let two pass each other at a time.

In fact, there was hardly any distinction between pavement and roadway at all, and you only knew when you were in the road by being hustled up against the wheel of a cart.

This led to quarrelling and fighting as to which should

take the path, and it generally ended by the weakest going, not to the wall, as the proverb says, but into the kennel.

Even when they took to parting off the path by palings four feet high, matters were not much improved, and it was only like fighting in a narrow ally instead of the open streets.

Besides this, the pavement was obstructed by steps, scrapers, shop boards, glass cases, and hampers, admirably adapted for knocking one's shins against; while overhead, sign boards, barber's poles, and low projecting roofs threatened to come down heavy upon the devoted nob of the pedestrian.

Then the footpath and road alike were mostly of round stones, so awfully knobbly and bumpy that the soberest man in the world could not walk straight on them, unless he walked straight into the puddles and gutters, which meandered like picturesque lakes and rivers down his majesty's highway.

On wet days it was particularly delicious, for the rain spouts poured down beautifully upon the head of each passenger, very much astonishing his cocked hat and feathers, and indeed spoiling his clothes *in toto*.

The carriage-way was so full of ruts that it was like travelling in *Rut*landshire, and even the king was sure to be stuck in the mud on his way to open parliament, unless he had the road made on purpose beforehand.

Not till 1762 was this state of things put a stop to by driving an act of parliament through the streets, and laying down the law and a new pavement at the same time.

Besides this, the number of thieves, footpads, cly-fakers, wipe-grabbers, and high-tobymen in the London streets was something alarming to contemplate.

You could not go to see the pantomime or visit your grandmamma at Christmas without a troop of soldiers to guard you, and a body of watchmen and link-boys to clear the way.

No gentleman could come home from a festive party without being ordered to "Stand and deliver!" and if he was too drunk to *stand*, he had to *deliver* all the same.

This took place even in broad daylight, and to lose one's way in a November fog was to be lost indeed.

When Dr. Johnson, a great Londoner of that day, made his celebrated proposal— "Let us take a walk down Fleet Street," he knew it was a rather dangerous walk to take, but as he was very big and strong—a particularly muscular Christian—and always left his purse at home and took a thick stick instead, the gents of the road were afraid to tackle him.—(*Observe the Initial Illustration on page* 289.)

What with discharged soldiers, sailors, cadgers, crimps and others, there were a good many—or rather a *bad* many —dangerous characters in London at that period, and as no regular police were known, only a lot of doddering old watchmen, who always made it a rule to be asleep when wanted, these desperadoes could do pretty well as they liked.

Some novelists have tried to make heroes of the highwaymen and other thieves of those times ; but it takes a great deal of making, let me tell you, for, in reality, instead of being the fine dashing captains we read of, they were mostly a set of hangdog ruffians, who didn't dare show up in daylight.

The notorious Turpin was a butcher by trade, and Maclean, the "fashionable highwayman," who boasted that he never robbed anybody under a baronet, was only a runaway counterjumper with his creditors after him.

Others were ruined rakes who, having run through their

property and been cut by their friends, had to cut and run altogether, and took to the road because they had nothing else to take to.

Turpin was for a long time the terror of the North Road, and he was always allowed to pass toll free—in the first place, because he jumped over the gates, and next, because the tollgate man, if he asked for the coin, knew he would only get a discharge in full from one of the desperado's pistols.

There once stood an old oak near Finchley which Turpin used to hide behind, ready to pounce out upon his prey, and the trunk was so riddled with shot holes that the greatest *riddle* of all was how he managed to escape the bullets.

As for the celebrated ride to York, it is all a myth, a flam, and an invention, for though there was a road from London to York, Turpin never *rode* it in that short time, any more than the American crew *rowed* from London to New York.

Turpin was had up at last for unnecessarily shooting some poor chickens, who had never done him any harm, which was certainly "murder most *fowl*," and being overtaken by retribution and rope, was "worked off" at York in 1739.

It was very capital punishment, and did for him beautifully.

LXI.

MORE ABOUT THE "GAME OF GRAB," AND THE ROBBERS OF LONDON.

ANOTHER of these miscreants was one named Hawkes, and as of course *hawks* can fly, this particular bird of prey was called the "flying highwayman."

However, when he was taken, it was proved that his wings were not quite strong enough to enable him to fly away, though he did take an *excursion in the air.*

Jack Sheppard was another unmitigated jailbird, and no more like a hero than a tobacconist's Highlander is like a Scotchman.

He was brought up as a carpenter, but instead of sticking to his plane and saw, his hammer and nails, he became *hammerous* of felonious fame, and proceeded to *nail* things that did not belong to him.

He went, as his biography tells us, "from bad to wuss, from wuss to wusser, and from wusser to wust," till he became the leader of scoundreldom, and all the black *sheep* in London followed this *Sheppard.*

Notorious as a prison-breaker as well as a law-breaker, the most unbelievable stories are told of this Jack.

Put into the roundhouse, it is said that he cut through the ceiling with a shilling razor, and got out.

I do not quite believe this, though, razor or not, he certainly did manage to *cut it* somehow.

The next escape was from Newgate, where, they say, having sawed through his ponderous fetters—half a hundred weight at least—he broke through a strong iron door, and a wooden post nine inches thick, scaled a wall twenty-two feet high, and away !

If you think this is rather too much to swallow, take another case, where Jack is represented to have got away from his cell with astonishing *celerity*.

Though fastened to the walls by iron staples, he managed to *file* his chains, *chisel* his jailers, dig through the wall with the broken links, even under the *lynx* eye of the warder, break through about half a dozen strong doors, get over spiked walls, out on to roofs, through inhabited houses, and so clear off.

There are recorded many other escapes, which all escape my memory, but they are all so incredible as to raise a strong suspicion that Jack Sheppard's flights from prison were only *flights* of imagination.

However, they got him safe enough at last, and his only way of escape was into the next world—it was certain that he was hardly *fit* for *this* one.

The well-known thief-taker, Jonathan Wild, was called " the great," and very properly too, for he was the greatest scoundrel that ever lived.

His plan was to enter into leagues with all the thieves and cut-throats for *leagues* round, watch them night and day, share all their plunder, and threaten to hand them over to destruction and the beak if they dared to turn honest.

When this had gone on long enough to get all he could out of them, Jonathan turned them over to the gallows for a big reward.

He was ready to swear black was white, and blue was mahogany colour, if he could get any poor wretch hanged and pocket the accruing bonus.

It is highly gratifying to know that Jonathan fell into his own trap at last, and had a fine opportunity of seeing how he liked it.

Never did the Calcraft of the period perform a more laudable day's work.

One of the last of these gentry was Jack Rann, celebrated as Sixteen-string Jack, but though *Jack ran* pretty quickly in his last chase, he found that all his sixteen strings could not save him from the last string of all, which, on this occasion only, he wore round his neck.

You will see that all the noted highwaymen and other depredators came to the same end—viz., a rope's end.

It was always the old story over again, as Tom Hood sings—

> " So he was tried, and he was hung,
>   (Fit punishment for such)
> At Hangman's *Drop*, and none can say
>   It was a *drop* too much."

Well, luckily, we are entirely rid of all those gentry now, and if any great grandson of Dick Turpin were to try and stop one of our metropolitan trains, he would find himself, as the Yankees would say, doomed to everlasting smash in half no time.

Certainly those were terrible hanging days.

It did not matter which of the commandments people

broke, or even whether they broke any at all, they were strung up all the same.

For a dozen or twenty men to be hanged each Monday morning was a matter of course, and to be as regularly expected as one's breakfast.

It must have been a splendid time for rope manufacturers, and a particularly busy time for John Ketch, Esq., who had to engage ever so many assistants to help him, besides a new "drop" made on an improved principle.

Some of the great suburban highways—Edgware Road, for instance—were thickly planted with rows of gallows trees, and if any of them were cut down, it was thought to spoil the view very much.

Gibbets were also stationed all along the Thames' bank, and added materially to the beauty of our prospect.

Our grandfathers—and grandmothers too, for that matter —were of a great deal stronger nerve than we are, and instead of being shocked at all this, considered it a pleasant little excitement.

Hanging was thought nothing of.

Why, in those days there used to be rich *hangings* even in the king's bedchamber, and a lot of "lardydardy" fellows used to *hang* about the royal court.

An execution was looked upon as the finest sight in the world, and ladies used to go in thousands, and take front reserved seats opposite Newgate on grand days.

The authorities still used to stick heads on Temple Bar (much to the prejudice of the owners) as coolly as we now stick heads on our letters, and people went up to look at them at a penny a peep.

But turning from this exquisitely amusing and cheerful subject, markest thou not, O acute reader, that the historic recorder hath now glided, glode, or glidden from the reign of

George number two, to his grandson, the third of that illustrious appellation.

He was not so German as the others, having been born in England, and being able to speak the language without any other impediment than a stutter, which sometimes made his words knock together in their hurry to get out of his mouth first. (*For his Portrait, see Initial on page* 299.)

Despite this, he was a very tolerable sort of king, who meant well if he didn't always do it, and did well if he didn't always mean it.

His reign was longer and his wig shorter than those of his immediate predecessors, and he took rather less snuff than those illustrious monarchs.

This alone would have endeared him to a loyal and patriotic people.

———

LXII.

BUILDING SPECS. AND STREET SPECTACLES.

HE improvements in London during this time were literally immense.

New buildings were run up everywhere, and many old ones, which had survived the fire of London, obligingly came down of their own accord.

Dozens of new streets sprang up every day, and so many squares were built that people thought London would soon be like a chessboard—all squares.

Clarendon House, Apsley House, and Portland Place were erected, and the Royal Academy founded.

Cold Bath Fields, Trinity House, and the Albany Chambers arose in all their glory; and numerous charitable institutions were formed, in particular the Superaunuated Asylum for Widowless Orphans, and the Benevolent Society for Teaching Ducks to Swim.

Westminster Bridge was built, not entirely without expense, and Blackfriars Bridge also, at the cost of £150 a foot, the architect receiving for his labours £300 a year and

LONDON STREET MUSIC, LAST CENTURY.
(See page 306.)

the valuable privilege of bathing in the river between the hours of five and seven on winter mornings.

London Bridge also showed signs of caving in, and it began to dawn on people that it was time to have a new one.

They thought of it for sixty years, and then began building.

Meanwhile it was patched up with as much despatch as possible.

About this date the range of buildings known as the Adelphi was built by two brothers.

The word Adelphi means *brothers* in Greek, and by the same rule, Haymarket means *sisters* in Latin (?).

These brothers were twins, and so much alike that they used sometimes to eat each other's dinners and pay each other's bills by mistake, and one often forgot which he was himself until he had consulted the other.

FEARFUL DISASTERS IN LONDON—GENTLEMEN OVERCOME BY THE EARTHQUAKE.—(*See page* 294.)

Whene'er I take my walks abroad, and happen to pass the Adelphi, I shed a couple of twin tears—exactly alike, of course—from either eye as I think of the founders of that noble edifice, and reflect that had they only lived till now they would have been one hundred and thirty years old.

London has lost many a pleasing sight and sound which enlivened her streets in those enviable times when George the Third was king.

No more do we see the dancing bear, the performing pony, the penny peep show, and the street harlequin perambulate our thoroughfare.

And then the sweet harmony produced by the good old cries of London.

All the street folks had their particular cries then—the apple-woman, the orange-girl, the cherry-ripe seller, the costermonger, the small coal man, and a host of others, including the cries of the street children, which were rather squally.

The dancing bear ambled gracefully along to the strains of the drum, fiddle, horn, and bagpipes, and then there were drums, flutes, and hurdy-gurdies galore.

Hogarth (the great painter of London life at this time, whose pictures were almost as comic as ours, perhaps more, " though we say it as oughtn't ") has given us a particularly lively picture in his " Enraged Musician."

The scene is the street.

The musician, who has just tuned up his violin for a classical prelude, is looking out of window when he hears a concert just outside that beats his out of time.

LXIII.

THE ENRAGED MUSICIAN—THE CELEBRATED COCK LANE GHOST. —UMBRELLAS INTRODUCED.

IN that inimitable picture we are speaking of, there is a woman singing street ballads, a hungry man playing on a clarionet, a milk-maid crying, "Milk below," in a be(*l*)lowing voice; a dustman with his bell; a post-boy blowing his horn; an energetic lady from Billingsgate crying the best mackerel; a youngster performing a rataplan on the drum; a knifegrinder whirring away at his grindstone; a small dog who is doubtless big enough to bark; and a little maiden amusing herself with a rattle.

All this is going on just under the professor's window, while a church in the distance gives us to understand that the bells are ringing a merry peal, and two cats on the opposite roof are arguing the question with prolonged and piercing "wows;" the musician, somehow, don't seem to appreciate the beauty of this fine oratorio; perhaps to his experienced ear it sounds a *leetle* out of tune.

One of the first sensations of the new reign was the celebrated Cock Lane Ghost, the earliest rapping spirit ever introduced into a free and enlightened metropolis.

It first manifested itself in the house of a Mr. Parsons of Cock Lane, whose daughter was its chosen victim.

In the room where the child reposed, mysterious knockings, rappings, and tappings were heard, seeming to proceed from the walls or the bedpost, and defying detection.

The neighbours all flocked to see, or rather hear the phenomenon, and a consultation of doctors and clergymen was called.

They found the child lying in bed, and it seemed to them very much as if the father, who acted as showman, was *lying* too.

He said he thought the ghost was that of his departed second cousin's sister-in-law, and that though invisible to the eye, he regarded this rapper as he*r-apparition*.

The doctors sounded the wall, but could find nothing the matter with its lungs, tapped the bedpost, but got nothing out of it, and tried the patient with homœpathy, brimstone and treacle, cold drawn castor oil, and other surgical appliances, but in vain.

They removed the girl to another house, but the rappings began there just the same.

Even a strong mustard-poultice fixed to the wainscot failed to draw out the ghost.

The mystery kept on for years, and caused an immense and ever-increasing sensation all over London, until one doctor, acuter than the rest, made the discovery that the child had swallowed the knocker off her doll's house by mistake, which was a patent one, and wound up to go on forever.

She was cured eventually, though the doctors all agreed it was the strangest case they ever undertook, and declared they never wanted another one like it.

A similar noisy ghost made itself audible at Stockwell a little afterwards.

This disturbed spirit could be heard in the dead of night haunting the kitchen, rattling the crockery, and drawing corks in the wine-cellar.

In the morning, bottles of beer and wine would be found empty, and various eatables gone.

The fearful and inexplicable mystery kept on for weeks, till at length the mistress of the house, lying in wait, found a big guardsman in the kitchen cupboard in the act of pocketing a cold fowl.

It appeared that a too confiding cook had entrusted him with her bunch of keys.

There was rather of a tableau, but from that day—or rather night—forward, the invisible ghost was never heard in *that* house.

It is highly interesting—nay, quite touching—to reflect that in 1764 lightning conductors first came into general use, though *'bus* conductors were not introduced till many years afterwards.

It is also startling to know that at a shortly subsequent date umbrellas were first seen in London.

Previous to this time, any person who valued his or her dress had to take a coach when it rained, or take shelter under a waterspout, but now one John Macdonald, a footman, was the first man in London who made a practice of carrying an umbrella.

At first he was laughed at and followed by crowds, but as he still held out, and used to drop the heavy knob of the handle upon the nobs of those who jeered at him, they after a time let him alone, and thus he persevered, holding his umbrella up every day, whether it rained or not, till people agreed that, after all, there was some sense in not getting wet.

And so an article at first declared to be only fit for

"fools, women, and Frenchmen" (what a mixture!), came to be patronised by all.

It is a glorious institution, for what is a Briton without his umbrella?

As miserable as a Chinaman with no pigtail.

All honour to John Macdonald, who ought to have been raised to the peerage under the title of Lord Gingham, and given, as crest, a golden parasol on a rainy background.

Umbrella-making is now a large branch of manufacture.

Thousands are made every year, and the number of those lost, or lent and never returned, passes all computation.

In 1766 there was an awful tempest in London, which did fifty thousand pounds worth of damage, and then dishonestly refused to pay for it.

The same year the King of Denmark came to visit us, costing the country only a hundred pounds per day.

However, he taught us the last new style in cocked hats (the "Denmark cock"), which was of course worth the money.

In 1768, the lord mayor first left off wearing a full-bottomed wig.

Hooray!

LXIV.

THEATRICAL, POLITICAL, AND BALLOONICAL.

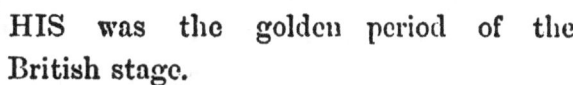

THIS was the golden period of the British stage.

Theatres had sprung up like mushrooms, and many actors arose who could not only promise but perform.

But none came up to the celebrated Garrick, who seemed as if he could act any *Garrick*ter (!), and never descended to *Garrick*ature.

It is true they did not understand dressing for the parts in those days, for they acted "Macbeth" in a periwig and high-heeled boots, with an elegantly-laced plaid waistcoat.

Hamlet sported a cocked hat and walking cane, and Richard III. stormed through his part in a swallow-tailed coat and tremendous cravat.

They would rather have astonished Shakespeare, had he been there to see.

The fairs and public gardens—Ranelagh, Vauxhall, and Marylebone—previously described with such startling minuteness, still went on.

St James's and other parks were thrown open to the people, principally because it was found impossible to keep them out.

Mrs. Salmon's noted waxworks, set up in Ann's time, flourished till late in the century, when the old lady died, aged ninety, leaving a hundred and fifty wax figures to mourn her untimely loss.

Early in the reign of King George III. a magnificent statue of that monarch was planted near the Royal Exchange, on horseback.

People recognised who it was meant for at once, especially as the name was put underneath.

Otherwise, it might just as well have been Julius Cæsar, for it was dressed in a Roman military habit, and carried the usual rolling pin you may notice on all similar statues.

I do not know why, for George III. was neither a Roman nor a general, and so little did he know about the use of rolling pins, that he never could imagine how the crust got fixed round the apple dumplings without showing any join.

All readers of " Barnaby Rudge " are aware that in 1780 London was convulsed from centre to circumference by the riotous proceedings of Lord George Gordon, a Scotch Peer who, being rather *cracked* himself, determined that the peace should be *broken*.

His parliament petition being refused, he stirred up the roughs of the metropolis, and, as Lord Macaulay says, " raised Old Harry."

They mobbed the Houses of Parliament, blocking up every approach, attacked the Archbishop of York in his carriage, with a cry of " No Popery ! " and though his grace smiled benignantly and replied, " Of course not, my good people ; who said there was ? " he had to descend, dive through the crowd, and seeking refuge in a pastrycook's, ate buns until the row was over.

Then they set upon Lord Mansfield, and kicked his shins till they were like the French flag—red, white, and blue—

pitched into several other noblemen, bishops, and other grandees, and stole the Duke of Northumberland's diamond watch—all for the good of the Protestant cause.

Finding all this was deliciously exciting, the crowd paraded London, attacking all Romish churches, chapels, and religious edifices, broke into private houses, and public houses as well (which made them worse still), knocking down pulpits, altars, pews, and benches, and all other ecclesiastical appurtenances.

Guy Fawkes was burnt in effigy, without waiting for the Fifth of November.

Roman candles were burnt at both ends, so as to get rid of them all the sooner.

This sort of thing kept on for above a fort-night.

Nobody was safe even in his own house, though many wrote on their doors: "No Popery here ; apply at the next street."

Lord and Lady Mansfield, seeing the unwelcome visitors marching up to their town resi-

GREAT SENSATION : THE FIRST UMBRELLA IN LONDON.
(*See page* 309.)

dence, just managed to get out of their back window as the rioters rushed in at the front, and escaped spiflication by the very skin of their teeth.

However, the mob played off the fiend's own vengeance upon the unoffending house and furniture ; they tore down the pictures, tore up his lordship's clothes, split up the grates and fire-irons into splinters, and burnt them as firewood, destroyed the wine and swallowed the bottles ; in short it is hard to say what they didn't do.

Next the mob broke into Newgate, and several other prisons, setting free all the culprits and fellow rioters that had been therein incarcerated.

The prisons were then devoted to blazes, and thirty-six fires were going in London at one time, which were rather too many even for that cold weather.

The soldiers turned out in thousands, the Riot Act was read, and five hundred pounds reward was offered to the ringleaders of the riot to come forward and be hanged peacefully, but all in vain.

The mob thought they would combine pleasure with profit by breaking into the Bank of England and appropriating its contents, but the mild persuasions of twenty thousand soldiers, armed with muskets, induced them to give up the idea, and console themselves by smashing windows.

At last these innocent pastimes were put a stop to ; the indignant Britons dispersed, and the good citizens of London could again go to bed without the fear of waking up murdered in the morning.

LXV.

MORE ABOUT THE LORD MAYORS.

ON a memorable day in 1784, the soul-stirring cry of " Ah bah loon !" was first heard in the metropolis.

Balloons were soon all the rage, and it became fashionable for ladies and gentlemen, who were already high up in the world, to go up some two or three hundred feet higher.

In 1789, the front of Guildhall was done up, at an immense cost in whitewash, and the interior was decorated with a splendid painting, representing our old friend Wat Tyler having his brains knocked out.

You see in these hanging days, they not only hung men but pictures ; the only difference was that pictures were hung because they were good, and men because they were bad.

Talking of Guildhall, you will perhaps like to know how its occupants, the lord mayors, got on all the time.

Well, they got on bloomingly.

A splendid new coach was built for them in 1757, and a few years after the lord mayor, his lady, and his entire household were provided with new clothes, utterly regardless of cost, which was exactly £621 13s. 9d.

The lord mayor of 1776 had the misfortune to be stopped at Turnham Green by a single highwayman, and robbed of all his valuables.

The city sword-bearer was in the carriage, but he was afraid of using his beautiful ornamental weapon, for fear of spoiling it.

So the robber got off with his booty, and rode off triumphantly to Kew, where, *kew*riously enough, he met the vicar and robbed him also of everything, including a packet of sermons.

Let us hope that he took them home and read them, and was thereby led to reform, give up "the *road*," and take to the right *path* instead.

One lord mayor, Alderman Kennet (inventor of the renowned Kennet ales), began life as a waiter, and kept on waiting until it was his turn to become king of the city.

It was said that habit was so strong in him, that at the Guildhall dinner he stood behind his own chair instead of sitting on it, and kept on saying, "Bottled ale, sir? Yessir. Coming directly, sir!" etc., as per usual.

Another lord mayor was a brewer, and called "Mash tub" in derision.

Sir William Staines, another of them, first started in life as bricklayer's labourer, and certainly carrying up hods of mortar seemed great *odds* against his ever becoming lord mayor, nor is a builder's ladder exactly like the ladder to fortune, though it does consist of a succession of *steps upward*.

But Staines *did* get to the top of the ladder at last, and rode in his coach on the 9th of November with the best of them.

It was this exemplary man, who, on being told that his only son had fallen off the roof of a house, exclaimed—

" Great heavens ! run and see if the poor fellow's watch is broken !"

(This was a touching instance of parental feeling, and would almost draw tears from an onion peeler.)

From these examples, gentle peruser, thou canst see that the proud position of Lord of London is open to all, great and small, short and tall, poor and rich, and every free-born Englishman has a right to the lord mayoralty—*if he can get it.*

What beggar-boy can look upon his lordship as he rolls by in his gilded chariot, in all the pomp and circumstance of glorious mayoralty, and not feel a thrill of ambitious delight, at the thought that, poor and ragged as he is, *he* might be lord mayor, too, if they'd only elect him.

Many a poor boy has come to London with nothing in his pocket but holes, and ended by wallowing in bloated opulence.

We all remember the American who " came to New York with only one shirt to his back, and in course of time *accumulated ten millions.*"

Fancy wearing ten million shirts !

Yes, 'tis an immense advantage to begin life with nothing at all.

So go, reader, and do thou likewise.

Throw away your unnecessary cash, put on rags, and walk into London with exactly sixpence and a hopeful heart.

Work your way up by degrees, and on the day you are enthroned as lord mayor, send us an invitation to the dinner, in gratitude for our invaluable advice, and we will come.

Some of the lord mayors of the eighteenth century were, however, less to be praised ; for there was Alderman Hamet, who, in 1797, refused to become lord mayor at all when he was elected, and was therefore very properly condemned to live upon turtle-soup alone for the term of his natural life.

Indigestion marked him for its own, and for declining to be *mayor* during the *day*, he suffered a perpetual *night-mare* ever afterwards.

But the worst of the mayors was the notorious Jack Wilkes, who flourished about a hundred years ago, more or less.

Jack was a terrible fellow, and so awfully ugly that people used to put their shutters up whenever he walked by, for fear the children should be frightened into convulsions.

He squinted so fearfully that you never could tell whether he were looking at you or at the man next door, and his very smile made one think of battle, murder, and sudden death.

However such a being got to be lord mayor at all seems a puzzler, but probably he put on a frown, and frightened them into electing him.

However, there is one good thing Wilkes did; he stuck up for liberty, especially liberty of the press, for there was not any before his time.

It was thought almost as bad as high treason for newspapers to report the parliamentary debates, and the subject caused a great many unparliamentary debates before it could be settled.

Jack Wilkes was not the only one put in prison for saying what he really meant, and at last the government got tired of trying to put it down, so that now we have the glorious privilege of telling a good deal of truth, though not too much, for fear of libelling somebody.

The *Times* and the *Evening Courier* were started, and

though they were thought wonderful at the time, they were as insignificant compared with our modern papers, as the baby hippopotamus is to its late lamented papa.

LXVI.

CONCERNING THE FASHIONS, COSTUMES, DRESS, HABITS, AND HABILIMENTS OF THE PERIOD.

ITH regard to London fashions, ladies continued to wear the fly-caps, mob caps, long waists and bell hoops, with all the paraphernalia thereto appertaining, as hereinbefore mentioned, and at one time the trains were of such a length that the ends were sometimes lost in the extreme distance.

Often might a lady be observed walking in Regent Street, while the further portions of her skirts were in Piccadilly.

A fashionable dame, in order to be quite *a la mode*, one hundred years back, was recommended to get for her head-dress a bushel of false hair, done up with a pound of pomatum, ten yards of ribbon, and about five of gauze.

The dress to have two dozen wide flounces, and a train not less than seven yards long; boots, three inches in the heel.

How beautiful! and HOW comfortable!

Men's coats continued to be made much in the same style until there was a change in the fashion.

For years the coat-cuffs were worn so large that gentlemen

frequently lost themselves in them, and had to be pulled out by their valets.

This was found to be inconvenient, and the cuffs gradually dwindled until at last nothing remained but two buttons to mark the spot where once they dwelt.

Dazzling waistcoats and coats of blazing splendour were still in wear.

One Lord Villiers, an overwhelming swell, had his coat stuck all over with pearls and gold medallions ; the lining, we suppose, consisted of bank notes sewn together, and each button was a separate guinea.

In this style of fashion a man might carry all his money about with him, and let people see at a glance how much he was worth.

Extreme fashionables, " macaronies," as they were called, went to great lengths.

Some dandy M. P's would saunter into the house with their faces rogued, and carrying large nosegays.

They only wanted a big fan and a scent bottle to complete the picture.

Our old friend the cocked hat was now worn all sorts of ways, sometimes being pulled down over the face like a spout, sometimes hanging down behind like a coal-heaver's neck-protector, sometimes dome-shaped, square, flat, or three-cornered.

About a century ago round hats were introduced, and the half-moon hats, which never reached a *full* moon, came in for evening dress.

Wigs were still worn on the head, it being feared that they wouldn't look well on the feet.

We will not, however, discuss this matter, never having seen them on the feet ourselves ; but even those for the head were not destined, as we will show, to *stand* much longer.

LXVI.—(*Continued.*)

WIGS were worn in every variety of shape, from the bob-wig to the poultice wig, and the frizzly skull-coverer ; but as time went on, wigs went off by degrees, and got smaller and less conspicuous, till many enlightened geniuses contented themselves with powdering and plastering their hair till it was almost as uncomfortable as a wig itself, and tying it in a bag or a queue pigtail behind.

The poor wigmakers made a *wig*orous resistance against these new-fangled fashions, which spoilt their trade, and they even went in procession to petition the king not to ruin them by taking to wear his own hair.

PORTRAITS OF SOME OF THE LORD MAYORS—ALL FROM LIFE.
(*See page* 318.)

The monarch's reply was truly sublime.

"Nations," he replied, "may be hurled to the abyss of destruction, stars may fall, and the very universe be shaken to its foundation, but through all these mighty changes I'll stick to my bob-wig."

And so he did.

You mustn't suppose that a *bob*-wig was one that only cost a shilling; it was so called from the way its curls bobbed about, and from its generally "bobbish" appearance.

Anon both *beau* and *belle* adopted a style of dress that made them look like trussed turkeys.

What with high collars, tight neckcloths, tight lacing, and tight fits of all sorts, the fashionables of that age must never have dared to breathe at all when in full dress.

And then the high-heeled boots, making the ladies stoop forward in a style almost as idiotic as the Grecian bend of our times, which makes them hobble like a tame kangaroo or a superannuated giraffe.

The French revolution caused quite a revolution in dress as well as everything else.

That of ladies was so fearfully and wonderfully made as quite to baffle description, and inspire terror.

LXVII.

CONCERNING COSTUMES, COACHES, AND CHIMNEY SWEEPS.

WE have spoken of the stage, and now we will say a little about the stage coaches.

You are perhaps aware that there were no railway trains before steam, if not, rely on it as a fact.

In travelling, our ancestors took, on an average, twenty-four hours to our one.

The Edinburgh coach journeyed from London in ten days in summer and twelve days in winter, and the very rapid express couldn't do it under nine.

The "flying coach," as it was called, went at the break-neck pace of five miles an hour.

Sometimes the coaches didn't get over more than eleven miles a day, so that people who were in a hurry had to walk.

The "Highflyer" coach took twelve hours to do forty miles, and was rather proud of it.

The diligences, or "dilies," and "long coaches," a sort of 'busses, went still quicker, and when the first-class mail coaches reached ten miles an hour, it was thought that the world was coming to an end.

People were afraid that such frightful speed would take their breath away and bring on apoplexy.

What with the jolting and robbers, and bad roads, travelling was delightful indeed.

The old coachmen were never in a hurry, and argued that if you didn't get where you wanted to go to-day, you might next week—*weather permitting*—and wasn't one day as good as another?

Before this time, wondrous to relate, the world had actually contrived to exist for six thousand years or so without any Jack-in-the-Green, though Maypoles and maids dancing for garlands, and other May Day sports had not been unknown.

But now an affecting incident caused the institution of the great sweeps' festival.

Mrs. Montague, a lady of great wealth in Montague Street, happened to lose her only son, aged sixteen months, three weeks, and eight and a quarter days.

She left him under the seat of a hackney coach while she went shopping, and had so many parcels when she came back, that she didn't perceive the loss, though she felt sure, on looking over her luggage, that she missed *something*.

It was only in the middle of the ensuing night that she remembered (with, ah! how much grief!) the real facts of the case.

She rose, raised the house, sent servants in all directions, rang the bells, and advertised in that very morning's papers, offering the tempting sum of three and sixpence reward.

All, all in vain!

The infant heir of all the Montagues, like the aristocratic nose of his afflicted mamma, *refused to turn up*.

Years passed, and still he came not, and grief had taken up its residence as a yearly tenant in the heart of the bereaved parent.

At length it began to dawn upon her that the chimney wanted sweeping.

In her one absorbing sorrow she had not noticed that circumstance before, but now the descent of soot reminded her of it forcibly.

With her as-*sent* the sweep was *sent* for, and his boy was despatched to make an as-*cent* of the *cent*-ral chimney.

For in those days, you must know, they used to employ boys—the smallest they could get—to climb up chimneys and bring down the contents, and this one, I suppose, found the chimney a size too big for him, and so lost his hold and tumbled into the fire-grate of Mrs. Montague's boudoir.

"Great gracious!" exclaimed the lady, "how you frightened me! Go back the way you came instantly. But stay, child, your appearance, though sooty, is interesting. Who were your parents ?"

"Never had none," was the reply of the dark infant.

He spoke from internal conviction.

"And who brought you up ?"

"I never was brought up at all, mum; I was only dragged up," he replied. "I have been sweeping chimneys for my master, Mr. Flue, ever since I can remember; perhaps longer."

"Poor juvenile ! And can it be indeed thus ? Here is sixpence ; but no, I will give you that to-morrow. Ah! had my son lived, he would have been just your age and size, though I hope not so awfully black. Tell me, have you a green gooseberry mark on the back of your neck ?"

The sweeper's boy rubbed off some of the soot from the region indicated, and then, dexterously slewing his eyes round, looked at the back of his own neck, and answered—

"No, mum, I ain't !"

"Then you are indeed my long-lost son !" she exclaimed,

and forthwith folded him to her white satin dress, which was thereby spoilt for evermore.

The next day (May 1st) the now washed youth was publicly owned as the recovered heir.

His old friends the chummies were invited to a grand spread and picnic in the grounds of Montague House.

From that day the event was annually celebrated by the festival of Jack-in-the-Green.

The introduction of improved and new brooms (which proverbially sweep clean) has caused some *sweeping* reforms in the sooty trade, and small boys are never allowed to climb chimneys now, in this *clime* at least, and certainly the practice was a *climax* of cruelty.

LXVIII.

THE WONDROUS NINETEENTH CENTURY.

WE have now reached the wonderful nineteenth century.

Everybody calls it wonderful, and it certainly is a distinguished period, for WE live in it.

But let us now look back seventy or eighty years.

Things were at this time like the tea at two-and-four, rather mixed.

On the Continent Buonaparte was pitching into the world in general.

In England the deep *Pitt* and the knowing *Fox* were prime ministers, and there was a constant struggle between the Whigs and Tories as to which should be *whig-tory-ous* (victorious ?).

London was getting on very well indeed, but still open to a great deal of improvement.

The robbers and highwaymen were not all hanged yet, though the authorities tried their best at it by "working off" several dozen at the Old Bailey ever Monday morning.

The old watchmen, or "Charlies," were still as sleepy as ever, and let all sorts of crimes be done under their very noses.

Fast young fellows, out on the spree, used to come behind them, or upset their watch boxes, and then all they could do was to kick and yell out, which generally led to a row, and the "Charlies" walked off any such guilty persons as couldn't afford to give them a tip.

Citizens always used to take their plate and cash with them on going out of town, or else leave them at their respected uncle's, who never charged more than five hundred per cent. for the accommodation.

The policemen of course were not born yet, and in place of our detectives they had the Bow Street runners, who were sharp fellows too.

The chief of them was John Townsend, who, as he always wore a red coat, was considered a *scarlet runner*.

The streets were still rather hard lines to have to walk upon, until Alderman Staines benevolently undertook the paving at the public expense.

Swords being no longer worn by gentlemen, there was a falling off in the number of people killed in the street; but duels still went on now and then in the parks.

A fearful one took place between Colonel Lennox and the Duke of York.

It appears that they had a quarrel because the colonel

had heard somebody else say that he knew a party who declared that the duke had said something which the colonel didn't approve of.

They fought accordingly.

One fired in the air, and the other had forgotten to load his pistol, and the wounds consequently were not fatal, and the surgeon declared that both patients might with care recover.

Fashionable folks generally dined at four o'clock, unless it happened to be earlier or later.

Poorer people dined earlier, and some poor wretches didn't dine at all.

Gambling still went on like all vengeance, and nothing was so aristocratic as to lose all you had at cards.

Pinks of fashion were no longer called fops and gallants, nor often beaux, but macaronis, bucks, bloods, or dandies, and the female specimens were nicknamed "dandirettes."

The macaronis generally sported top-boots, striped waist-coats, and sugar-loaf hats, and always carried two watches, one to tell what time it was, and the other what time it wasn't.

Wigs had disappeared, and even hair powder became, like *gun*-powder, an exploded article, for a tax being laid on it, every true Briton thought it his duty to cheat the revenue.

So a lot of noblemen conspired to cut off their own hair and pigtails.

This fearful deed was performed at Woburn Abbey, the seat of the Duke of Bedford.

He, with several viscounts, marquises, etc., having engaged half-a-dozen barbers in their *barbarous* plot, went into the lavatory, had a complete shampoo, and came out with hair as short and frizzly as niggers.

From that hour powdered hair was doomed, and rough heads, called "Brutus" or "Rufus" were all the go.

They say that some revolutionists in France took to going about in Roman togas, and other classical *togary*, and though after all they didn't look much like Romans, they certainly were *Rum'uns*.

Ladies' big hoops now collapsed, and they piled most of the material on their heads instead.

Hats as big as umbrellas were adorned with birds of Paradise, sham cabbages, and other mineral ornaments.

Chains were worn as big as cables, with golden birdcages, eggs, scissor-cases, gridirons, and other tasteful bits of jewellery hanging from them, and tassels, bows, ribbons, and veils, *ad libitum*.

In 1802, Madame Tussaud first appeared in London with her life-like figures.

She finally settled in Baker Street, where, like her predecessor, Mrs. Salmon, she lived to the age of ninety, a proof that waxwork is very healthy work if you only stick to it long enough.

It was only a little before this that the pretty time-honoured custom of decorating Temple Bar with human heads, was done away with.

Many people thought it a great pity, as the Bar looked so bare, and nothing like so lively as in the good old days.

One of the first sensations of the new century was an invasion panic.

It was feared that the great Nap. wanted to catch England *nap*-ping and that Buonaparte was coming over to *bone a part* of our territory.

So a number of volunteer corps were started in a great hurry, and though they were hardly as smart as our modern riflemen, and armed only with lumbering old matchlocks and muskets, they had hearts of oak, and were determined to die in defence of their country or perish in the attempt.

London alone turned out twenty thousand volunteers as quickly as if it had been done by machinery.

Old King George reviewed them in Hyde Park, and though it rained *hard* nothing could damp their *ardour*.

However "Boney" didn't come after all, and in 1802 grand peace rejoicings took place.

One hundred and fifty thousand pounds were spent in fire-works in three days only, which shows how easy it is to get rid of money, if you only give your mind to it.

Except the burning of the two principal theatres, and a few other events, nothing happened for several years.

In 1810, the patriotic and popular Sir Francis Burdett was walked off to the Tower of London for having called the House of Commons a parcel of old women, about as fit to govern as a lot of broomsticks.

This was considered very high treason, and all the more atrocious because it was so cuttingly true.

The same year that irrepressible wag Theodore Hook played off his great Berners Street Hoax.

This was a plan to serve out an old lady he didn't like, who lived at No. 56.

LXIX.

HOOK'S HOAX—GEORGE'S GRANDEUR, AND BRUMMEL'S BOUNCE.

MR. HOOK sent off letters by the hundred in the old lady's name to all the tradesmen in London, ordering goods of every imaginable description, and timed them to arrive at her house nearly all at once.

The consequence was that on the appointed morning the thoroughfare was blocked up by carts, carriages, wagons, trucks, wheelbarrows, and pedestrians; and the entire neighbourhood was in commotion.

No "Derby" ever brought together a greater crowd than this *Hoax*.

Among other things were five pianos, three cradles, and a first-class coffin, just made to measure.

The old lady naturally thought that the whole world had suddenly gone mad, and she was nearly driven out of her own senses.

Hours passed, and still they kept coming and coming, and the row outside was something awful.

Presently arrived no less a personage than the lord mayor himself, who said he had just received a note asking him to come, as the case was very urgent.

Meanwhile Mr. Hoak, seated at an opposite window, was enjoying the fun with all his might.

All London was soon in a wild tumult.

Traffic was stopped in Berners and Oxford Streets for the rest of the day, and it was not till about ten at night, when the knocker and all the bells of poor No. 56 had been wrenched off by being so much used, that the last of the tradesmen had discovered their fool's errand and departed.

Nobody knew who was at the bottom of this gigantic practical joke, but some people had their suspicions, and Mr. Theodore thought it wise for a time to take his *Hook*.

In 1811, Prince George of Wales was declared regent.

In consequence, everything was named Regent after him; Regent coats, Regent collars, Regent cravats, Regent Circus and Regent's Canal.

Regent's Park and Regent Street were also set out; and a pretty *set out* they made of it.

This was the heyday of fashion in London, for this majestic prince—afterwards George IV.—was overwhelmingly great at levees, drawing-rooms, and all sorts of state festifications.

The ladies flocked to his assemblies in such numbers, out of sheer admiration, that he was obliged to order them to leave off big hoops and trains so as to give more room.

Prince George the Great was noted for his gorgeous appearance.

He was as good as a tailor's model, and, if a trifle too stout (for it took four lifeguardsmen to lift him into his saddle), he was just the figure for a *heavy* swell.

He it was who first cultivated mutton-chop whiskers.

He also invented white kid pantaloons, which fitted like a glove and never showed a wrinkle.

How he got into them seemed a mystery, and how he got out of them another.

The secret was that the garments were hung up on a line, and the intended wearer, going up a ladder, dropped gradually into them.

When he had got about half way two valets, one on each

side, helped him on very carefully for fear of splitting the material.

Thus it took about three hours to put on a fashionable pair of trousers, and nearly as long to peel them off at night.

Even at that it was dangerous to walk fast in them.

Then, what with padded coats and stays, and cravats as high and tight as a brick wall, his majesty must have felt about as comfortable as a hog in armour.

No wonder he looked rather puffy and apoplectic about the face, and extremely suggestive of a tendency of blood to the head.

Of course he moved along as if his joints wanted oiling very badly; but this was thought very graceful.

The dandies of the day imitated him, and practised what they called the "Regent's lounge," instead of the "Roman fall."

They made awful guys of themselves, and seemed to be all collar and coat-tails.

The latter appendages were as long as those of nigger minstrels, while the vest was so short as to be a mere *vest*-ige.

In fact the dress both for the ladies and gentlemen was as stiff and tight as if they had been melted and poured into it.

This sometimes got them into a ridiculous fix.

On one occasion the Regent was talking to a fashionable lady, who happened to drop her handkerchief.

As her ladyship had a bad cold, this was awkward.

The prince, of course, would have picked it up most politely, but he did not dare to risk it.

The lady, for similar reasons, was also afraid, and so, after standing gazing at the dropped handkerchief pathetically for a while, they had to ring for a servant to come upstairs and pick it up; for the fact was, neither of them was *dressed for stooping.*

The foremost leader of fashion at this period was the celebrated Beau Brummel, a great pal of his royal highness. (*For Portraits, see Illustration on page* 336.)

Brummel's boots, hats, coats, trousers, and especially his cravats, which took an hour and a-half a day to fix, were the admiration of the universe.

He was once the son of a pastry cook, but when he came in for £30,000, he cut that connection at once, and became so awfully aristocratic that he thought even port wine was a vulgar beverage, and the sight of one of the "lower orders" made him turn pale.

When a beggar said to him—

"Please tip us a copper, yer honour, if it's only a ha'penny."

"A what?" exclaimed the horrified beau. "Fellow, I don't know the coin."

And he always used to wash his hands after touching anything less than half a sovereign.

When someone offered to treat him to a glass of mild ale he fainted outright.

He was the exquisite who declared he caught a cold by being put into a room with a damp stranger.

Another time a friend met him limping along Bond Street, and, when asked what was the matter, he said, dolefully—

"Fact is, my dear fellow, I've hurt my leg, and the worst of it is it's my *favourite* leg."

Somebody once asked Brummel how much a gentleman ought to spend upon clothes.

"Haw, well," replied the beau, putting up his eye-glass, "it might be managed for £800 a year, *if you're careful.*"

Brummel's cheek was something tremendous.

He used to invite himself to people's houses whenever he liked, and poke his fun at dukes, viscounts, or any other grandees, in the coolest style.

Once, when dining with the heir to the throne, he tapped him familiarly on the shoulder, and said—

" *Wales,* ring the bell."

The prince thought he was going a little bit too far, so he did ring the bell, and ordered Mr. Brummel to be shown the door.

Next time they met, H.R.H. pretended not to see him, so Brummel, turning round to one of his companions, pointed over his shoulder to the prince, and asked very loudly—

" I say, who's your fat friend ?"

The regent turned beetroot colour with rage, and wished he had had the power of cutting Brummel's head off, without judge or jury.

Brummel was pretty well the last of the beaux, though Sir Lumley Skeffington was another nearly as extensive ; and a still more recent star of fashion was Count D'Orsay, of whom I *dorsay* you've heard (oh ! !).

He introduced white waistcoats and covered himself with glory.

LXX.

AN ICE FAIR IN NASTY WEATHER.

IT would be impossible to tell all the improvements now made in London.

How old Vauxhall and Ranelagh were done away with, and various new theatres built, how squares and streets stretched out in all directions, how a new road was laid down from Islington to elsewhere, and other neighbourhoods in the

LONDON STARS OF 1811 : THE PRINCE REGENT, BEAU BRUMMEL, &c.—(*See page* 334.)

same quarter; and how many charitable institutions were founded, such as Millbank, Pentonville, and Cold Bath Fields, where people suffering from a propensity to crime might be cured free of all expense.

For all who appreciated being nearly frozen to death, the great fair on the Thames in 1813-14 was a genuine treat.

It began two days after Christmas, and lasted six weeks.

The river was not only frozen *over*, but frozen *under* as well to a depth of about a yard and a half.

The weather was a caution to barometers.

As the rhyme of the period hath it—

> "Fust it rained and then it blew,
>   And then it friz and then it thew,
>   And then it friz *horrid!*"

The snow kept on coming down for eight whole days without even leaving off for meals.

The thermometer sank 320 below freezing point.

DISTINGUISHED FOREIGNERS IN LONDON—OVERWHELMING POPULARITY OF MARSHAL BLUCHER.—(*See page* 343.)

Butter became so hard as to be bad for the teeth, and wouldn't melt in anything less than a furnace.

Brandy got frozen into chunks, and had to be sold by the pound.

The hands of all the clocks were covered with chilblains, and cats fought like grim death for the warmest corner in the kitchen fender.

Out of doors it was worse than awful.

All the pipes, even meerschaums, were frozen hard, and the plugs wouldn't come up for any money.

Traffic was almost entirely stopped, avalanches of snow came thundering down off the roofs every three minutes, and icicles several inches long hung from the noses of all the coachmen who ventured on the box.

The fog was fearful, pea-soup was like double-distilled crystal compared with it, lamps had to be used all day long, and even then it was rather darker than pitch.

H. R. H. the Prince Regent, going out of town, got " fog-logged " and ran up against the monument when he thought he was in Piccadilly.

All London was in for it, Islington was turned into *Iceling-ton*, the Green Park was *white* with snow, Houndsditch and all the other ditches were frozen, and Temple Bar began to resemble a huge twelfth cake, the snow having well whitened its top and quite filled up the gateway.

St. Paul's looked like its own ghost—all in white.

Old Father Thames was quite transmogrified, and seemed like a cross between Switzerland and the Polar regions.

LXXI.

FAIRYLAND (AND WATER) ON THE THAMES.

THERE were mountains of snow, and buildings of ice, and islands made of both together, that floated about, and crashed up against each other like thunder.

The great thickness and hardness of the ice may be judged from the fact that one nigger actually broke his head open when he fell on it! He had often been hit previously by cannon balls and they didn't hurt him.

However the citizens determined to make the best of it, and consequently got up a fair.

Shops, and booths, and tents were fixed up, at which all sorts of things were sold.

Licenses were granted for public houses on the river, and everybody, even on Sunday, was considered a *bona fide* traveller.

Fried sausages, eggs, and 'taters all cooked on the ice were dispensed in large quantities; a newspaper was started, and had a large circulation of about a mile square.

Chestnuts were roasted whole, and so were sheep.

People gave sixpence a-head to see them roasting, and a shilling a plateful for the meat.

This was the celebrated "Lapland mutton."

One 'cute fellow fixed up a notice outside his shop—" The desirable premises next door to be let on reasonable terms; *ninety-nine years' lease ;* thirty-six feet frontage; on solid ice, warranted three feet thick. A splendid investment for anybody just starting in life."

The frozen-out watermen set to making paths across the river; not in the usual way, by sweeping away the dirt, but by laying dirt down.

Of course, passengers were *told* that they would be *tolled* for going across, for the men said it wouldn't be *fair* to let anyone pass to the *fair* without paying the *fare*, not even if they belonged to the *fair* sex, so that the watermen *fared* very well themselves out of it.

Skating?

I should think there was indeed.

Everybody skated—dukes, dustmen, and donkey drivers; grand ladies, grenadiers, and greengrocers, ministers, milk-

men, and millionaires ; peers, pork butchers, and pick-
pockets—all joined in the merry-go-round on the ice.

Some people never took their skates off for weeks, but
slept in them, and skated miles and miles in their dreams.

The ice would have borne anything, even an elephant
laden with iron.

If Louis XVIII., the Claimant to the French throne at
that period, a twenty-two stone man, had only been a little
more active on his pins, he might have skimmed along on
that ice like a swallow, without the least fear of coming to
a dangerous part.

People wrapped up of course ; plenty of *muffs* were to be
seen everywhere, and huge bundles of fur were visible skating
as *fur* as the eye could reach.

It was capital fun !

But this couldn't last for ever, you know.

Accordingly, on February 5th, the weather seemed making
up its mind for a thaw, and when it began to *rain*, people
thought it was time to *mizzle*.

The ice cracked, and a temporary printing establishment
began floating away, with all the men inside ; thus their
type and their business were both suddenly broken up.

" The ice and snow are going fast," observed one spectator,
a humourous individual.

" *Ice*-see they are," answered another jocular party ; " so,
of course, it's *snow* use our staying here, and we had better
go at once."

And go they did.

The ice islands and snow mountains, and all the rest of it,
that had made the fair look like *fairy*-land, and put one in
mind of the transformation scene of the " Icy Realms of Old
King Winter," which we sometimes see at the pantomimes
—all these soon cracked up, and " like the baseless

fabric of a vision, left not a rack behind "—except a precious mess.

There was a general skedaddle; all the shops and boats broke from their moorings, and got carried down the river with whoever happened to be in them, so that the Thames contained a large *floating* popululation.

Ever so many highly desirable establishments bumped themselves to bits against London Bridge, and it was a week or more before the wreck was all cleared away and the great frost fair was over.

———

LXXII.

814 : GRAND VISIT OF FURRINEERS, MOSSOOS, AND OTHER ILLUSTRIOUS STRANGERS.

 THE next big events were the rejoicings over the downfall of " Boney," and the visit of the allied sovereigns to London.

They came each attended by his *suite*, forming altogether a *sweet* spectacle.

There was the Emperor of Russia, the King of Prussia, ever so many princes; the Hetman of the Cossacks, the Waywode of Bulgradocia, General Schtopflszkoff, Count Mangelwurzel, and all sorts of Tschoffskis, Gotschakoffs, Woronzoffs, and Popoffs imaginable.

Louis XVIII., who had been staying over here as a refugee, under the name of Mounseer Smith, and giving

French lessons for one shilling a head and no extras, was also present, to take a last farewell ere setting sail for the throne of France.

Never was London in such a state of festivity.

There were illuminations, fireworks, races, reviews, triumphal arches, fancy temples, balloons going up, and various choice drinks going down, all day.

The royal, imperial, and serene visitors were *feted* within an inch of their lives, and taken everywhere—to Covent Garden, St. Paul's Cathedral, Punch and Judy shows, oratorios, &c., besides parties, balls, banquets, and concerts without end.

Occasionally they went to bed, but there was very little time for that, and many found that it saved trouble to sleep in their clothes, and not take off even their decorations.

The banquet at Guildhall was the splendidest ever seen.

It cost altogether twenty-five thousand pounds—the value of the gold dishes alone was over two hundred thousand pounds—and no less than one hundred and fifty pounds was spent in laying down gravel outside the door.

They must have *piled it on* pretty thick *in the bill.*

Healths were drunk in English, French, German, Russian, and Polish, and responded to in Polish, Russian, German, French, and English.

Nearly all the company were warriors, more or less, and each wore his particular distinctive costume, so that though everybody was in uniform, there was no *uniform*ity.

Some of these foreigners were rather uncivilised chaps.

The Russians looked rather greedily at the candles, and the attendants kept an especially sharp eye upon the Hetman Platoff, a wild and predatory Cossack, for fear he might try to carry the *plate off* when they were not looking.

Wherever the illustrious strangers went, they were mobbed right and left, and particularly old Marshal Blucher, who was very popular here.

He found it quite a nuisance at last.

Everybody wanted to shake hands with him, and often he had to hide behind the trees in Kensington Gardens till the crowd had passed by.

He appreciated the people's friendship, but declared it was worse than facing the French.

When he first rode through, he was delighted with the riches and magnificence of London, especially the jewellers' shops, and exclaimed—

"Mein Gott! vat a city to plunder!"

After the feast, it was found that a good deal of the eatables and drinkables were still left; so the lord mayor determined to kill two birds with one stone by giving a grand special spread in honour of the Duke of Wellington.

His grace came, and received quite an ovation, and lots of presents.

When he returned from Waterloo next year, of course he was a greater hero than ever.

He was smothered with laurels, laudations, and, above all, received a big shield, which, though it was never intended to use, looked magnificent when hung up in his grace's front parlour.

The prince regent was present, and paid the duke some of the handsomest compliments ever strung together.

His royal highness said that though he had never been to battle himself, he had worn so many different sorts of uniform in his time, that it came to pretty much the same thing, and he could enter into the duke's feelings exactly.

Beyond this, for few people should forget Wellington and Waterloo—as if they ever could!—several statues were raised to him in London.

A number of ladies clubbed together to erect the celebrated Achilles statue in Hyde Park, near Rotten Row.

It's a splendid bit of marble, like life itself, but it seems a pity that the funds wouldn't run so far as to provide it with any clothes.

Other statues were fixed up about this period in the metropolis, and in particular we ought to mention the Duke of York and Nelson columns.

They are remarkable for the fact that, try how you will, it is impossible to get a good view of the figures on the top.

Going up in a balloon on purpose, and having it anchored just at the right level, might enable you to manage it.

The Nelson column was intended from the very first to have four lions to guard it.

Landseer was the man for lions, and when he had finished them—it only took twenty-five years—he became quite a lion himself.

They quite took the shine out of the renowned lion on the top of Northumberland House.

Bye-the-bye, the latest news is that this venerable and majestic edifice is very shortly to come down.

Alas! and woe is me!

'Tis sad to think of.

For centuries it has belonged to the Percy family, a family so ancient that they are supposed to trace their descent from the Medes and *Percy*ans.

It is built in the Babylonian style, the architect having

been Mr. Christmas, probably the identical Old Father Christmas, whom we very often read about, but very seldom see.

The inside is splendid, containing lots of paintings by the old masters, some of them so old that nobody can make out what they are.

It is said that once the duke, having fallen out with the

PRESENTATION TO THE DUKE—THE SHIELD OF HIS COUNTRY.
(*See page* 343.)

prince regent, insulted him by having the lion turned round with his tail towards his royal highness as he came by.

The prince, seeing the *stern* of the lion thus conspicuously, looked *stern*ly at it, and said—

" Let's (*s*)*turn* back !" which he did.

LXXIII.

THE NORTHUMBERLAND LION, AND OTHER LIONS OF LONDON.

WE have heard that the lion's tail is seen to wag at twelve o'clock on every first of April, but as our informant was a known joker, we expect that this *wag* of the *tail* is merely a *tale* of a *wag*.

However, we respect that lion from the very bottom of our soul, and deeply lament that although he is *standing up*, he will soon be a *lion down*.

It is generally supposed that he is of stone; others assert that he is of lead—many tame lions are *led*, you know, with a chain—but no doubt when he is removed, they will hold a *post mortem* examination upon his remains, and we shall know for certain.

Bridges being wanted for London, Waterloo, Southwark, and Blackfriars were begun with speed as soon as the needful could be raised.

It is not generally known that Waterloo Bridge was built on the model of the *bridge* of the Duke of Wellington's nose, which was declared by architects to have a magnificent Norman *arch*.

In the very middle of the Waterloo rejoicings Lord Elgin arrived in London from Greece, bringing with him the celebrated Elgin marbles, which were not easy to play with, as they weighed at least three tons each ; in fact they were Grecian statues, and were taken to the British Museum accordingly.

One, of Jupiter, is in splendid preservation, except that the head, left leg, and right arm are lost, and considered very much like him.

One of the greatest agitations in London, in the year 1815, was the story of the pig-faced lady, who was said to be living in one of the principal squares.

She was reported to be wonderfully beautiful, all but the face, which was exactly that of a fine prize porker.

Her riches were tremendous, and she was fed daily out of a golden trough with a silver spoon.

Forty thousand pounds down was offered by advertisement to whomsoever would marry her.

Several fortune-hunters came forward, but their courage failed them.

After the first interview they fled, and henceforth could never pass a pork-butcher's shop without a shudder.

What became of the pig-faced beauty is not known.

She faded away into oblivion, though for a long time afterwards they professed to exhibit her at " penny gaffs."

In point of fact the whole story was a gigantic sell, and probably the only foundation for it was that the lady was a descendant of Lord Bacon, or a relative of the poet Hogg.

In 1816 the first steamboat arrived in the Thames, having come all the way from Glasgow in twenty hours.

People flocked down to see her, and when they heard about the wondrous speed of the steamer, they took to *esteem her* very much.

Among other immense events, the building of the Coburg theatre, now affectionately known as the " Vic," ought never to be forgotten by grateful Londoners.

Literature now went ahead amazingly; newspapers flourished, the *Times* began to be printed by steam, and to add to all this enlightenment, gas was first used in the London streets.

You may *gas* what an effect it had on those who saw it for the first time.

This was the great period of the clubs, and the number of them in London was now prodigious.

There were the Oddfellows, and the Humbugs, the Mulberries, and the Eccentrics, the Three-bottle-men's club, the No pay, no liquor club, the One-eyed club, and the Sublime Society of Beefsteaks.

These were only a few, besides White's club, and Boodle's, and Poodles, and Tom's, and Bill's, and Bob's, and Jack's, and ever so many more.

Nor were benevolent institutions neglected, for some charitable citizens founded the Refuge for Destitute Millionaires, the Asylum for Decayed Teeth, and the African Institution, which was a place where superannuated street niggers might lay aside their *banjoes*, and rest their weary *bones*.

In 1821, London was all alive with the coronation of King George IV., and by George, it was a coronation !

It took five hours to get the crown on the king's head, and the whole affair cost a quarter of a million, or fifty thousand pounds an hour.

The lord mayor was there, of course, and handed the king some wine in a gold cup, after which his majesty gave him back the cup as a little keepsake.

His loyal lordship declared that he would never part with it, except with his life, and even then he wouldn't.

LXXIV

OTHER EVENTS OF THE GEORGE-THE-FOURTHIAN ERA.

THE same year the lord mayor's coach was relined, and the horses had new harness, and their shoes were newly soled and heeled.

The intelligence of this great event spread throughout the City, and all true Londoners wept tears of joy.

This reminds us that the House of Lords was also thoroughly repaired at the same time, and the noble peers had to sit on the stairs to conduct their debates, being determined that business should be carried on as usual during the alterations.

The king ordered a splendid new throne to be got up, with a canopy over it to keep the rain off; he also had the Wool-sack fresh stuffed with the very best sawdust.

You know that the "Woolsack" is the seat occupied by the lord chancellor, who sits on it for six thousand pounds a year.

Anyone wouldn't mind getting "the *sack*," if it were *that* kind of one.

More improvements in London; oceans of new buildings raised, old Bedlam pulled down, and new London Bridge begun from the designs of Mr. John Rennie (or *rennie* other man), the lord mayor laying down the foundation stone, and the public laying down the money.

Regent's Park was now getting so awfully aristocratic that scarcely anyone under a baronet ventured to walk there, and even *he* had to take a carriage.

Several *ramas* were got up in London, viz., the diorama, the cosmorama, and ever so many panoramas.

Barker and Burford's was the most celebrated. It represented the battle of Trafalgar so naturally, that many of the spectators began to feel sea sick, and to imagine themselves hit by cannon balls.

"Waterloo" was also beautifully done—it was as good as being there, all but being killed—and "Napoleon's retreat from Moscow" was life itself.

The ice and snow sent the audience home shivering and laid them up with a severe cold for days afterwards.

On March 6, 1822, there was a phenomenon.

A circular south-west wind blew the waves of the Thames till they formed a number of little islands, which were, of course, instantly taken possession of in the name of his Britannic majesty.

They thought of appointing a governor and civil and military council, but before they could do so, the islands disappeared.

About the same time, more or less, London was honoured by a visit from the far-famed Polish Count Boruslawski, who was introduced to the king.

The count, instead of being lanky and tall, as most *Poles* are, was the smallest man of his size ever seen for sixpence a head, which was the price charged for looking at him.

Indeed, some short-sighted people who came to have a look at the noted dwarf, declared the affair a swindle, as he was so tiny they really couldn't see him at all.

So the smallest gentleman in Europe was interviewed by the greatest gentleman in Europe, who presented him with a watch and chain in proportion to his size.

This came economical, and was, of course, very different

from giving a giant a gold watch and chain in proportion to his size, which is rather expensive work.

And among our other distinguished visitors at this time were the king and queen of the Sandwich Islands, who arrived in 1824.

They were taken about and made a great fuss of, and their names—Kamehamehahaha and Kamehamehulahilaholahee—were in everybody's mouth.

That sublime anthem " The King of the Cannibal Islands," was composed in their especial honour and played to them wherever they went, and whether they liked it or not.

For a while they enjoyed themselves muchly.

But London fogs and the small-pox together proved too much for the poor darkies, and they went home very much more dead than alive.

Of course, the reader knows that the Sandwich Islands were so named from the sandwiches that grow there, ready cut, on the far-famed Bread-fruit tree, and form the principal food of the natives.

In 1824 there were awful times in the City.

Forty-four banks went to smash all at once with a report like an earthquake.

A general panic took place ; bankruptcy right and left nobody would give anybody else any credit, and even those who paid ready money were looked upon as suspicious customers.

This, of course, led to the building of the National Gallery, the Royal Academy, the General Post Office, the Thames Tunnel, and several other hospitals, and, above all, the " Zoo " in Regent's Park.

This was really a " sweet boon " for London.

Before there was nothing but travelling menageries, from

which the animals sometimes used to escape, and occasionally some quiet family would find a lion or tiger walking into dinner, or be disturbed in the middle of the night by an African baboon trying to get in at the window; incidents rather apt to frighten nervous people.

But now the whole of the animal kingdom were accommodated with spacious lodgings in the park, and all of them, from the golden eagle to the ring-tailed golopossums, could live happy ever after.

There all is peace and happiness.

The wolf never devours the lamb, nor does the lion eat the tender antelope, nor the boa-constrictor swallow live babies, *because they never get the chance.*

Up to this time London travelling locomotion had been nothing but slow-commotion.

No trains, cabs, or busses to be had ; nothing but lumbering old hackney coaches, with broken springs, and wheels coming off when least expected, which shook and jolted the passengers about like so many potatoes in a basket.

LXXV.

OTHER AND STILL MORE HISTORICAL OCCURRENCES.

ONE very fine morning in 1820 the first cab was seen in London, and was hailed with delirious joy.

Not till ten years afterwards was the omnibus started, and then people began to think they really were flying along "like a bird."

LXXV. (*Continued*).

WHAT would people have said to the Underground ?

As King George IV. retired from town for good (or for bad), as he got older, we needn't say much more about him.

He added to the extent of the metropolis, for he built a good deal in his time, and perpetrated some of the ugliest edifices in the universe.

Even his own residence, Carlton House, was not much to look at, for all it cost so much, though there were some pretty adornments and curiosities inside, among which may be noted the throne of the King of Kandy, captured in India, and composed of sugar candy throughout.

SOME DISTINGUISHED FOREIGNERS WHO HAVE VISITED US.
(*See Page* 366).

George IV. was certainly a liberal patron of trade, for he didn't care how much he spent or where the money came from.

The tailors must have loved him as a father.

His clothes, even when old, fetched the scarifying sum of one hundred and fifty thousand pounds, and one cloak alone was lined with sable to the tune of eight hundred pounds.

You see King George knew his own value.

He wasn't worth much in himself (probably about £0000), so he put it all on the *outside*.

In 1830 came King William IV. to the throne, the main reason for his so doing being that the throne wouldn't come to him.

His coronation was a most cheerful and brilliant spectacle, and the late Lord Lytton, who was there at the time, describes the populace going mad with joy, and crossing sweepers shouting—

"Bravo, my boys! there's good times coming! Everythink's to be set right, and beefsteaks is a-going to be a penny a pound! So chuck up yer hats, and hurrah for King Bill!"

Still, yet, nevertheless, notwithstanding, there was a good deal of discontent about in various quarters of the realm, especially in Ireland, where they seemed to have laid in an extra stock.

London wasn't altogether in the happiest state, and His Grace the Duke of Wellington seems to have got into *dis*grace with them, for he was about as unpopular as the high price of coals in the present day, and equally hard to get rid of.

The lord mayor had invited the king to his November feast, according to the good old custom, and it was expected that the show, the feed, the speechifying, and the bestowal of honours would surpass anything that had been seen since the last time.

But somebody sent an anonymous letter to Wellington, telling him that if he dared to go too, he had better bring his shield, and a hundred or so of his Waterloo guards with him, or he would be mobbed to death.

Soldiers began to be seen about the streets, and the water in the Tower ditch was turned on, as if preparing for a siege.

The duke's residence, Apsley House, soon had reason to be called *mishaps*ley House, for all its windows were smashed, and nothing but Providence saved the eagle eye of the great commander from being bunged up, and his eagle nose from being irreparably damaged.

So he determined not to go to Guildhall, and as the king wouldn't go without him, neither went.

It was even reported that the annual procession and feast at Guildhall would be given up, and many an alderman and " man-in-brass " wept at the thought.

However, it all ended by the king turning out the ministry, which turned out the very best thing he could do.

The time-honoured show showed up as brilliantly as ever, and it was even darkly whispered that the turtle-soup was better than usual.

In 1831, his majesty King William, with Queen Adelaide, went in state to open the new London Bridge, accompanied by the court, corporation, and companies of our mighty capital.

Everybody was there, so was everybody else.

Suns shone, drums waved, and flags were beaten.

The lord mayor's barge was present, and seemed much interested in the proceedings.

The ceremony at the bridge was a long one, but nobody wished to *abridge* it.

Those who stopped away from the sight lost a great deal, and so did those who went, for they had their pockets picked.

The spectacle was quite nautical, and we have heard, upon good authority, that if Lord Nelson had not died twenty-six years before, he would infallibly have been present.

The king, standing majestically upon the parapet of the bridge, and waving a golden trowel, declared the bridge "open," and that anybody could now go over, which wasn't true in a literal sense, as, what with the soldiers and the crowd, it was impossible to move.

However, three cheers immediately arose from the assembled millions who sang—"It is, it *is*, yes, it is our opening day!" and drank the king's health in glasses of well-filtered Thames water.

The Reform Bill agitation, in 1832, was so tremendous in London, that many people could neither eat, drink, nor sleep during the fifteen months the government took to consider the measure.

When it received the royal assent, and became law, exhausted nature gave way, they wept tears of joy, "liquored up," and went to sleep for a week at a stretch.

We ought here to note, among City events, the fitting up of Crosby Hall as a first-class dining place, 1834.

The founding of the fire-brigade in 1833.

The burning of the Royal Exchange.

All the time it was on fire the great clock kept on playing —"There is na luck about the house!" which was true, for there wasn't.

Extent of damage £150,000 3s. 11¾d.

LXXVI.

THE WIND-UP OF THE MARVELLOUS HISTORY OF GOG AND MAGOG.

THE reader will doubtless wonder what has become of Gog and Magog, the famous City giants, who for so many centuries had stood like so many *sentries* at Guildhall.

Age had by this time pretty well doubled up the old boys, and they had of late retired a great deal into private life (for they had always been of a *retiring* disposition).

Consequently they didn't know much about what went on in the world, or even if anything went on at all.

They had never heard that locomotives were taking the run out of horses, and railway companies were being started "like steam."

It was November 10th, the day after the Lord Mayor's Day, and the fog was so thick that you couldn't see the end of your nose, much more an inch beyond it, when the two old giants went out for a walk.

They were wrapped in their own thoughts and great-coats, and walked with sticks and respirators.

They had got about a mile out, in a very unfinished neighbourhood, when they came upon a deep cutting across a field, which (to let the reader into a secret) was the newly-made line of the Nor'-Nor'-Eastern by Sou'-Western Railway.

"Hullo!" cried Magog. "What do you call this? It

looks like a dry ditch with a lot of iron lines laid down. What's it for?"

"I'm squashed if I know, brother Magog," was the reply. "And look here at these poles with wires running through them."

Of course he spoke of the telegraph posts, which were about their own height.

"I should say," said Magog, reflectively, "that those wires are to keep the posts up."

"And what are the posts for, then?"

"To keep the wires up."

"I tell you what they keep up," said Gog, putting his ear to one of the poles. "They keep up a sort of buzzing noise, as if they were bad in the inside."

Magog caught hold of one of the wires with his immense hand, which was enveloped in a white Berlin wool glove.

Instantly he felt a profound shiver throughout his frame.

He let go, and to his amazement, saw these words upon his fist—

"Dearest,—Home to dinner at six o'clock. Boiled mutton and turnips. Yours ever, Harry."

It was a telegraphic message sent by Mr. Jones in the City to his wife, and it had thus been stopped on its journey, and *got printed off upon the giant's hand.*

As, however, neither Gog nor Magog could read modern English, it was all Greek to them, and they believed it was magic into the bargain.

"Well, I *am* flabbergasted!" they exclaimed, in a breath. "Wonders will never cease. However, let's walk down the lines a bit, and see where they go to."

They hadn't proceeded far, when one of the porters shouted to them from the bank—

"Hi, you sirs! you're trespassing.   If you don't look out, you'll run up against the 12.45."

"The 12.45!   Whatever does he mean by that?" asked Magog.

"Never mind him," was the answer.   "Shan't a free-born City giant walk where he likes?   Rather!   Come on."

And they went on; and the porter, who was rather scared at their size, didn't care to say any more.

Presently they came to a tunnel.

"Oho! here's a cave," cried Gog; "and what a long one!   I can't see the other end at all.   Hark!"

And they felt a terrible trembling of the ground under them.

"Good Gog! whatever's this a-coming?" exclaimed Magog, grasping his brother's arm.   "Look!"

And they did look.

The ground trembled and jarred like an earthquake; a hollow sound was heard in the tunnel; two red eyes were seen in the dark opening, and then, with a rush and a roar and a rattle, an enormous monster burst out of the opening.

"Stand back!" cried Gog.   "It's a fiery dragon coming out of his cave; he'll run over us.   Look at his eyes (the lamps) and his fists (the buffers), and, by Jupiter! he's belching smoke and blue blazes out of the top of his head."

"A dragon?   So it is," replied Magog.   "I thought those varmints were all exterminated.   How it shrieks!   And there are two men riding on his back (engineer and stoker). They must be enchanters.   I've killed many a dragon in my time, and I'll have another go in, old as I am.   Now, come on."

And, collecting all his strength, the aged giant raised his

staff, and made a spring at the dragon, with the intention of giving him a topper.

Instantly a hundred eyes were thrust out of the dragon's *sides*, which were full of *holes*, and at the same time it gave such a piercing shriek as would have stunned twenty giants, and rushing by, was out of sight in a moment.

Magog fell down flat on his face.

The very wind of the monster in rushing past had been so powerful as to knock all the wind out of *him*.

"Oho, oho !" groaned Magog, " I'm killed, I'm murdered ! That dragon's the awfullest I ever saw ; and if there's many this size, I don't want to live any longer."

Gog raised him up, and leaving the iron road, they proceeded to toddle on, with their nerves very much shaken.

They were soon accosted by a sharp-looking gentleman in black, with green spectacles and a white choker, who carried a case of surgical implements and another of medicines.

" Dr. Livingstone, I presume ; no, I mean Gog and Magog," says he. " I presume I have the honour of addressing the renowned City giants ?"

" What's left of us, at least," groaned Magog, "and that's not much now. Who are you ?"

" My name is Professor Quackington, of the University of Katzenellanbogen. I can cure every complaint under the sun, and many more. You're both out of sorts—general debility. I'll set you to rights in two twos, with my celebrated mesmeric elixir. Come, it's only twelve and sixpence, bottle and stamp included."

" What will it do ?" asked Gog.

" What *won't* it do ? The first thing it does is to send people to sleep, and then, whatever they've been suffering from, when they wake up, they find a perfect cure," replied Quackington.

"Well, call on us at Guildhall to morrow afternoon," said Magog, "and we'll give it a trial."

———

LXXVII.

THE LAST OF GOG AND MAGOG CONTINUED.

ACCORDINGLY Professor Quackington *did* call the next day.

He found them alone in the great hall.

They told him they didn't feel much better yet.

"Cheer up; you'll both be as young and brisk as kittens when I've done with you," said Professor Quackington, M.D., giving his bottle a shake ; "only you must have a good long snooze. My fee to send you to sleep is a guinea, and for waking you up again two guineas. Mind, nobody can wake you up but me."

"All right," said Magog ; "you won't desert us, I know, as some of the payment depends on your return. Here's your first instalment, but after that remember it's no cure no pay."

So Gog mounted the pedestal in the corner of the hall where he was wont to stand, and Magog took up the corresponding position on the other side.

"I rather prefer to go to sleep standing up ; I've been so used to it while on duty as sentinel."

Then the professor handed them the elixir in turn.

It must have been rather strong, for a quart of it began to have an immediate effect upon the gigantic brethren.

"It's a-working," exclaimed Magog. "Good night, brother Gog, I'm off. How do you feel?"

"Better already," was the reply, "but rather drowsy. I shall be able to sleep like a top."

"You *are* a top," said the jocular professor, "for you're *a-top* of the pedestal. Now, good bye. Next Tuesday I'll call to administer the reviving dose, and if you don't feel all right again, I'll give you free leave to call me a tremendous humbug."

"Good night, Brother Gog," said Magog again.

"*Bob swore,*" answered Magog.

(N.B.—He meant this for French).

In four minutes both giants were as fast as door-mice, but with the exception of being quite motionless, they looked as wide awake as ever.

(They had learnt that trick when serving in a police capacity).

The professor surveyed them through his green spectacles, chuckled to himself, and then began to explore the apartment.

He left Guildhall soon after.

The lord mayor was rather concerned to see the inactivity of the two giants.

He commanded them several times to wake up, but all in vain.

They didn't.

Days, weeks passed, and there was no change in the condition of the patients.

The professor never came back.

From that day to this he has never been seen.

A number of the best silver spoons, and other articles of

plate, disappeared mysteriously just at the same time, and have never been seen either.

What became of the distinguished mesmeriser remains still a mystery.

Perhaps he forgot all about his gigantic patients.

Perhaps he thought it hardly prudent to put in an appearance.

Perhaps he emigrated to Nova Scotia.

Perhaps he's on the railway; perhaps he's dead; perhaps alive; perhaps he's on the sea; perhaps he's——

But why speculate?

He went, and returned not.

And as nobody else had the secret of resuscitating the giants, they remained mute and quite still on the top of their pedestal, and they are *still* there now.

Every known means have been tried—spiritualism, red-hot pokers, trumpets, and all other kinds of *rows*, but nothing could *rouse* them.

Will they ever awake again? Time will show.

It may be that in a hundred years or so the effect of the draught will have passed over of itself, and Gog and Magog will arise, literally " like giants refreshed."

Indeed there is a report at Guildhall that on the night of every 9th of November, when the feast is over and all is still, the two gigantic brothers wake up to life, come down off their perches, and indulge in an hour's cheerful talk, and a loving cup of the best Irish whisky, going back to their perches, like Hamlet's ghost, when the first slice of daylight is served up.

As your chronicler never sat up all night on the 9th of November at Guildhall, he cannot personally vouch for this as a fact, but doesn't see why it shouldn't be as true as spirit-rapping at least.

Even if it isn't, why lament?

Perhaps, after all, it is best to let the poor old giants rest in peace.

They have had their day, and done good service, and deserve to sleep the slumber of the just.

Besides, if they were to be revived, what an expense they would be to keep in these dear days.

Why, it might even add something serious on to the income tax.

LXXVIII.

THE HOUSES OF PARLIAMENT AND OTHER ZOOLOGICAL COLLECTIONS, &c.

THE new Houses of Parliament were also begun about this period, the old ones having got into such a ruinous and higgledy-piggledy state, that members often lost themselves, and found their way into the refreshment department instead of the committee room.

It should not be forgotten, as a national event of great importance at this period, that the fine old time-honoured custom of washing the lions of the Tower of London on the first of April was done away with; for three reasons—

1st.—Because all the other *washing* in the tower was *put out;* and why not that of the lions?

2nd.—Because the washing of lions is a disagreeable and dangerous process.

3rd.—Because there were no longer any lions there to wash.

So henceforth don't be taken in by people who assure you that the ceremony still goes on.

We have already mentioned the "Zoo" at Regent's

Park, but there were at that time also the Surrey Zoological Gardens.

They were called gardens because they contained all the *flowers* of the animal world.

Thus the giraffe, from its height, might be considered the *hollyhock* of quadrupeds ; the tiger resembles the *tiger-lily ;* the snakes were certainly *creepers ;* and the lion in a rage resembled a *passion-flower.*

They used to have concerts at the Surrey Zoo, until it was found that what with one thousand singers, the band, and the organ, and the animals joining in from a near distance, it was altogether too much for even the most devoted lovers of music.

At present there is only one zoological collection in London, except that at the British Museum, which is interesting, but not lively.

The animals there don't cost much to keep, and it's no use going at any time with the hope of seeing them fed.

None of them, in fact, have been known to eat anything since they have been there, though they were all *well stuffed* before they came.

They are perfectly harmless, and an infant six weeks old might play with them and not get hurt in the least.

We have often found ourselves there, with a raging hippopotamus in front, a ferocious rhinoceros in the rear, and a camelopard, twenty-two feet high, in the near perspective, and got off without any damage.

Most of the great institutions in London have been rebuilt within the last forty years.

The march of improvement has been a double-quick one.

We live in truly wondrous times.

Our railways surpass anything ever known amongst the Anglo-Saxons.

Our Thames embankment is unique, and not to be "dittoed" in the whole world, for where will you find a *Thames* embankment abroad?

Our river steamers, it is true, might be slightly improved without being too luxurious, and if a quantity of fresh air were pumped into the Underground Railway every morning we should be very grateful.

There are few other things to complain of, and even if there were, it wouldn't be much use complaining.

The newspaper world has made seven-league strides of late years.

Look at the London newspaper press, it is downright wonderful!

Why, the *Daily Tall Giraffe* alone uses up, every year, ten million reams of paper, and one hundred tons of newsboys.

Since the good old days of Waterloo shoals of foreigners have settled in London. They like it so much that some of them won't go away until they are pressed for rent, when they disappear suddenly.

They have discovered that London is a nice peaceful place to live in, and that we don't have a revolution every week, as is the custom in many other countries.

Lastly, but not leastly, among the metropolitan improvements there is one recent as to date, but venerable from its historical associations, we mean the erection of the BOYS OF ENGLAND office.

So now, with tearful eyes, we say our last words and make our bow.

Reader, the best of friends must part, and the same very novel remark applies to the worst of enemies.

May you be happy!

FAREWELL!

www.ingramcontent.com/pod-product-compliance
Lightning Source LLC
Chambersburg PA
CBHW080724020726
47503CB00010B/2774